THE GODDESS AND THE HAWK

CHIARA GALA

Identifiers:

ISBN 978-1-7392997-0-5 (paperback)

ISBN 978-1-7392997-1-2 (ebook)

Published February 2023

CONTENT WARNING

The Goddess and the Hawk is an Adult Fantasy Romance. This book contains mention of violence, death, murder, strong language and cursing, explicit sexual activity, gore, torture, BDSM, miscarriage, drugs, gang violence.

Please only read if you are comfortable with these topics.

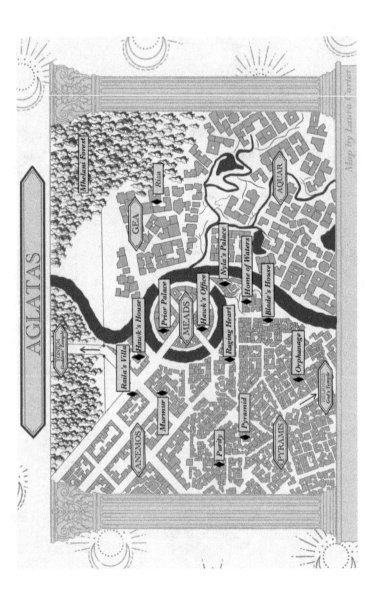

To those who chase sunsets and Love like hearts don't break.

L'Amor che move il sole e l'altre stelle.

— Dante Alighieri

PROLOGUE

There was a God and a Goddess.

Whilst there were two now, there had been many. There was once a Goddess, then another, and then another. There was once a God, and then another, and many others after that.

But there had been only two energies. Always.

Always the same energies.

Over and over.

Searching, choosing, merging.

And then, repeating everything from the beginning, all over again: searching, choosing, merging.

For millennia.

On Exanthea, there were two deities — not two gods, though — two utterly divine, everlasting energies. Each picked one of the People, a *vessel*, and merged with them for the rest of their days. The divine fused with the non-divine, making one a God or a Goddess for a lifetime.

Then once the vessel dies, the energy finds someone else.

Again and again and again.

Over and over.

For where there was always a God, there was always a Goddess.

Goddess Serabel was now in the 20234 year of Exanthea, the 61st vessel. God Aarush was the 55th.

CHAPTER 1

A mala loved the sun, but she wasn't sure the sun liked her back.

Nonetheless, if the sun was shining, it was going to be a great day. She could sense it in the air and the soft breeze whirling around her body. Murmuring the final words of her prayer, she rose to her feet and bowed her head once more toward the altar, taking a moment to check if the other priestesses were still praying.

It wasn't going to be a great day because she believed in luck, or in signs, or superstitions — no, it would be a great day because the sun gave her enough strength to create one.

A slight smile rippled on her lips as she gently walked away, not turning her back to the altar until she was out of the kneeling priestesses' way. Reaching the entrance of the temple, she took a last glance at the bright, ethereal room, sending her gratitude to the Goddess. Amala stepped outside onto the white marble porch surrounding the temple, breathing the cool air that encircled the Yonium — the calm after the storm. A storm, like the one she'd witnessed the previous night, happened only occasionally, maybe a couple times a year during the

rainy seasons. But they were never something one could get used to —
not if they lived at the temple, anyway.

Carefully avoiding a puddle visible on the marble surface, Amala slid
her bare feet off the cold floor, and towards the stairs leading to the
grounds. The porch was raised, only slightly above ground level, but
enough that — in times of celebration — the priestesses could stand
on it and celebrate their rituals in front of the people reunited outside
before the temple.

As she walked down, Amala finally faced the sun, allowing the warm
light to shine upon her. Her smooth skin glowed beneath the light's
embrace, her soul beaming as she rested a few moments, her eyes
scanning the horizon: the temple was built next to the river, the sound
of rushing water a constant background noise in the priestesses' life.

The Apàle didn't flow next to the temple the same way it did in the
city; in Aglatas, not so far away, the Apàle was quiet, placid, serene...
and on the other side of the city, next to the *other* temple, it was even
more tranquil.

Next to the Goddess's temple, the Apàle could be impetuous and
turbulent. And sometimes, in the rainy season, it could overflow and
flood the shores. It had almost happened the night before; the moon
cast a silver glow onto the earth's fury as raindrops melted with the
current. The priestesses had rushed to protect their botanic gardens and
greenhouses, ensuring the animals were safe before retiring inside the
temple and closing the doors for the night.

The Apàle hadn't overflown though and, despite the puddles
spreading across the marble path, this morning's sun was so powerful,
that it would dry the mess before noon.

The sun was Amala's favourite part of the temple: it stood there,
shining so bright and proudly; she could see it appear at dawn, rising
above the trees of the forest.

Mhelani Forest circled three quarters of the Yonium: it was a beautiful, dense forest, rich with many varieties of trees and plants and flowers. Animals roamed freely, safe from hunting, and sometimes deer came to the border, curiously attracted by the sweet chants of their rituals under the moon.

That same moon scared her, sometimes. As if it could see all of her and reveal her deepest secrets.

She glanced at the borders closer to the greenhouse, searching for any familiar faces among the trees: deer weren't the only inhabitants of Mhelani. The Centaurs kingdom was there too, built within the wilderness. Centaurs had lived in the forest for centuries, from way before Amala was born, and she'd gotten used to their presence around the temple since childhood.

They weren't common at all in Aglatas: some of them might have lived there, if necessity required so, but most of them were extremely attached to their tribes and customs, not to mention their hatred for the modernity of the city. Perhaps, that was the reason why centaurs and priestesses got along so well: they shared the burden of an ancient lifestyle, a lifestyle they both had chosen to pursue, despite the modernity and technology blooming in Aglatas and all around them.

Amala knew that if she walked to the city, she would find cars, buses, and railways; phones glued to people drinking coffee outside of a bar whilst working on their laptop or shuffling out of a supermarket with their hands full of groceries. But there, at the Goddess's temple of Yonium, things were different. When Aglatas had started to evolve, some centuries before, the Goddess had decided she didn't want to reside in the city anymore and retired to her temple where she'd required the priestesses to maintain their current lifestyle and keep it throughout the centuries, regardless of what progress or aid the rising technology could bring them. The priestesses obeyed, and nothing had changed since.

Amala didn't miss it: she knew about it, of course, and knew that if she were to go to Aglatas, she would get on a bus and pay with her credit card. She understood the bare minimum use of technology, but she had never needed to learn it properly.

She was fine reading paper books rather than electronic, tending to the cows rather than buying milk, washing her clothes in a basin rather than a washing machine. She loved her life at the temple; the promise of an easier existence, spent away from her Goddess, had never appealed to her.

Born at the Yonium, raised among other priestesses, she'd sworn herself to the Goddess as soon as she'd been old enough to make her own choice, and had spent every day since honouring the great, supreme energy that was Goddess Serabel.

And after decades spent at her service, Serabel made Amala her High Priestess.

For the first decade of her life, she had known nothing of the world outside. She didn't need to. She had her Goddess at the temple, a beautiful home, and many, many priestesses she considered her mothers and sisters. Amala loved her lifestyle and had wanted to remain a priestess for the rest of her days.

But when she grew older, her mother — who once lived at the Yonium herself — had encouraged her to pursue her other dream: healing. She didn't want to become a healer simply because of her power. She was gifted, as everyone was, yet her power — if learned the correct way — could make her a skilled, brilliant healer. Amala came from the people of Air and had learned to control the wind since she was young. Channelling that energy into healing would only help deepen and strengthen her own power.

So, Amala had gone to Aglatas to study.

She had become a healer, and, after that, a midwife.

That had been her dream since witnessing a priestess giving birth at the Yonium. She had sat with her mother, far from the labour but close enough to understand what was happening and had spent her whole time watching the women assisting the birth.

To help bring life into this world seemed such a beautiful way to spend her days.

Amala had been a priestess and a midwife her whole life and, a few months from now, at one hundred and twenty-one years old, she would celebrate her eleventh year as High Priestess.

High Priestess Amala tucked a silver-white strand of hair behind her ear and stole another look at the sun, shining bright in the blue, peaceful sky.

She was supposed to take care of her Goddess soon.

Glancing back to the temple, she indulged under the sun for a few more seconds. Her soul lightened as her heart felt heavy. Why did she love the sun so much? Why did the most beautiful thing in the world have to be something so beyond reach? And not because the sun was unreachable.

But because, whilst the Sun was the thing she loved the most, Amala was High Priestess to the Goddess of the Moon.

☼

Amala reached the Goddess' rooms but lingered outside the doors for a moment. She felt blessed, as she always did, when she felt Serabel's divine energy surround her. What a blessing, indeed, to be the Goddess' High Priestess. She carried a tray with a goblet of carved, coloured glass, and a glass carafe of hibiscus tea. With absolute care, she used a spark of power to keep the tray afloat, as she gently knocked on the door. Her wind could keep anything hovering in the air for hours: it was one of the most common tricks for people of Air, but it wasn't

Amala's favourite. She preferred channelling her power into healing, or summoning breezes that whirled around her to keep her warm or cool.

Amala knocked on the door again. She would never enter without her Goddess' permission; she knew Serabel was probably busy, so she patiently waited until she heard a familiar, gentle voice beckon.

"Enter."

The Goddess' rooms were beautiful: they were big, with high ceilings and tall windows, much like the ones downstairs in the altar room. The antechamber had sofas covered in soft, creamy pillows, and fluffy carpets that were a delight to step on. A glass door opened on an ample terrace facing east, where Amala loved to watch the sunrise. She liked the window in her room more, but there was magic on that terrace.

A smaller door — now open — led to the Goddess' bedroom. Amala entered, announcing herself with a knock on the wooden surface. She bowed her head toward the Goddess, then waited quietly beside the door.

Serabel, the most beautiful woman Amala had ever seen, gracefully gestured to the people she'd chosen to spend the night with, as if inviting them to leave. Five in total: four males and a flustered female whose eyes lingered on Amala's body. Serabel instantly noticed.

"My beautiful High Priestess shall not be joining us," she simply said. Amala cocked her head.

"Why not?" the petite female breathed, eyes now fixed on her face. Amala took a step toward her and softly brushed her cheek.

"I have a busy day, beautiful. Maybe another time."

She said nothing else as her Goddess' lovers left. Each of them bore that glow — the glow she'd seen so many times, in all the people Serabel shared her personal time with.

When the last of them had left, closing the door behind them, her Goddess spoke once more. This time, her voice was quirky and amused.

"You have nothing to do today."

Amala scoffed. "I'm *busy*."

"Yes, avoiding the multitude of people who wish for your attention."

She could say nothing to that. It was true. Amala didn't like to entertain relations within the temple perimeter. If she was sharing a moment with someone, it would likely be outside of temple grounds, perhaps hidden by the trees of Mhelani forest. Centaurs and priestesses weren't an uncommon pairing: the centaurs lived just around the temple, and for the many priestesses who were born and raised there, centaurs were the first example of a male they had ever seen. Yet Serabel had strict rules about centaurs' behaviour regarding her priestesses, but still allowed them to have their fun.

Amala poured coconut oil on her palms and began to massage Serabel's shoulders. Her Goddess was utterly beautiful. Serabel had glowing, dark brown skin that gleamed under the moonlight, her shiny black locks were thick and tightly coiled, forming a halo of curls around her head. Now, she rested back her head, soothed beneath Amala's touch.

For minutes, neither of them spoke, unhurried through the ritualism of their morning.

Then, the Goddess broke the silence, "You could have joined," she said tentatively, "Even if they weren't your type."

Amala couldn't hide her blush.

No, a part of her instantly said.

Her Goddess had asked the question many times. She *wanted* Amala to join. But Amala... she had never taken her up on the offer, not once. How could she? How could she ever deem herself worthy to share such a moment with her Goddess?

Serabel knew her thoughts about it, but never ceased to ask. At first, the offer was frequent, perhaps hoping she could convince her but she asked less often now, knowing it was all in vain.

Amala would never say yes.

"I still don't want males, my Goddess. But if you require me to be here, I'll be honoured to watch next time."

"Such a big favour, from you and your voyeurism…" Serabel gently teased.

"I love watching people sharing intimate energies in a deep, personal moment. I love passion."

"I know, Amala."

She quieted, and Amala hoped she wouldn't mention it again.

It worked for several more minutes; Serabel enjoyed Amala's touch on her tense shoulders and seemed uninterested in keeping the conversation going. When the High Priestess paused, pouring more oil on her hands, she spoke again, and Amala sighed a breath of relief.

"You look cheerful today," the Goddess said, "Are you happy the sun is back?"

"It was a *week*. One entire week of clouds, and rain, and thunders and *dark* and—"

"—I know, I know. I'm sorry you had to deal with it."

"I'm sorry you don't like the sun." Amala retorted.

"I'm Goddess of the Moon."

And Amala, her High Priestess.

Yet, she couldn't help but love the sun more, and feel guilty for it.

Amala didn't speak as she finished taking care of her Goddess. She did it every morning, attending her rooms, bringing her breakfast, massaging her body, and helping her get ready. Serabel didn't need the help, but loved the attention, and maybe loved the fact Amala was the one giving it to her.

"You look incredibly beautiful, my Goddess."

She meant it: Serabel wore a white dress that contrasted perfectly with her dark, soft skin. Her body was elegantly and sensually wrapped in white strands of silky fabric, interlaced around her torso and swinging around her bare, beautiful legs.

She smiled. "Thank you, my lovely Amala. Are you having a good day so far?"

"Dawn Call was good. Lots of strong energies from many of us, and — of course — the sun is back."

Serabel sighed, "Well, I am sorry to ruin it for you, but I have some news you won't like."

"What?" Amala asked, arms dropping to her side.

"The God is coming here today."

☼

Amala hadn't always been this friendly with her Goddess. Serabel had been there from the day she was born, though it had taken Amala time to accept she wanted to be her *friend.* She knew it now.

For a while, when she allowed that feeling of deep unworthiness to rule inside of her without question, she often wondered if the Goddess had been this close to her previous High Priestesses.

Amala was her seventh, and Serabel had ruled as Goddess for almost a thousand years.

The People Amala came from could live unbothered for centuries, but some would tire with the unchanging world, choosing to reincarnate. Their body would leave this realm, but their soul and energy would not: they would be reborn into somebody else and start anew.

It wasn't the choice of all, but the choice of many. Some of Serabel's former High Priestesses had decided this too, but Amala couldn't conceive how one would give up the greater honour of their life. She could never disrespect the Goddess by choosing to reincarnate, to endure a life apart from her.

When she entered the altar room, the priestesses were chanting: naked and sitting on the floor in a circle.

Threads of gold and sparks of light tethered between them, snaking from each to the other, binding them in sisterhood. Remarks of their choice and their life.

Only a woman could be a Goddess' priestess. At the Yonium, acolytes became sisters after their first ritual, and were welcome to join a lifestyle made of passion, sensuality, and unbound emotions.

They had no need for clothing: the priestesses could wrap themselves in pure white robes, but most of their rituals required them to attend free of any attire, shining in nothing but their own skin.

Every day was a celebration of creativity, of that pure feminine energy that birthed and shaped the world. Amala had been born in that energy too, and she didn't wish to ever leave.

As she made her way to the kitchens, the clear voices of her sisters followed, honouring their Goddess.

Mistress of the Night,
Lady of Water flow,
Surge when lovers fight,
Stand when shadows grow.

Bringer of life,
She's both and she's neither.
Holding the knife,
That makes her moon-breather.

For carrying a secret,
So deep in her soul.
For her heart beats so strong,
That two make her whole.

Goddess, keep shining,

Let the story be told,
Let the light be blinding,
Let the power unfold.

Amala repeated the familiar words, trying to rid the unpleasant feeling in her stomach since Serabel told her the news. The God was coming to the temple, and she didn't like to admit how irritable that made her.

She didn't like to be irritable at all.

Down in the kitchens, she sat on the floor with her back against the cold wall, eating her strawberries in silence.

"What's with that face?"

She looked up.

A smiling, blond priestess with eyes like bright green sparks peered down at her. Hebex was a rose with a bunch of thorns and a thousand fluffy petals. The petals made her friends feel safe, and the thorns kept away whoever tried to harm those she loved.

"God Aarush is coming here."

Hebex groaned as she sat next to Amala, stealing a strawberry from her bowl. She sucked on it for a moment before taking a bite. "I knew that. I'm sorry I didn't tell you."

"You *knew?*"

"Medyr told me! But it totally slipped my mind when he went down on me. Sorry."

"That's fair. Priorities," Amala chuckled, taking a bite of a particularly red strawberry. The sweet taste lingered on her tongue, and she curved her lips into a smile.

"I thought you'd be happy. It's sunny again," Hebex shrugged. She closed her hand into a fist, resting it under Amala's face; when she opened her palm, a small daisy bloomed.

The High Priestess picked it up and tucked it into her hair.

"Feel better now?"

"I sure do."

Like Amala came from the people of Air, Hebex came from the people of Earth.

Each Element had its own district in Aglatas and was ruled by a Protector. Since power was hereditary, chances were that families would settle in a district and reside there forever.

Children learned to control their power at an early age in school and could develop it with further education; the extent of each power varied, and there wasn't a precise pattern. Still, most people from the same element followed similar paths.

But at the Yonium, people from all elements came together. Priestesses lived and worked together regardless of their power, helping each other, and following the same educational patterns.

Hebex, who had joined the temple almost seventy years before, was born in Gea, the Earth district of Aglatas, and had worked at the Earth Protector's Great Greenhouse since she'd finished school.

She had always admired the priestess' life though so, at thirty-five, she was initiated to the Goddess' temple. Whilst she hadn't received a priestess education the way Amala had, she had caught up quickly. The High Priestess — who, seventy years ago, was a priestess like the others — helped Hebex adjust to her new life.

Hebex could make flowers bloom from the palm of her hand and was remarkably skilled at harvesting; together, with the other Earth priestesses, she had made the Yonium's greenhouse blossom every season of the year. No element was represented more than others at the temple. Yet water was supposedly the most feminine element, whose energy was mostly inclined to align with the Yonium's customs.

Another priestess joined them in the kitchen. She sat on the floor before them, a mug full of milk in her hands. "Morning."

Her voice didn't match her appearance. She had curly, dirty-blonde hair, and a heart-shaped face with smooth sweet features. Her bronze skin glimmered as the sun traced it through the windows.

She was a person one would expect a dulcet, melodious voice from — honeyed, almost. Instead, she was sharp and bold, unafraid of speaking her mind, and absolutely unapologetic.

"Good morning, my love." Amala said with a smile.

"Slept well?" the priestess asked.

Her hand sneaked into Amala's bowl and grabbed a strawberry.

"Seryn!"

"What? Hebs can have some, but I can't? I've known you for longer," she stated, biting into the fruit. A red rivulet dribbled from her lower lip. She licked it, wiggling her eyebrows. "What put you in a mood anyway?"

She hooked a finger in one of Amala's crystal waist chains: she wore two, always hanging around her hips. The upper one was made from sunstone, the lower one carnelian. Seryn — who had always been passionate about crystal healing — had gifted her both years before, and Amala never took them off.

She sighed now, wrinkling her nose, but Hebex replied instead. "The God is coming here."

Seryn's brow rose.

"Now?"

"Today."

"Oh." She waited a moment. "Priests, too?"

Amala shrugged. "Serabel didn't say. They're coming to discuss Madakahiri, so I guess Medyr will be here. A bunch of the others, too."

"Alright," she seemed to think for a second. "I'll take Teleia to the river."

Teleia was Seryn's mate. She was a beautiful, tall, and graceful woman with incredible blue eyes, yet not blue like Amala's. Teleia's eyes weren't icy or cold, but blue like soft waves rocking to shore, a caress to help you fall asleep.

They had met at the temple.

Teleia had joined the temple some decades ago and, though her blue eyes remained the same, she was still early in her transition. She had changed much over the years, but Amala could have sworn she had always looked like that. Incredibly, utterly beautiful, and feminine.

Teleia wasn't born a woman: it had never happened before, a transgender woman made priestess to the Goddess. Amala didn't know why it was never the case before that, but she knew Serabel would have allowed, had the occasion presented in the centuries before Teleia.

She wasn't sure how the former Goddesses would have acted, of course, but Serabel would have done it. The same way she had welcomed Teleia in the temple the second she had asked. Seryn was extremely protective of her mate, and Teleia didn't always like to be around the God's priests.

"They won't be here for a while, anyway," Amala added. "I suppose they'll drive."

She couldn't disguise the hint of disapproval in her voice.

It was very common, for the Yonium priestesses, to disagree with the use of technology made from their counterpart temple.

The God's temple. Helioneis.

Situated on the opposite side of the city, where the Apàle flowed calmly in a plane and trickled closer to the sea, Helioneis was beautiful. An oasis of sun and light and warmth, where God Aarush was worshipped, honoured, and celebrated.

Amala loved the God's temple, but she loved the Yonium more. Regardless of the sun, her temple was her home... and Helioneis didn't share with them the rule of an older lifestyle. They had evolved with time and technology, and many priestesses found it strange that an environment so like theirs could be, in fact, so different.

Seryn's hand snaked to clasp Amala's wrist. She gasped at the warm feeling.

"Fuck, sorry," Seryn said, letting go. Steam came out of her palms, a shimmer of fire at her fingertips. She raised her mug innocently. "I was heating the milk."

Seryn came from the people of Fire. She was fierce, determined, and an absolute badass.

Sometimes Amala wished to be more like her.

The priestess clasped her wrist again, her hand now warm, but cooler. "You look very nervous. Maybe take the edge off, before they arrive? You will hate it if he teases you *because* of it."

Amala wasn't one for unsolicited advice, but she appreciated her friend's words.

God Aarush had the annoying habit of teasing her relentlessly since she'd been made High Priestess, and she was feeling *very* upset at the idea he'd do it in her own home.

She stood up, placing the ceramic bowl on Hebex's lap.

"Alright." She said, "I'll go take the edge off. Enjoy the river."

☼

"*Fuck,*" she groaned, a sweaty strand of hair falling in front of her eyes; she tucked it behind her ear just to feel it return a moment later, her whole body moving forward as the grip on her ass tightened, hands pushing her against the tree. She placed her palms against the trunk to balance herself, but—

"Hands."

A command.

She was about to object but then, again, she felt that tongue lapping against her sex and the only thing that came out of her mouth was a loud whimper. She obeyed, placing both of her hands behind her back as she felt *his* hand blocking her wrists, pinning her arms in place.

He slammed her body against the tree, and Amala screamed as her nipples hit the harsh wood, then moaned as he continued tasting her, dipping his tongue inside, before licking all the way back to her clit; his lips suckled right there and she started panting faster as her release beckoned. And then he bit her: his teeth pierced her clit, gently but decisively, then pulled softly; his hand squeezed her ass one last time before moving to her back and softly brushing her sensitive skin...

Amala screamed again as she came, her nipples scraping against the bark, whilst her hands remained pinned behind her back, forbidden from moving a single inch as he devoured everything that came out of her, licking that sweet, intimate flesh whilst she rode the wave of her climax. He didn't let her go as her breath turned even again, her soft pants quieting.

She could feel him smiling against her sex: "I—" her voice was hoarse. He released her hands and Amala wrapped her arms around the trunk, not able to support her own weight yet. After a minute, she turned to him and leaned against the tree: the centaur rose from the ground, and her eyes followed as he stood tall in front of her. She blushed slightly.

"Kanaan," she murmured, his dark eyes staring into her very soul, "Come here."

He lowered his head to her level, and she kissed him, her lips brushing softly against his. Her tongue teased him, asking him to join her. Kanaan kissed her back, wrapping his arms around her hips as he lifted her up, pressing her body against him. Amala tasted herself on his tongue and she sucked on it as she enjoyed every drop. She always thought she tasted delicious and was always satisfied when her lover approved. Their mouths kept teasing each other, with Kanaan paying special attention to her neck, nipping at her creamy skin, before she murmured: "I should go."

He didn't stop, and she cupped his face in her hands.

"Kanaan, the God is coming to the temple. I must go back." Her voice was sweet, and she pressed a soft kiss to his chin, whispering, "Put me down."

He obeyed, but didn't look happy.

"You still have time," he said, surveying her beautiful naked figure as she bent down to grab her dress.

Wrapping the robe against her body, she checked the sky before answering, "I should get ready. Can't be late."

He stepped towards her and Amala hesitated a moment before leaning in on the tips of her toes, and reaching his face for one final kiss.

"Thanks,"

She turned her back to him as she stepped onto the footpath, walking back to the temple.

The centaur was an amazing lover, and she enjoyed the time she shared with him, but he liked her in a way her heart wasn't ready to commit to, which was extremely unusual for her.

Amala loved to *love*. She had loved since her first heartbeat: it didn't matter who as she would give Love to everyone, at every moment of the day. Her heart was big, bigger than most, and her love was strong, fiercer than any love she had ever received.

A fierce lover, she was.

For every time she would share her energy with someone, she would give endlessly until there was no doubt on how strongly she loved; she hoped they would cherish that feeling forever.

Kanaan was different as she couldn't *give* him what he wanted.

Even if she wanted to, physical joining between the People and the centaurs was improbable. For centuries, the People had joined with every creature, and now pure races barely existed anymore. Some People bore traits from their ancestors — fangs and wings and scales and claws — and some bore none. Some clans of pure races still remained, somewhere, but nowhere near Aglatas. Except for the centaurs: they couldn't reproduce themselves with the People, which was why their own kingdom relied on the hope that they mated with each other. Even if Kanaan had a thing for Amala, she was certain his mate would be another centaur.

She should know. She had a gift for spotting mates from miles away.

But a mate was a given for the People. For the People, and every creature on Exanthea. Everyone, sooner or later, would find theirs. And Amala dreaded the moment when it would become so clear, that the love she had would never be returned in the same way.

Perhaps... she dismissed the thought with an annoyed gesture of her hand.

She was needed at the temple. Hurrying on the steps, the Sun gleamed on the white, lucid walls, light and warmth enclosing her home in a way that rarely happened. The sun shone every day, but not like this.

But she didn't have time to linger in the confusion because, as she stepped foot inside the Yonium, the God of the Sun was there.

CHAPTER 2

A mala entered the temple and stared at the sight before her: the God was there.

The God.

Him and Serabel faced each other, and she stilled for a moment to take in their beauty, to contemplate the marvellous sight of two deities: Aarush was the Sun, and Serabel the Moon.

Aarush embodied everything that was male. Serabel everything female.

Aarush was Earth and Heat, Fire and Warmth. Serabel was Water and Air and all things cold.

He was God of Lust and Blood. She was Goddess of Love and Sex.

He was Stillness, Bloodshed, Invention, Courage.

She was Creativity, Birth, Fertility, Flow.

Not opposites in everything, yet each had dividing powers and features to reign over. It was a blessing to see them together. They glowed: Serabel beamed of moonlight that followed her during the day, while Aarush's albino skin was crafted of pure daylight. He was tall, his muscular chest visible through the white robe he wore. His presence was the feeling of slowed time and, suddenly, Amala could feel every droplet of sunlight on her skin, could savour each grain of that golden warmth which burned through the room.

Serabel saw her first, drawn by her recognisable scent of sweet cinnamon, and smiled. The High Priestess stepped closer then, and when she had reached the pair, she knelt.

Simply bowing wouldn't do, not in this instance. Not in her temple, in front of the Goddess' altar, beholding the two most powerful beings in the entire world.

"I am honoured by your presence, God Aarush."

"Rise, my lovely Amala," Serabel replied sweetly.

Amala obeyed, eyes fixed on her Goddess. She was arching a dark eyebrow, full lips curled into a smirk: Amala could almost hear her thoughts in her own brain.

So innocent, so obedient... Serabel used to tell her.

She was. She would show kindness and respect and Love and humbleness to anyone, even when they didn't deserve it. Even to someone she did not like.

And she didn't like God Aarush.

The God had been chosen as the next vessel around fifty years before. He was a young male with a conspicuous inheritance and wanted nothing more from life except to have fun, enjoy the company of beautiful women, and fuck as many people as he could. And when he was appointed to be the next God... well, that had been unexpected. Not only for him, but for everyone else used to a divine God being a little more *divine*.

Serabel had taken it upon herself to educate him properly, so that he could fully understand the importance of his role, but that was taking a while. In fact, it had taken decades, and still Aarush never behaved like Serabel, nor the God before him. He was likely still adjusting to his new divine form. Meanwhile, however, he lived in a luxurious penthouse in

Aglatas on the top floor of the Raging Heart: his night — occasionally *sex* — club.

He was most definitely not the same as Serabel. But that wasn't the reason why Amala didn't like him.

She wouldn't judge him for that because it wasn't in her to judge people. She didn't like him because he belittled her *a lot* — constantly, even. Yet she was too respectful and humble to ever answer back.

She bowed her head to the High Priest on Aarush's side.

"Welcome to the Yonium."

"I haven't been here in a while," the God admitted.

I know, Amala wanted to say. The priestesses lived perfectly fine without his prying eyes and his incessant flirting. Aarush's gaze fell on her, closely surveying her body.

Amala wore a white robe which clung to her waist and a white piece wrapped around her chest. Her attire matched the silver-white of her hair that barely reached her shoulders and was never long enough to tie back. The robe concealed her front, which she never cared to hide unless visitors were present, but did nothing to cover her beautiful bare hips, or the sides of her dazzling, thick thighs.

"I know," Serabel nudged Aarush, that smirk from before returning to her lips. "She's gorgeous. Now, let's get to work. The Karale will want a complete plan of how you are scheduling Madakahiri. My lovely Amala, will you help Medyr with the rest, as I assist Aarush?"

"Of course, my Goddess."

Amala turned to the High Priest and waited until Aarush had followed Serabel away to smile at him. "Hello. How have you been?"

Medyr smiled back, sunlight reflecting on his blond hair, "We're still two months away from Madakahiri. I really don't know why the Karale wants us to deliver a schedule *now.*"

His voice didn't hide his annoyance.

"Harat is a busy man," Amala replied.

"Yeah, but I bet this is not Harat. It's Captain Mercurian, ever the asshole."

Amala giggled, "Yeah, probably."

"What should we schedule, anyway?" Medyr groaned, palm hitting one of the columns. "Madakahiri is the exact same thing every damn year."

Madakahiri, or the God's festivities, happened every year in spring. It was a celebration lasting seven days, each of them hosted at Helioneis from sunrise to sunset. A first ritual happened at every sunrise, followed by blessings and prayer. After that, the celebration transformed: it became a festival of light, with music and dances and drinking and chanting. Everyone came to Madakahiri. Traditional songs and dances combined with the year's trends, and spirituality merged with fun and amusements. There were games and challenges and often the festival shifted into more promiscuous scenarios.

The Goddess had the same kind of celebration in autumn during the Equinox: Verbamadeni.

The only difference was that Verbamadeni took place from sunset to sunrise, during the night, and its focus was not the Sun, but the Moon. Which was why Amala liked Madakahiri much more. The Sun never stopped shining on Helioneis, and she basked in the warm light for days without feeling any guilt.

Now, she chuckled at Medyr's irritation. "Just write it down formally. Aarush and Serabel will officiate *Numalu*, you and I will do *Narani*... the usual things. And maybe how many people we're expecting at Helioneis."

"Why are you always so organised? You've been High Priestess for way less time than I've been High Priest," he observed with a hint of admiration.

"I'm cut for the role," Amala winked. "I need to make Serabel's tea. Do you mind if we continue scheduling in the kitchens?"

He followed her downstairs, though he had been there enough times to know the way. But Medyr knew better than not treating Amala with the respect she deserved in her own temple, so kept beside her. The kitchens were mostly empty, aside from a few priestesses who took their cue to leave when the pair entered. Amala couldn't blame them: they weren't used to having males around and didn't like them interfering with their day.

She filled a pot with water, then looked around, searching for any sisters who could heat it through their power. No one was in sight. With a shrug, she resigned to lighting a small fire instead.

Medyr observed her as she grabbed a bunch of leaves from a bowl and got to work.

Amala liked to take care of her Goddess, and Serabel had recently been ill for several weeks. It usually happened with the coming of the rainy season, but this year was worse than usual, leaving her weakened and unable to join their rituals, even days after she had healed. Amala had been by her side every day to make sure she recovered swiftly.

She mashed Qelcena leaves with the ease of someone who knew how to work them quickly. She had picked them up herself, from one of the trees at the border of Mhelani forest. Qelcena leaves not only gave the tea an amazing, crisp aftertaste, but they preserved energy exchange, inhibiting one's energy so it could not be dispersed. It helped aid recovery and had been extremely beneficial, for Serabel, to mix with her tea.

"You're quite the maid." Medyr observed.

Amala winced as the silence broke.

"You don't make Aarush's tea?"

He huffed a laugh, "No, thank you."

"He's our *God*, Medyr."

"He doesn't live at the temple."

"So you're the boss?"

"Something like that. Your priestesses consider you the boss, too."

She waved him off but felt a spark of pride in her chest: she knew that already. Her priestesses loved her and always agreed she made an excellent High Priestess. All her sisters were happy to follow her guidance; they felt safe with her, and Amala always felt strong gratitude at the thought.

Medyr kept asking her judgement for minor Madakahiri details as she worked. She advised him, promising to share his burden of event organiser, and now poured tea into the carafe when someone called her name.

"Amala? Are you in here?"

"Yes!" she called back, but Hebex didn't wait for an answer before entering the kitchens.

"Have you seen Med—*oh*," she halted at the sight of the High Priest. "Hi."

They both chuckled: it was an unusual sight to see Hebex so flustered. Usually, she was quite confident, blunt even.

"I thought you—wait," the blond priestess smirked in Amala's direction. "Are you babysitting him?"

"Don't be a bitch, Hebs," he called out, a hand on his chest as he pretended to take it personally.

"Yeah," Amala frowned. "He's been High Priest for almost a hundred years, but still doesn't know how to plan Madakahiri."

Medyr snorted, "Very funny. It's not my fault *fucking* Captain Mercurian is asking for a formal schedule now, when it's two months away."

Hebex chuckled, throwing a half-glance in Amala's direction. One of her eyebrows wiggled, but the High Priestess smoothly waved her off.

"Off you go, lovebirds. Not in my room." She smiled as Hebex approached Medyr and kissed him on the cheek. He snaked an arm around her small waist. "I'll write down anything you need to remember, and I'll speak in your stead if the Captain behaves like an ass."

"Oh, he will." Medyr said with a smile of gratitude. He held out a hand and a rose bloomed on his palm, then appointed it to the priestess hair with tender touch — he came from the People of Earth, just like her. She kissed him again.

When he and Hebex didn't move, Amala arched an eyebrow.

"Not in my room, and *not* in the kitchens! Go have sex somewhere else!"

☼

"One more push, love," Amala said softly.

Her hands grasped the baby's head, gently but firmly. One more push and the rest of the baby would emerge. Her patient, a female named Chandana, let out a strained groan as she desperately pushed one final time. "That's it," Amala encouraged.

Her mate placed an arm around her swollen belly, supporting Chandana's body as the baby finally came out, caught instantly by Amala's firm, delicate hands. She pulled with care and expertise, until she was able to grasp its whole body, then carefully uncoiled the umbilical cord wrapped around the baby's neck: right then, the new-born let out its first cry.

Amala tried her best not to cry herself. It was her job, and she was used to it. Yet every time she assisted a birth and helped a new life enter the world, she felt overwhelmed. That feeling of pride and joy and everything that came with it... it was too much to explain through words.

"Boy," she murmured, enveloping the baby with a warm cloth as she looked at the mother. "You were amazing. Congratulations," she said, and gently brought the new-born to the mother's arms.

The woman gasped at the feeling of his new, soft skin: the bundle of joy now taking life in her embrace. The High Priestess enjoyed that moment, observing the love between mother and son as her chest subtly ached. Oh, that love.

That love was like no other.

She wished she could feel something similar. Not give it.

Feel it.

She wished for someone else to give her that much love.

Amala swiftly moved away as the newly-mother was surrounded by her mate and her family. She had chosen to give birth on the temple grounds, a choice Amala gladly appreciated. She was used to going wherever her patients wished: she was trained to assist a birth anywhere — in a hospital, at home, in the water, in an open space, but she loved doing it at the Yonium. She was born at the Yonium herself, and the feminine energy radiating from the temple was the perfect environment to hold and surround every woman, as they birthed new life.

Assisting birth at the Yonium brought her back to the days when that was her main task; she had started working as a midwife, helping the other pregnant priestesses, and creating some of the most precious memories.

There was a time when she was no one. And, some days, she missed it. She was only ever known for her incredible midwifery skills. She graduated, became a healer, and specialised in obstetrics: combining modern medicine and traditional healing. She was the first, after centuries, to commute both ways, learning and offering both to her patients. She applied ancient techniques, healing spells and energetic rituals, to new discoveries and research. She kept studying, kept learning. She had published papers and helped countless people.

She took pride in being High Priestess and being a midwife.

She wasn't sure though whether the people in Aglatas knew who she was. If she walked on the streets wearing her usual attire, people knew she was a priestess from the Yonium. But the aura of secrecy that surrounded the temple — for which one wouldn't know what happened there, unless they visited it themselves — made sure not everyone would recognize Amala in Aglatas.

She had always loved the way the Yonium wasn't broadcasted to all; it was a place of spirituality, and whilst Helioneis had succumbed to technology, the Goddess forbade the media to ever reach *her* temple. It made the priestesses feel safe and protected.

Amala had always found it quite ironic as she was extremely known in her field; everyone interested in healing knew that she was an extraordinary midwife: hospitals knew, doctors knew, specialised researchers knew... she was referenced in more than one case study, and in more than one book. That was *her* world, and she was extremely good at it. Not only did she have numerous patients in the city, but also in the forest, and the villages nearby. Many of the People would never put themselves in the hands of someone *different* for such a delicate moment as giving birth. Amala had found a way to make healing accessible to everyone and gained the trust of all her patients since their first visit. People trusted her — trusted her with their lives — and she had had every kind of patient in her life. That was her thing.

☼

An hour before sunset, Amala finally found a moment for herself. With the day spent assisting the labour, and the previous day receiving the God at the temple, she had hardly any time to breathe and stretch her body. Now she walked on the temple grounds on the lawn behind the greenhouse and reached her sisters who sat upon the fresh grass. She sighed as she laid down amongst them.

"Are you alright, my love?" Seryn asked. She was lying face up on the lawn, peering up at the sky; Teleia was half-asleep and curled beside her.

"All good," Amala confirmed. She turned to face the other priestess resting with them.

A beautiful dark-skinned woman with monolid eyes, a silver nose ring, and long lashes laid to her right; she was pregnant, clad in white robes that covered her breasts but left her swollen belly exposed. "I missed you, my beautiful Sinayla." Amala told her, crawling closer.

After Seryn and Hebex, Sinayla was the last of her closest sisters. All the priestesses were her chosen sisters, but the four had developed a special bond over the years. They were each other's family and, for Amala, whose family was not by her side, it was a blessing to rely on them.

Hebex was probably her closest friend: they were opposites in most things, but their energies had found each other and never left. Hebex was blunt, chaotic, and extroverted to say the least. She loved to talk and listen to other people talking. She delighted in asking questions and to watch people become flustered as they answered. She would have died for her sisters and was protective of each of them.

Seryn was Amala's oldest friend. Amala was the only one among the four born at the temple, but Seryn joined her not long after. She had always dreamed of being a priestess, but her family forbade it until she was old enough to make her own choices. Amala took her under her wing, and was her sister after her family cut her off. Now Seryn had mended the relationship with her relatives, but the bond between her and Amala had grown stronger since.

And Sinayla... she had joined them last, only forty years before. But she was a priestess already, accustomed to the priestess life. Only she was born and raised in a different temple: the Riza.

The Earth temple in Aglatas.

Sinayla and Amala met long before that, though. In their earlier years studying at university, they shared their first time together. For a few years, they were occasional lovers, but it stopped long before Sinayla joined the Yonium. And now she was pregnant — her mate, one of Aarush's priests in Helioneis.

"How was the trip back here?" Amala asked.

"Caelan drove me," Sinayla replied. "I'm fine, Amala. But yes, I promise this is the last time before I give birth that I will travel all the way there."

She knew Amala well and knew she would make a fuss. But that was a perk of having High Priestess Amala as midwife: she was amazing, but extremely careful when it came to her patients.

"How was the labour?"

"It was alright. Quite smooth, no issues," Amala listed quickly. "It went very fast once she started squatting. She gave birth to a boy. He's healthy and beautiful."

"Congrats, my love." Seryn whispered.

"You are so talented." Sinayla added for good measure.

Amala smiled with gratitude, her sisters were incredibly supportive when it came to her job.

She asked instead, "Is Hebs still at Helioneis?"

Sinayla nodded. "I think she'll stay there tonight, but she wasn't sure."

"Do you think Medyr wants them to be more serious?"

"He definitely does," Amala replied. "But he would scare her off, if he told her."

The only reason Hebex worked so well with her lovers was because she made a commitment to never commit to any man in her life.

Dozing off on the lawn with her sisters reminded her of simpler times, of afternoons that smelled like freshly baked bread, with hints of cinnamon and honeyed apples. The Yonium had been the only life she knew, but it hadn't always been a life void of pain and suffering — there was grief too, sometimes.

Amala peered at the sun, setting low on the horizon; the sky was turning pinkish with shades of crimson, and her heart instantly felt lighter at the view.

"See you at Dusk Call," she whispered as she stood up.

Her sisters said nothing, knowing better than holding her back in a moment like that: Amala didn't remember a day when she hadn't paused to watch the sunset.

Sunrise *and* sunset.

It was a moment she'd never miss; it was for her and her only, she rarely shared it with anyone else, and wouldn't skip it for the world. Amala loved the Sun so much that she *needed* to be alone with it, the moment it appeared in the skies, and the moment it left.

She ignored the sting of guilt in her chest that usually accompanied her thoughts. She had never looked at the sun and not felt guilty. But that feeling, for how restless it made her, was something she could live with, as long as she got to stare at the light.

CHAPTER 3

Aglatas was ruled by a Prior, and by the Karale.

The Prior was a governor in charge of the politics of the city, its expansion, and its borders. He oversaw everything that happened in Aglatas, and in the territories beyond.

The Karale was a council that convened every month.

Amala hated every single meeting. She didn't actually *hate* it, Amala was practically incapable to hate anyone or anything, but it definitely took a toll on her mental stability. Amala was used to dealing with people; she received and greeted hundreds of followers at the Yonium daily and interacted with all sorts of beings, like the pregnant females that required her midwife services — which often meant dealing with their families too, alongside their unwarranted advice on how to properly deliver a baby. But those people, overall, tended to like her — love her, even. They wanted to talk to her, and appreciated her presence and wise judgement.

The Karale was different: it consisted of fourteen members — the Prior, the four Protectors, the God and the Goddess, and all of their Seconds. Monthly meetings were hosted in the Round Room in the very centre of the Meads. Amala had never gotten used to it, nor had she ever spoke at the meetings, unless required to. They never cared about her being there.

Almost never.

Amala didn't belong there; where she was loving, sweet, and delicate, they were twisted, attached to power and territory. She was humble, they were arrogant. She was reserved, they liked to boast.

They wanted to rule, she wanted to Love.

She gave love yet they didn't want it. Well, some wanted *her*, but not in a way she would second. She'd rather no acknowledgment at all, compared to the looks she often received.

Hot High Priestess, they called her.

Amala had never commented on how disrespectful she found the nickname to be, unable to find the courage to talk back. It wasn't because she was a compliant person, Amala had never felt comfortable standing up to people who didn't know her well, and she had no intention of allowing them to know her either.

She felt guilty for thinking so low of the Karale: not *all* of the members were complete assholes, but no one stood up for her. But how could she blame them, when she wouldn't stand up for herself in the first place? Except for Serabel: her Goddess would always defend her. Although the Karale didn't respect Amala's authority, they wouldn't dare contradict Serabel's.

Amala woke up nervous that morning. She loved to wake up in gratitude, happy to live another beautiful day. Trying to seek comfort in the sunrise, she relieved some tension as she touched herself, her beautiful naked body splayed on the white sheets; the first rays of sun slowly filled the room and glowed upon her figure. She focused on Dawn Call, channelling her energy towards her priestesses, standing by their side, and setting her intentions for the day: happiness, and hopes and dreams fulfilled for them at the Yonium — and for all those who wished to use her energy as a starting push towards their goals. And Love. Love for everyone — Love for who needed it, who didn't, who wanted it, and those too scared to accept. Amala's Love was for all.

Still, that subtle sense of uneasiness followed her every step, still rotting in her chest as she knocked on the doors of Serabel's rooms.

"Enter," the Goddess' voice was harmonious, inviting her in.

"Good morning, my beautiful Goddess," Amala greeted, allowing the air to carry the tray in her stead. The door closed gently behind her. "How are you feeling today?"

Serabel was sitting on her bed, a silk foulard protectively wrapped around her head and hair; her long legs were concealed beneath the sheets, her naked upper body turning in Amala's direction, as the High Priestess pointed a hand to the tray and smoothly delivered it to the bed.

"Good morning," the Goddess said, rewarding her with a smile. "Much better than last week. I think the tea is working. And you?"

Amala set the tray upon the coffee table, pouring hibiscus tea in a glass decorated with the embroidery of a swan. "I feel much Love to share, I just hope to find people ready to receive it," she said, handing the glass to Serabel.

"Thank you," she sipped quietly as she studied the look on the High Priestess' face. At last, she sweetly whispered, "Sit with me."

Amala obeyed and sat on the edge of the mattress: it had taken her a long time to get used to that, to Serabel treating her as a *friend*... she used to hesitate many times before obeying such an order, yet now she felt at ease.

"I know you are nervous," the latter said, gently grabbing Amala's hand and placing a kiss atop of it, "But they do not deserve your attention."

"I wish they didn't give me attention, either."

"Do not waste your precious energy on them. You already know who is worthy of your love, and who isn't," Serabel said, taking another sip, "And do *not* say that everyone deserves your love."

"But it's true," Amala protested, "You know I can't choose. My heart is full; there is space for all people."

"Maybe focus on *someone* who *really* wants your love—" the teasing ceased as soon as Serabel spotted the look on her face. She snorted, "Soft spot?"

"Don't you dare." Amala rolled her eyes, huffing a laugh and determined to change the topic of their conversation, "I just don't like to have my day ruined from the words they say. I bet someone will say something stupid, forgetting I am a midwife."

Serabel chuckled, "Are we betting money?"

A nod.

"Ten silver oboli?"

Another nod.

"Aarush is my pick," Amala said.

The Goddess snorted: "Fair choice. My money is on Atalman."

The chit chat helped Amala calm down a bit: the soothing presence of the Goddess always seemed to lay a veil of brightness over the hard moments. After Serabel finished her breakfast, she stood and asked Amala to help her get ready.

With permission to touch her body, Amala gently rubbed coconut oil into her shoulders, then her back, before helping her comb her thick, curly hair. Serabel admired herself in the mirror as the High Priestess attached miniature amethysts to her strands.

"You are my favourite," she said, knowing the words would make Amala blush.

Amala did, but wore a pleasant smile on her face as she dared to reply, "I know."

☼

Normally they walked to Aglatas, but today the meeting would take place sooner than usual. Serabel saw fit to find a remedy to that. Amala stared at the two centaurs outside the temple, wondering if there was still time to change her attire. Dressed in white, a silky piece of fabric wrapped around her neck and breasts; a long robe clung around her waist, drifting down in two long pieces that covered her front, but left her hips completely bare and exposed. She wore that kind of attire on a daily basis, yet would have selected an outfit *with* underwear, if she had known they would be riding centaurs all the way to the city. Amala couldn't believe the Goddess had tricked her into this: a ride to the Meads with *both* her lovers. Serabel, on her side, seemed amused.

"Thank you for your service," she acknowledged both centaurs. Aries and Kanaan bowed to her.

Amala greeted them in turn, then gave the Goddess a side glance. She was *not* happy: "Why would you pick them? *Both* of them?"

The Goddess chuckled. "I told them to toss a coin to see who would carry you, to avoid this awkward moment." With a wiggle of her eyebrows, she asked, "Well, who won?"

Kanaan extended a hand to Amala, and she blushed.

"Please, be *nice*," she said, observing Serabel now mounted on Aries' back. She pointed at him, "You should be honoured that your Goddess is allowing you to carry her. It is a blessing indeed."

Serabel said nothing: she wouldn't dare undermine Amala's authority.

Aries bowed his head to the High Priestess, "I am honoured, and aware of the blessing." He paused for a second, as if pondering whether to say something else, but the look on Amala's face must have said enough as he quieted.

As she took Kanaan's hand and straddled his back, Serabel said, "We appreciate your help, but I would appreciate it even more if you would not tease my High Priestess. Today is already difficult enough for her."

She smiled softly, grateful for those words, and absently traced Kanaan's shoulders as he began trotting. His pace was quick, but not unsettling, and Amala found herself thinking of all the other times — several, in fact — where she had ridden him for a completely different purpose.

He'd go much faster then, and make sure her body smoothly slid onto his back and produced that delicious, continued friction that would bring her to climax in mere minutes. Kanaan — and Aries too — were always appreciative of her sounds of her pleasure.

The same sounds she was desperately swallowing now.

"What's with the cinnamon, my lovely Amala?" Serabel's voice teased, quickly tethering Amala to reality. Whilst she had kept her moans in, she couldn't say the same about her scent. Ignoring the furious blush on her cheeks, she adjusted her position in a way that would make her enjoy the ride a little *less*. Luckily for her, the centaurs ignored their exchange, and Amala busied herself by playing with Kanaan's dark hair as they rode to Aglatas.

On foot, it would normally take them an hour and a half to reach the city, and then another to reach the Meads at the very centre. Today, they reached the Prior Palace in little more than an hour.

Amala felt her heartbeat increasing its rhythm as she smoothly climbed off Kanaan, gesturing for him to draw closer before thanking him with a kiss on the cheek.

"A shame I can't ride you back," he said, gently stroking her neck.

"I have some appointments," she replied, "But I'll see you back at the temple. Perhaps tomorrow." Her sensual doe eyes sealed the deal as she said goodbye to Aries and wished the centaurs a good day, then followed Serabel inside the building.

It was beautiful: a rich palace with ancient architectural features which still included, somehow, modern and technologically advanced designs. All Aglatas was built like that: an ancient, fierce city progressing alongside the innovations throughout the decades.

She might have hated the Karale meetings, but she loved the location in which they were held.

The Goddess waited for her in the hallway as some officers registered their presence, likely notifying the Prior.

Amala was walking on Serabel's side when the Goddess turned to her and said, "Enjoyed my little surprise?"

She gasped, faking indignation. "Why would you pick *both* of them? I'd hate to disappoint one of them for the other." But a small, amused smile sat on her lips as they waited for the elevator.

"I thought Kanaan was your favourite."

"They're both good lovers. I believe Aries finds the vibe of High Priestess quite unsettling; we used to see each other much more before my ceremony."

Serabel raised an eyebrow, as the elevator doors opened.

"Good lovers? *Only* good?"

Amala followed her Goddess inside the elevator.

"*I* am an amazing lover. I wouldn't put them on my level." Amala answered with a smirk, but realisation hit her a second later. She stiffened.

The Goddess stilled too, as if she'd wanted to say something — Amala had known *what* — but she'd stopped herself just in time. They didn't look at each other as the pair slowly relaxed, then Serabel glanced at her, changing the topic.

"Behave," she murmured, "Even when they pick at you."

Amala snorted. "They always do, and I always behave."

But she was glad to occupy Serabel's side. Despite the unwanted attention she received when the Goddess walked next to her, it was difficult to focus on anyone else. Serabel was moonlight and beauty: an embodiment of all that was feminine; her rich scent was a taunting caress that made it extremely difficult for anyone around to not look, to not feel drawn to her.

Amala followed Serabel outside of the elevator, stepping foot into the hallway and proceeding towards the Round Room. All of the official meetings were held there.

She was Serabel's Second, but members of the Karale were latched to power in a strange way; they didn't like to acknowledge the God and the Goddess as the actual deities they were. Aarush and Serabel had the world's balance in their hands, yet somehow it was too much for the other Protectors to acknowledge it openly. Luckily for them, Serabel had no interest in being involved in the city's business, as long as she was given the divine attention she needed and deserved as Goddess.

Nonetheless, her presence to the meetings seemed to be required even when her judgement could do little to impact the Prior's choices, and Amala had to attend with her.

Two guards stood outside of the Round Room with slightly bowed heads; Amala wrinkled her nose in clear disapproval. They should kneel for a Goddess like Serabel.

They bowed their heads to Amala too when she passed, and followed Serabel into the room. She would have loved to greet them and share her energy, but the look on their faces as their eyes roamed her body instantly changed her mind.

"*Relax*," the Goddess whispered, sensing her tension, "It will be alright."

At her nod, one of the guards opened the doors.

They were on time, yet it seemed everyone else had gathered already. Two seats were left for them, Aarush and Medyr situated on their left.

On the right sat the Protector of Water, Nyla, with her Second, Ana, sitting beside her. She faced them, a kind smile on her face. Nyla was utterly beautiful: black hair and ivory skin, with her intense gaze surveying the room through her deep, dark green eyes.

Aglatas' Prior, Zale Harat, sat on his usual chair with his wings tucked behind him — he was one of the last in the city from a winged bloodline. The spot on his left was destined to his Second, but now free as he awaited his arrival. Amala assessed the other Protectors: Atalman and his Second for Earth; Jaren, Protector of Fire, the seat next to him empty as usual.

His Second, commonly known as the Phoenix, had never attended a Karale meeting, and Jaren probably liked to keep it that way. The Phoenix was utterly lethal: a killer, an assassin, a torturer and, occasionally, bounty hunter, who did all the dirty work for Jaren who amused himself whilst receiving updates every time a new target was hit.

Ten years later, Amala still had no idea what the Phoenix looked like, and she was glad to keep it that way. She was terrified at the sole idea of him, and glad — *so* glad — that she had never met him.

Her eyes fell on Raila, Protector of Air — her own power — and greeted them with a bow of her head.

"Good morning," Serabel spoke; her voice was pure melody blending into the Round Room, whirling around the members of the Karale, ensuring her energy reached every single one of them. She turned to the Prior, "Good morning, Prior Harat."

Every step full of delicate yet powerful elegance, Serabel moved toward the windows. She always sat there, Amala to her left and Aarush to her right. He greeted the both of them with a slight bow of his head. Serabel smiled back out of politeness while the High Priestess bowed, "God Aarush."

"Hello, pretty Amala." he replied, his eyes quickly glancing at her figure before stilling on her face, "I don't mind seeing you so often."

"*Don't*," Serabel lifted a hand, silencing him before assuming her position. She gestured for Amala to take her place at the table. "Amala is not *your* priestess to tease."

Aarush grinned, his gaze pondering Amala for a few more seconds.

"You get all the hot priestesses." He said finally, shrugging.

Serabel snorted, "And you get all the priests. I don't know how many times I need to tell you, you are *not* supposed to fuck your entourage, Aarush."

"And you would want me to believe you haven't done that?"

"Fucking my priestesses? No." replied Serabel calmly, giving a side glance to Amala.

Amala didn't dare reciprocate the look, but smoothly sat beside her Goddess, avoiding Aarush's gaze and moving her thoughts somewhere else. The Goddess' temple was a very open, progressive environment; as Goddess of Love and Sex, Serabel was devoted to a lifestyle that reflected those features, which included priestesses living naked — or close enough — with sexual intercourse occurring across the temple grounds: between priestesses or with outsiders, it didn't matter as long as it was consensual and enjoyed by both parties. Though the Yonium was flourishing with sexual energy, Serabel hadn't chosen a priestess as a lover in a long time; she had done so, in past centuries, but now only encouraged them to enjoy themselves with each other, not actively participating. She had tried with Amala, but they had only kissed a few times.

"Good morning, High Priestess." A voice to her right caused Amala to turn: the Protector of Water. She bowed her head in her direction, an almost regal gesture full of dignity.

"Lady Nyla," Amala repeated the gesture, "I hope you are having a beautiful day."

"You are always so nice," Nyla smiled, "And kind. Serabel should bring you more often." She addressed the Goddess with her chin, perhaps alluding to a past meeting Amala had managed to skip.

"The High Priestess' presence is highly required at the temple. She's the only one that can officiate certain rituals and guide the priestesses in their daily meditations. You would know that, if you came to the Yonium more than once a year," replied Serabel, her not-so-subtle teasing prompted smirks around the table. She noticed and looked at the other Protectors. "I understand you all underestimate what balance I bring to this universe, but it's in our best interest to keep that balance exactly the way it is right now. Which is why I cannot afford my High Priestess to fool around."

Amala retained herself from chuckling: Serabel never failed to remark on her role like that. She emphasised things, spinning sentences into warnings and leading her audience into a recalculation of her importance — her power. In case they had forgotten how much her contribution weighed on them all. Though half of what she said was untrue. Amala had many roles at the temple and yes, many rites needed her presence, but she had plenty of time to fool around. Serabel made sure to give her that.

"I think she would enjoy the city a bit more. If you ever come along this way, you could pay a visit to the Raging Heart." said Aarush with a wink, alluding to his club in Pyramis, the Fire district. He had never lived at the Helioneis, not a single day, yet the God's energy would have been worshipped at his temple with or without his presence. Serabel had spent centuries in the city, before deciding to retire at the Yonium.

"I do enjoy the city," Amala replied, her sweet, soft voice clear in the silence of the Round Room. "And I come here often enough. I just make sure to return before Dusk Call." She enjoyed Aarush's confused look, and could almost hear Serabel's voice, recalling the conversation from that morning.

Ten silver oboli.

"Often, you say?" Aarush repeated, his gaze sliding over Amala's figure, "What for?"

The High Priestess held his stare. Not in a challenging way, but in her usual kind, innocent, yet charming manner that Aarush adored. Medyr, by his side, was biting his lip trying to contain his laughter. It wasn't the first time Aarush had tried to charm Amala by 'forgetting' what she did for a living.

"I am a midwife," she smiled politely. "As I believe you already know. I have plenty of patients in the city, as I do in the forest. Speaking of," she turned to Nyla. "Your sister, my Lady, required my assistance for the birth of her child; I predicted it two weeks from now. I understand she would like to deliver in the Home of Waters?"

Amala couldn't hide the spark of pride that gleamed on her face; it always happened when she talked about her job, recalling the trust that people put in her.

Nyla smiled at her words, "Yes. Danua would love that. I was very pleased to know you would be assisting her, and I'll try my best to be there. I've already spoken to the priestesses in the Home of Waters to arrange the moving. They are happy to help."

"Of course. It's always a huge honour when a mother chooses to give birth in a temple. I am honoured. But," she halted, pondering how specific her next words should be. "I would advise moving there when the time is right. As a temple, the Home of Waters possesses a specific energy that could change the pregnancy's natural course. It's nothing dangerous, but Water is feminine, and the energy could stimulate the birth. I estimated two weeks, but if Lady Danua wishes to make it happen any sooner, she should try and move to the Home of Waters already."

The look on Nyla's beautiful face was grateful, appreciative, and somewhat admired, "You are precious, High Priestess. I consider my family very lucky to be cared for by your incredible gifts."

Amala blushed, "I appreciate your words."

Serabel didn't do anything to hide her smile; she was proud to show off Amala's qualities. She subtly nudged her High Priestess, tilting her head to Aarush as a reminder of their bet.

Amala scrunched her nose, her lips curving up victoriously.

The Prior finally looked up from his phone; worry contorted his features as he attempted to speak, hoping to regain control of the Karale. Before he could do so, the door swung open a final time, and the Round Room suddenly fell silent.

"I'm sorry to interrupt, boss. Your presence has been requested."

Harat spun to face the sudden presence which enraptured the Karale's attention. A male leaned against the doorframe, arms crossed, and dark hair tied up in a bun. His gaze explored the room, without focusing on anyone in particular, then returned to Harat.

"My presence?" the Prior asked, looking half confused, half relieved. Amala glanced at him, then back at the male at the door which probably explained why he was working so attentively on his phone only seconds before.

"Yeah. That's why I was late. I was dealing with it myself but... it can no longer be delayed." The male gestured with his head to the hallway, and Harat didn't hesitate before following him outside. The door closed beside them, and Serabel instantly turned to Amala.

"He is in a mood today."

Nyla shushed her, "I sense a fucking lecture coming."

She exchanged a brief glance with her Second, Ana: a stunning female with deep green eyes who was sitting on her right. Amala could have sworn the hint of a blush sparked Ana's cheeks.

No one said anything, but each of the Protectors looked around the table at the others, likely all wondering if the Karale had really needed to be summoned today. It was a monthly meeting to check the regular course of the city and the temples, and the only chance for the seven to gather. Whilst the Protectors occasionally confided in each other, providing advice or aid if needed, each had their own personal business to attend to. If something wasn't going well, Harat would solve the matter with the ones involved without mentioning anything further to the others, but he still liked each of them to know what was going on.

Amala was vaguely conscious of Serabel's flirting with Aarush as the door opened again and the male barged in, taking Harat's seat.

"Good morning," he said. He looked bored, placing both of his tattooed hands on the table. "One of you has interfered with my last investigation and I'd like to give them a chance to apologise to my face."

He surveyed the Karale with his wary gaze, his grey eyes pondering each of them. No one spoke. Amala knew they were not afraid of him, rather they waited for his next move.

The Protectors didn't like each other; whilst some had better relationships than others, they were not friends, and most communication ensued through their Seconds. The associations between Protectors were like doors not quite closed, yet ready to open if help or collaboration was requested.

But, even if they didn't like each other, none of them could hide that they liked him. *Him*. The male sitting in Harat's chair, continuing to study the group with those deep eyes of his.

Captain Mercurian.

He was Harat's Second and had held the position for the past century.

He had done several things in his life, including leading the city's intelligence department for at least thirty years. But, from the moment he became Second, he stopped all office work and was now solely in charge of all major investigations on the field. And whatever business Harat was currently attending to.

Amala had met him ten years ago at the first Karale meeting after becoming High Priestess, and had instantly understood why the others liked him so much. Captain Mercurian was just... intriguing.

Intriguing in an interesting, funny, and sometimes charming way, without ever stepping out of line. Never uttering a disrespectful word, but always saying the right thing. During all those meetings, Amala had probably spoken less than ten words to him, but she knew he had earned the respect of the Karale by helping each member at some point or another. And that respect — and *desire* — lingering in everyone's gaze was because, even after that, he had kept his distance, never revealing interest in their courts other than what his job required.

The Protectors liked to show off; they would have loved to have *him* by their side. Serabel had divulged to Amala that the Captain had received multiple offers of prestigious positions within their ranks, but had always refused without a second thought.

Nonetheless, he did his job perfectly, and the Protectors knew when they were in for a lecture.

"I believe that was me," Teun — Atalman's Second — answered eventually.

Amala exhaled a sigh of relief. She knew it couldn't be her, nor Serabel, but she had no idea if the High Priest had accidentally interfered with the Captain's business; she was thankful none of the *spiritual* ones — as the council called them — were involved.

But Teun held his piercing gaze, "I apologise. I didn't mean to meddle in your business."

"It's not my business. It's the city's business. You have inadvertently caused harm to by sending your squad *armed* into a residential neighbourhood with the order to shoot on sight any *unchecked* threat. I want you to personally visit the families." His voice was strong, brewing with a powerful energy, yet Amala could sense a kernel of... peace. Captain Mercurian might look like he wanted to rip the head off your body, but he definitely understood that his personal happiness and inner peace were not worthy of the troubles of the Karale, and he wouldn't mix the two.

Teun slightly bowed his head, "Thank you. I hope your investigation proceeds sufficiently, albeit my mistake."

The Captain gave a lazy grin as a ray of sun lit his golden skin through the window.

"That," he said, "Is none of your business."

He let his gaze wander once more around the table, then started again. "The Prior cannot attend today, so I will do the honours." His eyes quickly skimmed the paper sheet Harat had left on the table. "Madakahiri is in two months. What's the plan?"

Aarush didn't do as much as pointing at Medyr, more than happy with leaving the High Priest to deal with Captain Mercurian's questions.

"It's too soon for planning, Captain." Medyr sighed, leaning comfortably in his chair. A muscle in his jaw ticked. "It's going to be one week of celebration, as per usual. The first day is for all, from two to five for each Element individual, and the final two days reunited."

"I didn't ask for the schedule." Captain Mercurian replied. "I asked for the plan. I don't care how long it takes you to prepare a ritual, you may do it the day before if it suits. However, *I* cannot organise a festival in a day, which is why the Prior requires your logistical plan now."

"I believe the number of people involved will depend on the rituals," Medyr replied, glancing at Amala in an attempt to recall what they had discussed the day before.

"If *Numalu* is supposed to happen," she said, daring to look at the Captain for a second, "Then you shall expect the first day to be the busiest, ritual-wise." *Numalu* was a ritual of merging energies between deities and was said to be so beautiful that people from every nearby town and village would come to assist.

"*Numalu* will take place." Aarush confirmed, glancing sideways to Serabel. Amala knew of the beauty which accompanied such a joining and, whilst she had seen it before, she was eager to see it again. A memory was nothing close to watching it happen before her eyes.

The Goddess nodded. "My priestesses will join the celebration, but, if you're interested in logistics, a part of them shall stay at the Yonium for those who wish to come and pray, since Helioneis will be unavailable." Her eyes paused on Amala. "The High Priestess will join Aarush in officiating the ritual on the Air Day."

A moment of stunned silence followed Serabel's remark.

"I will?"

"Of course, my beautiful Amala. I thought you wanted to."

"I do," she quickly said, glancing at the God. "I just didn't expect God Aarush to accept."

"Why? He'd do anything for a shot at fucking you," Serabel shrugged, but realised her mistake a moment too late.

Amala's icy eyes widened in surprise, lips parting as she gasped.

Serabel's words were meant to taunt Aarush, not her, and yet... yet *she* felt embarrassed. She blushed, and Aarush didn't. Lowering her gaze, Amala did her best to conceal any hints of betrayal showing on her face.

She would have never expected her Goddess to put her in such an awkward position; Serabel *knew* better than this. She hadn't done it on purpose, of course, the jibe was not aimed at her, but it was Amala who felt embarrassed. And Aarush, ever the charmer, merely smirked and did not deny it. He hadn't agreed to this because he thought Amala worthy of officiating the ritual with him — of course he didn't. Amala mentally cursed herself for her naivety.

She *wasn't* worthy of a deity, and she never would be.

Serabel looked vaguely worried, but Amala kept her mortified stare fixed on the table. She hoped the meeting would finish soon.

Of all the times she had wished to speak up for herself, going against her Goddess was an impossible feat. Amala was unable to hurt someone's feelings on purpose.

The meeting ended, concluding with a summary of the previous month, and how it had been for each Protector and its people. Atalman had requested the Captain's help for some troubles he was having with a neighbourhood downtown; Raila had nothing to report for the people of Air, whereas Nyla and Ana had informed of some strange behaviour in the fountains of their court, powered by Water energy. They were waiting to see if the activity would extend to other public fountains, or remain concealed within the borders of their court, and Captain Mercurian could hardly feign his interest in the matter. Jaren grinned the whole time on his phone, and when his turn came, he seemed glad to inform them that the Phoenix's last mission had been a success. Amala shuddered at the mention of the Phoenix: Jaren's Second was a lethal weapon of death and that shiver was likely shared by all across the table.

Amala kept her distance as the Protectors exited the room, avoiding Serabel at all costs. She felt guilty for it, but wasn't ready to accept her apologies. It made her uncomfortable, the idea of her Goddess saying sorry — who was she to receive such explanations from a deity?

No one.

Medyr stayed behind, though, and approached her on the way out.

"Are you alright?" he asked. He knew how uneasy the meetings made her feel.

"I'm fine," she murmured. "I don't want to talk about it."

"Aarush is an asshole," Medyr shrugged. "He could have said something."

"Don't talk about our God like that!" She scolded, her voice a whisper.

"He *deserves* it, if he still hasn't figured you are not going to accept his offer..."

"Medyr, seriously. Don't bother."

But he went on, "I get it, Amala. That feeling of not being worthy of their attention or their love..."

Amala frowned. "You *don't* get it. If you had, you wouldn't have slept with my Goddess."

It had happened only once, from what she knew, and what had shocked her hadn't been Serabel's choice to sleep with Medyr... but the fact that he'd said yes.

He didn't do as much as wince at her words, "That's unfair. I don't know a single person that would say no if she asked."

Amala's eyes shot to him, challenging: "You know *me*. I said no."

"Are you angry at me because I slept with your Goddess?"

"She's your Goddess too. And I'm not angry. I just don't believe that you feel unworthy if you choose to sleep with her. I'd never choose that; I would live in regret forever."

Medyr gently brushed his fingers on her shoulder, but she didn't move. "Why regret?"

"Regret for not being the High Priestess I should be," she murmured, "I *honour* the Goddess. I could never dishonour her by... allowing her to have me. *Me*," she repeated, as if it wasn't clear enough that she felt so dreadfully unworthy of the attention. Medyr's eyes surveyed her, calmly but steadily. He wasn't wrong; some part of him understood her, but other parts didn't.

"Give yourself more credit, High Priestess Amala."

He left, leaving her in the middle of the hallway. Amala hated the way she was holding her breath.

Alone in the corridors, she waited a minute before finding her way back to the elevator: Serabel was already gone and had muttered something about meeting back at the temple, but Amala knew she planned to enjoy some alone time with Aarush. She wouldn't blame the Goddess for what she had said, even if it had embarrassed her. But Serabel knew better and was trying to prove a point. To *defend* Amala from Aarush because she knew, she *knew* Amala would never want Aarush, even if she had felt worthy of him.

Because she *couldn't*.

The High Priestess hurriedly entered the elevator and pressed the ground floor button. Lost in her thoughts, a voice behind her took her by surprise before the doors could close. She gasped, turning to find Captain Mercurian entering the elevator behind her. A slight smile curved his lips as he said, "Hello, Amala mate."

CHAPTER 4

A mala didn't smile back. She spotted the camera in the corner of the elevator, then looked back at him as the automatic doors closed.

"Hawk—" she started.

"For the thousandth time, Amala, there's no audio in those cameras. No one heard me. You can stop looking as though you want to murder me." He said, holding his stance.

"They can see my face," she retorted.

"Don't be shy, High Priestess," he teased, causing her to chuckle.

He halted, pointing at her expression, "There you go, a smile for me. See? That wasn't hard."

She huffed, glancing at how many floors separated them from ground level, "Did you have fun today? Playing Prior?"

"I enjoy my job thoroughly. Are *you* alright?" The slight worry in his eyes made her features soften.

"I'm fine," she sighed. She didn't want to talk about it. "What was Harat's business anyway? It sounded so... serious."

Amala was curious, and Hawk had never failed to provide juicy information when she had asked before.

"Just some family shit going on. His mate is pregnant, and he swore to answer every call. Which translates into *me* answering every call." He shrugged. "As I told you, I enjoy my job."

"Thoroughly," Amala echoed, causing him to snicker. "But really? Eset Harat is pregnant?"

She was surprised; she usually sensed new life long before the news came out, but Hawk held her disappointed gaze. "Don't worry, Amala mate. I'm sure she will ask you to be her midwife. If you are so sure you want to handle all that stress…"

"I endure that stress *daily*, Hawk." She exhaled, eyes dropping to the tattoos on his neck, "Eset's womb would just be womb number forty-four of this year. Of course, my stress can't match yours though, right? The powerful Prior's second, with such a fundamental job… picking up the phone."

Hawk let out a low chuckle, his eyes settling on Amala's figure, "Feisty High Priestess, today." She glimpsed a flash of his elongated canines, one of the hereditary traits of Hawk's blood.

"What time is your first appointment?"

"In three hours," Amala said, shuffling closer to the elevator doors as they approached ground level. "We *can* go, but I need some lunch before. I'm not gonna starve as you hogtie me from the fucking ceiling."

☆

Amala and Hawk Mercurian had history.

They met for the first time ten years before, at one of Amala's first meetings as High Priestess; she'd been rather dazzled by his looks, embodying her ideal type in full. Amala liked a male with long hair, and she had been subtly watching him throughout the whole meeting, before realising her attention was drawn by something else... something different than his hair. She couldn't understand what, but didn't force it and, as the meeting concluded, she'd returned to the temple, and tried not to think about him.

But for some reason, thoughts of him kept coming back. They were subtle, at first, and she had used the memory to meditate, trying to discover some sense in it.

And then, some weeks later, she'd seen him again.

During the Full Moon ritual, he'd come to the Yonium, and she was sure she'd never seen him there before. That ritual was the second Full Moon she'd embraced as High Priestess and, as she exposed her energy, scent, power, and divinity for all to see, to worship, to appreciate... she'd felt it again.

Amala hadn't looked at him, during the ritual, not even for a moment, but she embodied his scent: midnight wind, and a note of lemon, a delicious scent trying to merge with her cinnamon fragrance. Calling her.

Something was wrong, yet everything she felt was terribly right.

She had waited until the end of the ritual, as people began to leave the temple, then searched for him.

Where was he?

She couldn't spot him among the crowd, yet it shouldn't have been too difficult to see him. He was the only thing she could sense during the ritual, and she had exhausted an hour forcing herself not *to look at him, when her body and soul screamed to turn around, to become lost in his eyes.*

The feeling would not escape her — the feeling which told her exactly where he was throughout the whole ritual, but now was failing.

What feeling was that, anyway?

It was something new and unexpected, something she knew the name of but refused to voice: a subtle presence that wouldn't leave her be, but wouldn't taunt her either.

Had he left already?

He couldn't have. Not without saying hello. During the ritual, his energy had utterly consumed her.

Amala gave it one last try, surveying the crowd with hungry eyes, and... There he was.

Just across the marble path, eyes up assessing the Full Moon.

Had he been there all this time? How could she have missed him?

She didn't waste any more time now, and briskly trotted down the steps, rushing through the crowd to reach him before she lost him again.

If he had seen her arrive, he didn't let it show, but Amala's scent was so strong, she knew he felt it.

What happened next was confused in a blur of feelings she couldn't name; the crowd disappeared, as did the temple, the sky, and Mhelani forest all around. She no longer saw the moon.

There was nothing else but him. Her icy eyes melted into his grey, dark gaze, and then they spoke.

"Mate."

They said it together, and that word... Amala had not wanted to say it. She had not even sensed the word in her consciousness yet was unable to control her lips as she voiced it aloud.

As if her soul had said it for her.

They shared a look of surprise, as if they couldn't believe what had just happened. Was this the reason they felt so drawn to one other? Were they mates?

And then, she felt it: a thread crafted of strong wind and sunlight knotting around her soul and heart, pulling at once. By the way he suddenly moved, he'd felt it too.

Words failed her.

This beautiful male in front of her was her mate.

The person that would receive and accept her Love for the rest of her life.

Amala felt shy beneath his intense gaze. What could she say to him?

Whatever she decided would possibly be a moment he'd remember forever — was he feeling the same way? The same thoughts, the same uneasiness that ignited in a way that felt just right?

As that thread made of light subtly pulled once more, Amala decided to take the first step.

She had never been afraid to show her Love. If he was meant for her, perhaps there was a reason.

"Mate," her sweet voice drifted from her lips. "It's beautiful to meet you. My name is Amala."

Hawk Mercurian was her mate. But they weren't mated.

After making his acquaintance all those years ago, they had sat under a tree next to the Apàle and realised that, if they were mates, things in their lives would change. Also, they had realised that their mating bond was far from snapping; whilst the shimmering thread connecting their souls was there, it wasn't pulling just yet. It was a subtle pull, a merging of their energies that would grow into their souls, day by day, until one day it would snap and they would feel the need, the *urge* to mate. To be bound for eternity.

So, as they shared an apple under a Qelcena, they decided they would wait for the bond to snap and use that time to get to know each other. They both were more than happy to take things slow, but it hadn't gone the way they expected.

Ten years.

Ten years passed and their mating bond had grown, yes, but *never* snapped.

So, they had waited. Day after month after year, becoming each other's closest friend.

No one knew Amala better than Hawk, and no one knew Hawk better than Amala. Their friendship blossomed day by day, as their love had too, and now... well, now they were waiting for the bond.

They could both sense the time was drawing closer, but still made no move towards each other, as they had promised all those years before. They had never slept together, had never even kissed, but their friendship allowed them to indulge in all the other things mates usually did... as they *knew*, no matter what, they would mate and spend the rest of their lives with each other.

In fact, Amala and Hawk had a dog, rescued from the local shelter three years before. While it lived with Hawk in Aglatas, Amala saw Howlite often. Together, the pair had promised to see each other at least twice a week, *every* week, and to make sure they wouldn't skip that, they had an actual commitment.

"Do you think it needs to be tighter or—" Hawk asked, surveying her figure.

"It's just fine, tighter is going to hurt." Amala glanced at her wrists tied together.

"Are we pretending you wouldn't like it if it hurt more?" He raised an eyebrow as he observed her body. He was proud of his job: Amala was hanging off a wooden beam, red ropes around her chest, an intricate design following all over her body, her hips, legs and calves, with a single knot at the apex of her thighs.

Hawk observed her. Their commitment — rope-play class and practice — had started as a joke but ended up becoming an activity they were both extremely good at. Not to mention the way it had strengthened their friendship: seeing each other's body and learning to trust one another had brought them incredibly closer.

When they had the idea, a few months after meeting each other, they both still thought their mating bond would snap very soon, and rope-play sounded like a smart idea to a couple of horny people who thought they would sleep together in a matter of months.

At first, Amala was not opposed to the idea of rope-play becoming sexual. Only, it had never happened like that. Once it had become clearer that they weren't going to mate anytime soon, they'd both taken passion into their commitment, never having a second thought about its meaning.

Their rope-play was a form of art: art through ropes, bodies and trust, and Hawk was a master at it.

Now Amala rolled her eyes, scoffing at his teasing, "That's none of your business."

"Why? We both know you don't mind pain."

"Not your business!" she repeated, huffing a laugh.

"Not my business, but I'd like to know my *mate* is sexually taken care of," Hawk replied with nonchalance. He smirked, "You're still fucking that centaur, aren't you?"

Amala grimaced, "Not *fucking*," she tugged at her restraints as he shifted position, moving along her body so she couldn't see him anymore. "I can't fuck him."

Whilst she couldn't see him, she distinctly heard Hawk snicker, "I don't even want to know how sex between you and him is supposed to work."

Amala rolled her eyes, yielding to the ropes and resting her head on the knot holding her body upright, "It doesn't. Because even if Kanaan is a handsome male," she paused, picturing him in her mind, "The rest of his body is a *horse*. And the *size* of a horse. Do you need me to explain or?" Her soft laugh turned into a whimper as she felt Hawk slowly sliding a finger across her body, tracing her skin.

"Poor High Priestess," he taunted, "He can still go down on you, though."

"That he does. Now, please stop," Amala hissed, squirming in the ropes as Hawk's touch drew closer to her back. "Hawk," she repeated. "*Please*."

He halted, and was back facing her in a second, a grin on his face, "I'll spare you. But just because you admitted that the centaur makes you come."

"I never said that."

"I know you well enough to know that you wouldn't spend your time with him if you didn't enjoy it." Hawk raised an eyebrow, and the High Priestess curved her lips into a small smile.

"Fine," she said. "Enough with the ropes for today. I need my blood to fully circulate before I go back to my midwife duty."

Neither of them spoke as Hawk proceeded to untie her; he always did it with such delicacy and soft touches, making sure she got the aftercare she needed. He hoped she felt his gratitude as he continued loosening the knots that had turned her skin red, almost purple. His memory wandered back to the first time he'd done that; it had been the first time for both, despite not knowing each other long. They had laughed the whole time, trying to figure out the knots and the rules, and then — when Amala's hands were almost blue from the tightness around her wrists — she had suggested, "Maybe we should find a rope class, huh?"

And they had done exactly that. At first, they were hesitant, conscious that their faces would be recognized; that fear alone had kept them wondering if it was a good idea to keep seeing each other, but they had discovered how private, secretive, and reclusive that world was. Perfect for the two of them to enjoy without anyone else knowing.

"You okay, Hawk?" Amala's soft voice tethered him back to reality. "Are you overthinking this again?"

He finished untying the last knot and scooped her into his arms, lifting her sinuous body, "Yeah, I was. Sorry," he pressed a kiss to her forehead, "You alright?"

She nodded, placing her head on his chest.

Her fingers stroked the back of his hand, eyes trying to catch a glimpse. Amala loved to observe Hawk's hands. They were covered in tattoos, as his forearms were, and each marking told her something about him. On the back of his right hand, there was a human heart; black twirls of ink surrounded the heart, stemming from the base of his fingers down to his wrist. Letters were etched into each of his knuckles: *E D G E*. His left had a human brain encircled by the same patterns. His fingers were tattooed as well: on his index, a stylised hawk — from when he'd lost a bet — and on his ring finger, the word *senihsehs*. Amala wasn't sure what it meant, but every time she'd asked, Hawk had skirted the question. At first, it was *"I'll tell you when we finish our first full suspension tie."* And when they had, it became *"When you'll learn how to self-tie a corset"*. Then *"When you'll go a whole night without pulling a single girl"* and many others after, to the point that Amala still had no idea what it meant. Currently, the next target was *"When we'll mate"*, but she already knew he wouldn't tell her.

He had piercings, too: Amala nostalgically recalled when he used to wear a nose ring. Now, he limited to earrings.

"Do you want to be babied?" Hawk mocked, knowing after their sessions, it was usual for Amala to crave his attention. She nipped at his pectorals through his t-shirt.

"I'm okay," she grunted, "Take this off and make me happy," a grin appeared on her sweet face as she tugged at his t-shirt.

Hawk shook his head, revealing a flash of his canines, "Your midwife duty awaits, High Priestess."

"You did an amazing job today, Hawk. I think it was one of the best sessions we've done in a while." Amala replied, massaging her wrists.

"Thanks, Amala mate." He would have been the one massaging her skin, but didn't trust her to be on her feet after being suspended for so long: the only time he'd done that, she had fainted after two seconds.

"And for the record, I know you can hold it for longer. Spare me that bullshit, you just wanted to talk."

Amala laughed; she had gestured to him that she wanted to change ties soon after he'd finished the knots, so he had immediately removed the rope from her mouth, just to endure her voice mocking him for the remainder of the session.

"But yeah, it was great. Kind of hard to work when your sweet scent fills the room like that, I won't lie... but I made it through."

"I'm not going to pretend I don't enjoy you tying me up, Hawk." Amala winked.

A faint smile painted Hawk's lips, "I wonder what will happen when we put all of these sessions to practice."

In every other case, Amala would have blushed.

But not with Hawk.

She had never been able to hide her feelings from him.

It was her turn to smile, teasing.

"Keep wondering."

CHAPTER 5

Amala arrived to the Yonium an hour before sunset. She was tired, but at least the day was almost over: one more ritual, and then she could rest her energy, and refocus on loving her temple, her Goddess, and priestesses, rather than dispersing it to all around.

She was happy, though. Her visits had gone well, her signature glow swirled around her, as it always did after visiting her pregnant patients. The level of trust, confidence, and intimacy she had to build with each female... still, she couldn't believe people trusted her that much.

The sky was still blue, far from the pink stains that brushed the horizon — Amala's favourite moment of the day. Glancing around the marble footpath, Amala nodded gracefully at the priestesses who recognised her: a couple of them read under a tree, and another stood at the very border with the forest, talking with a centaur. The hour before Dusk Call was always a soothing, relaxing moment for the priestesses; almost done with their daily duties, they were able to recharge their energy before channelling it into the final ritual.

Amala didn't let herself linger on the temple grounds. As soon as she returned, she went up the stairs and reached Serabel's bedrooms, gently knocking on the door.

"Enter," the Goddess' voice was silvery, and her smile quivered when she saw the High Priestess, "Hello, my love. How was your day?"

"It was alright, my patients are doing well." Amala moved closer as Serabel gestured for Amala to sit beside her on the bed. She obeyed, the Goddess reaching for her hand and brushing gently on her palm.

"I'm sorry if I made you uncomfortable during the meeting, my lovely Amala. I meant to taunt Aarush, but I just ended up hurting you," she explained, her features soft as their eyes met.

The High Priestess curved her lips into a shy smile, "There's nothing to apologise for, Goddess Serabel... I appreciated your help." She tried to avoid recalling the feeling that shot through her body when Serabel uttered those words in the Round Room. Looking up at Serabel's lovely face, she forced herself to say, "Did you enjoy the rest of your day? You left the second the meeting finished..."

Her face said it all: the Goddess and the God had spent the evening together.

"I *must* apologise, Amala. I know you don't want to hear it, but I am sorry. I think you should be angry at me."

The High Priestess forced back the surprise in her eyes. "Angry? With you?"

"You should."

"I could never."

"Then I don't deserve you," Serabel replied simply.

"Alright, my Goddess. I'll accept your apology as long as you never say something like this, ever again." Amala sighed. "Now, tell me about your time with Aarush."

Her words of forgiveness made Serabel's eyes shine in a different light. Her voice felt reassured again as she replied, "I felt guilty, but he made me feel better. But honestly... I left earlier so that I could leave you free for the rest of the day."

Amala hummed, her cheeks slightly blushing, "There was no need for that."

"Oh, there was indeed," Serabel chuckled, "His energy was all on you, today. You would have known if you had looked up for more than two seconds."

"That's not true! He knows better than showing his interest in front of *them*."

The Goddess shrugged, "I didn't want him to starve."

A scoff. Amala rolled her eyes, "We have never even *kissed*, Serabel."

But she let herself zone out for a second at the feeling of his muscled arms around her small waist when he kissed her forehead.

Serabel let out a hum and Amala spun towards her, "What?"

"I don't even want to imagine how blue his balls must be."

This time, she let out a laugh. Despite her best efforts to conceal her friendship with Hawk from the world, her Goddess knew they were mates. Mostly because having a mate made Amala's intentions clear to Serabel as to why she refused to become her lover. Other than her, though, she had not told anyone. Not any of her sisters, nor anyone else.

Amala glanced at her wrists to detect any indications of their rope-play, but her skin was pleasantly normal, with no purple bruises adorning them the way it had happened so many times before.

Serabel followed her gaze; she knew about their commitment.

"You're fine. You know that you can tell me when you want to move in with him and then you're free, right?"

Amala instantly shook her head, "Being your High Priestess is the highest honour of my life. And Hawk knows that, even if we decide to... *mate*," her voice quivered as she said the word, "I would still want to live at the temple."

The Goddess moved closer to her, surveying her figure with those sweet eyes; Amala held her gaze, but wanted to cave into Serabel's power and embrace. Then Serabel was hugging her — hugging her like she would a friend, and Amala couldn't believe she was allowing herself this close to her *Goddess*...Serabel kissed her forehead, "I can *feel* it, you know. Your emotions."

Amala nodded. She knew.

And Serabel was right. If she knew already, why hide it? She braced herself as she released a breath, "I feel like the bond is growing. Like... the moment we choose to claim each other as mates is getting closer."

She said those words aloud for the first time since the thought had started haunting her; it started a few weeks before, after another rope-play session. The moment before she left his apartment, Hawk had drawn her closer, kissed her hair, and whispered, *"You are so important to me, Amala mate."*

She had beamed at his words, but hadn't said much in return, afraid to reveal more than she wanted to say. Instead, she relived the scene in her head the entire journey back to the temple. Amala and Hawk had exchanged many sweet words over the years, but she had never reacted like this.

"How do you feel about it?" Serabel asked, her voice was sweet and caring: the one of a mother. Amala loosened up slightly in her embrace, enjoying Serabel's warmth.

"It's Hawk. We both knew this would become real the second we knew we were mates. It just feels weird to know that... it *is* becoming real now. You see, when we decided to just get to know each other until the bond would snap in place, I never expected for things to go like this — enduring ten years of constantly teasing and mocking each other, ending up as dearest friends instead." Amala looked up at the Goddess, whose eyes were kind as she listened. "Hawk is *everything* to me. I'm not scared, but I'm not used to feeling like this. I can't help thinking...

will things be different? Because I love us, now. And I don't want it to change."

Serabel's unspoken words soothed Amala's body and mind as she lost herself in that pure, tender gaze: she had never forgotten that Serabel was an actual *deity*, but to experience such direct contact was always unexpected. The Goddess took care of the stress waves lingering in her energy, calming her down until there was nothing but untainted bliss in her thoughts.

"My High Priestess Amala is scared to love a little harder?"

Amala instinctively smiled, then. Such correct words reflecting whatever was going on through her head and heart.

"I'm not afraid of love. I'm afraid to love *him* so much... that it will be difficult to reciprocate."

"My lovely Amala," Serabel's voice was a soothing caress, "If there's one person that can love you the way you *deserve*... that's your mate. That's Hawk."

She wouldn't admit it then.

Not yet...but Amala knew the Goddess was right.

☼

"So? How did it go?" Seryn nudged her as Amala sat beside her, a small bowl in her hands.

"What?"

The priestess slowly smirked, "The meeting. What else did you do?"

Just some rope-play with my mate I never told you about.

"The meeting went well." She said instead, "I visited a couple of patients after that, including your sister. She's doing well, we'll be able to know the sex by next week."

Seryn gave her an appreciative look, "I'm so glad she chose you as her midwife... I told her so many times that you're the absolute best."

The High Priestess blushed at those words, but Seryn only smiled, adding: "It's true, Amala. And you know it."

Amala gratefully traced her arm. "She wants a boy, right?"

Seryn mumbled something, then sighed. "She didn't tell me, but I think she's afraid that a girl would eventually choose to join the Yonium."

Amala did nothing to hide the disdain painting her features.

"That's not fair," she scoffed, "A male could choose to join Helioneis the same way a female could choose to join us."

Seryn shrugged with impatience. "Velia thinks I will put her on this path—the baby, I mean, assuming she is a girl. That perhaps I will *inspire* her, maybe? To follow my choices."

The High Priestess scoffed again, beginning to eat the contents of her bowl: banana, strawberries, and mango.

"Regardless of what Velia thinks," Amala said carefully, sucking on a piece of strawberry. "Many people wouldn't want their children to join the temples. The perspective of spending the rest of their lives bound to a deity doesn't seem appealing, and I can understand that. You cannot know how it is, until you feel it."

"You've felt it since you were born, Amala, but we've been known in a different way. I've been wishing to join the Yonium since the first time I ever attended a ritual, but you know my family never wanted me to... I had to wait until I was of age before I could move here," Seryn explained, "And it took even longer to mend my relationship with them, after I made my choice."

Amala knew her friend's initiation to priestess life hadn't been easy, yet she had been by her side every day, trying to make things better for her as best as she could.

"I'm sorry if that has been hard for you," she said, reaching for her hand and gently stroking the back of it, "But I'm glad they accepted it, and I'm even happier to have you here. You can come with me, next week, when I visit Velia."

Seryn smiled broadly, gratefulness in her eyes, "I would love that."

Amala ate another piece of fruit, chewing slowly and relaxing her back against the wall, as Sinayla joined them.

"Not on the ground, my love," Amala reprimanded her as Sinayla began to sit, "Please, let me grab you some cushions." She quickly stood, leaving her fruit bowl on the ground, and left the room before the priestess could object.

Sinayla sighed, "She didn't have to."

But Seryn shook her head, "She's right, you should be as comfortable as you can! She'll never let you settle for less." Her tone was enough to settle the matter, and when Amala came back a minute later, she positioned the cushions comfortably for Sinayla.

"You are too kind, Amala," she said as she curled on the pillows, using one to balance her nearly giant belly.

"I'm merely doing my job," Amala said, gently stroking her hair, "How are you feeling?"

"Very tired, but I'm excited. I can't wait to meet her," Sinayla placed both hands on her womb, "I can't wait for her to grow up here."

Amala grabbed her bowl and slowly resumed eating; the taste of mango was pleasantly sour and instantly reminded her of lemon. Lemon. And Hawk. Amala sighed. If things were about to change, they should have talked about it. She should have brought it up; she wanted him to know that she cared, and wasn't pretending to be emotionally unavailable or uninvolved. She was scared. She took a mental note to tell him, or at least to try, and took another mouthful of mango.

"What does Caelan think of baby X living here?" Seryn asked Sinayla.

Amala subtly looked at the pregnant priestess, who nodded thoughtfully.

"We talked about it again today and we're sure. Maybe we'll alternate temples when she's older, but me and Xantara will live here, and he'll come to visit daily. Will Serabel let him stay here for the first few days?" she asked Amala, eyes slightly worried.

"You didn't ask her?"

"I'm afraid she's going to say no. I know that having a male here is unsettling for us all, I don't want to be the one to bring one..." Sinayla continued, blushing.

Amala interrupted her, "It's not unsettling when he's your mate *and* you're about to give birth to your child, my beautiful Sinayla. All of us bring males to the temple, for different reasons..."

"You don't."

"I don't." Amala complied with a smirk.

Seryn wiggled her eyebrows, a hand reaching for Sinayla's womb, gently stroking her swollen stomach.

"What about your Captain?" the latter asked.

Amala choked on a piece of strawberry.

Oh, she was in trouble. So much trouble.

"Serves you right — those fruits don't even go well together." Seryn mused, gently patting her back as she coughed.

"I like it," Amala spluttered, trying to shift the focus of the conversation.

Unsuccessfully, however.

Sinayla sneered, "Are you avoiding the question?"

"About what?"

"About *him*!"

Amala shrugged, accepting failure; her sisters would refuse to relent on the issue until she gave in, providing them with the answers they wanted.

"What about him?"

"How are things? When did you see him last?" Seryn asked, a smirk on her beautiful face.

Her sisters didn't know Hawk was her mate, but they knew about him. Over the years, Amala hadn't told them much, but had also been unable to hide her relationship with him as time went on: whilst Serabel knew the full story — mating bond countdown included — her sisters just knew Hawk was her friend, and that he had become more and more important to her over time.

The High Priestess sighed, rolling her eyes in exhaustion, "Today we had lunch together, and it was nice. Maybe I'll see him again later this week."

"Why don't you bring him here?" Sinayla teased, her hand playfully running up Amala's thigh.

"Not a single chance."

Both priestesses seemed to sigh in exasperation, before Seryn laughed, "You'd rather keep messing with Kanaan instead of giving *him* an actual shot?" Her tone was playful, but the question was serious, and Amala knew the weight it bore.

What did she want? She didn't know.

Fragments of her conversation with Serabel played in her head one after the other, almost blinding her — the memory of her energy and love: fresh, raw, and real.

Hawk is everything *to me.*

I'm not afraid of love. I'm afraid to love him *so much... that it's going to be difficult to reciprocate.*

She looked up at Sinayla, then Seryn, lips curved into a small smile as she opened her mouth to—

"High Priestess Amala!"

She whipped her head in the direction of the voice as Teleia entered the room, searching for her. "Two centaurs are here, and they wish to see you."

"Two at the same time?" Sinayla mused out loud. "Damn, Amala, you are busy." Her words invoked giggling among the priestesses, but Teleia shook her head.

"No," she clarified. "Not your lovers. A female and her mate... she believes she is pregnant."

Amala instantly stood, handing her fruit bowl to Sinayla, "Xantara will love mango, I bet," she said with a smile, brushing Seryn's hair before following Teleia out of the room. She could have sworn Seryn's gaze narrowed as they left.

Teleia guided her outside of the temple, where two young centaurs waited at the bottom of the stairs, on the marble path. Amala thanked the priestess with a kiss planted on her forehead.

"Thank you, my love," she said.

She quickly descended the stairs, eyes narrowing as she recognised the female centaur; her scent was sweet — freesia and blueberries and... something else — something different, *new*.

"Palana," Amala murmured, closing the distance between them, reaching for her hand.

"I'm sorry to bother you at such a late hour, High Priestess," the centaur murmured, "But I've... I've felt strange and I'd like you to assist me, if you will."

"Of course," Amala said. "Teleia mentioned you believe to be pregnant?"

The male centaur nodded. "My name is Keneti; I'm Palana's mate. We have been *trying* over the past few months, but this is the first time something is different. She doesn't feel good," he explained, and the High Priestess carefully listened, before returning her attention to the female.

"Did you miss your heat?"

Palana breathed, as if she was in pain, and Amala gestured for the pair to follow; walking on the grass surrounding the temple, the lawns were full of flowers and trees, brimming with delicious fruit.

"Lay here, beautiful. Everything is going to be alright," Amala said kindly, a hand stroking Palana's back as the centaur tried to sit down on the grass. Keneti helped her, his strong arms solid as he supported his mate into position.

"Yes, I did miss my last heat. But now all I feel is pain, cramps, and nausea. I'm not sure what it means. Helerai didn't have these symptoms at the beginning of her pregnancy, and all of what I'm feeling sounds so *human*," she carefully added, "I'm afraid something might be wrong."

Amala listened to every word, kneeling on the grass beside her, sending quiet tendrils of air to sooth her tensing skin and muscles. "Do I have permission to touch you?" she asked. "Will you allow me to?"

Palana nodded, but the High Priestess waited for her response.

"Yes. Do what you need," the centaur finally said.

Amala approved with a small smile of reassurance and proceeded to examine Palana's body. Her power acted with her, sensing the energy within her body: the muscles, bones, and the way her organs reacted to Amala's inquiry. Amala's energy was focused, careful and attentive to catch any hint, any whisper of an unusual pattern manifesting. The silence around them seemed to thicken, barely interrupted by Palana's slow breathing, as if each cost a great amount of pain.

Amala only focused further, every atom of her being concentrating on the female in front of her, feeling her presence and her body, the flowing of the blood in her veins, the laboured breath coming out of her lungs, the steady contractions.

"Well," she quietly said; her sweet voice was a whisper in the night, "You *are* pregnant. Congratulations." A smile instantly painted her lips as she saw the joy in Palana's eyes. The centaur looked up to her mate, who seemed equally incredulous.

Amala left them for a moment, allowing time to focus on each other, sharing the joy they would never forget in this moment. After a while, she continued, "It seems like you're having terrible cramps, beautiful Palana. And you were right, this is not a common symptom for centaurs."

"Is that bad?" Her voice betrayed incredible happiness mixed with a steady note of fear.

Amala quickly shook her head. "The major risk with centaur pregnancies is twins. Twins might cause problems, but you have only one life inside of you, and it's strong and growing. A single life is... safe. You are healthy and all is well. If you wish for me to assist you through the remainder of your pregnancy, we shall need a more specific visit perhaps, to assess everything else you may need."

"How far along am I?" Palana asked.

"I'd say almost two months. But I will be certain if you allow me to visit in a few days, I'll be more equipped for it."

The centaur absently nodded, one hand trying to reach for her belly and struggling as she couldn't.

Amala, still kneeling, continued to send the comforting tendrils of air in correspondence with her uterus, where the cramps were frequent and painful. "You are doing so well, Palana. This new adventure is going to be beautiful."

The centaur seemed to appreciate her words as she smiled. "What about the pain? Is there anything that I can do to make it go away?"

Amala considered. "Centaurs usually refuse modern medicine," Palana vigorously nodded in silent confirmation, "So I wouldn't advise pills or painkillers. A good combination of bloodstone and malachite could help you. You shall keep them on the painful area for a few nights, and it should help. But please, if you are in too much pain... don't disdain medicine. I'll never ask it from you unless it's the only way. But keep an open mind, just in case."

"Thank you, High Priestess. I am very grateful for your help."

"It's an honour to be chosen to help more lives into this world," Amala said, then helped Palana to stand up again. Keneti intervened, balancing her as the centaur struggled to stand still.

Palana breathed, "I am alright. I just need time."

Amala followed them back to the temple, her bare feet silent on the damp grass, the whole night silent too. She glanced up at the sky: clouds, thick and prepotent, covering the moon...

She blinked.

The moon was always there.

A strange quiet slowly possessed her body as she stilled her movements, searching for the moon in the sky. Narrowing her eyes, she tried to perceive the glimmer through the darkness of the clouds, the darkness of the very sky...

But the moon wasn't there.

Amala tensed, her energy focusing on the light, the *light*...

Then, something inside of her flickered. Energy flickered... not *her* energy, but that of Goddess Serabel. The Goddess' energy inside of her jolted, and Amala gasped in pain and surprise. The feeling was different, but not foreign. As she felt the jolt of power which didn't belong to her, nor her body... she knew something was wrong.

She barely opened her mouth in time to warn the centaurs when the ground shook beneath her feet, and she fell.

Wrong, wrong, *wrong!* Her mind screamed as she scrambled up as fast as she could. Everything was shaking, now. The earth was shaking, the temple trembled too and she could hear all of it — the energy crumbling.

She reached for her power, trying to steady herself: it was an earthquake, and her priestesses were still in the temple.

The Goddess was in the temple.

She didn't think twice before running; her power kept her focused, limiting the falls on the quaking ground beneath her feet. Amala didn't realise, didn't have time... the feeling inside of her, the energy becoming bigger, stronger: trembling, jolting, crashing, clenching, fighting...

Wrong, wrong, *wrong*.

She ran inside the temple; the columns shook and the windows vibrated, yet nothing fell, nothing crashed, nothing seemed to happen.

Glancing around, there was no sign of the priestesses. Her heart raced but she could barely feel it, because all the could feel was the incessant shaking, all around and in her very soul. Amala rushed to the stairs, trying to sense the energies — who was there, who needed help. Nothing.

Wrong, wrong, *wrong*.

The temple juddered, stronger than before, and Amala fell to the ground, landing against the marble. It hurt, but there was no time to feel pain; she didn't acknowledge it as she felt a strong pull — more like a whip — that sliced her whole body in half. She screamed in agony now. This was different, this was... breaking. Breaking her.

Amala's energy fought as she tried to fight the pain to run up the stairs, the temple continuing to shudder around her. Her head and body were on fire. It was *wrong*, so wrong, and she'd never felt that pain before, never, not even when—

No.

Not now.

Not now, she wouldn't, she wouldn't give in to *that*.

But the pain she felt... it sliced her brain in two, and her energy — the Goddess' energy within her — stopped fighting. And, as it crumbled one last, final time, Amala felt it dissolve as she darted, aiming for Serabel's room, for her priestesses...

The energy was dying.

She forgot how to breathe, the pain so steady it made it impossible for her to stop and realise what was going on, but then... it all stopped.

As she finally reached the hallway, the temple stopped shaking. The walls no longer screamed, and her energy was... quiet.

As if it wasn't there anymore.

All the priestesses — or almost — were in the hallway, curled up against the wall, outside of Serabel's rooms. Amala's eyes surveyed all of them, the slicing pain in her head *so* strong as she focused on counting each of them, ensuring they were all safe and present.

"Sinayla," she breathed as she rushed through the corridor, "Sinayla!"

"Amala!"

Her friend's voice erupted a sob in Amala as she found Sinayla, curled up on the floor, Seryn beside her with a hand on her swollen belly.

Amala kneeled next to her, hands on her temples, pressing into her skin to try soothing the pain. "Are you alright?" She asked.

Her friend nodded, tears streaming down her face. "You weren't here. I thought you..."

Amala shook her head. "I'm alive. In pain, but alive." She glanced around, "Are you *all* okay, my beautiful priestesses?"

She counted them again. They were all there, a breath of relief as she relaxed her shoulders.

Seryn's voice asked, "What do you think happened?"

Amala turned to her, "Where's Serabel?"

"She wouldn't let us in, Amala. Her doors are locked and none of us can undo the wards. We called you, but when the temple started crumbling, we just ran..." Sinayla explained, her voice barely a whisper.

The High Priestess rose, ignoring the pain as she rushed for the doors. She sensed the energy warding them and checked in with hers.

Empty.

So empty.

And wrong.

"Something is..." Amala tried to say, voice shaking, "Something is missing. Her energy is missing."

She felt drained as she directed her energy to undo the wards protecting the door. As High Priestess, her blood allowed that ability. To her, and her only.

But the Goddess' energy...

"What did you feel, Amala?" Teleia's silver voice asked behind her.

She didn't turn, focused on the doors in front of her as she answered, "Everything fell apart."

A brief pause.

Then, "And what do you feel now?"

The doors unlocked. Amala steadied, inhaling, searching for the moonlight scent of her Goddess Serabel.

This time, she faced Teleia.

"Nothing. I feel *nothing*."

Her heart was thumping in her chest, but she entered the doors, adrenaline coursing through her.

"My Goddess? Goddess Serabel?" she whispered, her voice hoarse. She cleared her throat, "My Goddess?"

Breathing, she walked through the antechamber. Empty with no trace of moonlight. Amala wanted to rush to the bedroom but her soul tried to stop her, to pull her back because this was all so wrong, wrong, *wrong*.

She fought it as she felt the presence of the priestesses behind her; some of them entered the room as she reached for the next door. Serabel's bedroom wasn't warded, not anymore.

She didn't check in with her energy and ignored the pain, swallowing down the agony burning through her whole body. Amala pushed the door open.

There was a shriek — a scream so loud she had no idea how her own voice could produce such a note.

No, no, no, no, no.

Serabel was on the floor. Amala stepped closer, tears clouding her sight, but she wiped them away as she dropped to her knees next to Serabel's body. Her chest and stomach were sliced open, as if someone had ripped, stabbed, and sliced right through it, to prolong her suffering as much as possible.

And blood... blood splayed everywhere — on the floor, on Serabel's white robes, on the bed sheets, and Amala's own knees, now.

She couldn't *breathe*. She was shaking, everything in her was shaking and shivering, but she fought it. Pushed through it. Kneeling, fighting the urge to cover Serabel's body with hers, Amala summoned her energy and reached for the Goddess.

But the energy was dead.

Serabel was dead.

CHAPTER 6

A mala wasn't breathing. She didn't want to. Didn't want to breathe, or exist.

Dead.

Her Goddess was dead.

Dead.

Serabel's body lay on the frozen floor: naked and covered in blood and ripped right through the middle. Amala couldn't bring herself to look yet couldn't keep her gaze from returning to the terrible view of her Goddess, as if watching her broken body would enable her to feel even the slightest ounce of pain Serabel must have felt.

Kneeling next to her body, Amala silently wept as she forced herself not to touch Serabel, not to embrace what was left of her. Her body was shaking, her throat bobbing as tears fell, yet she made no sound. She couldn't bring herself to utter a single word to acknowledge what had happened. She felt the priestesses behind her, all of them in complete shock too: some cried, some were leaving — as if they couldn't bear the view of their Goddess *slaughtered* on the floor.

Amala hadn't known a day of her life where Serabel hadn't been there. Had never known life without that pure, intense, majestic energy which had existed over the temple for centuries.

Energy that was now gone.

That energy was in her too and she had felt it jolt, tremble, then crumble to pieces. The High Priestess had a kernel of the Goddess' energy: the only other bearer of something so ancient and powerful.

And as she had tried to reach for it, to use and wield it to help her Goddess, it had been no use, because it had not been there. And now, as she tried one final time, all was confirmed. It was gone. *Gone*.

Something flickered inside of Amala then as nausea rushed through her, reminded by that same feeling outside of the temple, when she had instantly known something was wrong, before everything had gone to shit.

Time had lost all meaning; she had no idea how long the earthquake had lasted, or how long it had taken to finally arrive at Serabel's doors. Amala cursed herself for not being there sooner, for being unable to help her priestesses.

Or her Goddess.

Someone else was needing you, Amala, her energy whispered, *and you were helping them. As you always do.*

Though she wouldn't forgive herself so easily. She hadn't been there for them—

What would have changed?

Tears flowed down her beautiful face.

There was nothing you could have done.

Her energy attempted to rationalise her thoughts, but she needed to cry and mourn, accepting all faults and blame — it was the only thing that made sense. Blaming herself was the only thing to help her understand why this had happened. All of this, somehow, was her fault. She didn't know how, but she needed, *needed* —

Don't let your Ego get in the way, Amala.

Amala cried and, this time, knew the whisper was right.

She sobbed: her pale, bright skin now red with the Goddess' blood. Her fingers wiped away the tears, smearing it across her face...

The energy is not dead.

She felt that flicker again. And slowly, so slowly, the divine energy she had only known as hers from the day she became High Priestess merged with her own. Her whole energy — whipped and sliced and cracked open mere minutes ago — gently merged again, mending the wound, melding two broken parts with one another.

The last kernel of the Goddess' energy was hers. It had not died, it was hidden, only revealing itself now everything else was gone. Whatever happened, that kernel of power felt ready to emerge once more.

Amala sighed again: Serabel was gone, and her energy was there no longer to protect or ward the temple. Their *home* had been ransacked, robbed of their most precious thing... the Goddess they had all sworn themselves to.

The Goddess Amala had loved since the first day she was born.

But Amala's energy stayed the same.

Because for whatever happened next, she was needed. She was important — perhaps the only one ready to face whatever was to transpire. Amala knew, but gently wished in the silence to not think of it yet.

She would soon, but now...

Her eyes fell on Serabel's body again, and she couldn't stop the tears.

She hadn't known a world like this, none of them had. And she didn't want to know.

Amala cried in silence; she didn't know who was there or who wasn't. She heard people, yet heard nothing at all. Voices were distant, lost in another world. There were scents, but no feeling. Nothing which compared to the faint note of moonlight now leaving the Goddess' body.

The moon hadn't been there tonight. Did Serabel know that something was wrong? Had she tried to warn her? Had the moon fled, in fear of what was going to happen?

Minutes, tears, blood, sobs and murmured breaths: time passed, but she didn't know how much. She knew nothing at all.

Then footsteps, and the swift sound of wings. More scents, then voices, mixing and entering the room, and everything felt vain in her ears — everything felt meaningless as she wept in silence, tears running down her cheeks. But then she sniffled, and a different scent hit her: midnight wind and lemon, and the air seemed to swirl as she felt it drifting closer, wrapping her whole.

Hawk.

She lifted her gaze. For the first time since finding Serabel's body, she looked up, instinctively searching for him: there he was, standing next to the window. Harat, wings splayed, was there too with worry on his face. Hawk's eyes lowered to Amala's figure on the floor, his eyes finding hers. The High Priestess felt their bond pull — for a second, she wished to run into his arms and hide there, listening to his insistent whispers that everything would be alright.

Before reality hit.

Serabel was dead.

The Prior was there.

Her priestesses were there.

And yes, Hawk was there, but Amala couldn't bring herself to even stand.

She looked at him, tears still streaming down her beautiful face, and he knew. He knew what she needed: a craving for reassurance, which he desperately wanted to give.

Harat was talking, but Hawk stopped listening and reached for her, kneeling on the floor by her side. He didn't touch her as Amala carefully surveyed his movements, his eyes fixed on her, etched with concern. When he spoke, his voice was softer than usual; it was caring, as though they were the only two in the room.

"I'm here," he murmured, low enough so only she could hear him.

She slowly nodded, sniffed, then glanced at Serabel's body. She couldn't bring herself to speak.

"Do you want to tell me what happened?" Hawk asked. He questioned himself for a moment, then reached for her hand. He didn't care if people could see them: Harat knew. And she could reject him, if she wanted to.

But maybe she needed him.

And he was right. Amala instantly grabbed his warm hand, her small fingers freezing against his.

She nodded again, and opened her mouth to speak.

And said nothing.

More tears streamed down her cheeks as she closed her eyes, lowering her face to the ground.

Hawk sighed; it took all his self-control to not pull her into a bone crushing hug; he wanted to help her, to make her feel better, for her to know he was there — not for work, but for *her*. He would do anything for Amala.

But a bone crushing hug wasn't the move, not right now.

Instead, he said, "How long ago did you come back?"

Amala sniffed, her eyes returning to his once again, "Hours ago."

"Did you find her?"

The High Priestess closed her eyes, reliving the memory — fresh and painful in her mind. She nodded.

Hawk is here.

It's Hawk, Amala. Hawk.

You're safe.

"Was she here?"

Hawk wanted to talk about anything else, but he needed to ask these questions, and wanted to be the one asking them. No one else knew how much the Goddess meant to Amala. No one could understand the pain she was feeling right now, not even him. But he was the closest to understanding her feelings because he knew *her*.

And, God and Goddess, he would not let anyone else near Amala's side and didn't care if Zale thought he was biased. He didn't give a shit. He wanted Amala to feel safe.

"I—" she started, her voice a mere whisper. "I felt her die."

Hawk stilled. Without saying a word, he stared into her eyes, his expression and body language demonstrating to Amala: *I'm here and I'm not leaving*. He could not understand it, he knew that. Who could understand what she had *felt* as her Goddess died before her?

The Goddess she sworn and promised her life to.

Amala sniffed.

The Goddess that had been her only reason to live for most of her years. Her purpose.

The Goddess was...

Dead.

The Goddess was dead.

"For a second, I felt like I was dying, too," she added, as if it wasn't relevant. As if she'd exchange her life for Serabel's in an instant, if only given the chance.

In that moment, the only thing she wished was that their roles were reversed — that the High Priestess had died instead of the Goddess, so Serabel was here: living and thriving and smiling. Amala would rather have died instead, if her Goddess could live. But she couldn't reveal that to Hawk, she refused to give him such pain.

Hawk said nothing.

She squeezed his hand as hard as she could and he let her.

"Did you touch the body, Amala mate?"

Amala shook her head. "I—you taught me to never do that. And I never touched Serabel without her permission. I know she considered me her *friend*, but she is—was..." her eyes filled with tears once again, "My Goddess. My Goddess," she repeated in a whisper.

She reached for him without thinking twice, throwing herself into his arms and crying.

Hawk was there, arms wrapped around her and said nothing. He held her tightly as she wept. Amala needed him. Inhaling his scent, her breath slowly calmed. It took several minutes, but her tears eventually dried, and she peered at him once more.

"I want to be in charge of this case, Amala mate. And I will. But... they need to know what you mean to me. If they find out later, it will only mess things up." Hawk would have rather said anything else, anything at all, but he was on duty, and she had to know this. "Are you okay with me telling them?"

Amala stilled. She knew what he was doing, but wished he could simply be there for her instead. She didn't need him to be Captain Hawk Mercurian, she needed him to be Hawk. Her Hawk.

But the murder of a Goddess? She could only imagine what kind of investigation that would start.

She sighed.

"Do what you need, Hawk," she simply said. Amala no longer cared: the mates, people knowing, the investigation... nothing seemed to matter anymore. So many things were about to change, and she couldn't bring herself to think about any of them.

To focus on anything else would mean accepting that Serabel was dead. That her Goddess was not coming back.

Amala knew it was selfish, to pretend there was nothing to think about.

But she couldn't avoid it.

Tomorrow, she would think of it. Tomorrow she would embrace her High Priestess duty. Tomorrow could wait.

She could wait.

Hawk watched her as though he knew the thoughts unfolding in her mind, "They will need to question you, Amala mate," he said softly. "I don't know if they will let me do it, once I tell them you are my mate. But I'll ask if they can wait until tomorrow."

"Can I speak to the priestesses?" she asked, eyes wide.

Hawk nodded, and she breathed a sigh of relief: she needed them, and they needed her. Their High Priestess — the only one left to guide them now.

"I'll need you to leave this room, Amala mate," Hawk muttered, turning around to find Harat still there, his gaze fixed upon them, "Forensics is coming in. You can speak to the priestesses, but you can't leave the temple." Amala closed her eyes for a moment and, when she reopened them, new tears were there.

"And where would I go?"

When Hawk didn't reply, she leaned against his chest one final time. "Do you need me to do anything?"

Amala may not have been there for her priestesses when the earthquake happened, but she would be now. She would not allow them to be questioned, deprived of their mourning.

Hawk gently stroked her hair, "Take your time, Amala mate," he said onto her forehead, "I will need a list, just a list of who was here at the temple tonight. But you don't need to do that now."

Amala merely nodded.

"Please, can you come and say goodbye before you leave?"

Hawk placed both hands on her face and kissed her forehead.

"I'm always here for you, Amala mate."

☼

Prior Zale Harat watched Hawk from the moment they got there.

Hawk followed Amala out of the room, leaving her only when he was certain she had reached the priestesses. Only then did he face the Prior.

"What?" he asked.

Zale shook his head, "This is a bad idea."

Hawk raised an eyebrow, "Then put someone else in charge."

The Prior had every right to do so; the Goddess' death was his matter, and he had the power to step in at any given time.

"What, you're giving me attitude now?"

Hawk didn't care if it was disrespectful. He wouldn't endure one second of *anyone* refusing to understand Amala's grief right now.

"Listen," Hawk started, his voice low and serious, "I don't believe anyone knows what the priestesses are experiencing now. These people have sworn their *lives* to the Goddess, and now she's dead. No one ever thought this could happen. We don't know what they feel and, if I'm to lead this case, I will respect their mourning, their time, their habits, and their temple. Their home has been violated; their whole *lives* have. I don't believe we can relate to that."

He sighed — harsh maybe, but true. He couldn't place himself in Amala's perspective. How could he understand her pain? How could he feel what she was feeling? He simply couldn't.

"You are too involved with *her*, Hawk," the Prior said, then continued. "But I don't trust anyone else to lead this one. It's yours. You answer to me. This case gets priority, and you're off Madakahiri."

Hawk nodded. Good.

Not for the case, but for *her*.

Because as long as he was leading this, she would be safe, protected, and no one would undermine her authority as High Priestess.

"Thank you. I won't let you down," he said.

"You've never let me down. But you can't follow your heart, are we clear?"

"I've never done that," Hawk countered, but he knew why Zale said it. Amala had never been involved in any investigation before. And he had never felt the urge to protect her as much as he felt it now.

Zale observed him. "Anything I should know?"

"The bond is going to snap soon," Hawk said between his teeth. "And Amala can't stay here. The priestesses can't stay here. Until we find out what happened... they are not safe. Things must change," he sighed because he knew Amala would never wish to leave the temple. "I don't want to involve her. Not now. We'll need her, at first, to tell us more about Serabel. But after that..." He paused. "She will crumble if I fuck this up, Zale."

Zale nodded. He knew Hawk and knew what Amala meant to him; he knew they were mates but hadn't mated yet. Amala's behaviour within the Karale was impeccable; Hawk and Amala had barely interacted for ten years, never acknowledging each other by name, or ever caught alone.

Maybe that was why the Prior thought he was too involved, Hawk realised. Zale had never seen him and Amala together before. But perhaps Hawk was always like that around her.

"Did the Goddess know you were mates?"

He nodded, "Yeah, Serabel was rooting for us from the start. She never got to trigger our bond to snap, though. You know, being Goddess of Love and everything."

"Doesn't really matter if it's snapping now." Zale shrugged.

"Well, now is definitely not the time," Hawk sighed, "Make sure they don't alter the body?"

But the Prior just raised an eyebrow in defiance: "It's your investigation. You make sure of that."

CHAPTER 7

Amala had managed to fall asleep, exhausted from endlessly crying, though her sleep had not been restful.

She woke at dawn. Staring at the ceiling, her bedroom felt terribly cold as her naked body shivered under the sheets. For the first time in her life, the temple felt empty.

The energy of her Goddess no longer there.

She couldn't begin to process what that meant, that the Goddess was now vacant.

The energy had left, yes, but to find someone else. Someone worthy of the Goddess' energy. Someone that would *become* her, from that moment on. It was a long process. It could take weeks to find the right vessel, sometimes months. But the energy always found someone else.

It took months for the new vessel to embrace the energy, and even longer for the Goddess' ceremony. Amala sighed. It was her duty, as High Priestess, to serve the Goddess, whoever the Goddess was. But for some reason, the thought of having someone different than Serabel felt wrong.

She shivered while recalling her feelings the previous night as the temple crumbled.

Serabel had been Goddess for almost a thousand years. The world hadn't known another vessel for that long, and now it was...

Shit, she realised. It was all in her hands.

Amala took a breath, preventing her thoughts from consuming her as tears threatened to spill once again. No, she had to stay focused. Last night, she allowed herself not to think or process what had happened, but today she had to. It was her duty as the Goddess' High Priestess: to serve, protect, embracing the energy and the temple. To be the closest thing to the Goddess.

Over all those centuries, it had never been required. Until now.

She sighed again.

You got this, Amala, she told herself. Although she did not truly believe it, it was better than nothing.

What would Serabel tell her? She didn't know. She had never experienced anything like this, not many High Priestesses had. Vessels weren't a common thing — she was unsure how many vessels had existed from the beginning, but no one knew. Goddesses didn't die like that, nor did they die often. There had been many more High Priestesses than Goddesses in their history.

And she was... fuck.

The High Priestess was the *only* being that could identify the next vessel. It all depended on her.

You need to get up, Amala, she murmured softly to herself — her inner words were gentle today, compassionate — she deserved kindness too. *You can mourn in silence. No one can take that from you.* No one could take her guilt either. Yet, she was unsure why she felt so guilty. Whatever killed the Goddess would have killed her too if she had been there.

Amala tried to conjure some advice, or something that Serabel, or Dhara — the former High Priestess — or even her mother would say... but her thoughts automatically wandered to Hawk.

Hawk.

Hawk had been there when she needed him. He was the only, *only* person that could understand a fraction of her feelings. Not in terms of energy, or commitment, as all the priestesses felt that. While all had sworn themselves to the Goddess, for Amala it was different.

Hawk knew because she had tried to explain it to him when they first met.

Why do you love being High Priestess so much? He had asked. Such a Hawk question. Amala almost smiled at the memory.

There's no way I can tell you with a simple answer, she had said. *But I can show you.*

And so, she had. In all the time they had known each other, at the beginning of their friendship and beyond, she constantly showed him, sharing the beauty of what she did: the energy she felt, the divine connection that joined her and Serabel; the trust her priestesses devoted to her, and the way she saw the world as High Priestess. The Love she felt and the Love she gave.

But one time, as she explained, Hawk had told her something, now permanently imprinted on her soul.

The Love you feel and give, Amala mate... I think that's not you being High Priestess. It's just you. You would be like this, whatever your title.

This time, she smiled. That memory always evoked a rush of serotonin; it had been the first time in her life that someone understood her. She was grateful to Hawk for those words. Sometimes she still doubted it was real. Perhaps it didn't matter if she was High Priestess or not, maybe she didn't need to be a priestess at all, to embrace that Love she had felt from the moment she was born. That Love *was* her. It was Amala.

She shook her head. She couldn't afford to ignore reality any longer. One of Hawk's more favourite sayings came to mind, a phrase said countless times — not to her, but to himself. During every investigation, every time he was lost or stressed...

Amala knew what *he* would tell her now.

One step at a time, Amala mate.

She could do this. One last sunrise before whatever was next.

She stood up and began her day.

☼

The emptiness was driving her crazy.

Walking through the corridors — a routine from every day of her *life* so far — felt completely different, as if something was amiss.

But something *was* amiss.

The Yonium was soundless, the constant clinking of her anklets the only sound reaching her ears.

She had told her priestesses no Dawn Call would be officiated today; they seemed relieved at the news, and she couldn't blame them. All of them were used to Serabel, all shared that strong, deep sense of emptiness cursing each of their thoughts.

She found Sinayla in the kitchens sitting on the floor, a cushion behind her back, and a bowl in-between her legs. Her eyes looked vacuous, and she barely sensed Amala enter.

"Are you alright, my love?" Amala whispered, kneeling beside her.

Sinayla looked up, her grey eyes widening as she realised who Amala was, as if seeing her for the first time.

"Amala," she breathed, her voice was hushed, almost fearful of speaking too loudly.

Amala repeated her question, worry in her eyes as she surveyed the priestess' body.

Sinayla absently nodded as her hand reached for Amala's, beginning to stroke her palm. "I am so sorry." she whispered, her voice breaking.

Amala hugged her shoulders and kissed her cheek. "Don't feel sorry for me, Sinayla," she started, but was interrupted.

"I do." A strong claim, even if her tone was barely audible as she spoke, "I do feel sorry for you because no one can know how you're feeling. I can *try* to understand you, but I will never fully be able to and it *kills* me! I have barely slept, thinking of how you must be." She admitted, pain in her eyes as she surveyed Amala's face.

"I'm alright."

She would not allow Sinayla to pity her; each priestess was grieving, no one took priority over another. Serabel had been a part of all of them; being High Priestess did not mean a greater claim on the loss.

She had spent the past ten years making sure her sisters knew it: besides officiating rituals, besides the Karale meetings and being closer to Serabel... nothing had changed. Still, she was a normal priestess — one with more responsibilities, perhaps — but she was still the same as them; as Sinayla, Seryn, or Hebex or anyone else.

"Don't lie to me, Amala," Sinayla whispered, fingers stroking the back of her hand.

Amala sighed. "I don't even know what's next. What should I do? What should we all do? I..."

"We'll figure it out. But your feelings... they're *valid*, High Priestess. Don't shut them out because you're too busy caring for us," Sinayla interrupted, "Tell me how you feel."

Trust, loyalty, and friendship glinted in her eyes, as she watched Amala in silent devotion.

"Well," the High Priestess said, "I know everything happens for a reason. But this time I'm struggling to see *why*. Why would this happen? Knowing there must be a reason has always helped us to rationalise things, hasn't it?" Sinayla nodded. "So, what's the reason, then?" Amala continued, "Not only is she gone, but the only thing that remains of her is..."

Me.

Her sacred, divine energy in my fucking useless, unworthy soul, she wanted to say.

"You," Sinayla said, and her voice was sweet, caring, almost relieved.

"Me," Amala repeated, her voice attempting to disguise the disgust she felt, but the priestess noticed and raised a reprimanding brow.

"Are you going to say you are unworthy? Because I *swear*, you—"

"I *am* unworthy!" Amala countered, raising her voice. "She is—*was*—a Goddess and I'm... *how* can I be the only thing left of her? *Me*? What makes me deserve her energy, her power, her divinity?"

"Who do you think deserves it any *more* than you, then?" Sinayla replied, breathless.

Anyone.

No one.

Amala closed her eyes: she didn't know. She had no idea, but...

"I don't care. I know it's not me."

That. That she knew.

She didn't want to be worthy.

Sinayla said nothing. Amala knew she didn't agree, but her silence offered a truce: a truce she was more than willing to accept. She was grateful for the high opinion her friends had of her, but she wished the others would perceive her the way she saw herself, as one of them: nothing else, nothing more.

"I wouldn't want anyone else keeping that kernel of divine energy, right now," Sinayla's voice murmured after a moment, "I wouldn't feel *safer* with anyone else, nor would the others. You may disagree, but we are all relieved. This loss is devastating, for each of us. But it's different because you don't have Serabel anymore, but we still have *you*. And when I woke up this morning and the temple was *empty*, and I felt like dying... I thought: yes, Serabel is gone. But Amala is still here."

Amala's icy gaze widened in surprise at those words; she hadn't known how much she needed to hear that until then. Sinayla seemed to understand because she smiled. "It's true."

"Thank you," Amala whispered, squeezing her hand, "I am sorry Serabel won't be here for Xantara. I know you wanted her to bless the baby."

But Sinayla shook her head, "It will be fine... I've always wanted Serabel to bless my daughter, but I'd really love for you to be there."

Amala curved her lips into a small smile, "Of course I'll be there, my beautiful Sinayla. I can't wait for the day you become a mother."

"I *really* want *you* to help me give birth, Amala." Sinayla repeated, "But only if you feel alright with it." The High Priestess nodded.

"I said yes the first time you asked, and I'll say yes every other time," she said, "It's an honour, for me, and I cannot wait to meet baby X."

"Are you sure? That it's alright?"

Amala nodded again. "I promise."

Something unspoken lingered between the two of them, but their talking ceased as they squeezed each other into a hug, carefully minding Sinayla's belly. Amala caressed the swollen skin with gentle fingers, each stroke sending energy into the priestess' body, revealing her gratitude: for her, her presence, her words.

"Whatever's next, Amala," Sinayla whispered, "We'll face it together."

Amala met her stare.

"Together."

They stayed there for a while, hugging each other upon the floor.

And then Seryn arrived, joining them on the ground, pulling them both into a hug. She squeezed Amala between her arms, whispering in her ear how much she loved her, how much her energy was there for her. Amala sat between her friends, and life — for a moment — felt normal again.

Together. *Together.*

"What about your Captain?" Seryn said.

Amala instinctively smiled and instantly, they noticed.

"What about him?"

Seryn shrugged, "It was the first time I've ever seen you two interact."

Amala sighed. "I know it's selfish but, despite everything that happened, a part of me is glad he was the one who found me. I mean, the first who talked to me."

Sinayla didn't hide her smile, "Would you like to give him a chance?"

She didn't answer. She *knew* what she wanted to say, but couldn't bring herself to say it, not *now*, not with everything happening. Whilst the situation was temporary, the emptiness, the mourning, and the *pain* was not.

Instead, Amala said, "I am to be celibate until the energy finds the next vessel."

Seryn gaped, "What?"

She observed the surprise painted on both priestesses' faces as she slowly nodded.

"Yes," she said, "The High Priestess must abstain from intercourse until a new Goddess is found. The energy within me must be preserved and not shared."

"Are you serious?"

"It's fine. It will allow me to focus on mourning properly. I would not want to disrespect Serabel in any way."

"Can you touch yourself, at least?" Sinayla asked; she seemed worried.

Amala chuckled at the question, "Yes, I can share my sexual energy with myself, but nobody else." She carefully explained, "But this only applies to me. You are all free to keep yourselves busy with whoever you want."

Sinayla huffed a laugh, "I'm in no mood to keep myself busy."

Seryn finished chewing a piece of fruit, and lowered her voice before saying, "Do you think the next Goddess will be okay with Teleia?"

Amala had already thought about it, and had decided not to worry unless the problem presented itself. She did not want to worry Teleia. The priestess hadn't been alive for long enough to know how the Goddess' energy worked; the energy always picked the *best* soul, someone rightfully meant to be Goddess, to embrace the divinity, and yet plenty of Goddesses had done terrible things.

Goddesses of the past had banned the Charal tribe — warrior women sworn to the Goddess — and slaughtered any Charal woman that hadn't gone into hiding. High Priestesses of the past were complicit too, so Amala could only imagine what a soul like theirs would think of Teleia. But no, she told herself, there was no way she would let any Goddess disrespect Teleia like that; as High Priestess, she would do anything in her power to ensure she was the most welcome woman in the temple.

"The energy chooses the vessel because they *deserve* to be Goddess," Amala said, gently stroking Seryn's cheek, "I have faith that, whoever she is, will be as bright and beautiful and as altruistic as Serabel was. I will pray for Teleia to be safe with her."

Seryn slightly smiled, "Thank you."

The High Priestess softly nodded, gratitude in her eyes. "I love you, my beautiful sisters. I am thankful to have you by my side in a moment like this."

Had she ever told Serabel how much she meant to her? Had she ever told her Goddess how the main and sole purpose of her life was to worship Serabel's divinity: to be reliable, loyal, and devote her soul? To Love her until her final breath?

Amala couldn't remember and marked it in her soul as a reminder to never risk that again, to never retain from saying words of Love and gratitude, especially to her priestesses and sisters.

They heard steps and the presence of a unique energy, an unusual one. Amala's body tensed, then relaxed as she recognised the scent of midnight wind and a softer, yet strong note of lemon.

Her favourite.

She stood in time for Hawk to enter the kitchen, his voice preceding him.

"Are you here, Amala mate?"

Hawk entered, eyes falling on Amala's naked figure before him, then the other two naked priestesses still on the floor. And Amala, as a furious blush crept up her cheeks, begged the Goddess that they hadn't heard his words... but there was no Goddess to pray, not anymore.

Seryn's voice spoke a second later.

"What did he say?"

"Fuck," Hawk muttered, realising his mistake too late, as his worried glance fell on Amala's face. Amala flushed under his gaze and peered at her friends.

"Can I have your robe?" she gently asked Sinayla, gesturing to the white fabric discarded on the floor. The priestess handed it to her as Amala quickly wrapped it around her body, knotting it behind her neck before facing Hawk again.

"Good morning," she said.

"I am *so* sorry," Amala moved a step closer to him, her eyes urging him to know that it was alright. But he shook his head, "I'm sorry, High Priestess. I didn't know you had company."

She said nothing and turned to the priestesses: both of them intensely observed the interaction, as though close to unravelling a secret.

"This is Captain Hawk Mercurian," she gestured, "Hawk, these beautiful souls are Seryn and Sinayla. Xantara—" she motioned to Sinayla's belly, "Xantara is yet to be in our world, but she has been blessing us with her presence over the last few months."

Sinayla smiled wildly at that, a hand resting on her stomach. Seryn bit her lip as Hawk bowed his head in greeting, "Is he your mate, High Priestess?"

Amala avoided her sisters' eyes, and subtly glanced at Hawk. A faint smile painted on her lips as she said, "I've always known the Amala *mate* thing would fuck us up."

Hawk huffed a laugh, but couldn't hide his own smile. That gave Amala enough strength to face her sisters again.

It was fine if they knew the truth, she told herself. She could do this.

"Yes, Hawk is my mate." She explained, "But we aren't mated," she observed the surprise quickly painting their faces, "We..."

"Our bond hasn't snapped yet," Hawk came to her aid, and she offered him a grateful smile, "We are still waiting for that to happen."

Sinayla gaped. "How long have you known?"

Amala reddened.

"Since I met him."

"When was that, eight years ago?"

"Ten," she corrected.

"*Ten!*"

Amala hoped her sisters would not be angry. She had kept this for ten years and always knew they would figure it out at some point, but not yet.

"Please don't be mad if I didn't tell you before," she whispered, but Seryn's warm hand clasped hers before she could continue.

"Amala, it's your choice to share what you wish about your life."

"I should have told you— "

"You should not have done anything," Sinayla countered. "Don't think about it anymore. We can talk another time."

Amala pursed her lips, unsure. "Really?"

"Of course," she replied, as if it was the most obvious thing in the world. She looked up at the pair: Amala and then Hawk, a faint smile on her face.

Amala knew what she was thinking and exchanged a subtle glance with Seryn to ensure neither of them said it aloud. Turning to Hawk again, she wouldn't hide how good it felt to unashamedly reach for his hand and smile at him in front of others. His thoughts mirrored her own as he squeezed her hand.

"How are you?" he murmured.

Amala shrugged, instantly feeling small under his gaze. "I don't know. But I'm glad you're here."

Hawk handed her a small paper bag stashed in his pocket. "I got you this on my way here."

Amala took it and peered inside, biting her lower lip as she felt her cheeks turning pink once again.

"What's that?" Sinayla's curious voice reached her.

Amala looked at her and despite everything going on — the Goddess, the energy, the empty temple, the mourning, the pain — none of that could stop the biggest smile on her face as she answered, "A cinnamon roll."

CHAPTER 8

"**N**ame?"

A half smirk formed in the corner of Hawk's mouth. He told her this would be formal, but it still felt strange to follow the identification procedure. He left the Yonium five hours before, went home to sleep for a few hours, and then returned first thing in the morning before sunrise. Because he knew Amala would be awake, and hadn't stopped thinking about her, or how she was feeling. He just wanted to be there.

Hawk had caught her by surprise, and loved the expression on her face and even though it was selfish to think of *them* in a moment like that, he couldn't help it. Amala was talking to some of her priestesses when he found her. She wasn't crying, but didn't look great either. She must have cried the whole night.

He didn't know who the other priestesses were, but they must have finished their morning ritual because all of them were naked. They didn't look uncomfortable though, when he entered. Amala had felt less at ease, and Hawk noticed the way she had blushed whilst she covered herself. He had brought her breakfast from Aglatas.

She was still eating now, sitting in front of him in the kitchens. She was the slowest eater; even in that moment, chewing her apple, he wondered how a person could take half an hour to eat a single fruit.

"High Priestess Amala," she said, her voice full of pride as she pronounced her title.

Hawk paused, before noting it down on his laptop, "I need to write a last name here."

She shrugged: "Kora is—*was* a priestess. Faurn was a priest too. I never used a—you know what, just put Amala Abeile."

"Whose last name is that? Kyne?" He said. That wasn't the first time the matter sparked his curiosity. He searched for her last name in the archives at his office, but never found anything. He didn't insist on knowing, but now the question felt spontaneous.

She nodded. "Yeah. I don't use it, but it's what my documents say."

He wrote it down.

"I know when your birthday is, but I still need to ask you."

Amala snickered; she felt guilty for feeling so at ease with Hawk: safe, like everything weighed a little less.

"On the 16th day of the ninth month, on the 20113th year."

"Where?"

She curved her lips in a tiny smile, "Upstairs."

Hawk narrowed his eyebrows, "What?"

He knew Amala was born at the temple, but he never would have assumed it would be in the very room they were in.

"What do I write? Yonium?"

She shook her head, "Full name is the Goddess's Temple of Yonium."

"Can you describe to me what happened yesterday? What did you do?"

"The whole day?"

Hawk nodded.

"When I woke up, I prepared for the Dawn Call. I performed the ritual, then I helped Goddess Serabel to get ready. I completed my morning duties, which included checking on the new-borns — there's currently two — cleanse the main altar and harvest the vegetables for the day from our greenhouse. Serabel and I left the temple around ten, and Aries and Kanaan — two centaurs from Mhelani forest — escorted us to the Prior Palace in Aglatas. We attended the Karale meeting in the Round Room at eleven. After the meeting, I don't wasn't sure where Serabel had gone, but she later confirmed she had spent time with God Aarush." She paused. Hawk had told her to mention him, to not omit anything, and to refer to him only in the third person. After a moment of consideration, she kept going, "I met Captain Hawk Mercurian after the meeting at noon. We had lunch together in the Meads, then we went to a club in Pyramis. We stayed there until half past two when I left for my appointments; I assume Hawk went home. I had two appointments scheduled, one at three at the Fire Temple, and one at half past four in Anemos. After my appointments, I took a bus to the Northern Gate, and I walked the rest of the way back to the Yonium. I let Serabel know I was back, then I got ready for the Dusk Call. The Goddess didn't attend our ritual — she doesn't attend often, and I assumed she was resting." She sighed. Amala had felt Serabel's energy during the ritual, and it had been stable. Normal. Now she took a small bite of her apple.

"After the ritual, our evening proceeded normally. The Goddess stayed in her rooms, as she often does, and I didn't check on her, as per usual. Later at night, before retiring to bed, I was summoned by a female centaur from the forest. She believed she was pregnant and asked me to visit. Centaurs do prefer nature, so I let her stay on the temple grounds. It wasn't a long visit, but I was still outside, finishing my conversation with her, when I felt it…" Amala stiffened. She couldn't.

"Take your time," Hawk said, his eyes fixed on her as she slowly chewed another bite.

She could do this. Only one more time. One more time, and she wouldn't need to relive it again.

One more time, and they would have it: the recording and the transcript, and she wouldn't need to repeat herself. One last time.

"I have never felt anything like it. As High Priestess, my energy is bound to the Goddess. A small part of her energy exists in me. It jolted, then started trembling — *I* started trembling, and I knew right away something was wrong. I immediately left Palana and rushed back to the temple. I wasn't the only one who felt the shift: something was happening, and we could all feel it. But I felt it differently, I could almost feel what was happening to her... in *me*. I tried to fight that feeling to reach her, that's why it took me so long. The other priestesses were upstairs already, but they found the Goddess' rooms locked. Not with a key, but with her power: warded from within. They had to wait for me; I was the only one who could undo the wards, but..." she couldn't cry, and tried to resist, but soon the tears were streaming down her cheeks.

"By the time I got upstairs, the temple was trembling, and we were all scared. It felt like a massive earthquake, the temple itself was the very epicentre. Nothing happened, though. Nothing was destroyed, and we were all safe. But that was... the energy of our Goddess, leaving the temple. Leaving Serabel. When I undid the wards and managed to get in, I found her lying on the floor, and she was dead. I didn't even think that her killer could still be there, somewhere. I realised what I risked only hours later, when I kept reliving the scene over and over and..."

Hawk winced and she stopped. He shook his head, gesturing with his chin for Amala to keep talking, but she took a moment.

Amala hadn't thought of the killer still being there, but neither had he. Not until that moment. Hawk had focused so much on Amala's feelings, he didn't even realise how close to danger she had been. He was so close to losing her and the thought made him shiver. Amala seemed to understand as her eyes softened, interlocking his gaze with hers.

"No one was in the room. Only the Goddess. And she was dead. I had to protect my priestesses, so I sent my energy around to check. I didn't want to leave Serabel's side, but I felt the temple in me, and nothing—*nothing* from outside was there. The Goddess' energy was no longer, but nor was there energy from within. We were alone. Once I knew... I let myself go. I didn't leave Serabel's body for a second, and that's where they found me when they reached the temple."

She finally quieted as Hawk watched her: he could feel every ounce of the pain sparkling in her eyes. "Is that everything?" he asked.

"Yes," she murmured.

He nodded and stopped the recording. Amala sighed, more tears falling down her face. It was done.

"You did so good, Amala mate," Hawk said with a hint of sweetness purposefully omitted from his interrogation. She smiled through the tears and allowed herself another bite of the apple.

"Did you tell them I am your mate?"

Hawk nodded, "I told the precinct. Not all of them, just those who needed to know."

"What did they say?"

He pondered telling her the truth. In another moment, perhaps he could have pulled off a joke, but not now. Amala's doe eyes surveyed him.

"Nothing much. They congratulated me," he shrugged.

She huffed, crossing her arms, "Did they ask if you fucked me?"

Amala *knew* what people said about her. When he didn't answer, she added, "Did you say no, at least?"

"Now that's just *rude*, Amala mate."

She stuck her tongue out at him, a little smirk showing her gratitude for his presence.

They sat in silence for a while as Hawk tried not to stare, and forced himself to look away. He pretended to survey the kitchen but couldn't stop thinking about the female sitting beside him.

Her energy — usually so eager to be shared, to wrap around his soul — was now barely perceivable, her cinnamon scent weakened too. Hawk knew he made the right choice by assuming responsibility for the investigation; she felt safer with him, sharing everything with no fear of the repercussions. It would have been different for her, reliving the previous night with someone else. To expose her vulnerability as the only remaining thread to the Goddess' energy — the only representation the Goddess had at all. He knew Amala needed to mourn on her own yet a part of him, a selfish part, hoped she needed him too.

"I've done that list you asked me for," Amala said, suddenly remembering. "It's in my room, I'll get it for you later. But Hawk, I..." she paused, considering what to say next. "You know it couldn't have been any of us, right?"

Her words didn't come as a surprise, he had a hunch: a piece of memory in his mind recalling a past conversation with Amala.

"I think you told me, sometime ago?"

"Yes," she nodded. "When a priestess swears herself to the Goddess, the magic that binds them ensures we are bound to the Goddess and the Yonium. We cannot harm her or the temple."

Whilst it was comforting to know Amala trusted her priestesses, it made the rest of the case painfully complicated.

"It's not like I thought it was any of us, anyway," she added, as though the thought was immensely disturbing.

"I'll still have to run backstories about all of them," he said. "And I'm sorry if this will bother you, but—"

"Hawk," she interrupted. "I told you last night. Do what you need to do. None of us would have harmed Serabel, I know it in my soul. But you don't need to believe me, believe the oath. None of us can physically harm her in anyway. That's the rule. A Goddess' priestesses cannot wish her ill."

Hurt laced her words; Hawk knew it wasn't *him* she was angry at, but it broke his heart to see her so broken.

"Amala, I do believe you. I will follow the expected procedure, but concerning everything else, I will listen to you."

She stayed silent, unsure of what to say; perhaps she didn't want to say anything at all. He observed her face, subtly. She fidgeted in her chair, then asked nervously, "Can I go?"

He nodded. She didn't give him a second glance before leaving.

☆

Amala stood in front of the altar, the silence thick around her. She shifted her footsteps, as unsure of her position, but she knew it was a pathetic attempt to procrastinate what she should do next.

Tendrils of cold air gently aimed for the altar as she summoned her power, wrapping the breeze over the podium to cleanse every inch of the sacred table. After taking her time this morning, hours had passed before she decided to face it: the altar. The Goddess' altar. The emptiness was harder than expected. A priestess's life was ordinary, one could say: days articulated in the same slow and repetitive steps, rituals, prayers, offers and dances... but one element was constant throughout all the priestesses' lives. The Goddess' energy was there. *Serabel*'s energy was there.

A Goddess would outlive many priestesses during her time as a vessel, but the opposite was not so common; a priestess would see two vessels, only if she was unfortunate enough to witness her Goddess' death. Now, all of them had.

Amala didn't stop the tears this time as they slid down her cheeks — she hadn't cried from pain in a long time. A faint memory shot through her body like a burning arrow: a reminder of grief, heartbreak, betrayal, sorrow, and rage combined. She shut it down before it festered.

Daring to move closer, she continued to cleanse the altar, touching the smooth, cold stone. Her eyes fell on the candle displaced in the middle: she couldn't light it up again. It was her duty, her High Priestess duty, to make sure that everything in the temple functioned according to the rules, until the next vessel was ready. The next vessel... she forced herself not to think about it.

She wouldn't.

It was only of importance once the energy would manifest; only then would she worry.

But now... right now Amala only wanted to cry it out. So she did.

☆

Amala was unsure how long she stayed at the altar, tethered to reality by the sound of her thumping heart, the only thing keeping her company as she knelt before the podium and wept. Soft footsteps echoed behind her.

Amala sniffed, wiped her tears and regained composure.

"Amala..."

The High Priestess turned to the voice, her eyes still blurred from the tears, though Hebex's beautiful form was easily recognisable as she approached. The priestess knelt by her side but didn't look at the altar, those green eyes remaining fixed on her grieving sister.

"Amala. It's almost sunset," Hebex said, gently stroking her bare shoulder. "No one would ever ask you to miss that. Not even for this."

The High Priestess sniffed again, her eyes meeting Hebex's. She barely nodded.

"Dusk Call..." she tried to say.

Hebex shook her head, "No Dusk Call today. We are allowed to mourn. *You* are allowed to mourn."

Amala said nothing: there was no need for words; both priestesses knew rituals were superfluous, now, especially as Amala possessed the only kernel of Goddess' energy among them.

Hebex offered a hand and they rose together. Watching each other a moment, the priestess pulled her into a hug. Amala startled for a second but returned the gesture, Hebex's skin was warm and her scent — honey and roses — engulfed her like a sweet caress.

"I've been searching for you this morning," Amala murmured. "I had to tell them you weren't here yesterday. When did you come back?"

Hebex's body stiffened, and the priestess drew away from the embrace; her face bore no trace of the kind smile before. She looked guilty.

"I've..." Hebex sighed, shutting her eyes, as though she suddenly couldn't stand the sight of Amala.

When she spoke again, her breath was uneven as she fought to let the words out, "I've been avoiding you since I came back. But I knew you would never wish to miss the sunset, but—I can't. I *can't* have you looking at me like that. Like—" she paused.

Amala's face softened. "You deserve to express your feelings and grief."

"I *don't*," Hebex said between gritted teeth. "You know where I was, what I was doing. This is my fault. I left the temple unprotected because my energy wasn't here. Whoever did this, it was easier for them to get in because *I* certainly didn't contribute to keeping them out!" The priestess' voice cracked, her body shuddering as she allowed the tears to spill.

Amala pondered what to say: it was true. Hebex's absence had made the temple more vulnerable, but the same could be said for all the other priestesses who were missing at the time of the murder. The High Priestess hadn't thought for one second that it was their fault. The priestesses' energy was the same: Hebex's level of protection wasn't higher than the one Seryn could provide, or anyone else. Except her.

Amala's energy held more power than theirs — just in quality of High Priestess — but apart from that... it was a matter of quantity of energies, never of quality.

"Hebex..." Amala pronounced her name with such love, "You cannot, you *must not* fall victim to guilt. Several of you were missing last night. Never would we have imagined Serabel's energy would be unable to prevent such evil intentions from our home. We couldn't know," her doe eyes met Hebex's again, "It is not your fault. Take it back."

Hebex shook her head and withdrew her hand.

"I can't ease the guilt like that," the priestess said. "Not if I think of the reason that kept me away..."

"We are entitled to nights off," Amala countered.

"You never took one."

"That is not true, and you know it. I am far from perfect, Hebex. I feel like the whole world is crumbling around me; I am the only one keeping that energy alive, right now..." she pointed to the altar, her eyes lingering on the extinguished candle, "It's a lot. But we can deal with it together."

Facing each other, they cried in silence: no judgement, no embarrassment — never, not between them, because no one could understand a priestess' life better than a priestess herself.

Then, when Amala glanced at the sky through the windows and found it a delectable shade of pink, she finally turned to the door, and didn't look back as she aimed for her sunset.

☼

Hawk wanted to say goodbye, but when he strode for the altar room and glimpsed at the pink sky through the windows, he knew Amala was likely watching the sunset, and he wouldn't interrupt her in a moment like that. He had never done such a thing, and wouldn't risk it today.

"Wait!" a voice stopped him as he reached the main doors. He turned to face a young priestess swiftly running towards him. Her blond hair was decorated with fresh daisies, her petite body undulating in her movements and creamy skin wrapped in the usual priestess attire: exposed and on display.

"Is there anything you need?" Hawk gently asked.

"I was hoping you could answer that," she said, bowing her head. "I'm Hebex. I wasn't here last night when *everything* happened, and I wish to help you. They said you were overseeing the investigation."

He stilled. While her eyes were red from crying, her expression was determined — desperate for Hawk to accept her help. She needed to feel useful, to do something to benefit the situation.

He extended his arm, "Hawk," he said.

She shook his hand, her tiny fingers an immediate reminder of Amala's.

"I know," Hebex said, and curved her lips into a small smile. "Aren't you our High Priestess' booty call?"

Hawk snorted, "I wish."

"She told me about you," the priestess continued, eyebrows raised. Hawk started: *what* had Amala told her, exactly? That they were mates? Only Serabel had known about it... until that morning, when he let it slip in front of her sisters.

He didn't really know what to think, but replied, "Yeah? What did she say?"

Hebex shrugged, "That you two are friends."

Oh.

Of course. He almost scoffed. Friends. They were friends, though. Amala was his best friend, and he was sure the feeling was reciprocated.

Hebex smiled back, "Will you think about my offer?"

He thought of all the paperwork waiting for him back at the precinct.

"Yeah," he said, "Could you help me with the priestesses' files? Let's just say that distinguishing between you all is a nightmare. I keep losing count and getting confused. I assume you will be better than me?"

"Sure." Her voice trembled with pride, knowing she could provide some service, "Of course. When?"

"Do you know where the precinct is?"

She nodded.

"Great. Come over tomorrow morning and ask for Captain Mercurian."

"Thank you. Amala is outside by the way, enjoying the sunset." Hebex added, gesturing to the doors with her head.

"Thanks," Hawk replied. "But I think I'll head home. See you tomorrow."

And without saying anything more, he left.

CHAPTER 9

The next day it rained. Starting during the night, thick dark clouds coated the sky from the very early hours of the morning. Hawk's mind immediately slipped to Amala, as though he hadn't thought about her enough lately.

He still felt sorry for calling her 'Amala mate' in front of her sisters, but he couldn't believe Amala had been fine with revealing the truth. Yes, it happened by accident, but she had seemed fine with revealing it — happy, even.

But she wouldn't be happy now, Hawk thought as the rain tapped against the windows in the living room. He was comfortably seated on the sofa with Howlite's head in his lap and absently stroked behind her ears.

Howlite didn't mind the rain, but Amala hated it. There would be no sunrise today, clouds covering every inch of the sky since dawn. Hawk wondered sometimes: what did she do without the sunrise? When the embers hid behind the clouds? He knew Amala well enough to know she wouldn't let a change in the weather affect her day, yet also knew sunrise was fundamental for her soul. Never had she missed one.

"Are you even listening?"

Hawk raised his head, peering at the man seated on the couch opposite.

"Not really."

The male across from him snickered, then took another hit from the joint between his fingers.

"Still thinking of hot High Priestess?"

Hawk snorted in annoyance: Blade Hendrix was, supposedly, his closest friend. Or he would have been, if not for Amala.

Blade was what people called handsome: tall, quite broad, perfectly smooth dark skin; his hair was dark, short, and curly, yet impeccably soft. His utterly symmetrical face was adorned by a pair of deep, feline eyes, and a shaved, square jaw that ticked when he focused. He could rarely say more than two sentences without uttering a stupid joke, hence why Hawk had wisely decided not to bring him to the temple when interrogating Amala, or the rest of her priestesses.

"Yeah," he said, shrugging. He *was* thinking of her.

"How's she doing?"

"Like shit, Blade, how do you think she's doing?"

"Easy, man." Blade raised a concerned brow at the sudden shift in Hawk's behaviour.

Hawk seemed to realise it too as he frowned.

"Sorry," he grunted. "She's not doing well, and I can't help. I have no idea of her feelings or how hard this must be for her, and I'm stuck in this fucking investigation."

"Why did you take it if you hate it?"

"Because those priestesses are about to be kicked from their temple! Their Goddess is *dead* and the rest of the world is on the verge of a fucking unbalance."

Blade released a low breath. "Shit," he said. "I hadn't thought of that."

The God and the Goddess retained Exanthea's balance merely by existing. If one died, the balance would crumble. They were *both* equally needed; a vacant deity meant that, until another vessel was found, the world walked on a precarious edge. Everything keeping Exanthea stable — love, values, respect, and morals — tended to weaken, falling prey to lesser energies. Morals were especially targeted during an unbalance, with crime rates steadily rising opposed to normal times.

"I wouldn't have thought of it either," Hawk admitted, "But Amala talks a lot about the whole balance thing. So, I started thinking. Do you remember when the former God died?"

Blade nodded. "Yeah, it wasn't even that long ago."

"Fifty years is a *lot*," Hawk countered.

"Well, you're three-hundred years old. Yes, it's a lot, but it hasn't happened where both God and Goddess died in such a short period." Blade explained. "Serabel and God Darnen reigned together for centuries, and then both died in a matter of decades. If you think about it this way... fifty years is a short time." He grabbed the television remote to turn down the volume.

Hawk watched him closely before asking, "Do you think there's a chance the deaths are related?"

"Whoever did this may not have even existed when God Darnen died," Blade shrugged. "I'm not saying they're related, but I wouldn't rule out the option. Not yet."

Hawk absently tapped his knee. Blade's words mirrored the same idea forming in his mind once he found Serabel's body two nights before. No one expected it, but when God Darnen died, criminality thrived in Aglatas as they awaited the vacant vessel. Back then, Hawk would never have known how the absence of a God could shift Exanthea's moral balance.

"Listen, I've thought about it," he sighed. "The last unbalance was close enough that everyone alive then remembers how it was, including the ones who benefitted. Whoever lived it up when God Darnen died is as good as guilty right now. If we have nowhere to start, all the people gaining advantage from the last unbalance would be a damn good place to begin."

Hawk's thoughts were clear and yet Blade didn't seem to agree. He was muddled, a frown marked on his forehead.

"That's a whole lot of people, Hawk."

"I know, that's why we should hurry before the unbalance brings them what they want. By then, we'll be deep in shit anyway."

Blade hummed around the joint between his teeth, taking another frustrated hit. Throughout the one hundred years Hawk had known Blade, he had always smoked.

Hawk wasn't born in Aglatas, but came from Tabara: an island in the Pandora archipelago, located in the Southern Sea. The archipelago was well known for the obstinacy of its People who decided, centuries before, to never uniform with the increasing modernity and technology of the world. They lived like those in ancient times, refusing any form of aid from modern medicine, architecture, or anything else. The People of Pandora had a not-so subtle hatred for every invention or upgrade Exanthea had undergone in recent centuries.

It wasn't simply a lifestyle, like the Yonium priestesses, it was more like a dictatorship run by ancient clans ensuring no Pandoran would ever leave the archipelago — no cars, no phones, no technology of any kind, no sexual protection. No way in and no way out.

Hawk had been curious as a young boy and his family failed to realise that perpetrating hate against Exanthea only piqued his interest to explore the world. He had tried several times to find a way to leave, but had only managed to convince his parents after signing up for the army. Finally, he had left at sixty years old, with the promise of coming back soon after he finished his military service.

But he had breathed Exanthea's true scent once and forgot Tabara completely.

That was real life, then.

That was how it felt to embrace the world.

Hawk had completed his training and served in the army for years, trying to procrastinate, and avoiding his return home. When he returned, there was only one thought in mind: compromise.

Though he soon discovered there was no compromising with his family. There was no way he could leave Tabara without leaving them. But when his family left him with a choice: an eternal life stuck in Tabara, or a free life in Exanthea — completely alone — his mind was made.

People of Pandora were tied to family values more than anyone else, and yet Hawk's curiosity for life prevailed. After spending years apart from his family, he became accustomed to what life would be like, if they decided to cut him out. He never expected it to happen, but it did. And he had been ready. Hawk had always known his crave to explore the world would never meet his family's expectations, though it hadn't made the separation less painful.

Blade's voice brought him back to the present. He took another hit before saying, "So, the only way for things to go back to normal is if we find a new Goddess, right? Until then... we'll have to make sure no one fucks up."

"I already told Zale," Hawk replied. "We're working on it."

"Can hot High Priestess tell us who the next Goddess is?"

He whipped his head in Blade's direction so fast that his friend burst out laughing.

"Yes."

"But?" Blade tried to hide his grin but couldn't.

"No buts. She can and she *will* tell us once she knows. But I will not pressure her, nor is there reason to. She would never hide it." Hawk said. "If I ask her, though..."

"She's going to think you only care about this investigation," Blade finished for him. "Which, listen, would be actually helpful, right now. Rather than having you acting like the biggest simp history has ever witnessed."

Hawk didn't reply but shot him a glare that said enough. The door opened and both whirled in the direction of the foyer. Howlite jumped from the sofa, running to meet whoever had arrived. A male spoke and Howlite must have hurdled at him as his voice cursed harshly. Blade and Hawk laughed.

"Be nice to Howlite," Hawk warned.

"I *am* nice."

The male appeared: jacket still on, paired with shades. Cairo looked like he had stepped out of a movie; his skin was tanned, his eyes clear, and a faint beard coated his sharpened jaw. After successfully starting his career as a sniper, he had met Hawk on a mission and had worked with him ever since.

When Hawk moved to Aglatas, he knew no one and had nothing. But he was a quick thinker and took an opportunity when he saw one. After taking part in the annual Air Games — and winning — he made a name for himself in the city. The Games ensured a place in the Protector's court for the winner, but Zale had heard of him, and chose to hire him instead.

"Was he actually nice, Howlite?" Blade inquired as the hound came back; she trotted towards him, hopping onto the sofa again. He pet her, raising his gaze to Cairo, now sitting beside Hawk.

"How much longer will she rule this house?" Cairo asked.

Hawk snickered.

"As long as she wishes."

Hawk was very fond of dogs. He used to have two as a boy, long ago before he knew of life beyond Tabara.

Amala had picked the name Howlite. She said the hound was striped the same as the stone; it had been her first thought when they entered the shelter together. Howlite was the best addition to his life. Not only that, but she brought him and Amala closer, to the point where she visited his flat at least twice weekly now.

Cairo cocked his head, "Is Naressa here?"

Blade snorted, but Hawk shot him a glance that said *enough*.

"No, and she hasn't been in a while."

Hawk's thoughts wandered to the red-haired beauty he was lucky enough to call his friend. Naressa completed their group: she worked in forensics and was so brilliant that several police districts around Exanthea had tried, at some point, to offer her a job. She was a burning flame of red hair with curious cat-like eyes; her scent was sweet like vanilla, and her attitude fiery as hell.

"Breath of relief, Cairo?" Blade snickered. "She told you Hawk was her favourite, right?"

Naressa had been Hawk's lover for some time, but was Blade and Cairo's too. She alternated between the three of them without ever interfering in their friendship. They didn't mind, but mostly chose not to talk about it.

"Yeah," Cairo seethed, eyes narrowing.

Naressa was smart. Smart enough to keep the three of them hooking up with her. She had initiated a silent competition of sorts by lying about her 'favourites'. Blade knew Cairo to be her favourite, whilst Hawk believed it to be Blade. Only recently, after two years of hook-ups, had they figured it out. Hawk didn't care: Naressa was his friend and he never expected more. Not when Amala was in his life.

But Cairo...

Cairo liked Naressa more than he cared to admit. Not that he ever said a word about it.

He dropped the topic now, glancing at Hawk and then Blade, before nodding at the laptop on the coffee table. "So, what did I miss?"

"It depends," Blade said. "We covered the usual."

Cairo pondered it for a second, "Hawk simping on the hot High Priestess?"

Blade grinned wildly, "Exactly, you missed nothing."

Hawk snorted, allowing a faint grin before frowning once more.

"Listen, I'll take the mocking *any* day, you fuckers." He said, "But she's experiencing the worst moment of her life and—"

"He gets touchy when you talk about her," Blade explained to an amused Cairo.

Hawk refused to look at them; he wasn't protective of Amala, usually. Simply because he didn't need to be, she had the Goddess to protect her and she could take care of herself. But now, he was struggling to understand how she was feeling and questioning how to be there for her. His friends belittling the situation she was in? He couldn't stand it.

Cairo seemed to understand his feelings, tapping his shoulder, "Sorry, man. Didn't mean to disrespect her."

Hawk gave him an appreciative nod, and Cairo pointed to the laptop.

"What's our next move, then?"

"Naressa said it will take a while to run all the tests on the body," Hawk sighed.

It was bad. Bad enough that they had low-to-zero evidence to work with. "Meanwhile, we got almost *nothing*. No weapon, no details, no DNA... the only thing we have is motive, or at least a possible reason, with a shit-long list of people who *could* be involved."

"Great. Fucking great," Cairo muttered.

"So do we just raid all the gangs involved last time?" Blade asked, horrified.

"How *many* gangs are we talking about?"

Cairo took the laptop from Hawk and quickly read the notes taken over the past few days. "Well, shit."

But Hawk shook his head. No matter how many gangs could possibly be involved — big or small — there was no way they could come close enough to the two main ones dominating the last unbalance.

"Yeah about that," he started, pointing at the notes on the screen, "Minor gangs may take us less than a week probably, but…"

Blade's jaw twitched. "What?"

"Embers are going to be a nightmare to check out," Cairo replied.

"Embers are untouchable. Dragons too," Hawk shrugged at the surprise on his friends' faces. "Listen, I'm in no mood to ask Jaren for favours, and there's no way we can get to the Embers without talking to him first. And the Dragons…"

"Aren't they based in North Aquar?" Blade asked. "I could get the info in five minutes." Withdrawing his phone from his pocket, Hawk's voice stopped him.

"No," his tone was low, almost harsh. "Listen, this must stay confidential… the Dragons are under the Protectors' care now."

Meaning they couldn't raid them without involving the Protectors with their own circle of alliance and, perhaps, the whole Karale itself.

Cairo looked surprised. "Does Nyla run the gang?"

"Ana does," Hawk replied. "And she's a fucking bitch."

Blade alternated his gaze between the two males.

"You can do it, then," he said, pointing to Hawk.

"What?"

Cairo glanced back, confused, while Hawk simply shook his head.

"You're no fun, Hawk," Blade grinned, looking at Cairo. "Ana has a thing for the Captain."

They both burst into laughter as Hawk rolled his eyes, exasperated. His friends loved to mock him; Hawk was so busy thinking about Amala, he rarely noticed when anyone else was interested.

"Okay, quit it," he ordered. "If you want to talk to Ana, be my guest. She'll shred you and send me the pieces in a box probably. And I don't need any new home décor. I'll talk to Aarush, first."

"Why?"

"Because he had a thing going on with Serabel, he could help with the bigger picture."

"How do you know he had a thing with the Goddess?"

He shrugged, "Amala told me."

Cairo thought about it. "Did she tell you anything else? Anything that could be a possible lead?"

"No, so for now your best chance is to make eyes at Naressa and see if she can get our answers any faster."

"I would have done that already, if she hadn't turned me down for *you*." Cairo scoffed.

"She'll come around," Hawk reassured him, a faint grin returning to his features as he added, "She likes none of us, anyway."

CHAPTER 10

Two days later, Hawk worked at his precinct office as the sound of distant footsteps forced him to raise his head from the paperwork, his first break in hours.

There was a soft knock at the door.

"Enter," he said.

The door opened as Hebex shyly swept in, "They told me to come here," she said, "I didn't mean to bother you."

Hawk nodded to her in greeting, "You aren't. I asked you to come," he replied. "How are things at the Yonium?"

The priestess gently closed the door, but didn't move from where she stood. "Busy. We all are. I'm not ready to meet people. But we *must*, so…"

The temple was about to host Serabel's funeral ceremony that night: the priestesses were working endlessly to make it happen, so Hebex had needed to postpone their meeting.

"How's she doing?" Hawk asked, his eyes settling back on the paperwork to hide his thoughts of Amala. Yet he stole a side glance to

INGRAM EVEN THE GODDESS AND THE HAWK COPY COPY 125

the priestess, witnessing the corners of her mouth curving upwards in a smirk.

"She cried a bit less, today," Hebex replied, "But I think she's terrified to host the ceremony and perform the ritual. She feels lost."

Hawk said nothing; since the interrogation, he hadn't spoken to Amala. He knew she needed time and space. Not him. It had barely been two days, but it was difficult to suppress the urge of going to the Yonium and checking on her. He had been close to do it, more times that he liked to admit, but he was finally going to the temple today, for the funeral.

Everyone was going.

Aglatas' citizens would reunite together to celebrate Serabel one final time. Hawk knew Amala hated it: the fact that most people ignored the temple, yet would fake pretences to attend the Goddess' funeral. Right now, she was probably livid. Even if the High Priestess dreaded the moment, Hawk couldn't hide his happiness at her conducting a ritual once again. It had been four months since the last time she allowed him to attend.

"Do you have a specific role, tonight?" His eyes were kind as he added, "Take a seat."

The priestess obeyed, shifting closer to his desk, and sitting on the chair opposite.

"No," she replied, "Amala does most of it. Thank the God, she does. None of us will ever be ready. While we love and serve the Goddess, there's a reason why *she* is the High Priestess."

"You wouldn't want to be?" he asked, surprised.

Hebex's eyes widened, "God and Goddess, absolutely not! I would never feel worthy of it. I enjoy being a priestess; I wished to join the Yonium for a long time, and I was incredibly happy to do so... but I barely felt as though I served the Goddess *enough*. Most of us feel the distance," she paused, "We all embrace our divinity but at the same time, once you're conscious of how *much* the Goddess is... it's difficult to feel worthy of the place you occupy. That's why we have a hard time when Aglatians don't show the respect She deserves. We barely feel worthy of her, yet they take her for granted every day..." A soft pain surged behind her eyes.

Hawk nodded; he knew what she meant because Amala had told him countless times before.

As if knowing where his mind wandered, Hebex added, "Take Amala, for example. She is the best of us, no doubt. None of us will deny it, we know no one has the same passion, the same love, or attitude for what she does. She is born to share her energy and her Love with everyone and *anyone*. I would be surprised if Serabel — or any Goddess for that matter — had a better High Priestess than her. And still she feels unworthy. You can agree that it's crazy." Hawk nodded again.

"Serabel *loved* her," Hebex continued, "The Goddess held her in the highest regards. She would have done anything for Amala. She..." Lowering her voice, she briefly glanced at the door to make sure no one could hear, "She asked Amala to be her *lover* so many times. But the hot High Priestess always said no."

Hawk knew. He knew Serabel — and many others — had tried to seduce Amala. She refused most of them — the important ones, anyway: all those possessing a title, or a role of power in Aglatas. He repressed a smile and said nothing.

"I didn't know you called her that too."

The priestess snorted, "Everyone calls her that but we never say it in her presence." She chuckled, "Even *Serabel* called her it when Amala wasn't around to hear."

This time, Hawk snickered.

"Not everyone," he countered, "I never call her that."

"No," Hebex gave a feral smile, "You call her Amala mate."

Hawk paused, brow furrowing. Just a few days before Hebex had called him Amala's friend, yet now...

"Relax," she added, reading his thoughts from the look on his face, "She told me. I guess she wanted to even the field now that Seryn and Sinayla know."

Hebex was still smirking as he relaxed back in his chair, now more at ease.

"Very well," he said, "I imagine you will have to be back in time for the ceremony, so we better get started. First, I tried to read your file, but they are currently making copies and will bring everything to me soon," he glanced at the door, "So I have no idea about your alibi. Care to tell me?"

Hebex blushed but Hawk held her gaze, eyebrows narrowing as the priestess lowered her head. She didn't expect such a question, and likely hoped he had read her file already.

"I—" her voice dropped as she rubbed her cheeks, now boiling with embarrassment. "I was at the God's temple with High Priest, Medyr. He and other priests can confirm this too." She bit her lip, quietly. Hawk raised an eyebrow: Medyr? He resisted the urge to roll his eyes. He had no idea what the priestesses saw in him.

"You two have a thing going on?" he asked, surprise evident on his face.

"I guess," she pondered for a second whether to feel embarrassed, "Whatever, I was with him, and we felt the earthquake from Helioneis. We realised something was wrong, along with the other priests — and priestesses — that were there."

"Wait—" Hawk stopped her, "How many of you priestesses have a thing with priests? Is that common?"

Hebex chuckled, "It happens. Don't worry, Amala prefers centaurs, so she can be a pillow princess."

He snorted as Hebex wiggled her brows, satisfied her joke had landed. Hawk glanced back at the endless pile of paperwork they had to get through.

She sighed.

"Let's get into it, then."

☼

"Damn, your memory is good," Hebex said.

"You can't do this job if your memory sucks."

They had spent the past hour checking files and matching alibis; Hawk was surprised by his recognition of many of the priestesses.

"What about her? How does she feel now the Goddess is dead?" He pointed to the picture of the stunning, dark skinned, pregnant priestess. Sinayla. They had met for the first time in the kitchens several days ago, but he knew of her from Amala's stories: she may have not spoken of him to her sisters, but sometimes she couldn't help but tell him about them — her memories, the life shared at the Yonium.

"It's not like there's much she can do," Hebex said, "But she's happy Amala is there. I think she would be much more stressed without Amala, even if Serabel was still with us. She wouldn't wish for anyone else to be her midwife."

Hawk said nothing: he knew Amala was a pillar in her priestesses' life, a constant presence that made them feel safe and protected, understood. He only wished she could rely on them just as much.

"So you're all sorted out, but I might need some assistance figuring out some connections. Can I ask for your help, if that's the case?" he said at last.

Hebex nodded instantly.

"Definitely. I'm going back to the temple now, but I'll see you there?"

Hawk nodded.

"Thanks for your help," he said, "See you later."

Not that his brain would let him focus on Hebex during the commemoration. Amala would be there, and, although it had only been a few days, damn he missed her: her quiet smile, her eyes which lightened every time she saw the sun, and the cinnamon scent which swirled around him whenever she was happy.

He absently registered the sound of the door closing as Hebex left his office, but he didn't lift his gaze, nor switched his thoughts from the High Priestess whose soul was bound to his.

CHAPTER 11

F or the first time since she could remember, Amala was dreading the sunset.

Because today, and today only, the sunset meant the day was over, and that the commemoration was coming. Her Goddess' funeral. Their final goodbye.

The last time they would address her as Goddess. She would be remembered as such, of course, but it would be different: from then on, she would be part of history, not reality. Not anymore. Amala couldn't stand it, knowing she would be the one to say those words, to consecrate whatever was left of the Goddess to oblivion. She had cried all day, hoping for time to pass slowly so night would never come. Now, however, she tried to set aside her thoughts and grief and remain composed for tonight. Amala didn't care what they thought of her. While she was not embarrassed to cry, she made herself a promise and wouldn't allow any negativity to affect her last salute to Serabel.

Since she was to officiate, she would provide her Goddess with the best commemoration she could and, if something was to transpire, it wouldn't be grief or sadness. It would be Love.

She welcomed Hebex after a gentle knock on the door: the blond priestess entered with a grim smile.

"How are you holding up?"

"Can I say I'm shitting myself?"

Hebex laughed. "Yes, yes you can."

The High Priestess sighed as her sister aimed for her bed, gracefully laying across the white sheets. Amala asked, "How was Hawk?"

She couldn't see the priestess's face from her position, but detected the smirk in her reply.

"Handsome."

Amala scoffed as Hebex's fingers gently brushed her arm. For a moment, she pondered how to reply: whether she wanted to play it safe or show her true feelings for him.

"I know he's handsome," she finally said, turning towards her with a slight smile on her lips. "Was he nice to you?"

Hebex nodded, toying with the jewel of her belly button piercing — a habit Amala found dangerously addicting.

"He's so worried for you, Amala..."

"He shouldn't be."

"I am, too."

Amala sighed. "You have far more important things to focus on, my beautiful Hebex."

She tried to shake her head but halted at Amala's serious look, so let it go instead. She knew better than to tease or pester her today of all days.

Instead, she pressed her lips together. "Do you want to know if Hawk said anything about you?"

The High Priestess huffed a laugh and lazily stretched her beautiful body on the mattress. "I already know he did."

"Do you want to know what he said?" Hebex tried again.

This time, Amala nodded.

☼

She took a deep breath, trying to relax her muscles, and settled in that position for five minutes. Tension oozed from her body. Inhaling, she welcomed the air into her belly, her body, and locked it inside, legs stretched and chest lowered to the ground.

I am High Priestess Amala.

I am High Priestess for a reason.

Serabel believed in me; my sisters believe in me.

She allowed herself to exhale, body relaxing along with her breath.

Hawk believes in me.

He did. They all did: Hawk and Hebex and Seryn and Sinayla and all her sisters, all the priestesses that trusted her guidance, her protection, her energy, her very soul.

They believe in me, so I believe in myself too.

I can do this.

She inhaled again, held it, then exhaled. Her body melted with the ground as she felt the temple within her, melting with her energy, as Amala and the temple became one.

You got this, Amala.

I've got this.

One last breath, and she slowly rose. She hugged her frame, thanking her body for supporting her, and her anklets clinked together as she slipped into her robe, the white fabric swinging between her thighs. Amala wrapped another piece around her neck and breasts; she should officiate naked, but she didn't feel like it.

It didn't matter; her soul would be the same, whether she was naked or dressed.

Feeling every inch of the cold marble against her soft feet, she reached her sisters downstairs. The silence was filled with stress, but Amala fought against the negative emotions as she aimed for the altar. The extinguished candle laid atop it, surrounded by flowers the priestesses had chosen.

At last, she faced her sisters, and all others in the room. She scented some of them, yet kept her eyes downcast.

God Aarush was there, and Medyr. Some of the priests had come from Helioneis; she recognised most of them, a warm smile painting her face. They had come. Her heart beat faster as she bowed to Aarush with reverence.

"Good evening," she murmured, "Thank you for being here. We are all appreciative, it is such an honour for our Goddess." Her attention shifted to her priestesses as she searched for Sinayla.

Amala always checked on her, and there she was. Sinayla stood next to Caelan, her mate, and Amala nervously bit her lip as she took in the sight of them: he kept a hand on her swollen belly, caring about nothing except his beautiful, pregnant mate. Amala couldn't blame him: pregnant Sinayla was stunning, and her scent was thick with that note that anticipated something new. A baby.

Amala lifted her gaze, eyes quickly skimming across all of her sisters.

"My beautiful priestesses, I can sense your emotions," she said gently, "We all feel anxious and I won't ask you not to be. Embrace your feelings as they are always valid and I'm grateful that you feel safe with each other — and safe enough with me — to express the true sentiment of your soul. But I wish to honour our Goddess one last time, by cherishing all the Love she gave us."

She paused. Took a breath. The words were clear in her mind as her throat tightened, the tension dangerously threatening to strike again. Amala breathed, fighting against it.

One more breath: she would speak the truth for her sisters.

"I am terrified. To officiate this ritual in front of so many people who only cared about our Goddess in this very moment alone... it's not how

I would want to honour her. I swore myself to Serabel, we all did, and my grief is personal. But I wish to share the Love I have for this place and for my Goddess. I lived here since the day I was born, but Serabel has been the foundation of this temple for a thousand years. She has been the core of the Love experienced throughout the world for centuries. Not many of those people are here, now. Yet we are. For some reason, we are the ones left to commemorate her, and I will speak and express my Love — for all the ones that loved her and aren't here to say it. We have been lucky, my beautiful sisters, to feel her Love for us, and I beg you to think of those moments tonight." Amala's eyes met Hebex's, glimpsing the tears sliding down her beautiful face. "I'm not asking you not to grieve or mourn. But if you feel like sharing your energy... share the Love you have for her. Let us share our Love with the rest of them."

At last, she quieted as her words shifted the emotions around her. Amala's heart was lighter as she breathed in relief, savouring the energy of her sisters and sending soothing tendrils to all of them.

"You shouldn't be terrified, Amala."

She lifted her gaze to Teleia's trembling voice as the blonde female looked up at her with gentle, deep blue eyes.

"You shouldn't be afraid of officiating this," Teleia repeated again, a new edge to her voice. "They can think you're hot High Priestess as much as they like. I don't care if that's the sole reason they came tonight — it won't make you any less worthy of our Love. You are our High Priestess and our *sister*, and I think no one could embrace this role better than you. You may not choose to believe my words, but Serabel thought the same."

Those words were true.

And it was a truth she wouldn't allow herself to believe unless someone else was brave enough to tell her. She *was* worthy, and the Goddess had chosen her for that reason. She gestured Teleia to move closer and, as she took a step towards her, she was pulled into a hug.

It was more than words could express, right now, for the gratitude bursting in her heart.

Amala turned to Aarush at last and bowed her head once again.

"We agreed that I will be officiating tonight to say whatever is necessary to say. We do not wish to host a big or long ceremony, and we will have our private commemoration when we're alone. But if you wish to speak at any time, we will be thankful for your intervention."

Aarush's intense gaze pierced her whole figure; Amala prayed he wouldn't say anything, or comment on her as he used to at any given moment. She didn't even know who to beg: the Goddess was... not there, and the God was... him. Yet she released a captured breath as he replied.

"Thank you for your kind offer, High Priestess. Are you saying you *allow* me to say something?"

Amala bit back a groan of frustration — not his usual teasing, but there was a subtle note of banter there.

Allow.

He was playing mind games with her — the last thing she needed. Yet Aarush was right. He was teasing her, indeed, but his words were true. It didn't matter if he was a God and she wasn't, the High Priestess was the sole representative of the Goddess. In her absence, no one else had more jurisdiction over the Yonium. Aarush knew and Amala knew, too. But for him to *say* it, to challenge her authority in front of Serabel's altar in an attempt to play with her emotions. Amala pondered letting the matter go, as she always did. While she didn't care if he picked on her when she was alone, she wouldn't let him do it in front of her sisters — or before the altar of their Goddess in the middle of *their* temple — their *home*. Serabel always commented on the spark she knew Amala had somewhere within her.

Here it was.

She took a breath, her icy eyes now fiery as they landed on his.

"I would not play power games with me in here if I were you. If you wish to be back in charge, I can *allow* you to leave." Her voice was sweet once again: pure cinnamon, sugar, sunlight, and *power*.

She distinctively noticed Medyr gape at her words as Hebex fought the urge to smile, biting her lip.

The energy felt lighter once again: her priestesses felt the challenge and channelled their energy towards her. And Aarush... she didn't know what he implied with his taunt, but he looked satisfied — as if he wished to see that spark too. As though he knew the spark had always been there.

"I won't speak at the celebration. But thank you for the offer, High Priestess Amala."

☼

Amala pretended to be alone.

She didn't know who was there or who was watching — she spared not a single glance. Not the Prior, not the Protectors, not even Hawk. Not once did she turn to the crowd.

She kept her gaze fixed to the altar, on the candle which burned every day since the moment she was born, now extinguished. Amala faced her sisters, searching for the strength she needed to get through this.

Mistress of the Night,
Lady of Water flow,
Surge when lovers fight,
Stand when shadows grow.

When the priestesses started chanting, she released her energy: for a second, it almost felt like Serabel's scent of moonlight was there with them.

She missed her. Oh, she missed her so much.

Bringer of life,
She's both and she's neither.
Holding the knife,
That makes her moon-breather.

Bringer of life: her beautiful Goddess of Birth and Fertility. Both and neither: herself, as a person, and a divine being merged within her soul forever. Both a goddess and a soul, but neither without the other. How many people had loved her moon-breather Goddess? How many priestesses had chanted for her? Who had been the first ones to do it, and why were Amala's sisters the last?

She had loved Serabel.

A millennium of priestesses had loved and honoured Serabel.

Amala reflected on all the People her Goddess had helped. Of all the People her Goddess had loved. She thought of the warrior women who had sworn themselves to the Goddess' energy millennia before Serabel, blessed by a past Goddess, then slaughtered by the jealous ones who followed after. Those women of Moon who could make a Goddess' army — all dead now, killed in a massacre lasting for centuries, despite their constant loyalty: the Charal tribe, whom Serabel had helped as much as she could...

Amala would bear the grief for all of them, too. The grief and the memories. She allowed herself to think of them: the High Priestess before her — a sweet, kind soul named Dhara, that she had loved like a mother and a sister — the priestesses that had sworn themselves to Serabel, the Charal women who would have wished to, but couldn't do so. The people her Goddess had helped, the women whose children she blessed, the temple itself, and all that had blossomed under her guidance, power, and energy.

For carrying a secret,
So deep in her soul.
For her heart beats so strong,
That two make her whole.

And lastly, herself: Amala had sworn her life to the Goddess and her energy. Though whoever was next, it wasn't Serabel. And if Serabel wasn't Goddess anymore... she allowed herself to think of her as a person one final time.

Serabel's thick curly beautiful hair that Amala had decorated with crystals every morning.

Serabel's shiny eyes that had looked at her with love, lust and friendship.

Serabel's lips that Amala had kissed more times than she wanted to remember, reminiscing on the taste of moonlight on her tongue.

Serabel's love. It had never felt as big as Amala's, but it had been strong. One of the strongest loves someone had ever given her.

When Amala officiated her first rite as High Priestess, her Goddess had been there — not as her queen, but as her friend.

A friend Amala had never thought to deserve. And yet she knew, rather unbelievably, Serabel sometimes felt as though she did not deserve Amala too.

Goddess, keep shining,
Let the story be told,
Let the light be blinding,
Let the power unfold.

CHAPTER 12

H awk didn't mind his job most of the time, but some days he really hated it — for two reasons. First, when the lack of clues gave him a fucking headache, and stressed him to the point of insomnia for nights in a row. Second, when the investigations required him to do something that, in his normal life, he would *never* do.

So, as he stood outside of Aarush's sex club on Tuesday afternoon, it took all his will power to stay calm and keep his mouth shut as the bouncer suspiciously looked him over. He flashed his ID and raised an eyebrow in unspoken question before entering the club.

He hated this place. Sometimes he wasn't sure if his dislike for Aarush was his own, or born from what Amala had told him throughout the years. She wouldn't say a bad word about him, of course, but what she *didn't* say exposed the differences laid plainly between the God and the Goddess. Where Serabel had been attentive, Aarush was careless; where she was kind and loving, he was wicked and found fun in a lifestyle which deemed him unworthy of the divine — unworthy of the godly energy he possessed. Like this nightclub.

He preferred his kingdom to be built within the city, rather than claim Helioneis as his true home and residence, despite the many faithful priests and followers waiting for him there. Like the priestesses, they swore themselves to him the same way Amala had done with Serabel. Instead he indulged here, in this sinful place of which he had full control and power.

Yes, power. Because of all the delicate and subtle things he, as God, wielded... he seemed to care only about that one: the raw power that flowed in his veins and soul.

Aarush wasn't worthy to be God, Hawk had told Amala once.

He knew she agreed, yet she didn't say. She would never say such a thing — it was blasphemy. Instead, she looked at him with a faint smile on her lips, and replied, "If the energy picked him to be vessel, there must be a reason. We don't know how long he will be God but, whatever his path will be, will lead us to greatness at the right time. Divine energy never fails."

He wasn't sure he believed her, but she was certain of those words., and had made it clear more than once. And, two nights before, she had seemed to believe that the divine energy hadn't failed with her, either.

During the celebration, Hawk had observed her carefully, wondering if she wore a persona or embraced a different side of herself he had never seen. Amala's figure was so delicate before the altar, silver-white hair matching the immaculate colour of the marble, of the very moon... and her icy eyes were deep and full of sincerity and Love. Pride.

Amala *knew* why she was chosen to be High Priestess, as though no one could have embraced the role better than her — at least, that's how it seemed. Head held proudly the entire night, Hawk didn't dare go closer to her or ask how she was doing.

Amala hadn't looked for him either. It had been a week since they last spoke and he missed her. Though he also knew that giving her time and space was the best choice so she could heal. If she wanted to mourn on her own, he'd give her that.

The look in everyone's eyes as she was officiating: admiration, appreciation, lust, but no understanding. Not even Aarush — who should have, at least, shared part of her pain — looked aware of the grief in Amala's eyes.

But Aarush's mind was occupied with other matters, like how many people he could fuck at the same time: his main business at the Raging Heart.

That was the only reason Hawk was there on a Tuesday: the quietest day of the week and his only chance to speak to Aarush without interrupting his numerous appointments. Or orgies. But apparently, he was wrong. As he entered the room, the music became soft and sensual, less vulgar than the sounds arising from the others.

Sitting on a throne, Aarush held a female on his lap, with three others sitting around him. He twisted from time to time, giving attention to each of them: tracing his fingers across their bodies, touching their lips, and whispering in their ears. His throne was crafted of black onyx, adorned with soft black pillows — a couple now discarded on the floor.

Hawk thought Aarush wanted to look as though he enjoyed this more than he actually did: he seemed tired, the face of someone who hadn't slept well in a while, and not for a fun reason. Aarush's attention wavered from the women as Hawk stood by the door, uninterested. His greeting was nothing more than a nod of acknowledgment.

"I heard you wanted to see me, Captain?" His gaze found Hawk while his hands roamed the brunette on his lap.

Hawk kept his chin high. Aarush liked to play games but had never disrespected his authority.

"Yes."

"What do I owe the pleasure of this visit to my sanctuary?"

Hawk frowned, "You call *this* a sanctuary? You have a temple at Helioneis."

"Different types of sanctuaries never killed anyone, Captain."

"Yeah, speaking of killing..." Hawk started, "I wondered if you could answer some questions?"

Aarush paused, the female on his lap frowning at the sudden lack of attention.

"Am I under investigation?"

"Not yet, unless you give me a good reason to investigate." Hawk shrugged, "I'd like to know your perspective on things. You knew Serabel very well, and your insight might be useful."

The God recovered his usual smugness rather quickly, allowing his hands to roam free once more. His mouth curled as he threw a glance at Hawk.

"Not interested."

"Name your price, then."

Quick, steady answers. That was how one could win with Aarush. A moment of hesitation was a victory for the God: he loved to elicit doubt, second guessing, insecurity. Hawk wouldn't allow that. He didn't like the idea of allowing Aarush to choose a price, but he would not beg for answers. Simply knowing what the God would ask in exchange would give enough information on what he knew, and how much he valued it.

Aarush seemed to ponder the request, a wicked smile slowly painting his features.

"What about hot High Priestess?"

"What about her?"

It took him every ounce of self-control not to flinch at the mention of Amala. Not only her, but the nickname. One day, Hawk would raise hell against Aarush to ensure he finally gave his mate the respect she deserved.

"Can't she help you?"

"She already is. I need your point of view too."

"Bring her here."

"What?"

Why did Aarush want Amala at the Raging Heart? What did she have to do with any of this? How did he just happen to mention — and know — of Hawk's dearest thing in the world? Hawk looked up at Aarush, confused, but faced the wicked and cruel smile of the God.

He wouldn't change his mind.

"She's my price. Bring hot High Priestess here and have her dance for me. Then, we'll talk."

☼

"We skipped a whole week," Amala commented.

Hawk said nothing. Though he hadn't mentioned the absence of their sessions, not with everything that happened. But he couldn't lie, he missed this. Them. They were so used to those two moments every week — just them together — they ended up relying on their sessions more than they cared to admit. Because no matter how crazy the investigation was, or how shitty his days could be, he always had that moment to look forward to.

"I'm sorry if I asked you to take a break."

"Don't even say that." Hawk snorted. "I would have told you to take a break, even if you hadn't."

It was the truth. There was no way he would let Amala endure the mental effort of being a rope bottom while she mourned the Goddess. She still mourned, but today she allowed herself a distraction.

"Don't overthink it, okay?" She murmured. In this precise moment, "I'm okay. I'll tell you if I want to stop, but it's *my* cue. If you constantly check in, I'll just get nervous." She pleaded. Desperate not to think of anything else for a while.

Hawk nodded, "Promise, Amala mate."

She gave a small smile, hiding a yawn as she took her long skirt off. "What are we doing? Can I keep this on?" she gestured to her top.

Hawk nodded. "Let's start easy. Reverse prayer."

"Keeping the priestess vibe? I told you I wanted to distract myself," Amala laughed as she positioned her arms behind her back.

"A week is enough for your skin to forget how the ropes feel. So, we'll take it slow," Hawk said, positioning himself behind her. He started to bind her arms, his work steady and methodical. "Did you talk to Hebex?"

"We didn't speak much. She told me you asked for her help?"

"Yeah," he wrapped the rope twice around her left arm, bending it, and pinning it to her back, "She helped me to file the priestesses. I needed to sort out their alibis."

Her body tensed under his hands. Hawk paused.

"Why her?" Amala's voice was a soft whisper, as though she didn't want to show how much the thought startled her. Yet she couldn't hide the hint of jealousy that sparked within, hitting Hawk's chest too.

"What do you mean?"

He couldn't see her face, but he could have sworn her doe eyes widened as she replied, "I could have helped you with that. They are *my* priestesses, I—" Amala grunted as he tightened the tie around her wrist. She didn't finish her sentence, Hawk unable to keep the grin from his face.

"I know you were mourning, Amala mate. Hebex begged me to let her help; she felt terrible that she wasn't there that night."

"Did you find out where she was?" Amala's voice betrayed something like a huffed laugh.

Hawk paused, "You *knew*?"

She chuckled, his fingers tracing along her back, circling a specific spot he knew would drive her crazy. She choked on a breath, her back arching as she tried to escape his touch.

"Hawk!" she pleaded, "Please."

He resumed tying her arms but repeated, "How long have you known?"

"At first, she didn't tell me, but then I figured it out. She's been hooking up with Medyr for a year." Hawk finished the reverse prayer tie and let her body go, admiring his work.

"How do I look?" She asked, tilting her face to the side to try and catch his eyes.

"Delicious."

"Shut up."

"You asked."

She chuckled, "I'm sorry I didn't tell you where she was. But I'm glad she has an alibi that checks out."

Hawk snorted, "I still can't get over the fact she was with *him*."

"You have always had such an aversion for him," Amala retorted.

"Yeah, since you told me how terrible he was that one time you—" Amala burst out laughing. "He *never* deserved that chance, c'mon."

She couldn't hide her amusement as she finally managed to face him, looking into his eyes as her own sparkled with delight. "Are you pissed at Medyr because he got to fuck me *one* time, while you never have?"

Hawk gaped, surprised she would call him out like that. Amala was only ever this blunt with him — portraying the High Priestess to the rest of the world — but he still didn't expect it.

She wiggled her eyebrows, "Am I right?"

"I never understood why you gave him a chance," Hawk raised his hands in defense, and Amala chuckled again.

"It happened once, Hawk. We performed a rite together and our energies merged well together. It just happened. It was years ago." She rolled her eyes, a grin on her beautiful face as she read the expression on his, "And *no,* it wasn't good. Is your pride still intact?"

Hawk snorted again, "Very funny."

"You know I like when you're vulnerable with me, but being insecure because I slept with Medyr *once...* there's no need to feel like that, Hawk."

She smiled but he shook his head, unamused, "I'm not insecure. I'm *jealous.* There's a difference." As he started undoing the knots, his face came dangerously close to her ear as he whispered, "He didn't make you come, right?"

Amala scoffed, rolling her eyes. "He didn't," she confirmed. "So you guys are even."

"We can solve that right now."

She laughed as her body followed his touch to ease his movements.

"Actually," she breathed. "We can't. I am—"

Hawk stilled, realising what he had said. Suddenly, she couldn't feel his touch anymore. He moved in front of her.

"Amala mate, I didn't mean to—"

"Hawk."

He paused again, blowing out a breath.

Amala shook her head. "It's alright, I don't mind the teasing. I meant to say that I am celibate."

If Hawk was suddenly shocked before, it was nothing compared to his reaction now. His jaw dropped, exposing a flash of his canines.

"Celibate?" he repeated, his voice not as steady as he expected.

"Celibate," she confirmed. "Until the next vessel is found."

"Oh." He hesitated.

Amala anticipated his next question, "It's not all the priestesses, just me."

Hawk shrugged. "That doesn't really help. You're the only priestess I want to fuck."

Their faces were mere inches apart, cinnamon and midnight wind merging with their breath.

She narrowed her eyebrows, icy eyes sparkling, "I'll stop teasing if you stop taunting."

Hawk grinned.

"Deal."

CHAPTER 13

Amala did not want to sit in the middle of the Round Room without Serabel by her side. For days, she had been dreading the meeting, with several reasons why: every member of the Karale had seen her at the funeral. They had watched her officiate, performing the ritual she prepared to honour the Goddess, and now... they wouldn't tease her, would they? They wouldn't dare to address her as they usually did — not *now*, not after Serabel's death.

Though if they did, no one would stand up for her today.

Amala slowly walked to the Meads, using each step in an effort to calm down. She took her time to reach the palace and proceeded even slower once inside the building. Now, sat at the round table, her gaze absently wandered outside the window to avoid focusing on the empty seat on her left. Serabel's seat.

"I believe today's meeting has one main purpose," the Prior's voice forced her to look back. She took in the sight of each member of the council as they nodded in agreement.

Today, everyone was there — besides the Phoenix, of course — and Serabel's absence could be deeply felt throughout the room.

"Captain Mercurian is in charge of the investigation on the Goddess' murder and death. Your collaboration will be required today to make things easier," Harat nodded to Hawk, who sat in his chair as though he didn't want to be there.

He had already told Amala the purpose of this meeting so, when he spoke, she wasn't surprised.

"You and your priestesses can no longer live at the temple."

He tried to sound gentle, while knowing the words would hurt anyway, no matter how kindly he voiced or phrased them. Amala had known already, but now, as he finally said it aloud before the Karale, it felt different.

It felt official.

She sighed. She didn't ask why because she knew, but Atalman probed instead.

"Why is that?"

Hawk turned his face to him, a scoff barely audible as he rolled his eyes. He made no effort to hide his dislike of them: the people who, throughout the years, had continuously disrespected his mate. While they didn't know Amala was his mate, sometimes he allowed his mind to envision what would it be like if they ever found out. What would be the look on their faces? Finding out that the hot High Priestess — the innocent, kind-hearted, beautiful priestess that they had all tried to bed for years — was in fact *his* woman. Hawk's woman.

He sent the thought away. Not today. Today his task was to protect Amala, to ensure the meeting ended with no sign of their bond. She would never forgive him, if he exposed the truth against her will.

"The Yonium is not safe." Hawk answered, "If someone managed to get in, to pass the protection and wards, it would be chaos. It is no longer safe for the priestesses to continue living there. Not while we conduct our investigation. We still have no motive as to why the Goddess was murdered. And the priestesses remain alone in that temple without Serabel's energy to protect them. Have you ever considered the killer might strike again, as they remain unprotected?" Hawk's words were harsh, each one a slight stab to Amala's heart. He was right. The temple — her *home* since the day she was born, had felt different lately. Without the Goddess, everything was different.

She couldn't blame Hawk for wanting to keep her safe: the Yonium was her home. But to walk, sleep, and live there knowing a killer had managed to get in... Officers and centaurs, trained to protect them, patrolled the perimeter now, but she hadn't felt safe since. Hawk was right, they couldn't continue like this: until the mystery was solved, they needed to move somewhere else.

Aarush looked at Amala, "Do you believe your priestesses would accept to be hosted at Helioneis?"

She smiled.

"You are very generous, God Aarush. But will you be able to accommodate all of us?"

"Our temples are the same. Open to those in need, and ready to receive more divine beings," he said. Amala held his gaze, "What about our rituals?"

If anyone in the room believed the rituals were unnecessary now that Serabel was dead, they had the common sense not to voice it. They had no idea of its importance. The Goddess lived much further beyond the actual vessel. It was a balancing energy necessary for the wellbeing of the universe.

"So, you've got Dawn and Dusk Call, right?" Medyr asked.

Amala moved her eyes to Medyr and nodded. They understood each other; he'd always been the easiest one to talk to in the Karale. The one that felt the same as she did. Bound in their roles, Amala was grateful for his friendship; after sharing much sacred energy over the years, even before she was High Priestess, their spirituality sealed the bond between them. They respected and cherished each other, ready to help in a moment of need.

"Yup," she said, popping her lips. Only with Medyr would she drop the formalities. "You do sunrise too, right? And then the Highest Sun is at noon," Amala continued.

He nodded, "Would it be okay if we joined dawn and sunrise together?"

Amala thought about it. She would love to attend their sunrise rituals without having to officiate her own Dawn Call, praying as a follower of the God instead. It was entirely her choice and responsibility what the priestesses would do from now on.

"We shall join your First Ray and perform our Dusk Call later on in the evening. We would be honoured to attend your rituals and meditations." Amala decided.

"It is settled, then." The Prior intervened. "The Goddess' priestesses are to temporarily move to Helioneis for the time being, until further notice. What should be done about the temple?" He looked at Hawk.

Yet Amala intervened before he could answer, "I can ward it," she offered. "No one will be able to get in unless I personally undo the spells."

"That works," Hawk said quickly. It was better if no one felt tempted to enter the Yonium while he continued the investigation and the forensic team had already gotten everything they needed from the crime scene.

The High Priestess seemed to hesitate. She looked at the Prior, swallowing once before speaking again. "I don't mean to insult God Aarush's generosity, but I cannot officiate Moon Rites at Helioneis."

Medyr looked vaguely confused, "Is there a rule? Because of the Sun?"

"Oh, no," Amala chuckled. "Because of the males. New Moon and Full Moon are sacred, but only females can witness and take part in them while the Goddess is…"

Dead.

"Vacant," she finished.

Amala would never avoid their most sacred rituals. She would give up Dawn Call to enjoy the sunrise, but the Moon Rites… they happened only twice a month but were essential. Nyla's sweet voice, on her right, turned Amala's head.

"The Home of Waters could host you."

"Oh."

Amala's eyes widened as she pictured herself officiating in such a polar environment to what she was used to. The Home of Waters was a beautiful temple, but it held a specific feminine energy. Being Air, Amala preferred a more neutral space for her prayers. Yet she was most appreciative of Nyla's offer, and nodded. "I would be honoured."

The Protector of Waters curved her lips into a smile as Amala dared to ask one more question.

"Could your temple offer a place to the priestesses that do not wish to live at Helioneis?"

She did not ask for herself, nor did she wish to take advantage of a Protector's generosity, but not all of her priestesses would be comfortable living at the God's temple.

"What do you mean?"

"We have always lived among us. We are all female. If I ask my priestesses, many will be grateful to live at Helioneis, but some would not want to live among males."

Nyla slowly nodded, as understanding slowly painted her features. "Of course, then. They are welcome to live at the Home of Waters for as long as they need."

Amala sighed with relief, glad to be assured of the safety of all her priestesses. The previous night, she faced them too and informed that the Yonium was no longer safe. Luckily, most had agreed. They all loved the temple, yet it felt strange to live there now. They had the option of returning to their families in Aglatas, reside with the centaurs in Mhelani Forest, and now Helioneis and the Home of Waters.

"Captain Mercurian requires absolute collaboration from each of you," the Prior regained control of the conversation, nodding to Hawk as he started explaining what he needed. Amala glanced at Medyr, who smiled back as she allowed herself time to zone out. Her life could continue while living at Helioneis: enjoying the sunrise and sunset, assisting her patients and priestesses, and her meetings with Hawk. Her body soothed, melting into the chair as a glimpse of sun shined across her features and she reclined her head back, enjoying the feeling.

"... That'll do it," Hawk's voice. "And then there's the issue of the High Priestess."

Amala froze. Opening her eyes, she looked at him, confused. "What issue?"

"Where will you be staying?"

Amala imperceptibly raised a brow: what was he saying? He hadn't mentioned this last time they spoke.

"At Helioneis," she said, "With my priestesses."

"No," he said, his voice a little harsh, "You can't."

She stiffened. *What?*

But Hawk shook his head firmly in decision; briefly looking at the Prior, then to her again, there was no trace of solidarity in his eyes.

"We don't know what happened to Serabel. We don't know how her killer got into the Yonium... you can't afford to live in another temple."

"I can't, but my priestesses can?"

"It's different."

"It's *not* different," she countered.

"It's fucking different, *Amala*!"

She blinked, her lips parting slightly in surprise.

Hawk had never called her by her name in front of the Karale. In fact, he had barely spoken to her at all. She continued to survey him, still shocked.

Hawk's eyes slightly softened as he sighed, "If *you* go to Helioneis and something happens to you, none of the other priestesses have your powers. None can communicate with the Goddess's energy. None have been trained like you have." He paused. "You are powerful, High Priestess, but you are also *too* important for such a risk. Your priestesses will be safe, I promise, but we cannot take our chances with you."

"She'll be fine at our temple," Medyr said, glancing at Amala.

She mentally cursed — not Medyr. Not Medyr insisting to Hawk she should go to Helioneis. The Prior seemed to share her thoughts, only his sneer was subtle.

"I said no." Hawk countered, raising his voice. "There's no way she's going to that temple."

Halting Medyr's words with a dismissive gesture, Hawk's eyes met hers.

And so did Medyr's.

Amala fought an amused smile.

"Captain Mercurian makes a fair point. I do trust your temple, Medyr, and I am sure my priestesses will be safe. But—" she considered Hawk for a moment. "Will I be able to see them? To visit?"

"Every day, if you need."

Amala could not help but hesitate: how could she do such a thing? Leave her sisters behind?

The Prior caught her frown and added, "Your safety is a priority right now, High Priestess Amala." His voice was full of power and pride as he continued, "We'll make sure you can visit the temple whenever you want. But you will need an escort to ensure you are always safe."

In his words, something clicked.

Amala blinked, almost amused with the revelation as she repressed a laugh.

"Am I to live under the supervision of someone else, then?" she bit her lip, eyes challenging the Prior.

Harat nodded, "We will make sure your escort keeps you safe."

She scoffed, shaking her head. The *audacity*.

"And let me guess..." her eyes shot right to Hawk who met her stare. And grinned.

☼

"So, you're not coming with us?" Sinayla asked, a smirk on her face as she finished packing her bag. Hebex smiled too as Amala rolled her eyes.

"Don't look at me like that," she said, "I'm feeling so guilty. I tried, I *really* tried, but God and Goddess, I am so mad!"

Both priestesses snickered.

"Mad?" Sinayla repeated, amused. "I've never seen you mad, before."

"Well, I am now!"

"Because your Captain cares about your safety so much to provide you with extra protection?" Hebex replied in attempt to calm her down. The High Priestess shook her head.

"It's not like that," she tried to say, but was interrupted again.

"Listen, I'm not going with them either!" Seryn said, pulling her into a hug. "And it's fine, Amala. No one would blame you for this..."

But Seryn had a reason to go somewhere else, a reason to pick the Home of Waters rather than Helioneis, whereas Amala had no reason to leave them, no reason to make such a choice.

She grunted.

Don't lie, she told herself.

They were her sisters, right? Her closest friends.

"I'm afraid," she admitted, eyes watching the floor, unable to meet the gaze of her priestesses. "Our mating bond is going to snap *very* soon. I can feel it in my bones, in my veins, in my soul. I didn't like him hiding the truth from me, but I understand why he did so." She would have never said yes if he had told her alone.

Even if she wanted to.

Yet Amala was grateful Hawk had made that choice, because she likely would have never found the courage to make it herself, to follow her heart and be with him — and Howlite.

"Are you afraid to be... tempted?" Hebex asked quietly, trying to understand.

Amala slowly shook her head.

"I'm afraid to fall for him." she confessed as a blush crept up her cheeks, finally voicing the words only Serabel had known.

"Why?" Sinayla scoffed.

"Because I shouldn't let *him* be my priority right now! I want to properly mourn my Goddess without such feelings. I will never forgive myself if I become distracted by Hawk, even if he is my mate," she carefully explained, daring to meet her friends' gaze.

Hebex looked surprised. "You wouldn't be able to keep *Love* away from you, no matter how hard you tried, Amala!"

Sinayla chuckled as she nodded in agreement, Seryn too.

"Is this why you're mad?" The latter asked, a grin on her lips, "Because you're trying not to fall for him, and his plans have messed up yours?"

Amala burst out laughing. It was a weird way to summarise how she felt, but—

"Yes," she answered, allowing to light up her eyes.

That, and also the fact Amala had loved many people in her life; with a heart crafted of sunlight, she had Loved so much and no one could ever match it in return.

"It's all right, then," Sinayla replied. "We'll check on you daily. Every time we see you, we'll let you know if we think you've fallen already, or if you still got a grip, alright?"

She didn't want to, but she laughed again: she had feared that moment for days, weeks. To leave her temple — the unknown perspective awaiting her and her priestesses, yet now... the Yonium was her home, but Hawk was her home too.

And maybe *that* perspective was worth a shot.

CHAPTER 14

H awk found Amala three hours later.

Standing outside of the temple, he observed the multitude of people leaving the temple: priestesses, People who had come to pray, forensic officers who had disbanded their setup on the murder scene before the Yonium was about to be warded... steps tapping against the marble became background noise, merging with the mixture of voices together. He would have loved to go there more often, yet Amala only allowed him to come every few months: he was Captain Mercurian, and too many people knew what he looked like for his presence to go unnoticed.

But what if I'm a faithful follower of the Goddess? He asked, all those years before. *Wouldn't that excuse my presence?*

Amala had laughed, soft and sincere: *You are three-hundred years old, and you've never cared before... I'd say it would be suspicious if you suddenly turned up right when the hot High Priestess Amala performs her naked rituals.*

He'd given her a point for that. And so, he obeyed. Even if he rarely came to the temple, he knew Amala longed for him to see her during those rituals, to reveal her truest self. When she unleashed her power, not merely officiating, but embracing the Goddess' energy — almost *becoming* the Goddess' energy — Hawk knew every single person who had watched Amala was incredibly lucky. Amala was more than a priestess, perhaps more than a High Priestess. She was the temple: her energy a sweet, yet powerful caress that could heal your soul in seconds.

His mate.

The sound of hooves against the marble floor raised his head, instantly more conscious of the reality around him. *Centaurs.* He spotted them at the bottom of the staircase as Amala exited the Yonium, closing the heavy doors behind her. She had a bag swinging across her body, still dressed in her usual priestess attire.

As she approached the centaurs, Hawk shifted closer. He had a plan. Knowing Amala was most likely mad at him, he thought it would be better if *she* spotted him first, rather than approaching her himself. It had seemed a good plan — a good plan that went to shit the moment he saw her with those males.

"Fuck," he muttered, approaching them with no control. *Fucking mating bond.* And fucking jealousy. Hawk had never been jealous of Amala before, but they had hidden their feelings for too long and now the moment was drawing closer. They both knew it too.

So, Hawk felt justified to cut into their conversation before it even began.

Amala saw him a moment before he reached her: her expression changed, her smile faltering as she raised a challenging brow, halting him with a gesture of the hand. "What the hell are you doing here?"

She tried to raise her voice, yet failed to sound anything less than sweet as she trained her features to appear angry. Hawk considered her attitude and decided to give her the satisfaction of yelling at him. He deserved it, after all.

"I thought I could pick you up." Hawk replied, eyes steady on her face.

"Why?"

Hawk hadn't thought this far ahead. Without a good excuse for standing there, he felt incredibly stupid. He wanted to apologise, but doing so right now would only make things worse: Amala wouldn't appreciate if he mentioned what had happened in the Round Room in front of any more people.

"Help you carry your bags?" He shrugged. "I honestly thought you had more stuff with you."

Amala glanced at her bag, "Most of my clothes are underwear," she explained, "It all fits in one bag." Hawk couldn't disagree. She hooked the bag from her shoulder and handed it to him, "Here you go."

An awkward silence fell on the group as Amala sighed, shifting uncomfortably.

"This is Hawk," she nodded her head towards him. "Hawk, meet Aries and Kanaan." Her eyes sharpened as she locked eyes with her mate: a brief, yet powerful glance, so familiar that he could hear the words behind her stare: *Don't. Call. Me. Amala mate.*

He wouldn't do that. Hawk stared back and knew that she was right, he would. He felt incredibly jealous standing before two centaurs — two centaurs who had fucked his mate — while he was unable to claim her as his.

He braced himself, breathed, then looked at them instead: his eyes fell on Kanaan first. Kanaan — Kanaan who was still fucking Amala.

Hawk could hardly believe he had held back over the years, without feeling the need to *slaughter* anyone who touched her. This feeling now was perhaps an escalation of all the times he had felt no jealousy at all.

Facing Amala, he said, "Kanaan looks an awful lot like me."

A smirk instantly appeared on her face. She bit her lip, shrugging, "Forgive me if I have a type."

Hawk grinned, feeling slightly more at ease and, if Kanaan understood the innuendo, his face revealed nothing. Maybe Kanaan was smarter than he thought. Definitely smarter than him.

"We'll miss you, High Priestess," the other centaur, Aries, stepped slightly closer to Amala's side.

"You can visit the Home of Waters, if you still wish to attend the Goddess' rituals," she replied. "But I know you wouldn't come to the city. I'll come back to visit Palana and Helerai soon."

"You assist female centaurs too?" Hawk asked, surprised.

"I assist every creature." Amala said, her eyes a silent command to ask nothing further. "There are two beautiful pregnant females in their tribe." Turning back to the centaurs, Amala continued, "Thanks for coming to say goodbye. I appreciate it. I must go now, but if you wish to contact me, just..." she halted, pondering what to say before turning to Hawk. "Are letters okay?"

"I'll give you a phone the second we leave, but yes, they can send you all the love letters they want."

Amala shot him a disapproving glare before saying, "Give them your address, then."

She was brief in her goodbyes, not stepping closer to the centaurs, or making any moves that manifested physical contact. With one last glance at the Yonium, *her* home, she followed Hawk along the marble path.

"A phone?" she said, falling into step beside him.

"I'll have lots of stuff to do, Amala mate. And I'd like to be able to contact you at all times."

She said nothing. Both of them knew they were pretending everything was okay because, once they had the talk, there was no turning back.

"You should never compare centaurs and anthropomorphic creatures in the same sentence, you will end up offending them. By describing us as *human* because we have a human body implies they are animals. Which they are *not*." She quickly explained, her pace hurried with her words. "You behaved well."

Hawk didn't look back, unfaltering in his steps. "I'm sorry I didn't tell you about staying with me, Amala mate. I— "

"—Forgive you." She interrupted him. "I forgive you."

Her tone was quick with conviction, a clear indicator she wished not to discuss it again. "Let's not talk about how sneaky you have been. Just, how much freedom do I have?"

"All the freedom you need. I just want to know where you are. And maybe drive you around myself, if you don't mind."

The small smile rippling on her lips told him she didn't.

Strolling through the marble lane onto the short footpath in the woods, they finally reached the parking lot, not uttering a word as they approached the grey SUV. Hawk sat behind the steering wheel, leaning into the leather seat: fake leather, he had promised Amala when he bought the car three years earlier.

"Fasten your seatbelt." he said, but she interrupted him.

"Hawk," she knew how much he loved to hear his name from her mouth. "Talk to me."

Her eyes were clear and face sincere. He definitely knew what she was referring to.

"You be honest," he countered.

Amala nodded: "I promise."

He braced himself, thinking of what to say. But it was Amala, his mate, not someone he should be afraid to offer his thoughts to. "Lately, it's been different. I feel jealous and happier than usual every time I see you. I feel like I'm going crazy. And I can't stand it, Amala mate. I can't stand that you're mine, but you're not, that I can have you more than anyone else but at the same time it's like I've never had you for real."

Amala gasped softly, not expecting those words, though never more ready to receive them. She felt the same way. This morning, she had thought of him as she touched herself and, when she watched the sunrise, she wished he was by her side appreciating the same view.

"You have me, Hawk. I am your mate forever."

He sighed hearing those words, then locked his eyes to hers, "I am so sorry I yelled at you at the meeting. I wanted to shut up, but I also wanted to rip Medyr's head off. He thinks he has some leverage on you because he's a priest and fucked you once. But you are *my* mate."

Amala chuckled a genuine laugh at his words. Reaching for his hand, she rubbed her soft skin against his.

"I have a feeling he'll know that I'm yours soon enough."

Hawk grinned, and Amala melted in her seat, knowing he saved that grin only for her. The honesty he was talking with... she swallowed dryly as she took the courage to voice her next thought.

"It's my turn to apologise. I've felt our bond growing deeper too, stronger every day. I should have told you sooner. I want you as my mate, and I know we're trying to hold back until we can no longer avoid it, but I'm okay if we keep going like this. I just don't think we have much time left. But know that, when we feel it, we will make it happen."

She rubbed the back of his hand. Amala was celibate now, but this wasn't about that. This was about them as mates, not lovers.

"Do you want it to happen?" he closed his eyes, enjoying her gentle touch.

"Of course, I do." She murmured. "Do you?"

He nodded.

"It happens when it happens." Amala said. "Okay? And when it happens, we'll be ready."

He opened his eyes and squeezed her hand in gratitude.

"Let's go home, Amala mate."

☼

Hawk opened the door as Amala entered before him; she barely had one foot into the apartment before Howlite pounced.

The big hound, white with black stripes — similar to the shades of howlite stone — tried to lick her face as she fell onto the floor, laughing.

"Hello beautiful," she murmured, scratching behind her ears.

The last time she saw Howlite was last week, but the hound was always happy when Amala arrived.

She stood up, accepting Hawk's outstretched hand.

"Thanks," she said.

Amala then paced the apartment which had become all too familiar over the years. Yet she thought of this place as home, second to the Yonium. It wouldn't take too long for her to settle here.

"I still feel bad for leaving them alone," she murmured.

Hawk gently lifted her chin and kissed her jaw.

"They'll be alright. They're with Medyr," he said, the tone in his voice prompting a laugh from her.

She clasped her small fingers around his, moving her face out of his reach.

"I really want to enjoy this, staying here," she murmured, looking around, "And I don't want to make it difficult for you, driving me around with this case ongoing. I can take care of myself—"

"I know you can."

"—And I *need* to take care of my sisters."

She didn't want to depend on him — to feel utterly useless.

Hawk read it on her face, his features softening.

"You can do as you wish as long as we make sure you're safe," he said tenderly, tentatively brushing his fingers against her cheek, "I'm happy you're living with me, Amala mate. How many drawers do you need for your things?"

She shrugged, "Probably one, perhaps a few crutches for my dresses. Do you mind if I sleep on the sunny side?" she asked, eyebrows knotting.

Hawk stilled, his face an alteration of surprise and confusion.

"What?" Amala said, biting her lower lip.

"You *actually* want to share a bed?"

Now she looked confused — embarrassed even.

"I—you don't want to?"

Their eyes met and they burst out laughing.

Hawk's gaze was gentle, focused solely on her face as he replied, "I thought you didn't want to force things."

He hoped she could detect the honesty in his words: he would always let her set the pace of their relationship, whatever was going on between them.

"I'm not forcing things. I feel safer if I sleep next to you," Amala replied, face sincere as she traced his knuckles gently. "And there's no sun in the other room."

He smiled, "You can have the sunny side, then."

Hawk carried her belongings into the bedroom, Amala's eyes brightening at the mention of the sun. She observed him while she slowly followed, taking in the view of his apartment. Amala had always liked his house. It wasn't big, but cosy, and Hawk did well to keep it tidy. Her eyes landed on his bed and a sudden thought hit her.

"What if you want to hook up?"

"Just say the word and I'm ready."

"*Hawk!*" she scoffed as she tried her best not to chuckle.

He raised a questioning brow, amused by her reaction. "You mean with someone else?"

"Aren't you seeing Naressa?"

"Did you just forget everything we said in the car?"

He enjoyed the sight of her face as a red blush crept up her cheeks. Amala blushed a lot when she was around him, but her eyes betrayed her thoughts — she meant it. She *actually* felt guilty if her presence prevented him from sleeping with someone else.

"I still plan to be celibate for a while," she shrugged. "So, I thought you may want to keep yourself occupied."

Hawk snorted at the thought of *looking* at anyone else with Amala around. *As if*, he almost said.

"I'm not hooking up with Naressa — at least not regularly, Amala mate."

Amala shrugged, "Why not?"

She *really* was a tease.

"Because she alternates between me, Blade and Cairo depending on her mood."

And because I like you, he mentally added.

Amala pursed her lips together and considered.

"What if you feel like hooking up with her, though?"

Why was she insisting?

"Were you there in the car when we said we would see how things could be between us? Or have you forgotten already?"

"We *never* said that!" she snapped back. Her eyes widened as regret hit her seconds later.

He wouldn't fall for words spoken out of fear or anger. Hawk knew better than that and knew *her* better than that — enough to realise she didn't mean it. Taking a breath, he considered. Amala was celibate anyway, which would allow her to focus without pressure or fear of any change between them. And it would probably be torture for him, waiting for her to sort out her feelings as if his soul didn't depend on hers… but it was better this way. So that, when she was ready, it would be for real.

"What if I share your commitment, then? I'll be celibate too."

The words came out of his mouth before he could double check if they made any sense.

Hawk regretted them a moment later, mentally cursing himself. Amala surveyed him with those icy eyes of hers.

"I didn't mean to disrespect you, Amala mate..." he reached for her, afraid she would reject his touch.

She didn't. Stilling, she allowed Hawk to gently brush her shoulder as she looked into his eyes. Into his soul. A small smile appeared on her lips.

"You don't have to, there's no sacred energy that you need to protect. I mean," she corrected herself. "Your energy is divine, too. But you are free to share it with whoever you wish."

He didn't know why and had no clue what his brain was doing but he repeated, "I'll do it."

Amala's eyes brightened, though she added, "You're free to pull back whenever you want."

She moved towards his bed and lazily dropped into the mattress, stretching across the soft sheets. Hawk studied her closely: her body splayed across his bed — a view he would get used to very soon.

"There'll be no need."

CHAPTER 15

T hat feeling wouldn't leave him alone. Two days had passed since Amala moved in and Hawk felt inexplicably and unexplainably moody. He had felt that way for a while but, over the last two days, the feeling had somehow intensified. He was irritable, tending to view things in a negative perspective: overreacting and approaching life in a way that didn't feel like him. It was strange, considering Amala now lived with him — a dream come true. She lived in his house: sleeping on the other side of his bed, eating breakfast with him, and helping him clean the dishes. The absolute bliss of the domestic routine he had dreamed of since the day they met.

When he apologised for his moodiness, Amala only shrugged it off.

"It's normal, Hawk. The Goddess isn't here to balance love anymore," she explained, "And we all feel the consequences of that."

You don't look affected in the slightest, he had wanted to say, yet knew it was untrue. Amala might not appear affected by the unbalance, but she remained extremely unsettled by her Goddess' death.

Then there had been the phone call, and Amala had worried for real.

Someone had been killed. There had been a riot — one of the minor Water gangs fighting over territory — but the situation had escalated quicker than usual. Such things were expected when a deity died: the line between good and bad fading. When the Goddess was missing, it was almost natural for morals to deviate compared to normal times.

Amala had been quieter than usual once learning of the news. That morning, as they had breakfast together on the kitchen island, she barely looked at him.

"Are you alright, Amala mate?" Hawk gently asked, observing her microscopic bite of the cinnamon roll he had bought.

She nodded slowly, so Hawk returned to his mug of coffee and took a sip.

Then gently she said, "I feel guilty that those people have died. I feel like it's my fault for not having figured out who the next vessel is."

Hawk started to interrupt but she quickly added, "I know it's *not* my fault. Rationally, I know. Yet some part of me feels guilty, knowing it could have been avoided."

"You said it takes time."

"It does. Only one person is worthy enough to embrace such energy, so it's a long process to find out who it is."

"I still can't believe, among all the people in this world, the divine energy picked Aarush."

Amala choked on a small piece of pastry that she, somehow, was still chewing.

"Hawk!" she scolded. "That's *blasphemy.*"

"Sorry."

Amala smiled, then took another bite.

"What are you doing today?"

"Visiting Pyramis with Blade and Cairo."

"Do you have a lead?"

He shook his head.

"No, it's not a lead. It's a micro clue that will hopefully turn in something more promising."

Amala hummed but didn't question him. Instead, she took a sip from her glass. "You know what? It's worth living here compared to the Yonium because I can finally have *this*," her eyes sparkled as she drank again. Hawk chuckled. Amala loved juice, but couldn't have it at the temple unless she made it herself, from the fruit picked from the trees. With a nostalgic smile, his mind wondered back to some years ago, when he had visited the Yonium and was offered a glass of peach juice — handmade by her.

It had been surprisingly sweeter than he expected, and even with a hint of cinnamon. He had pondered whether to ask if she had added some, but decided to keep his dignity. Whatever was left of it.

Swallowing another sip, she smiled. "I'll see you later, then?"

And Hawk couldn't describe the way those words made his heart thump in his chest.

☼

"Are you sure you want to park here?"

"It's not my car," Cairo shrugged, tapping on the steering wheel.

"Just because the precinct lent you the car, doesn't mean you can leave it in the worst street of Pyramis." Hawk scoffed.

"It's not like it says *police*, dude," Blade sneered. "But the second they get word of us, this car is gone. Forever."

"Yeah, it'll probably be gone way before that, if you park it here." Hawk remarked.

They didn't look behind as they crossed the street. Hawk loved to drive. He could drive for hours: from Aglatas to all around the villages in eastern Babylon and back. Driving took his mind off things, allowing him to explore a world once forbidden.

Mostly, he liked to drive outside of Aglatas. Despite becoming acquainted with the city and its districts over the years, he never ventured into certain parts unless his job required it. Blade, on the other hand, was born and raised in Pyramis and had great knowledge of the district, especially the area surrounding Jaren's pyramid. He had spent days hiding there after school to avoid the fire bullies that searched after him.

"This way," he grunted, heading down a narrow alley.

Hawk knit his brow, "Are you sure?"

"I'm high, not dumb." Blade retorted, "Yes, Captain, I remember the way."

Hawk swallowed a laugh as he followed him, Cairo behind. Pyramis was opulent in an extravagant way. Every single detail was immensely cared for: the immaculate pavements, the elegant buildings, the clean, neat and — all functioning — streetlights. Everything was lavish: gold drainpipes and window fixtures, shops' shutters made of delicate bordeaux etched with silver lines. Even down the street, onto the road, one could glimpse sparks of gold all around.

The small alley they now passed through channelled the same decadent energy.

Blade led the way, his slumped posture readjusting to gain composure as he tried to hide he was a massive stoner.

The pyramid was even more lavish. Hawk refrained to go there, even when dealing with Jaren for other matters, but he couldn't ignore the electricity buzzing in the air as they drew closer. It felt richer, smelled richer. The palace was monumental. He lost count of the stories long before his eyes reached the top. On a clear day, the Pyramid could be seen all the way from the Prior Palace in the Meads. There were guards outside, too. Hawk scoffed. The prick loved to show off his wealth, but armed guards patrolling the building? He frowned as the three of them stopped in front of the gates.

One of the guards spoke first.

"What is your business here?"

That morning, Hawk had woken up with the intention of being on his best behaviour. With his strong dislike for Jaren and his ways, he was in no mood to deal with him. Luckily, his friends knew this and took the lead.

"We're from the Priory. Is Jaren home?"

The guard observed Blade, unable to tell if he was serious or not. Blade merely grinned.

"We demand an audience with Protector Jaren," Cairo complied. He was better adjusted to the formalities certain people required in Aglatas, mostly because Hawk had sent him to deal with several unpleasant situations on his own.

A quick check of their documents was enough for the guards to let them in, as one guided them through a maze of corridors and staircases. Every time Hawk had come to the Pyramid, he was shown a different path: he suspected Jaren had no intention to let his guests memorise the palace grounds.

Today, the Protector rested on a balcony. Its ceiling was a canopy of red flowers, some scattered on the ground. From the scent, it must have been amaryllis.

Jaren stood from the couch — a gesture easily mistaken for kindness, though Hawk knew it was another move to state his dominance. They would have to bow to him.

Bow.

Hawk knew it was coming, but he really hated the bastard.

Biting his lip to avoid a snarky retort, Hawk slightly dipped his head. He didn't need to; Harat had given him absolute authority over the Protectors — and anyone else — during the investigation, but he didn't want any trouble. To go against Jaren's will in his own palace wouldn't be worth it.

"Your presence was unexpected, Captain Mercurian," Jaren's snarky tone caused Blade and Cairo to repress a snarl. Hawk didn't look at them but relaxed in his stance, silently urging them to do the same.

Quiet.

Hawk had never cared what Jaren thought of him and wouldn't start now. The Protector was a selfish, despicable male who found entertainment by tormenting his fire subjects. Hell, his Second was a trained assassin whose sole purpose was to punish as many people as possible.

"If I wanted a formal meeting, I would have called in advance," Hawk replied, gritting his teeth. "This should tell you enough."

His voice was steady, but not rude; proud but not insolent; powerful but never disrespectful.

"Am I right to believe you need my *help* in your investigation, Captain?"

Hawk snorted at his choice of words.

"I'd hardly call it help, but yes, I do require your assistance."

Jaren flashed his teeth in a quiet sneer, but there was no mocking reply. A slight hint of amusement simmered in his charcoal eyes, deep and fuming like perpetual cinders. "If you are asking for my most prized weapon, the Phoenix is currently not in Aglatas."

"Thank the Goddess," Blade muttered, the words mirroring Hawk's own thoughts.

"We're not here for the Phoenix," he tried to retain his composure, holding Jaren's gaze, "We require access to the Embers."

The tension which followed was palpable. The silence deafening. Cairo's breath was ragged behind him; peering at Blade whose dark eyes were trained on Jaren. No sign of how stoned he truly was — Hawk had to give it to him, it was quite a remarkable skill.

"What do you need from the Embers?"

Jaren's voice was raw, unable to hide his annoyance and, perhaps, fear. Hawk understood, though. Jaren was safe as Protector, but he didn't want any dark shit within his gang to be uncovered.

"The Embers gained half of their popularity when God Darnen died. They owe most of their influence to the past unbalance. I wouldn't be surprised if they have something to do with what's going on right now."

"Are you saying my gang is behind Serabel's murder? Accusing us? *Me*?"

Hawk beheld the Protector and raised a brow, allowing him to see the bitterness in his eyes. "No one raised any accusations against you Jaren but, if you don't shut the fuck up and comply, we might. We need immediate access to the Embers and we thought of coming here first. Unless you would prefer us to go ahead and begin the raid?"

Jaren released a low breath, a glimpse of his scales flashing through. The Fire Protector kept a glamour on his skin, but it was well known that Jaren descended from a powerful ancestry with shifter blood and, while he couldn't shift himself, the scale came with the heritage.

"Fine."

☆

"Play nice, will you? Do that and I promise I won't kill you."

Things hadn't gone exactly how they had planned. Jaren had allowed them access to the Embers, but with the condition Hawk would get them to talk on their own. Jaren refused to help. It was their own responsibility to get in.

Hawk expected it. The Protector had agreed to their request because he knew better than going against Priory orders, but would never make it easy for them to get what they wanted.

They had a plan though. And it worked.

The only reason Hawk preferred Jaren to play mediator was to avoid a bloodbath. Him and his friends had no problem fighting their way in but it could be easily avoided, had the Protector not loathed them so. Instead, they raided the Embers' warehouse, frightening off those within it, and threatening the rest if they didn't collaborate. Some were now locked in a room to gain the information they needed.

Hawk refrained from chuckling at Cairo's voice, unaccustomed to seeing him play the part of scary torturer. His specialty was killing from afar and, of all the people Hawk had worked with, he had never met someone with the same skills. Cairo could shoot from a mile away, landing the perfect hit. Though he wasn't equally experienced in hand-to-hand combat.

"I'll ask one last time," Cairo said now, "Are you going to tell me the truth? Or should I remind you where you were the night of the murder?"

"Fine," the man blurted, eying Cairo's dagger. "I know absolutely nothing about the temple. I've never been there."

"It's true," the woman admitted. "When the former God died, business boomed. We had tons of new deals every week, but it was never a thing for us to *make* it happen again."

"Are the same deals ongoing now?"

"With different people," she shrugged. "But essentially, yes. We have recently received lots of new clients."

"So, you'll forgive me if I say this gives you an incredibly good reason to make it happen again?" Cairo replied, but Hawk knew it was in vain. They had checked the temple perimeter and found nothing reconducted to the Embers. And yet—

"I think someone hired you," Hawk slowly interrupted. "Either before, or after, the Goddess died. Someone came to you with a request."

The woman said nothing. The man, with Cairo's dagger pressed below his chin, gulped.

"Listen, you have wasted our time already, so my patience is running low. *Extremely* low. You better give us what we need now, or I won't ask so nicely again." Hawk bared his canines, and the man had the common sense to look away, shuddering.

All it took was Cairo to press the dagger deeper into his skin before he gave up.

"Fine, fucking Goddess!" he cursed, "We got hired!"

His demeanour instantly relaxed as he gave up the information. Hawk's eyes narrowed as Blade grimaced at his side. They exchanged a brief glance, then refocused their attention on the terrified man being held against the wall. The woman sighed: half disappointed, half relieved.

Blade spoke first.

"Who hired you?"

"We don't know, I've never known."

"Never?" Blade's face was questioning, glancing at Hawk.

"Let me sit down, for the fucking Goddess, and I'll talk. I swear it." The man said, his eyes hastily alternated between the pair, trying to see which one he could ask for mercy. None of them would, but Blade allowed him to catch his breath, monitoring every movement with unreadable eyes.

Once he felt more comfortable, the man returned their stares: regret and fear mixed on his face. Hawk barely hid a grin, pointing to the man as his patience ran low.

"Now that you're all comfy, talk fast. You said *never*. How many times have you been involved with this... buyer?"

The man shook his head again, "I don't know if it's one person or many. We never approach first, it's always them."

"How long?" Hawk asked, baring his teeth.

"A while," he admitted, "But it's never the same guy who reaches out. Everything is anonymous. We tried to figure out who it was, but nothing worked."

"That's bullshit!" Blade spat, "The Embers don't deal with strangers. You would never settle for the lower hand." He kept an eye on his phone, typing down before stashing it back in his pocket.

"Usually we don't, and that's what we told the first guy who came here. But they came back and insisted. They offered us more," the man said.

Blade caught Hawk's expression, then asked, "How much more?"

The man shrugged.

"Triple price. Triple price to do whatever favour they asked of us."

Triple price meant whoever the buyer was, had money to spare. Hawk sighed. The Embers were not cheap; too many had fallen for their deals without realising what it meant to be indebted to a loan shark.

"You're gonna tell us exactly what they asked for."

"The first time, it was easy. Just some non-accessible records from two hundred years ago — or something like that. We delivered soon and they paid well. Then, the second time they wanted some reserved information — about some dagger I don't really know about. I wasn't the one who worked that deal. And then..."

He glanced at the woman, dubiously watching on.

"Jaren is going to kill us."

"Jaren fucking authorised us to raid you, so answer the damn question." Cairo seethed.

"Fuck, fine! Blueprints. They wanted blueprints."

A thick silence followed the revelation as Hawk's gaze met Blade's.

"What blueprints?"

"They wanted blueprints of the Yonium. It was urgent, they said. They would pay quadruple our prices if we managed to give it to them in a week."

"A week?" Hawk said, "When was this?"

The man pondered momentarily. "A month ago? A month ago, or something like that. It was the last time we heard from them."

Hawk's heart sank. A month ago was not nearly long enough for someone to plan a murder based on blueprints, not if they wanted to cover their tracks.

"But we couldn't make it in a week," the man added, "So we got our normal tripled rate. It took us days to get our hands on the information."

"How did you do it?" Blade asked, trying to hide his curiosity.

"It took us a while. We had no clue how to get what they wanted, but Jaren told us to get the deal done. But that fucking temple is on zero records, there's nothing about its structure. We tried to approach a couple priestesses..." Hawk's blood boiled as he pictured Amala, now safe in his house, being bothered by this asshole. His hands tightened into fists as the man kept going, "Then we just figured we could use Helioneis' plant."

"What do you mean, Helioneis' plant?"

"Helioneis and the Yonium are the same. Their structure is the same. In every wall and floor."

"How did you get *this* information?"

"Helioneis is different from the Yonium. They have a fucking website, cameras and all. You know, the second you go *modern*, everyone knows your shit."

Blade's phone buzzed. He glanced at the screen and nodded at Hawk with his chin. "We'll catch her if we go now."

Hawk hummed and shot a look to Cairo.

"I'll finish here and send you all the info in a minute," he assured them. Cairo was the best at writing detailed reports, never missing a single piece of information.

Hawk followed Blade outside.

"Does she know we're on our way?" he asked.

"Oh, she has no idea we're coming. Get ready to share your secrets."

CHAPTER 16

P yramis wasn't so bad, Hawk decided.

Though he always seemed to go there to interact with people he hated, but it was worth it to take a walk along the opulent streets of the district, the temperature always slightly warmer than the rest of the city. The sun created a delightful game of lights and shadows across the facades of the high, elegant buildings.

Blade on his side, they walked along the immaculate pavement, passing the most luxurious neighbourhood into a less wealthy area; while the buildings didn't lose their height, the facades grew dirtier, and the streets and fences less sophisticated. Blade stopped in front of a big building with chunks of plaster falling from the walls and a huge hole indented in the window as though someone had thrown a rock at it. On the contrary, the front courtyard seemed immaculate.

Hawk turned to Blade, an indecisive frown on his face.

"Are you sure she'll be willing to help?" he quietly asked.

His friend nodded vaguely. "She'll do it. She owes me big time, anyway."

"You owe her for not killing you when you were a teenage dickhead," Hawk countered, but followed Blade's lead as they approached the front gate.

He kept his distance, aware that — even after centuries — Blade always had mixed feelings about coming back here. Hawk observed his friend's trembling fingers as he buzzed the intercom, looking away when he spoke through the microphone. Hawk didn't try to make conversation as they walked inside, lingering a few steps behind as he let Blade set their pace. The orphanage was well kept, regardless of the outside. But Hawk knew it hadn't always been like this.

When Blade was just a kid, thrown in here with his sister, the orphanage was indeed falling apart. Aglatas had almost no technology and the building lacked any funding to be kept up to date: too many children and barely anyone willing to adopt them.

Blade didn't often tell the history of his childhood. It had taken him decades before he felt comfortable enough to even tell Hawk.

Blade and his sister were twins, born in Aquar from young parents that had make a mistake: they didn't have money, could barely afford rent, and whatever they earned, they gambled. Social services found Blade and his sister locked in their basement at 3 years old and took them to the closest orphanage. Which would have been a blessing, had the orphanage been anywhere else but Pyramis. Spending their childhood bullied by the other children because of their difference in power, Blade had spent every day trying to protect Wahine. Going back to the orphanage always felt traumatic for him, even though Wahine now worked there.

The pair had been adopted by an older couple when they were 10. Adopted by two women who found they were mates long after their fertility window, yet they wanted to offer a better life to more than one child. Blade and Wahine were lucky: their mothers were wealthy, so they had moved from the orphanage to one of the richest areas of Pyramis.

Blade thought his suffering would end after leaving the orphanage, but attending Pyramis' poshest school somehow made things worse.

Blade had taken it worse than Wahine. He was too kind for this world, but never complained about his life, even if he didn't appreciate his teenage years. Instead, Blade was eternally grateful to his parents, though his life had been hell. Yet things perked up once he joined Aglatas' firefighters where, decades later, he met Hawk.

Wahine was different. She was fiery, intimidating: a force to be reckoned with. She had one goal and had worked all her life to achieve it — graduate and work until she could afford to buy the orphanage, to give all those kids a better life. All the children who were not fortunate enough to be adopted, ended up joining the Embers. Wahine had seen it coming and started a whole business to prevent them from harm: now, most Embers' members were indebted to her, and she used the upper hand to keep them at bay.

Hawk was well acquainted with Blade's family: his parents were incredible people, always willing to help and support their children. They were genuine, interested in everything that their children liked or did, and willing to learn about it merely for the purpose of having something to talk about with them. A common interest.

Wahine Hendrix was quickly walking past their direction when she spotted them, a frown of confusion on her face. She paced the last steps to reach them.

"Blade!" she blurted, her steady voice softening a touch for her brother.

"Hey, little drop," he opened his arms and there was no waiting as she threw herself at him. Blade lifted her up, Wahine almost squealing in surprise with a big smile painting her face. When Blade put her down and turned to Hawk, her eyes shimmered.

"Well hello, Captain," she said, bowing her head. "You look well. You were miserable when I saw you last — when was that?"

"Two months ago," Hawk replied, already knowing where this would go

"Two months ago," Wahine replied, "And now you look very happy, even with a dead Goddess and everything going to shit. What happened?"

Blade snickered and Wahine whirled on him.

"What?"

"His mate agreed to move in with him," Blade smirked, throwing Hawk a look.

"You found your mate?" Wahine gaped.

Hawk rolled his eyes: Blade was *dead*. His friend was so terrible at keeping secrets it was probably a miracle this was the first time he had shared the truth about Amala.

But they needed Wahine's help; he knew Blade was feeding her information on purpose, regardless of fraternal love or affection. Wahine was simple to work with: a piece of gossip for another.

This time, the piece of gossip in question was Hawk's personal life.

"I found her a long time ago. But we're not together," he added before she could ask.

"And do I know her?" she insisted, not even bothering to mask her curiosity. "Is she the redhead that works with you guys?"

Blade choked on a laugh, and even Hawk fought the urge to grin.

"No, it's not Naressa," he said, "But I guess you might know her."

"Does she work with you at all?"

He shook his head. "No. She lives at the Yonium."

Wahine gasped.

"A priestess?" She moved her gaze between him and Blade, eyes flitting manically between the two. "A priestess... poor woman, what a hard time she must be going through... they had to leave the temple, right? Is that why she moved in with you?"

Hawk nodded. "Yes. She could have moved with the other priestesses in Helioneis, but the Prior and I agreed to keep an eye on her. She's fundamental for whatever concerns the temple and the Goddess." That was as much as he would reveal. Wahine should have pieced it together by now. And indeed she had as she gasped again, bringing both hands to her mouth.

"Hot High Priestess is your mate?!"

Blade burst into laughter, but Hawk shot him a glare, turning back to Wahine.

"High Priestess Amala," he corrected, "And yes, she's my mate."

Wahine was ecstatic — delighted, to say the least.

She opened her mouth to probe further, but Blade halted her. "We need your help, little drop."

Her smile faltered. "You came all the way here because you need something?"

"Of course not. I'll stay around after," Blade promised. "But we might have a job for you."

Wahine considered, eyes again darting between the pair.

"What do *I* gain?"

Hawk sighed. "I'll tell you about Amala."

A smirk.

"Deal. Let's go to the Den."

☼

The Hendrix siblings were good at drugs. Drugs and poisons.

Blade could identify any substance in moments, and gain access to any drug he liked whenever he liked. He knew where to find and create it, but had never liked people knowing he was the mastermind, so Wahine was the face of their business, whilst he operated behind the scenes. On the one hand, she was Wahine Hendrix: director of the orphanage.

On the other, the Mistress of Venoms.

That was the name coined within the Aglatas underworld: an expert of poisons, building an entire kingdom from it. She dealt anything: legal or illegal drugs, drugs one couldn't find anywhere else, poisons, potions, powerful venoms, elixirs made on request, and more. Anything vaguely dangerous, she sold it.

The Den was her kingdom: Hawk followed her through the narrow alleys of Pyramis' periphery, and watched the street slowly embody the elegant, residential boulevards. Wahine didn't hesitate before entering a tall, ornate building, and taking the stairs to the basement.

Wahine held the door open for them as they stepped into the ample room. It was sophisticated; the lights were dim, but Hawk could see most of the place: it was as decadent as the rest of Pyramis was — fake columns, immaculate wooden cabinets, a stylish fireplace surrounded by soft, lavish armchairs. At the centre of the room sat a mahogany bar: Hawk knew very well those bottles contained no alcohol, but an endless array of deadly poisons. Wahine made her potions directly on the main counter, as though she was bartending.

"Drink?" Blade asked.

"I'm alright," Hawk checked his phone and found Cairo's report: it contained everything that the Embers had told them, with additional details Cairo added to simplify their future workload. He quickly read through it while Wahine followed Blade to the wooden cabinet where *actual* alcohol was kept, carrying two goblets.

"How much have you smoked today?" Hawk heard her asking.

"Way more than you'd approve."

"Blade!" She scolded, gently bumping his shoulder.

Hawk comfortably sat on an armchair as he waited for the twins to join him. Once they were in front of him, tender flames crackled in the fireplace as Blade started.

"Alright little drop, let's talk business."

Wahine's eyes narrowed suspiciously. "Is this about the Goddess?"

"In a way."

"Was she poisoned? I think your friend is clever enough to figure poisons out without my help," she stated practically. Hawk nodded: Naressa had her fair share of knowledge on the matter.

"We're still waiting for the blood tests. Naressa is running them again; she found absolutely nothing on the first try. No poison. Nothing that could give even half a clue."

"Oh," Wahine said, tone curious. "So, what do you need then?"

Blade tapped his fingers on the counter. "How many of the Embers still owe you a favour?"

Wahine laughed. "All of them. If I call one back, I'll make sure to get them back in debt soon enough."

Hawk thought Amala would love Wahine, taking a mental note to introduce them soon.

She took a sip from her goblet. "Is it information, money, evidence?"

He shook his head.

"No, we need blueprints."

☼

Hawk closed the door behind him, bracing for Howlite to launch. Only she didn't.

He couldn't see clearly in the semi-darkness of the foyer, but when he reached the living room, he froze. The dim lamp on the coffee table was the only source of light as Amala slept on the sofa, Howlite nestled beside her.

The laboured breathing of the hound was the only sound as he stood still, indecisive about his next move: part of him wanted to snap a picture, while the other wished to never move again and behold this scene for the rest of his life.

Treading quietly, he slowly moved towards his bedroom, yet the attempt was short-lived as Howlite sensed movement. Instantly awake, she jumped off the couch. Amala whimpered in confusion, suddenly awake and as she twisted on the sofa, her soft voice murmuring, "Hawk?"

"Hey, beautiful," he said, eyes resting on her face. Her cheeks were red, eyes swollen, hair ruffled as silver-white strands tangled in her brow. "Was it a good nap?" he asked, petting Howlite behind the ears.

"Very good. Howlite is so *cuddly*," with a sweet smile, she added, "How was your day? You look tired."

He nodded, striding for the adjacent sofa and sitting beside her. "Could have been better, but it was good."

"How was Pyramis?"

"Rich," Hawk said, and she giggled.

"We live in the Whisper, Hawk: you're one to talk."

We live. Hawk's heart skipped a beat when he heard those words. We. *We*.

"Did you speak with Jaren?"

Hawk nodded, failing to hide a grimace. She noticed. "Was it bad?"

"It was useless, but we spoke with the Embers and they talked."

"The Embers?" Amala's voice dropped an octave, the hint of a shiver in her words.

Hawk's smile was reassuring. "Everything went fine, Amala mate."

"But the Embers are *ruthless*, a—and the Phoenix—"

"The Phoenix wasn't there," Hawk repressed the urge to reach for her, to pull her against his chest so she was safe in his arms. "We were safe."

Amala shuddered, face unconvinced. Howlite jumped beside her again, slowly relaxing as Amala began to stroke her back.

"Yes," she whispered, "Hawk almost *left* us today. He could have died and left us here in his fancy house. And I would have given you all the food you wanted, beautiful." Her eyes shifted to him, a sparkle in her cunning ice gaze, "But he's here now."

Hawk snickered and said nothing, content with looking at her instead, observing each of her movements: the way her silver-white strands framed her face, or how her pouty lips moved sensually every time she spoke. Every word she uttered.

If Amala knew he was unashamedly looking at her lips, she didn't show it.

"Dinner?" she asked without looking at him.

"You didn't eat?"

Amala's head whipped in his direction, "You did?"

She was blushing and biting her lower lip. Then glanced away, embarrassed.

"I ate something on the way back. Sorry, I should have checked if you wanted food."

"I thought we'd cook something together," she whispered, the embarrassment in her voice was palpable now.

"What do you want to cook?"

"Nothing now."

"Amala."

She raised her head, eyes meeting his.

Hawk would happily drown himself in those eyes: sharp, sweet, bright like the sun.

"What's going on?"

Hugging her knees tightly, as if she wished to make herself smaller.

"Hawk, I've never lived like this before. I have nothing to do, no one to talk to — there's no vegetables."

"Vegetables?"

A nod.

"You know I don't eat meat. But you don't even have potatoes. What the hell do you eat?"

She was right, he knew. The priestesses at the Yonium raised their own animals — cows and sheep, mostly — but refused to ever eat one. Amala would not start now, no matter the circumstances.

"I'll do groceries tomorrow." He started. "I'm sorry I—"

"I just... I think I miss the temple. Just a bit."

Her voice was low, almost guilty and ashamed to admit it. Her hand reached for him on the opposite sofa as he extended his own, brushing against her petite fingers. They sat like that for a while, the sound of their breathing beginning to steady as she sent her power around the room, travelling like a warm breeze. There was a faint note of cinnamon, and Hawk couldn't help but smile as he felt it.

"I'll buy you strawberries," he started.

"And pomegranates?"

"And pomegranates. Whatever you want, Amala mate." He took her hand, "I'll make it feel like home. I promise."

CHAPTER 17

H awk kept his promise. Two days later, Amala woke before sunrise aching with desire, and bare legs beneath the sheets. She stretched her body, moaning softly, halting only when she heard Hawk's muffled laugh by her side.

She turned towards his voice, her whole body tilting as she leaned to face him.

"Sorry," she whispered, "I didn't scent you."

He curved his lips in a lazy smile, "It's because *your* scent is everywhere," he groaned, voice hoarse as he spoke for the first time that morning.

Amala smiled back, rolling into the sheets, and facing the ceiling again, "Sorry about that."

"*I* am sorry, Amala mate," Hawk said, his hand sneaking closer to her body. He idly traced the skin on her thigh "I should have remembered you need your... little *moment* in the morning."

She chuckled. "I'm just used to it, I guess. I've skipped it for four days now though, so I'm about to explode."

Arching her back, she enjoyed his touch on her skin for a brief moment, before scoffing. "Stop that. It's a *myself* moment, you don't get to make me come."

Hawk's laugh prompted shivers through her body.

"I know," he withdrew his hand, reaching for the bottom cabinet of the nightstand. He pulled out a small bag and passed it to Amala. "As promised, this is the first step to making this feel like home."

She stilled, upper body rising with her breasts exposed above the white sheets. Amala grabbed the bag and peered inside.

"No way," she murmured, gaze instantly settling back on Hawk.

He grinned, his canines making a brief appearance.

"*No* way," she repeated. "You know I've never used one before, right?"

Plucking the small vibrator, she handed the empty bag to Hawk as he snickered.

"I suspected. So, I did some research for you."

"What kind of research?" she caught him peeking at her breasts, yet said nothing.

"It's a clitoral suction stimulator, I believe."

Amala couldn't believe it. Of all the things he could have done to make this place feel like home... she didn't expect this.

Shifting closer to him, the warmth of their naked bodies merged beneath the sheets; Hawk placed his hands on her hips, pulling her closer, and she hooked a leg around him. She placed her head on his chest, inhaling his scent as she said, "Thank you, Hawk. This means a lot."

He hugged her, stroking her hair. "I'm happy you like it, Amala mate."

She pondered for a second whether to move but Hawk decided for her, dragging his hand closer to her back. She immediately stilled, then rushed to move away.

"Easy, High Priestess," he said. "I'm not trying to get you in the mood."

She bit back a laugh then as she returned to her side of the bed, the first rays of sunlight slowly approaching from the window.

"No need. I'm already in the mood." She smiled teasingly, "Close the door when you leave."

☼

She lazily stretched her body, walking towards the kitchen when she spotted Hawk on the couch; his head was turned towards her as a particularly intense ray of sun hit his face, lighting up his features. Amala sighed at the view: he looked delicious. Him and the sun together... suddenly, she found her new favourite thing.

Amala changed her mind and walked closer to him, stopping abruptly a few feet from the couch. She sniffed, then looked at him and a smirk formed on her lips. "Were you touching yourself?"

Hawk bit his lower lip, canines showing. "You want a lie or...?"

His husky voice made Amala shiver as she took a step closer, stopping right behind him. Her hands reached his muscled shoulders and rested there. "The truth, please."

He snickered, "Yeah, I was." There was no trace of embarrassment in his voice as he continued, "You are one loud woman, Amala mate."

She didn't blush and he loved that. As he had loved to hear her moans and pants, perfectly audible even through the closed door, sweet and rich as he pictured Amala touching herself on *his* bed, squirming in *his* sheets, thanks to the gift *he* had given her. Yeah, of course he had touched himself.

Her gaze wandered around the living room, "Where did you come, then?"

"Are you looking for proof of my release?".

Her hands played with his hair strands, twirling them around her fingers.

Hawk didn't move, but added, "Don't worry about me, I came."

☼

Hawk's day had been incredibly boring as he tried desperately to find a lead. Things didn't improve though so, when Blade invited him to smoke a joint by the river, he did. Perhaps it would be best to calm his nerves.

It didn't go as planned as Blade challenged him to jump *into* the Apàle; when he said no, Blade jumped himself, destroying a child's sandcastle.

"I'm telling you, that kid was a crier." Blade told him an hour later.

"You destroyed his sandcastle. I'd say he was allowed to cry." Hawk handed him the keys as Blade reached for the door of his apartment.

"He cried because he wasn't able to hurt me with his pathetic use of fire." Blade countered, "Who the fuck uses fire power next to a river, c'mon."

They entered the apartment, Hawk following behind.

"Very mature of you, to challenge some eight year old."

Blade said something, but Hawk wasn't listening. Hanging his jacket in the closet, he aimed for the kitchen as the sweet smell of chocolate filled the air; some light music played in the background, and... Amala was dancing next to the island, moving her sinuous body in time with the music as she mixed something in a bowl.

He wanted to gesture to Blade to be quiet, but his friend had froze the moment his eyes found the High Priestess. Of course, she wore no clothes: merely a white thong and a silky piece of fabric wrapped around her neck and breasts.

He didn't want to interrupt, but she sensed him and spun to face the pair with a look of surprise.

"Oh, no, you're back already!" she blurted. Was she blushing?

She set the bowl down on the island, then glanced at the oven, "I was cooking brownies for you. I wanted it to be a surprise."

"Consider me surprised," Hawk beamed. He wished he could hide how much he melted at her words. But to see her there — caring for him, cooking for him — it was better than anything he had imagined.

"What are you baking in that one?" he pointed to the other bowl.

"More brownies," she shrugged. "I wanted them to last for more than a day. If I made only one, you would finish it by dinner. Hi Blade," she smiled, as though suddenly returning to her role as High Priestess. "You look so confident today. I'm happy you feel good with yourself."

This. There were many things Hawk loved about Amala, but *this* — he couldn't explain how much his heart pounded when she was so herself, so Amala. Pure Love, ready to share her Love with everyone.

Blade startled; her doe eyes glowed as she spoke to him and it took Hawk a second to remember that Blade wasn't used to someone who cared this much — someone who cared so unapologetically. Someone like Amala, so radiant and... Hawk needed five minutes to himself. Why couldn't the fucking bond just snap already? Instead of taunting him every single time he saw his mate. He was having a boring day, sure, but it was definitely better to think about Amala in his office, rather than having her standing a few feet from him, shining in those few last rays of sun that glistered on her through the windows. He sighed — who was he kidding? This was a thousand times better.

Blade loosened up in his stance, throwing a smile in Amala's direction.

"Hello, pretty High Priestess."

She returned her attention to Hawk, "How was your day?"

"Incredibly boring," he said, as she turned once again to keep mixing whatever was in the bowl. She prepared a second tray, covering it in baking paper before pouring the contents of the bowl inside, the sweet smell of chocolate filling the kitchen.

"Are you drooling over the brownies, Hawk?" Amala teased, carefully using a spatula to even out the tray. "Or me?"

Hawk tensed, praying his brain would focus before Amala and Blade noticed his scent shift. He tried to relax. "Can't it be both?"

Blade cut him a glance, as though criticizing Hawk for ever complaining about his life. Hawk shrugged; his grin said enough. They both watched as Amala put the new tray into the oven and took out the one that had just finished baking.

"Twenty minutes," she whispered to her phone, setting the timer on. She lifted her gaze, this time taking in more details as she observed the pair. "And you, Blade? Having a good day?"

"Can't complain," Blade clicked his tongue, "I fell into the Apàle, though."

"You *jumped*," Hawk corrected, eyeing the way Amala chuckled at his words, "How did your visits go?"

Her smile was radiant as she replied: "Seryn's sister is having a boy. And—*ooh*," she whipped her head to the bedroom's door, the familiar sound of claws scraping against wood resonating through the wall, "Look who's up. She looked so happy to have all the space on the bed."

Hawk strode to his room, opening the door as Howlite pounced, full weight forcing him to the floor. She looked pleased that her surprise landed as planned as Hawk laughed from underneath her.

"I didn't realise I took her place on the bed. You should have told me."

Hawk's voice was muffled as Howlite licked his face clean, "You didn't take her place. I did." He tried to pull himself up, petting the hound to calm her. "She used to sleep on my side. I moved there because you wanted the sunny one."

Blade couldn't pretend he wasn't curious, "So, you two are sharing a bed?"

Amala gave him a weird look and ignored the question. Reaching for Hawk and Howlite, both still on the floor, she kneeled next to them to pet the hound.

"I am sorry, baby girl," she pouted, aiming for a kiss. "I'll spoon you as much as you want, I swear."

The familiar sound of a camera flash resounded and the pair turned to Blade. He looked vaguely guilty, hurriedly stashing his phone back into his pocket.

"You looked cute," he shrugged, "Family picture."

Hawk focused on not grinning as he knew Amala fought back a blush. Howlite seemed the only one at ease as she continued to pant, taking turns to lick both their faces.

Amala quickly rose, then did a spin as a ray of sun marked her skin.

"Oh! Sunset! Can—can you check the brownies, please?" she faced Hawk, waiting for a nod. Then she ran to the balcony.

CHAPTER 18

The two brownie trays rested on the counter; Howlite seemingly interested in whatever was airing on the TV. Hawk was half-slumped on the sofa, checking something on his phone. Blade laid on the other couch, booted feet propped on the coffee table, while he gazed in the direction of the balcony.

"So," he started. "You had the audacity to complain about your life today?"

Hawk already knew he would have to fight his way out of that conversation.

"All right, before you begin," he countered. "I'd appreciate it if we could talk about anything but her."

"And why is that?"

"Because she's been the only thought on my mind for the whole fucking day, that's why," Hawk grunted, glancing at the TV. He heard Blade snicker.

"Does she know?"

"That I'm drooling over her while I wait for the moment the bond finally snaps? For the moment I can finally tell her how much I need her?" Hawk's words were a low hiss. "I haven't told her yet, but I think she figured."

Blade couldn't hold back his laughter: his friend was *definitely* fucked. Hawk snorted something like *shut up*, gesturing for Howlite to hop onto the sofa beside him.

"If you ever complain about your life *again*, dude," Blade repeated.

But by the look on Hawk's face, Blade knew he was about to let loose. And he did, recalling exactly how stressful his day had been: from waking up next to Amala, knowing how aroused she had been as she used her new vibrator to pleasure herself in *his* bed; failing again at finding new leads, smoking on the bridge, finding her in his home — naked and baking brownies — knowing he couldn't touch her and not hiding how much their proximity was driving him crazy.

"Doesn't help that every single time she speaks to me she will mock me about how much I got it bad for her, and that every time she does it, guess what? I like her even *more*. Therefore," Hawk concluded, "I have every fucking right to complain."

Blade didn't say anything as he listened to Hawk rant about how miserable he felt. He knew everything already, but knew it was important for Hawk to let everything out. So, Blade let him. And, once he finally calmed, he peacefully shrugged his shoulders.

"Seems like you're living the dream, Hawk."

He pretended not to hear, ignoring Blade's words as he changed topic. "I need to get to the God's temple tomorrow. I need something, if not a lead, something close to one."

Blake looked at the balcony door as the last rays of sunset filtered through, finally departing from the horizon, "What are you hoping to achieve at the temple?"

"I don't know, but the Goddess' temple perimeter looks fine. I'm guessing if nothing is wrong outside, maybe inside we can find what we need. At least before we get our hands on the blueprints."

"The temple is warded. I mean, hot High Priestess can help with that but—"

"She won't do it," Hawk cut him off. "And I won't ask her to relive what happened by bringing her there. I already checked the Yonium. I was thinking if we go to Helioneis, maybe I'll spot if there's anything different in the structure? Anything evident, at least."

Blade shrugged, "It's a start."

"Barely," Hawk hissed, "But better than nothing."

"How many priestesses moved to the God's temple?"

Hawk thought about it; the Goddess had a great number of priestesses, so many it had been a nightmare to gather their alibis, even worse ensuring their alibis checked out. He knew many wished to stay at the temple, but Amala had convinced the majority to stay at the God's temple instead. It was familiar enough to give their lives some normality.

Some priestesses didn't like the idea of living among males, choosing to attend the Home of Waters, while others wished to stay closer to Mhelani, and had moved into the centaurs' realm. The centaurs were loyal to the Goddess, sworn to help the priestesses in their times of need.

In return, the females at the temple blessed their kingdom and poured their energy and magic into the forest, connecting it to its very roots and ensuring it would flourish. He summarised the information aloud as Blade calculated the numbers.

"So, around sixty priestesses at the God's temple, and the rest are split between Home of Waters and the forest," he nodded in thought. "Plus one hot High Priestess in your bed." Pausing, he added, "And we're sure the priestesses are clean?"

"They cannot harm the Goddess in any way, it's an energy stronger than power itself. They're bound to it from the moment they swear themselves to her." Hawk recalled, "I sorted all their alibis and backgrounds, if we'll ever need it. Hebex helped a lot."

"Who's Hebex?"

"Amala's Second? Well, Amala's best friend."

"And can we trust this Hebex?"

"She's alright. She's involved with Medyr, the High Priest." He exhaled, "And I think we need to speak with him tomorrow."

"Medyr?"

"Yeah, as well as checking the temple. He — well, he was in Amala's current position when the former God died. His opinion *is* valuable." Hawk didn't like coming to this realisation, but knew better than letting a petty grudge hinder the case.

"Cool. So, Helioneis tomorrow," Blade's gaze wandered back outside the window.

The balcony door opened, a gentle breeze floating in from outside and filling the room. Amala hurried back in; the goosebumps on her body a visible indicator of the cold weather.

Hawk made a point to look anywhere but her nipples, now completely visible as they peaked against the smooth fabric of her top. She aimed for the spot next to Blade as Howlite sprawled across Hawk and flashed the pair a smile, "I need to go to Helioneis tomorrow."

Her words left them momentarily confused.

"What?" they said in unison.

"What?" she repeated, "I—it's New Moon, I need to bless the altar. I'll officiate the rite at the Home of Waters tomorrow night. But the main altar, where we channel our energy, needs to be blessed before that," she explained. "Is that a problem?"

The males exchanged a brief look.

"We need to go too." Hawk broke the silence.

"Why is that?"

"I don't want you involved in this case, Amala mate. Not this soon. Whoever did this will *know* I'm searching for them, and I don't want them to have easy access to you because of what you know."

She looked at him through her icy doe-like eyes, "Oh—are you *protecting* me?"

Was she mocking him?

Hawk snorted, "Yeah, because I'd like to keep you around. You bake good brownies."

Her beautiful face beamed, "Did you eat them?"

"Not yet, we were waiting for you. How was the sunset?"

Amala's gaze drifted to the balcony as she recalled the moment. Hawk never knew what she did during her personal time watching the sunrise and sunset. She prayed, he imagined, but perhaps a different kind of prayer. Not to the Goddess, not to the God — but to the sun itself: a separate entity.

"It was powerful," Amala murmured. "The wind loved it. It was a bit chilly but I loved it too. And the sun was glorious. Sometimes I feel like the sun shines more near New Moon. I know it's not true, but I thought that all the time, when I approached my High Priestess ritual. Because—" she paused and turned to Blade. "Do you know the rite?"

"No one taught me about it in school," he replied with a shrug.

Amala chuckled. "They should."

"Does it happen on New Moon?"

Hawk nodded; he hadn't studied it in school either, but he knew about it. Amala had told him the story of her rite. It was one of his favourite things to listen to. The way she beamed, emanating pure light as she revisited the memory was priceless. A part of him hoped she'd tell Blade the whole story, so he could listen to it again.

The High Priestess curved her lips into a kind smile. "Only on New Moon, yes. It's a powerful ritual. Very feminine."

"How does it work?" Blade's feline gaze betrayed his interest as Amala glanced in Hawk's direction, as though reading his mind. She knew he loved this story.

"Do you want the story of the rite in general, or mine?"

Blade didn't hesitate. "Yours."

She seemed satisfied with his answer — perhaps, even a tad flattered. Sending a cool breeze around them to lull them into the story, she started.

"The Goddess makes a small cut on the priestess—it's very small, but it's symbolic. It signifies the physical pact that binds a High Priestess to her Goddess. It binds me to serve her, embrace her, to *be* in her place when needed, kind of like I'm doing now. I'm protecting what remains of her energy as the divine energy searches for the next vessel." Amala paused briefly; Hawk could see in her eyes the memory of Serabel's dead body. Shaking her head to send the thought away, she pointed to the side of her right breast. Right under her soft skin, there was a faint scar. "My cut was made here," She blushed as she added, "Serabel said she wanted to mark somewhere she liked to look at. When blood flows from the cut, the rite officially starts. I got my final blessing, then all the priestesses left the temple.

"The Goddess is always the last one to leave as she leaves part of her energy behind — the truest, most powerful element of her energy. Then, she wards the temple. The priestess has to spend the night of the New Moon inside, alone with the Goddess' purest energy. It's very intense; I took months to get ready for it as I was madly scared of the dark. You see, New Moon means no moonlight, so the temple is pitch black. That energy is powerful. And, on the night of my rite while I was alone in the temple, my period came. It wasn't supposed to come then, but it did. So I was bleeding from my cut, but also myself and... the Goddess' energy loved it." Amala paused briefly, her icy eyes quickly assessing their reactions.

Hawk was in awe, as usual, listening to her sweet voice narrating one of the most intense and important moments of her life — a pure blessing to his ears. The fact she decided to share such memories with him was enough to make him grin, thanking the Goddess for blessing him with Amala as his mate.

Blade's eyes contained a spark of admiration too; he had always admired Amala.

"The divine energy *loved* it," she repeated with a soft smile, "Loved that my femininity had decided to come out for her. So, I spent the night awake and the energy spoke to me. We slowly fused together, the energy merging with mine. And I merged with the Goddess. And, when the sunrise came, my blood had drawn the shape of a yoni on the floor. I used my new-born energy — that kernel of divine power — to undo the wards and open the temple: that was probably the most important moment. Every High Priestess merges with the Goddess, but every High Priestess is different. So, the energy that breaks the wards is always unique. My energy opened the temple and Serabel and the priestesses were outside waiting for me as I stepped out—" she halted, her voice trembling with emotion at the memory.

Hawk's eyes were attentively fixed to her, listening to every word and every detail, as she now held his gaze, shuddering from the intensity of that look.

"And?" Blade murmured, not bothering to mask his eagerness to learn more.

Amala swallowed. "And they knelt for me. For *me*. And Serabel — Goddess Serabel took my hand and *bowed* and said, '*I bless you, High Priestess Amala*'." She didn't stop the tears now, lost in the recollection of the memory. Hawk knew it had been the most incredible moment of her life.

To live for the Goddess and to hold part of the Goddess *inside her*, to be recognized as her High Priestess... it was the greatest honour of Amala's existence. She let out a long, low breath, swiping the tears away with her fingers.

"Sorry," she murmured. "It's a very emotional story for me. But that's it. I've been High Priestess ever since." And now her Goddess was dead, the memory was probably worth so much more.

Blade watched Amala, this time with no trace of smugness, "Thank you for sharing that with me."

Amala still had tears on her face when she moved the brownies from the kitchen to the coffee table. She didn't talk further of her rite, but that spark of pride remained in her eyes all evening. Hawk thought it indeed was a blessing to see that side of her again, after mourning with no interruption.

A part of him still hung to the unanswered part of Amala's story. The whole reason she had told the story in the first place. Waiting until Blade left, when they were both in bed together with Amala curled in-between the covers, he asked her.

"You never said *why* the sun shines more on New Moon."

He heard her breath catch, as if she hadn't expected to hear his voice again before falling into slumber. Or perhaps she was already asleep. He considered letting it go, but her answer came in a whisper a moment later.

"Because there's no light at night. I always pretended the Sun was shining twice as much, to make up for the moon's absence. I feel so blessed when the sun shines on me," she admitted.

Hawk's lips tugged upwards into a faint smile, but she couldn't see him.

"I think the Sun is blessed to shine on you, Amala mate."

CHAPTER 19

"I've never gotten used to their *technology*," Amala spat the word like she was afraid of it. "I just think it's strange. One day we mourned the God's loss, and the day after Aarush had decided to modernise the temple..." she let herself linger at the memory, but Blade interrupted her thoughts.

"You personally knew the former God?"

Amala blinked, "Of course I did. I've lived at the temple since I was born. Serabel always said she knew I would become her High Priestess since the day she helped my mother give birth to me. Yeah," she assessed Blade's look of shock, "Serabel wasn't a midwife but, as Goddess of Birth, she could be helpful. It wasn't a very difficult birth, I believe, but Kora never spoke much about it." Amala shrugged, not sure whether to continue.

Blade glared at her from the passenger seat; he called shotgun the *second* he saw her that morning: splayed on the couch petting Howlite. Bursting into the apartment and claiming he wanted brownies, Amala had replied, "What's shotgun? And your brownies are already on the counter."

She made him breakfast, leaving brownies and ice cream ready for his arrival and, as he laughed at her ignorance and explained the meaning of 'shotgun', she muttered, "Well, it's not like me and the priestesses ever raced to climb inside a car."

Blade kept forgetting she had lived at the temple her whole life and while she regularly visited the city, she was not a proper citizen of it.

Now peering at her through the rear-view mirror, full of pride while she sat in the back, he asked, "Why do you call your mom by her first name?"

Hawk muttered something like *shut up*, but Blade didn't pay attention. Amala looked uncomfortable. "It's weird. We... we all call each other by our first name at the temple, it's just the way we're used to. But Kora—mom. I call her mom now when I see her."

"Where does she live? You were born priestess, weren't you? Isn't she at the temple?"

Amala smiled at his interest.

"Kora was a priestess and Faurn, my father, was... he was God Darnen's High Priest. I'll try to keep it short because my parents had an amazing, *long* love story..." She couldn't hide the spark of happiness at the memory of her parents in love, "Faurn and Kora met during a ritual. Fell in love. They never lived together, each at their own temple, but they loved each other deeply and often visited. When Faurn got Kora pregnant, Serabel was incredibly happy: a priest and a priestess together, creating a family... that's why I was born a priestess. They always agreed on that. And then, well, Faurn died." She paused briefly. "I was thirty-two and Kora changed a lot. It felt very weird to be around her for a few years, but I don't like to talk about it, because I can't blame her for taking time to process everything. But it all just changed again when she met Kyne."

"Kora and Kyne were mates. Are mates. Kora asked Serabel for permission to leave the Yonium and the priestess life. She gave back the

Goddess' protection and moved in with her mate. And then they had Ayan, my half-brother. They lived near the Fire Square—well, I hope Ayan has moved out by now." Hawk snickered, "Hawk and I had a bet on when he finally would. As for Kora and Kyne, they are still very much exploring their mating bond and relationship."

"Are you happy for them?" Blade asked.

Amala instantly nodded, her eyes shining, "Of course I am!" she exclaimed, voice brewing with happiness. "Kora found her *mate*... and it made everything right. Faurn was not her mate — they were in love, but not like Kora and Kyne are. So, she could finally move on. I think when she met Kyne she realised she didn't love the priestess life, not anymore. She may have loved it before but — without Faurn — it felt very difficult to keep that life going."

Blade's face bore confusion as he pointedly said, "But she had you at the temple. Wasn't that enough reason to keep going?"

"Not really. We are all each other's mother and sister. Kora started being my mother much more, once she left and started her new life," Amala said. "I am really happy for her. I feared her disappointment for choosing the temple life in the past, but I think she's proud of me."

"Of course she is, Amala mate," Hawk's voice was a sweet purr, as if he had known her thoughts for a lifetime.

Blade turned to him, "And you? Have you met her family?"

He nodded, "I know Ayan and I've met Kora and Kyne a few times. But they don't know we're mates," he specified before adding, "Maybe Ayan knows."

Blade returned his attention to Amala: "Do you get along with your brother?"

Amala frowned, she didn't want to talk about it. For several reasons. The topic evoked a storm of bad memories as she felt her heart pace, sighing. Blade wasn't aware of her change of mood as she bit the inside of her cheek, deciding to offer the funnier version of the story. Or at least the one that didn't make her sick.

"Ayan and I are fine. We used to fight a lot over stupid things, but we haven't had a good argument in a while."

"What did you fight about?" Blade asked.

"Over girls, mostly," Amala shrugged with honesty. "I might have stolen a few from him. Never on purpose," she added, hearing Hawk's snort.

Blade barked a laugh, "That's so unfair, hot High Priestess! To your *brother*?"

"It wasn't my fault!" She protested. "One time, his new girlfriend broke up with him on the spot as soon as she met me. I didn't even speak a word to her!"

"Ah, yes," Hawk echoed. "The Night of Breakups."

Amala chuckled, but Blade was suddenly suspicious. "The what?"

She laughed with Hawk, the memory surging to mind. "Three years ago, I was dating this girl, Besa. Hawk was dating Isabel. One night, Ayan wanted us to go out with him and his new girlfriend. He wanted to introduce her to us, but it went downhill fast..." She paused, glancing at Hawk in the driver's mirror.

Blade's eyes were amused and Hawk cut in, "Ayan's girl took *one* look at Amala and decided she wanted her rather than her brother. Ayan got mad, and Besa was naturally jealous, so she freaked out. Then Ayan's girl made a move on Amala — Ayan lost it and Besa broke up with her on the spot." He was laughing now, Amala with him.

The next part was her favourite. "I was shocked and sad, to say the least..." she continued. "So, Hawk thought it would be nice to check on me rather than return home with Isabel. She thought it was an excuse for us to fuck now I was single, so she broke up with him too."

Blade burst out laughing, head snapping in Hawk's direction.

"That's why you and her broke up?"

He gave a single nod, canines flashing in amusement as Amala chuckled, unable to keep a still face at the memory of that night. It was probably one of the moments that had shaped their relationship the most, bringing her and Hawk so close.

"Isabel was delirious that night. She knew I usually have multiple partners, so I don't know why she thought I'd fuck Hawk because I was single."

"She probably had the thought for a while," Blade replied. "You guys are subtle, but I get why she would be jealous of your relationship."

"Well, she never figured we were mates." Amala observed.

"I didn't figure either." Blade reminded her.

He hadn't.

Hawk had asked Amala's permission to tell Blade a couple of years after they met, mostly because he felt guilty: Amala was becoming more important to him, and he wanted Blade to know who was quickly escalating the ranking, and why. Amala allowed the revelation, knowing it was an excuse; the bond wasn't the reason for their friendship. It had never been the bond. It was them. Amala and Hawk were perfect friends for each other, mating bond or not. This — their friendship — would have happened even if they didn't want to fuck each other's brains out.

It was a shame now her celibacy was in the way of that.

☼

Amala was acquainted with the God's temple: it had been a part of her childhood to attend weekly visits to her father and, as she had grown up, to attend any merged rituals the Gods wanted them to officiate. She loved Helioneis: it stood in the middle of a plane, built in grey stone and creamy marble creating delicious shades of orange during the sun's peak hours. It was ancient, just like the Yonium, but modernised like

Aglatas. The Apàle flowed tranquil and placid down the stream and, not so many miles later, would merge with the sea.

The grounds surrounding Helioneis were sandy, but not dry. Whilst the Goddess' temple was an oasis in the woods, this one was more tropical: the air smelled like salt and flowers, and the breeze was a gentle warm caress. And the sun — the sun was always shining, its light drizzling on the temple walls in droplets of gold.

Amala admired Helioneis in humming calm as she entered the altar room. Her heart felt steady and, somehow, serene. Guilt lingered in her stomach: she shouldn't feel good because of the sun, not on any day, and especially not when her Goddess was dead.

Adjusting the sheer robe on her waist, she spotted Hebex under the colonnade. She gestured to Blade and Hawk to follow and Hebex spotted their approach, a broad smile painting her lips as she shifted closer, "Good morning, High Priestess," her eyes hesitated on the two males. "Good morning."

Hawk bowed his head. Blade watched him first before imitating the movement.

Amala beheld Hebex who seemed amused by their behaviour. The priestesses always found it entertaining when people first arrived at the temple: the divine power and energy had a way to throw one off, if they were not accustomed.

"You look great," she whispered to Amala, making no effort to hide how avidly she studied her body, "Kind of... relaxed. What's going on?"

Amala's eyes widened, as if Hebex's words had revealed a great, untellable truth. But she lowered her voice so the males behind could no longer hear, whispering back: "Hawk got me a vibrator."

With a wild grin on her face, Hebex squealed in delight, "No way!"

"Shh," Amala gestured with her hand, a side glance to the figure standing behind her. Though she had a feeling Hebex's excitement was well matched with Hawk's intuition, and that — if she dared to turn —

she would find him there with a faint grin on his face. Perhaps a flash of canines. They seemed to emerge when she was around him. Amala's mind wandered just a couple of times, at the thought of those beautiful fangs gently piercing the skin on her neck. She had been subtly looking at them all the time in those past few days, and her body tingled in anticipation of the delicious pain she would feel—

"Cleansing or blessing?" Hebex asked, her voice tethering Amala back to reality: those green eyes gave her a look that knew far too much.

"Both," Amala replied, "Do you want to help?"

"Your wish is my command, High Priestess,"

Amala faced the two males, "I'll call High Priest Medyr for you."

Ignoring the scowl now on Hawk's face, she made a point to look at Blade instead. The two males exchanged a glance.

"You reckon he will actually help us?" Blade asked.

Amala shrugged, but Hebex nodded. "Unless you piss him off, then he would have every right to kick you out of here."

"Aarush is never here, Medyr oversees everything. Ask nicely, and he will definitely be happy to help." Amala explained, then met Hawk's gaze. "*Nicely.*"

"You don't trust me in the slightest, Amala mate, do you?"

"Not when it comes to Medyr," she said carefully.

Hebex burst out laughing, eyes shimmering as she turned to Hawk. "Are you jealous of him? Because he fucked Amala?"

Blade howled and even Amala hid a chuckle of surprise.

"Pretty much." Hawk answered.

Hebex grinned wildly, amused.

"If the Captain plans to hate everyone who wants to fuck hot High Priestess, he's in for a long list."

This time, Amala couldn't hold back the laughter. Then nodding to the males, she travelled under the colonnade, the pair following behind as Hebex led them to Medyr.

Another priest was talking with him and Medyr looked up when he heard them approaching. He quickly finished his conversation and met them halfway, gaze lingering on Hebex before shifting to Amala. He smiled at the priestesses, "Good morning."

"Good morning," Amala replied.

"How have you been?" Medyr asked.

Amala made a point not to look at Hawk as she answered, "Coping. I'll bless the altar for New Moon, if you will allow me. Captain Mercurian and Agent Hendrix would like to ask you some questions."

His eyes sharpened on the two males behind her, as if trying to sense what kind of questions they needed to ask. But then, as his gaze returned to Amala, he replied with a genuine smile. "You may bless the altar and the temple. And sure, I will speak with them. Hebs, are you staying?"

Hebex quickly shook her head and replied, "Thank you, but I'll go with my High Priestess."

Without sparing a second glance, both women turned around and left.

☼

Hawk watched Amala walking away, her robe swishing with every step as her hips bounced.

Get a grip, his brain scolded, but he steadily ignored it and kept his eyes on her. How could he ever stop looking at her?

Even if he excelled at ignoring the voice in his head, he couldn't keep daydreaming on Amala as Blade's sharp elbow suddenly brought him back to reality.

"What?" Hawk asked, attempting to play it cool.

Blade didn't hide his grin. "High Priest Medyr asked what we are doing here."

Oh.

He found Medyr's eyes; it was clear he knew where Hawk's mind had wandered, as he cursed for revealing his affection for Amala so carelessly.

"We have been looking into the Goddess' murder. The High Priestess has been telling me about the unbalance and the research for a new vessel..." Hawk didn't want to admit about their lack of sources or clues, but he needed Medyr's help. "I'd like for you to tell me how it was when God Darnen died. You were already High Priest, and have experienced this situation yourself."

Medyr frowned, confused. "How would this help you?"

"Well, Aarush refused to collaborate unless I brought the High Priestess to his club. This is the only alternative which may provide the same insight."

The High Priest winced at the mention of Amala, and Hawk knew — no matter much he *hated* Medyr — Medyr would have never allowed Amala to fulfil Aarush's request, either.

"The unbalance is like a giant pressing machine. It is worse in the areas closest to where the God and Goddess reside, as their absence weighs more. Imagine a field of flowers ready to bloom, but something prevents them from doing so. It's the same when a deity dies: all the good things stop blossoming. It's not like only shit happens, but people tend to choose the wrong path more often."

"How long does it last?"

"It decreases once the divine energy picks a new vessel, but it can continue for a while if they don't accept their positions. It stops after the ceremony, and then you get the opposite tendency." Medyr said, "Basically, it sucks but then it gets better. Though, that might take a while to happen."

An increase of criminal activity *during* the case was the last thing Hawk needed. His usual duty was to cleanse Aglatas of criminal behaviour, but now he doubted he would ever have time to keep track of gang behaviour on top of his investigation. "Do you know how long it takes to find the next vessel?"

Medyr shook his head. "It's different every time. Once a vessel gets picked, they are the God or Goddess for the rest of their days... which can be centuries, even longer, as was the case for Serabel. The Goddess' energy is searching for the person that can best embody all of its values from now until eternity. It can take a while."

"How can it find a person that embodies only the best qualities?" Hawk scoffed, unconvinced.

Medyr snorted, "It won't. Have you met Aarush?"

To Hawk's own disappointment, he couldn't help but laugh at Medyr's words. He was half-sure Amala would have scolded him — both of them — had she been there. The High Priest continued, "It took me a couple of months from when Darnen died to when I first had the vision of Aarush. It will happen to Amala at some point, then it will be up to her to meet the new Goddess and begin the initiation."

"And the new Goddess can't refuse, right?"

"She cannot," Medyr confirmed. "But she doesn't need to embody her role in any particular way. She just *is*, it's up to her how she chooses to live after."

Like Aarush had done. Hawk opened his mouth to reply, but the sight of a beautiful pregnant priestess — her dark skin glowing under the sunlight — halted his words. Sinayla, Hawk realised, his memory quickly returning to that day at the Yonium finding Amala and her sisters in the kitchen.

By her side, a tall male — a priest — surveyed her figure as she slowly strolled by.

The priestess bowed her head to Medyr, then to Hawk and Blade.

"Good morning," she said. "How are you finding this beautiful temple?"

"It's... bright." Blade said.

Hawk subtly looked to him and raised an eyebrow.

"We appreciate you hosting us," he said instead, nodding at Medyr.

"It's an honour," the male in front of him said. Sinayla smiled at him, before turning to Hawk.

"This is priest Caelan, my mate," she introduced.

Caelan looked a lot like Hawk. Oddly similar. It was a strange resemblance, but soft steps approached before he could ponder it further. Distracted by a faint, sweet note of cinnamon.

"I'll see you tonight at the Home of Waters," Amala was saying, hugging one of her priestesses tightly.

Hebex reached them first.

"Altar blessed," she shrugged, "We're all set."

"What's next on your schedule?" Hawk asked, his voice was distant and uninterested; it was becoming increasingly difficult to keep track of who *knew* they were mates and who didn't. He looked around: Blade, Hebex, and Sinayla knew. Medyr and Caelan didn't.

Amala pursed her lips. "I'll go to the Home of Waters."

"But it's hours from New Moon," Sinayla observed.

"Lady Danua is due today. We have an appointment to check in before the ritual."

Hebex hummed, echoing. "Baby born on New Moon..."

Amala instinctively smiled, then reached for Sinayla's hand. "Don't pout, my love. You're next."

She avoided meeting her gaze but looked to them, "Shall we?"

Blade carefully studied her, "Can you perform a C-section?"

"Sure," she nodded. "I have two degrees, Blade. And a doctorate. I've been a midwife for a hundred years."

"How many babies have you given birth to?"

Her eyes widened, as if she wasn't expecting that question, and even Hebex by her side whipped her head to him.

"None," Amala tilted her head, "But I have delivered three-thousand, seven hundred and eighty-four children. Lady Danua's son shall be eighty-five, and I'm off to Ulbaros next week for another scheduled birth." She surveyed Blade, noticing his smile, "What's funny?"

"Are you telling me four thousand kids saw Hot High Priestess as the first thing in their life?"

Amala scoffed, rolling her eyes despite the hint of a blush appearing on her cheeks.

"Don't call me that in the temple, please." she asked politely.

"You know everyone calls you that, right?" Blade inquired, amused.

Amala waved him off.

"As long as they don't say it in front of me."

☆

It had been a bad idea.

Hawk kept telling himself that as he switched channel on the TV. Howlite jumped onto the sofa, nestling between him and the pillows. Blade's laugh brought Hawk back to the conversation.

"What's so funny?"

Blade shot him a look, "Everything is funnier than you, right now. What's worrying you so much?"

Hawk sighed, glancing at Blade, and to Naressa sitting beside him, and Cairo on the other couch.

"You need to leave before she comes back."

Cairo snorted, glancing to the other two to make sure they were all on the same page.

"What? You think she'll leave you if she meets us?"

"I'll pick her up once the ritual is done. You can chill here in the meantime but I expect you gone when we get back."

Hawk decided the day Amala left the temple: if she was going to be in his life more permanently, he wouldn't indulge in any bullshit. Not for the present moment. He would introduce her bit by bit when she felt ready. Because to do it now, all at once, catapulting her into his world just like that, would be a big statement. Bigger than they needed.

It wasn't like Hawk had hundreds of friends: he trusted a few people and didn't let many others in, but could count on the fingers of a single hand the people he would trust with his life. Zale, of course, had been by his side for a long time. Or better, Hawk had been on Zale's side, learning to trust with absolute faith his judgement and capacity. And the Prior constantly relied on him, too — never pulling rank on him because he knew to trust Hawk's every move.

And then Blade and Cairo, of course. His closest friends. Their missions required them to build up a good amount of trust in a short amount of time and after that it had been just natural, for them, to slide into reciprocated friendship.

Hawk would trust Naressa with his life too; they had met her at work and, besides being a great lover, she was also an amazing friend: never mixing business with relationships and always appreciating being his confidant. She gave great advice, not to mention the amount of times she helped with his investigations.

And then... her.

His Amala.

She was at the top of the list, but he liked to pretend he wasn't in such deep shit with her yet. Who he was fooling, he didn't know — definitely not himself, nor his friends.

"Growing protective, already?"

Hawk's eyes shot to Cairo, a wicked grin on his face at the taunt. "I'm pretty sure she doesn't want to meet you. Definitely not after her ritual."

"I would love to see her officiating, you know? You have barely told me *anything* about her..." Naressa chuckled, the hint of a smile on her face.

Blade suddenly looked very interested in his glass, taking a sip to pointedly refuse eye contact with Naressa. Cairo sent another grin in Hawk's direction but he accepted the taunts and prayed the damn God that his friends would drop it, and soon.

"I don't *like* her," he said to Naressa.

She hummed, looking away as Blade mouthed the word *mate*. Hawk bared his teeth at him.

They wouldn't spill it like that, would they?

Hawk knew it was a fool's hope; he should have told Naressa he had a mate years ago, but he couldn't bring himself to do it. First, because she didn't seem to care. And second, he had liked Naressa enough during those years to temporarily forget about Amala.

Sometimes.

"Is the celibacy a problem for her?" Naressa asked.

"I don't think so." Amala seemed perfectly fine, merely teasing him relentlessly with no sign of stopping.

Naressa pursed her lips, "Did she have to break things with someone because of it?"

"No, she wasn't in any relationship. She broke things off with a couple of her partners some months ago. The rest of them were casual." Hawk tried to remember the name of the last girl Amala had been seeing. Nothing came to mind.

"What do you mean *them*?" Blade asked.

"What?"

"How many is 'them'? At the same time?"

He knotted his eyebrows, a flinch of confusion. "Wait—you don't know Amala is polyamorous?"

Blade's face verged on the incredulous. Hawk was so used to Amala's polyamory, he found it strange when people didn't know about it. In the ten years they had been friends, Hawk had seen her with any type of partner. She loved to Love, and had loved amazing people in the process. He thought they were incredibly lucky to be chosen by her, even for a small part of their life.

"Wait," Cairo's voice said, bringing him back to the conversation. "Are you saying that if you and Amala ever get together," he pointedly avoided using the word 'mate' in front of Naressa, "She might still like someone else? *Love* someone else?"

He shrugged. "Yeah. I've always known."

He was fine with that, really. While it might not be his favourite thought, picturing Amala with someone other than him, the way she loved so fiercely was probably his favourite thing about her. And he didn't care if she loved someone else; Hawk would give up the world to hear her saying that she loved him, too.

CHAPTER 20

Whoever killed Serabel had done a fucking good job, Hawk decided the following day, because he had absolutely no idea where to start. Medyr had talked about months of research before finding the next vessel, so they were in for a long time.

He summed up everything he knew: the killer had infiltrated the Yonium to kill Serabel. To do so, they had required blueprints exposing the weak spots — and a way to keep their energy quiet, unsensed by the priestesses upon entering the temple. Not that it mattered, they killed the Goddess, and could have easily killed anyone else posing a threat in their path.

Hawk shuddered at the thought of Amala facing the killer. They had filed all the priestesses and were sure all had an alibi for the night.

Blueprints, then.

A task given to the god damn Embers: the worst gang in Aglatas.

Whoever had bought the blueprints either gave them to the killer or *was* the killer.

Hawk hummed, drumming his fingers on the counter. He reached for the fridge and grabbed some orange juice, pouring some into a fancy glass as he glanced again at his laptop, trying to focus on his notes. The display said six in the morning, which didn't lift his mood.

He was a morning person, but...

Howlite lay on the floor, her dark eyes searching for his attention.

"Sorry, love," he said, then proceeded to get her breakfast ready.

The hound had slept in the middle of the bed that night, which Hawk was thankful for, because Amala looked delicious after her ritual. She was beaming with energy and light and Hawk had fantasised about her the whole night.

And now he was trying his best not to focus on her soft moans travelling in from behind the closed door of the bedroom. His bedroom.

Their bedroom.

Hawk put Howlite's bowl on the ground and she dove straight into it. His eyes fell to his laptop again.

Buyer, he wrote at the top of the page, followed by a short list of everything he already knew. Whoever they were, they were rich enough to deal with the Embers, and stupid enough to keep doing so.

Stupid or desperate.

The first time the buyer had reached out was to gather records from years before, and information on an ancient dagger.

Then the blueprints.

It made no fucking sense.

He had searched the records from around two hundred years before, yet everything was okay. The Goddess and the God, the former one, Darnen, had been alive, with no sign of disruption in Aglatas.

The bedroom door opened, and Hawk gave himself away by instantly turning to Amala — a quick glance at her naked figure, then he returned to his laptop.

"Good morning," she murmured, kneeling to pet Howlite as the hound ate her breakfast. She looked at Hawk. "Sunrise."

She whispered the word, already heading to the balcony.

Now sure he would no longer get hard by hearing her moans through the walls, Hawk quickly moved to the couch, setting his laptop on the coffee table. Howlite, finished with her food, hopped to his side.

Hawk needed to figure out if there were any interesting occurrences during the 20031st year — as he picked up from Cairo's report about the buyer — that could potentially provide a lead. He took a sip of orange juice, trying to calm down. He felt nervous and moody, though understood it was because of the unbalance.

Amala tried to teach him how to make it better, showing him ways of meditation to recentre himself to reality. Grounding, or something, she said.

But it wasn't working, Hawk thought, as he gritted his teeth.

His phone buzzed.

Blade Hendrix:
Outside in 20. Please be there, I can't deal with naked HHP two mornings in a row.

Asshole, Hawk thought.

If Blade couldn't deal with her two mornings in a row, he should try living with her for—

He paused.

The rest of his life.

The rest of his life, *if* she accepted.

But if they managed to catch whoever killed Serabel and the priestesses could go back to the Yonium, would Amala go?

Would she stay with him?

He didn't allow himself the luxury of daydreaming and proceeded to pack his laptop and whatever he needed for work.

Knocks on the glass caught his attention as Amala stood at the balcony door; he opened it and she swiftly came in.

"How are you?" she asked, voice calm.

She was always calm after sunrise. As if the view of the sun washed away all her worries, anxiety, and fear.

"All good," Hawk said, eyes not meeting hers. "What are you up to, today?"

Amala smiled, and he could have sworn the entire room lit with it. "Lady Danua wasn't ready yesterday, but she might be today. The New Moon is a big influence for pregnancies and, after the ritual, I'll probably be at the Home of Waters for the whole day."

"Baby three thousand seven hundred and eighty-five, then."

"You remember?"

"I have a good memory," Hawk retorted, "I listen when you talk. Will anyone assist you?"

"Seryn is ready to help. Sinayla can't leave Helioneis much at this stage, and Hebex... Hebs won't come, probably." She mused, "She enjoys living with Medyr a bit *too* much."

He chugged the last of his orange juice, then headed for the bathroom.

"I'm leaving soon, but I'll..."

"See you later," she finished for him, a smile on her lips.

Hawk nodded. "Yeah."

He didn't say anything else, praying to the God and Goddess she couldn't hear the way his heart thundered at her words.

See you later.

☼

The Home of Waters wasn't as beautiful as the Yonium, but Amala didn't mind.

She loved how her temple was built, how unique it was — well, unique, besides having the same structure of Helioneis. But the Yonium was the home of the Goddess, it was special. The other temples in Aglatas were beautiful, yes, but they didn't come close. Amala had officiated in each of them during the Elemental festivities along the year. During those rituals, only the priestesses and bearers of specific powers could assist. Not many months ago, during the Air festivities, she had officiated at the Murmur: the Air temple in Anemos.

A nostalgic smile swept her lips as she remembered Serabel's wicked grin when she told her she would be sleeping at Hawk's.

Amala missed her. She missed her Goddess so much.

She reached for the powerful energy lodged inside of her, taking a deep breath. No sign of the vessel, yet.

Amala sent the thought away and entered the temple, eyes searching for Seryn, for someone to distract her from this dangerous thread of thoughts. The priestess sat on a padded bench, Teleia on her lap. Amala smiled at the sight of them kissing, waiting until they had finished before approaching.

"Good morning, my beautiful priestesses."

Teleia met her gaze: her beautiful blue eyes grateful for the mate by her side, her lips swollen by their kiss. She bowed her head, "Good morning, High Priestess."

Seryn murmured her good morning, tracing her fingers on Teleia's thigh. The priestess shuddered and ignored her, but the hint of a smile curved her lips as she asked, "How was your sleep after the ritual?"

"It was peaceful. I had one dream that threw me off, but then realised it was Howlite snoring."

Seryn cocked her head, "Who's Howlite?"

Amala knew she was probably blushing. "Me and Hawk got a dog three years ago," she admitted. She didn't know why she felt embarrassed, probably because she should have told them sooner.

Something important about her life kept from her sisters — oh, she dreaded the guilt now creeping up her chest.

"Really?"

Teleia's bright eyes were shining.

Amala nodded. "Yeah, we—I mean, *she* lives with Hawk, but I see her regularly. And now she sleeps in the middle of the bed."

Seryn raised an eyebrow, "You are sleeping with *him*?"

Amala shrugged, then carefully teased, "No, I'm celibate."

Her friend snorted. "C'mon! You share a bed with him!"

Amala rolled her eyes, searching for any support in Teleia. The priestess merely shared her amusement, shaking her head at Seryn.

"Yes."

She hoped Seryn would stop pressing, but her friend had other ideas.

"How do you touch yourself?"

Amala wasn't expecting such a question from her. Usually, Hebex was the one who loved to pry into the intimacy of her sex life.

"He leaves."

Teleia hummed as Seryn grimaced.

But before either could continue, Amala said, "Enough with the Hawk talk, both of you. We have a big day ahead."

They stood at her words as she gestured for them to follow.

CHAPTER 21

D anua's waters broke around midday. She didn't instantly realise though, but Amala had noticed the switch in her energy only when the labour was about to start. It had been swift and quick — one of the quickest labours she had assisted as of late — and she had loved the atmosphere around her. The priestesses had helped, supporting Danua with kind energies and beautiful words, making sure Amala had everything she needed. Lady Nyla had assisted too, her own power a calming wave that soothed the entire temple for the whole duration of the birth.

Amala had washed her hands repeatedly, but the border of her nails were still bloody by the time she met her friends at a small café by the southern border of the city, at the end of Pyramis. She had never been there before, but Hebex had asked Medyr for a nice place not too far from the temple — and this was his suggestion.

Sinayla and Hebex were waiting inside when Amala and Seryn arrived.

They hadn't spoken much during the journey; Seryn had given her space, knowing better than initiating conversation when her thoughts were so loud.

Now Amala greeted her sisters with a smile, "Hello, my lovelies. Did you have a good day?"

Her gaze lingered on Hebex, whose lips were still swollen. She spotted a hickey on her neck.

"Oooh, a love bite," Amala taunted, sitting beside her.

"You're one to talk," Hebex replied, without a hint of embarrassment. "Your mate has fangs. He'll mark you, if you let him."

Amala's thoughts instantly drifted to Hawk's canines. Not a single day had passed without her daydreaming about it, catching a glimpse of his fangs every time she caught him staring. She pretended not to see it, but continued to notice, having the hardest time to keep a straight face as her thoughts wandered to how good it would feel with those canines sinking into her neck.

"Not yet," she said with a secretive smile. "I hope our bond holds off until the vessel is found, once I can have sex again. I don't think I would be able to resist if it snaps now." Amala sighed, revealing to her friends the true feelings hidden beneath her words.

"Is Hawk being safe?" Hebex asked curiously. "Does he know he'll have to pull out forever? Or buy a ton of condoms?"

Amala snorted, "Hawk's been on birth control for years," she explained. "And he's clean."

Which was a great step forward, considering some of her male lovers couldn't stand the idea of women not on birth control. Birth control wasn't relied on at the Yonium, the priestesses grew up with no intention of altering the internal state of their feminine energy. Amala had never — and never would — taken hormones for the sake of sex. She was grateful Hawk would do it in her place.

Not that the moment would come anytime soon.

Sinayla asked sweetly, "Is it bothering you, to be celibate?"

"It keeps me grounded. It's a reminder of my grief." An admission she wasn't sure she wanted to make aloud. But her energy whispered that it was fine to share her pain with her sisters.

They were going through the same, after all.

Seryn's understanding shone in her gaze as she reached for Amala's hand and stroked her palm. The High Priestess watched the tracing of her fingers, a solitary tear running down her face as she sniffled.

"I hope you are all having a good time, my beautiful priestesses." Her eyes paused on Sinayla, "You are about to experience the most amazing moment of this journey," her gaze drifted to Seryn, "You and your mate are thriving in the Home of Waters. And you, Hebs — I know you are happy living with Medyr." She smiled through her tears, her energy embodying her friends in a honeyed caress. Her voice dropped lower, "But I miss Serabel a lot."

Attempting to ignore the ache in her chest — in her heart — Amala couldn't hide how much she struggled. Goddess Serabel had been a constant presence in her life from the day she was born: a deity, an inspiration, and a friend.

"I am with you, Amala." Hebex said, reaching for her other hand. "My energy is with you."

"I'm sorry you feel alone in your grief, beautiful Amala." Sinayla's voice was full of respect and understanding, "I won't pretend that our Goddess has been my main thought. I feel guilty, of course, but I am so relieved that—" she paused, a careful glance at Amala.

"You can say it, my love," the High Priestess whispered. "It's alright."

Sinayla nodded, then continued, "I am so relieved that Caelan is with me to face these last weeks together. I wasn't sure if Serabel would allow him in the temple, and I mean," she paused, sensing her friends' reaction. "I would've understood, but I am glad he will be there at the birth."

Silence followed her words as she lowered her gaze. Amala noticed, and said: "Sorry."

"Don't apologise, Amala, *you*—" Sinayla said right away, eyes sweet once again.

"No, sorry. Lady Danua just gave birth," she only said to explain herself.

Sinayla gasped. "*I* am sorry, then."

"Don't be. I'm alright," Amala promised. She showed her friends her bloodied hands, and they shuddered.

"Was it safe? The birth?" Sinayla dared to ask, resting a hand on her swollen belly.

"Yes, it was very natural. She squatted and pushed," Amala explained. "Baby is as healthy as a horse, the mother and mate are both happy. No need to stitch her up and three thousand, seven hundred and eighty-five beautiful souls are here because I pulled them out of their mother's vaginas." Her sisters burst out laughing and Hebex shook her head, tears streaming from her eyes.

"Lady Nyla was so happy," Seryn added. "And her Second was there, too."

"God and Goddess, the *gorgeous* lady with the green eyes!" Sinayla gasped, eyes widening, "What's her name again?"

Amala smiled. "She *is* beautiful. Her name is Ana."

"Is she nice to you at the meetings? Or a bitch like the others?" Hebex inquired.

Among them, she was the most protective of Amala. But they all agreed their High Priestess deserved much more recognition and respect than what she received.

That's why they liked Hawk so much, Amala knew.

They had noticed how much respect and admiration he had for her.

"She's nice, for now." Amala shrugged.

"Why now?" Hebex inquired, the edge of protectiveness to her words caused Amala to smile.

"She has a thing for Captain Mercurian," she admitted with a blush.

Seryn gasped. "No way!"

Hebex grinned, defensive, ready to strike in case the Water's Second did anything to hurt her. "And does she know he's *your* mate?"

She shook her head. "Of course, she doesn't know. No one knows."

Amala could trust her sisters, and trust wasn't the reason why she had kept Hawk from them... rather that Hawk meant so much to her, and she wasn't ready to define *what* they had. At least, until now.

Since moving into his house, her perspective had slowly shifted: she didn't feel out of place, or eager to return to the temple. She loved to wake up early, watching the sunrise from the balcony and loved to doze on the couch with Howlite. She loved Hawk's sleeping body beside her at night and how he poured Amala a glass of apple juice every morning, as though she was unable to do it herself. She loved how they had done their rope-play session the day before, then walked home together afterwards. She could see them doing that... long term.

Living together, being together...

Fuck, fuck, fuck.

Their mating bond was so close to snapping and destroying her celibacy forever.

"What's on your mind, Amala?"

She blinked as Hebex raised an eyebrow.

"I have only two things on my mind," she revealed. "Hawk and Serabel. Whenever I think of Serabel, I only see her dead, lying there in a puddle of blood. Whenever I think of Hawk, I remember I'm celibate and the reason why I must be is because my Goddess is dead."

She felt slightly lighter releasing the words. It was better like this, anyway. Better that her friends knew what she was going through.

"How much guilt do you feel?" Seryn asked cautiously.

Amala looked at them all.

"So, *so* much."

☼

Hawk wasn't the kind of person to complain out loud. Which meant that, in the occasions where he did, he likely had a good reason to. So, when Amala found him scowling at his laptop, she allowed him to vent.

"I found a whole bunch of nothing," he grunted, "I spent hours researching records from the 20031st year, but again, *nothing* — nothing interesting, at least."

Amala swallowed a laugh at his tone, leaning more comfortably into the sofa. Then Hawk's words clicked in her mind, and she froze with a hand in the air, the glass of juice forgotten.

"20031?" She whispered.

Hawk nodded as she bit her lip nervously.

"What?" He asked.

"It's the year of the last Charal persecution."

Heart heavy, she glanced away from him.

"I know, I read it. But I don't think it's related." Hawk said cautiously, "Why? Do you think it is?"

Hawk tried to meet her eyes, but Amala shook her head. "No," she said quickly. "But I *hate* to think about it."

"I didn't know you were interested in the Charal."

Amala took a sip of her juice; she looked confused, as though she didn't want to talk, but then said, "I studied them a lot. Their birthing techniques. I wrote an entire paper about them, but it was never published because—well, because it was about them."

"You admire them." Hawk realised.

Amala's voice was bitter, "Of course I do. The Charal women were amazing. I feel lucky to be able to study them, because in 20031, you couldn't. Nor could you before that. Dhara used to tell me—you know who Dhara is, right?"

He considered the name for a moment. "The High Priestess before you?"

Amala nodded. "She has been in the Karale for decades. Dhara became High Priestess in 20054. I was born in the 20113th year. The last Charal persecution, two hundred years ago, was started by another High Priestess, Dhara's former — High Priestess Bresha. She started it without Serabel knowing, but by the time she found out, it was too late. It had been years already; Bresha had been covering her actions so well that nothing could be done. The Charal were gone, and Dhara told me... Serabel felt so guilty. *So* guilty." She paused to take a breath. "She killed High Priestess Bresha and made Dhara her next Second, but she wasn't able to save the tribe. Dhara did her best to restore some of their beauty and traditions, at least the stories and what could be passed on... that's how I learned about them."

"Was Dhara a Charal?"

Amala gasped, as if Hawk's words were blasphemous.

"Goddess, no! If she had been, she would've been dead by the time Bresha started the persecution. Dhara wasn't Charal, but she admired them so much... And Serabel was researching the tribe. She was trying her best to restore them, to, perhaps, even reunite them again, but she had no idea if they were still alive. That's why she instructed Dhara for years, before sending her to find them."

Hawk looked at her, as if he was trying to see past her words. "Is this why you're High Priestess? Dhara left for... where, exactly?"

Amala shrugged. "I have no way of knowing. Serabel wanted her to find the Charal, but I don't know if she managed it. I haven't seen her since she left and... well, Dhara is the closest thing to a mother that I have, after Kora."

"And why are you so interested in the Charal women yourself? Wouldn't you have liked to go with Dhara, searching for what remains of them?"

Amala shook her head, "My heart can't bear the pain. I wasn't born during the last persecution, yet I cannot believe another High Priestess was the author of something so cruel. Bresha — and many other Goddesses and priestesses before her — what they did to those women is the only thing that has ever made me ashamed of my title and role. To bear any association to *them* is a taint I will never be able to wash away."

She wasn't sure she would ever be able to explain how she felt about those fierce women who lost their lives in the name of the Goddess. A Goddess that hadn't protected them, hadn't *known* they were in need of her. Her gaze lingered outside the window, but she absently heard Hawk ask.

"What would you do, if you met a supersite Charal woman?"

Amala gave a bitter-sweet smile. "I would hug her. Very tightly."

CHAPTER 22

One week later, Hawk knew every single detail of what happened in 20031 and decided the death of the Embers former leader was the most interesting thing to happen. If anything, it gave the buyer a purpose: to check what had happened to the gang and how their ranks had reformed, lasting till the present day. A way of knowing the type of people they eventually would deal with. Though he wasn't fully convinced, it was better than nothing.

Hawk liked his office in the Prior Palace way more than the one at the precinct, mainly because no one was there to annoy the fuck out of him.

Zale had given him the office during the first day working as his Second — two hundred years ago now — and had kept it ever since.

This office was his personal space, his sanctuary — he didn't like people snooping around: he liked to keep a photo of him and Amala hidden in a drawer, and some rope in the drawer beneath that, in case his High Priestess ever wanted to practice after a meeting in the Round Room.

He had tied her up once in his office before, on a day they wouldn't make it to the club in time and she needed to go soon, so she had snuck up while he made sure to freeze the buildings cameras that might have recorded her walking his way.

Hawk couldn't tell if it had been a bigger risk for him or for her, that day, to have one of their sessions in the middle of the Prior Palace. They hadn't gotten caught, thank the Goddess, and had practiced in religious silence for a couple hours before Amala had walked back to her temple... he relished the memory for a moment. Sometimes, he just couldn't wait for them to officially mate, so he could tie her up in his office way more often, and with no need to hack the hallway cameras.

He opened the first drawer and observed the picture of the two of them: standing next to each other as he leaned against the doorframe in his bedroom; she posed with a hand on her waist, the other arm in mid air, index finger pointing upwards. Several times she had tried to understand how the timer on his phone worked, unable to get back to him before the camera shuttered. Until that one take, when she was miraculously able to reach the doorframe, turning to the camera in time. Hawk spent the next hour laughing his ass off for how funny and concentrated she appeared.

That was five years ago.

And now she leaned against his bedroom doorframe every fucking day.

Hawk sighed, regaining control of his scent that threatened to betray him any second. Tucking the picture away and closing the drawer, he lifted his head to a knock at the door.

"Yeah?"

The door opened, and Blade and Cairo entered. The former walked with his usual swagger, the latter with the arrogance of someone who drew the eyes of all the female employers at Prior Palace.

"You're late," Hawk said.

"With a perfectly plausible justification," was Blade's reply.

Hawk simply waited, cocking his head to the side.

Reaching for the pocket of his leather jacket, Blade handed him a crumpled piece of paper: folded and unfolded too many times.

"Blueprints."

Hawk snatched it, laying the paper flat on the desk, then faced Cairo, "What's your excuse?"

Blade grinned, taking a seat. "Naressa was sucking his dick."

Cairo snorted, but shrugged in confirmation as he sat on the other chair.

"You know that we need her to work so we can progress with this case, right?" Hawk sneered, glancing at his friend.

"Don't be jealous, Hawk. I'm sure hot High Priestess will get you off later, if you ask politely." Cairo said with a smirk. Blade howled, and even Hawk bit back a laugh.

"She'd be very polite." Blade cleared his throat, "*You have a beautiful energy today, but it's sunset now, so I really can't. Please don't ask me again.*"

Hawk burst out laughing, Cairo following in suit as Blade grinned, satisfied with his impression of Amala. Hawk examined the blueprint on the table.

The Yonium was massive. He knew it was big, but nothing compared to how it looked on paper: hundreds of rooms, alcoves, staircases, pillars, more rooms, endless hallways and corridors.

"Wahine got this?" Cairo asked.

Blade wriggled his eyebrows. "She saved our ass. The guy who owed her this debt, now already owes her another."

Cairo whistled, "Your sister is badass. I don't know how she's able to keep threatening the Embers like that."

"She knows what she's doing. The Embers would never take it out on the orphanage, because so many of them came from there.

Then Wahine took control and ensured those kids had other life opportunities." Blade explained. He glanced at the paper again. "This is huge. What the fuck do they do with all that space?"

Hawk examined the planimetry, trying to orient himself in the temple space.

"What about this? It says there's a—what, some sort of secret passage?"

Pointing to a small arrow on top of the tunnel, below it read:

To Helioneis

"Well, shit." Blade commented. "Are the temples connected?"

Hawk's eyes remained fixed on the blueprints. How had he never known about this? Shouldn't he have known, at least? Or Zale?

The temples were *connected*.

A secret passage — a God damn secret tunnel travelling all the way from the Yonium to Helioneis.

On paper, there was no sight of the end, but the text was clear.

"We have to look into it," Blade muttered, noting something into his laptop.

Another knock at the door. Hawk realised it was Zale and sat more decently as he politely said, "Enter."

The Prior opened the door: tired, a hint of worry in his eyes as he lingered by the doorframe.

"Good afternoon."

Blade and Cairo instantly stood, bowing their heads.

"Good afternoon, Prior Harat," Blade said, offering his seat.

"Thanks, Hendrix. But I'm not staying. I just…"

"Is everything alright?" Hawk asked, gaze set on his features.

"Eset hasn't felt too good today. Cramps, and nausea. Could you—"

"Yeah," Hawk interrupted, quickly. "Yeah, no problem. She'll be happy to do it."

Zale's face visibly relaxed along with his wings, his energy calming.

"How is she doing by the way?" he wore a tentative smile as he asked.

"Better, overall. Yesterday she assisted Lady Danua as she gave birth."

"Oh, right!" Blade interrupted. "How did that go?"

Hawk shot him a glare; he should know better than interrupting the Prior, but Blade seemed interested to learn the answer. "She never shares details. Just that baby number three thousand seven hundred and eighty-five was born and healthy."

The Prior started, "She has assisted that many births?"

"Yeah, she's been a midwife for almost a hundred years." Hawk said, a note of pride in his words

Pride that didn't get past the Prior.

Zale smirked, taunting. "Have you mated her yet?"

Blade barely contained his snicker while Cairo sneered, eyes studying Hawk.

"She's celibate until the next vessel is found." Hawk hissed.

What was so funny about that? He turned away but knew damn well that Zale was sneering too, with his friends close to losing it.

"I know," he said, "Hilarious. Back to the blueprint," he ordered, pointing at the table.

Blade and Cairo exchanged a look, amused, but obeyed.

Hawk now turned to Zale for the final time that evening, "I'll tell Amala about Eset. I'll text you when I know something."

☼

He couldn't risk meeting her in his office — not the one at the Prior Palace and definitely not at the Precinct. She said she was at the Home of Waters, and while he knew the chances of running into Amala were high, he still decided to go. Probably for that exact reason.

Although he had lived in Aglatas for more than two hundred years, he had never set foot inside this temple. He was pretty sure he had visited the others, at some point: The Purity, in Pyramis, had been at the centre of his investigations far too many times — the people of Fire were renowned for landing in the messiest of situations. While the Riza was the only neutral territory in Gea, for instances where he had needed to speak with Atalman.

The Air temple, otherwise coined the Murmur, was where he would go if he wished to pray to the Goddess — which hadn't been often during his lifetime, but more so since meeting Amala. The Murmur was a beautiful temple, and he knew his mate loved it. She felt at ease, officiating in a familiar energy, the same way she felt uncomfortable to officiate at the Home of Waters. The strong, feminine energy of the Water clashed with hers, rendering it complicated to find a decent harmony.

Hawk understood what she meant as he entered the temple: the Water energy was everywhere. It pushed, whirling around him, trying to sense his presence — his power. He let out a gentle barrier of Air, soft wind shielding him until the Water had enough and left him alone.

She was waiting in the lateral hallway, where she said she would be. Her green cat eyes shimmered in the dim light of the corridor as Hawk cautiously avoided the main altar room to reach her.

"Hello, Captain," Ana said, her feline gaze surveying his entire body. He didn't move; in fact, he had considered whether exploiting the soft spot Ana had for him was a good idea. Yet Zale had pressured him into gathering a complete understanding of the gangs of Aglatas and their behaviour after Serabel's death. It was why he had to resort to Ana, and why it was fundamental to avoid Amala at all costs. Now that she lived with him, it would take all of his self-control to act distant, to pretend he barely knew her.

"Hello, Ana."

She took a step towards him. "How is living with the High Priestess going?"

He started, "I'm not living with her."

"Oh," she said halting, the hint of a smile on her lips, "I thought you were in charge of her safety?"

"I just make sure she doesn't die," Hawk said, shrugging. "Doesn't mean she lives with me."

He tried to sound detached, even *annoyed* by her comment, as though he didn't care if Amala lived with him or not. He wasn't sure if it was convincing, though Ana seemed satisfied enough. Cocking her head to the hallway, she gestured for him to follow. Hawk forced the thought of his mate away.

Get a fucking *grip.*

She led him to a small room — some kind of storage closet — much bigger than the one he had at his own house. Before she got any strange ideas, he started talking.

"I need access to the trends of the Dragon's deals."

"And you couldn't say this via text?" Ana smirked.

"I'd rather you commit with your words."

Her green eyes peered into his. "Why do you need my people?"

"I don't care what they're doing," Hawk said carefully. "But I need to check how the gangs are moving in the underworld now the Goddess is dead. We're really trying to avoid anything worse happening."

She pouted her lips, feline eyes quickly inspecting the room around them.

"So... market tendencies?"

"I don't need names," he specified. "Just numbers: the increase in deals since Serabel died, et cetera: some statistics, a general viewpoint. Harat wants to monitor the situation before criminality gets worse. Can you do this for me?"

Ana's beautiful face offered him a smile. A sensual one.

"Of course, Captain."

She moved closer. Hawk had half an idea to step away, but was also well aware of how much he needed this favour. He forced his body still as Ana placed a hand on his chest: she was closer now, enough for him to catch her scent of seasalt and water lilies. Though it quickly faded as the scent of cinnamon merged moments after.

He would recognise that scent miles away.

That, and the faint clinking of her anklets. Soon enough for him to prepare, but too late to move anywhere else as the door opened and Amala gasped.

She took in the sight of them with wide, icy eyes.

Hawk *knew* she wanted to raise an eyebrow, perhaps say *'Seriously?'* in the sweet voice she used to tease him with. Instead, she stilled, and bowed her head at them, blushing furiously.

"My sincere apologies, my Lady."

Ana smirked, evidently pleased to be caught in a closet with Hawk.

"Are you alright, High Priestess?" she asked, with an undertone of amusement.

"Yes, my Lady," Amala bowed her head again, "I just needed fresh cloths for Lady Danua."

She didn't look at him, not once.

"Go ahead, then." Ana said.

Amala made quick work of grabbing a stock of clean, white cloths.

"Is Lady Danua alright?" Hawk asked.

"Yes, Captain." Amala replied, her voice was shaking.

He had to give it to her, she was good at acting like she hardly knew him. Hawk's own soul was aching as their mating bond tugged desperately, yet Amala looked unaltered — almost *happy* to find him sharing a moment alone with Ana.

As if she didn't share a bed with him, touching herself at sunrise while he made her breakfast.

Wrong, *definitely* wrong thought, his brain said as his scent threatened to come out and fuck everything up.

"I'll leave you alone," Amala bowed her head respectfully.

She turned to leave, but Ana said, "High Priestess!"

"Yes?"

The Water's Second smirked. "You won't tell anyone that you saw us, right?"

Amala blushed, the portrait of pure innocence as she vigorously shook her head. "No, of course not, my Lady."

Hawk's mind left with her, but his body and attention remained with Ana.

"Nothing wrong with having a little fun." She said, eyes trained on his lips.

He knew what she was asking from him, and had known from the moment he arrived at the Home of Waters.

"Maybe," his voice dropped lower, "If you'll bring me what I need, next time we'll have some fun."

Ana blushed under his gaze, and Hawk knew it was done.

"As you wish."

☼

Amala waited for him outside. Smoking.

Hawk stepped closer and she exhaled, a cloud of smoke swirling in his direction.

Weed.

"Where did you get that?"

"Your neighbour saw me waiting, thought I was hot, and offered me some." She inhaled again.

He stole the joint from her mouth and took a hit himself.

"Hey!" she protested, smacking his arm, "Give it back, or I'll tell everyone that I found you in a closet with Ana!"

Hawk halted. Gave her the joint back. Amala's doe eyes glittered with amusement.

"About that..."

"What did you need so badly?"

"Just some stats on the Dragons. Even if we have a lead, we can never be too safe. They're a gang too, benefitting from the unbalance as much as the Embers." His eyes trailed her body as Amala snorted.

"You stoop so low, Captain."

"Yeah, call me *that* again, and—"

"Why?" She pouted, her soft lips so inviting, "Did you get hard?"

Hawk scoffed, canines bared.

"Almost." he said.

CHAPTER 23

S prawled on the couch, Amala and Howlite peacefully enjoyed the sunlight. Hawk couldn't resist, snapping a picture of them together.

"She's having a nap," he quickly explained to Cairo, trying not to sound overprotective.

"Why, did you keep her up all night?"

Great. Fucking great. Was there anyone left who wouldn't tease him about Amala's celibacy?

Probably not.

Cairo smirked, and Hawk refrained from punching him in the face.

"Can't wait to see why she's driving you so crazy," his friend taunted and aimed for the other couch.

Cairo had met Amala once — not like Blade, who had met her several times. Cairo had no idea of what she was like or how gentle, kind, loving, beautiful, and sensual she could be.

Get a grip, his brain urged.

Hawk ignored it.

The second Cairo sat, Howlite sensed his presence and woke, aiming straight for him. Amala rose from the hound's unexpected movements, eyes still half asleep. Lifting her head and then her body, the sun shone on every feature and curve, her creamy skin lightened from the warm rays, mixing with her sunlight scent. Amala looked delicious.

Searching for Howlite, her eyes fell on Cairo on the couch. She momentarily stilled and observed him carefully, spotting Hawk by the doorframe behind and relaxing her shoulders at the sight.

"Hello," she purred. Her voice was sweet and slightly hoarse. "Did you just arrive, or have I been rude for much longer?"

Cairo raised an eyebrow at the incredible kindness transpiring from her question — shocked at her genuine concern of sleeping while he was there.

"I just got here."

Amala curved her lips into a smile, "You seem to be in a good mood today. *Cairo*, right?"

With icy eyes surveying his face and the way she spoke his name, Hawk knew his friend was struggling not to melt under her gaze.

He cleared his throat. "The one and only."

Amala slowly nodded, eyes to Hawk; she smiled even more when she spoke to him. "How are you?"

He observed her sleepy face, puffy eyes and everything.

"Not bad."

"Not bad or good?" she insisted.

Oh, his mate knew how to get him. The subtle smile as she asked the question, her eyebrow slightly furrowed... little tease. He knew why she did it: she loved being happy and, right now, she couldn't be. Not as much as she used to. Mourning, grieving, and unbalance didn't do her any favours, but she would use any glimpse of serenity to feel a little happier and wouldn't let him do otherwise.

There's a big *difference between not bad and good, Hawk,* he could still hear her voice say. *Why should you lower your energy and avoid manifesting good vibrations? You're allowed to complain, but let something bad happen, first.*

Hawk rolled his eyes. "Fine, I'm good. Do you want lunch?"

Amala let out a small victory smile, slowly stretching her body. Hawk was ready to bet she would ask him for strawberries.

"Do you have strawberries, by chance? And—" she brought a hand to her stomach and gently massaged her skin, "Oh, finally. My blood is coming. Can I free bleed?"

She looked delighted, observing her belly and womb with interest. Hawk already knew about Amala's monthly habits: she was proud of her bleeding and attached to her rituals. Though it didn't make it less odd, especially as Cairo intervened.

"Free *what?*"

Amala cocked her head, looking at him.

"Bleed," she repeated, "Let it flow. I was taught to let it flow — it's very disrespectful to our bodies to conceal it. It's a beautiful state of being and it must be cherished as such." Her face lit up with a smile as she explained.

Cairo didn't give up on his puzzled facial expression. His own wind — he came from the People of Air, too — now paced up around him, a faint echo of his scent of rain and grapefruit.

"You let it flow... where?"

Amala's brow furrowed. "I just... bleed. I make sure to clean all the time. We all do like that, at the Yonium." She paused, firmly unsatisfied with his reaction, "It's fine, whatever. I'll need to buy a moon cup."

Gracefully, Amala excused herself, heading to the bathroom, Howlite following behind.

Hawk kept his eyes fixed on her until she disappeared, before meeting Cairo's mesmerised gaze.

His friend raised a brow.

"What the fuck, man?" Cairo said, lowering his voice.

"What?"

"Now I get why we call her hot High Priestess," was all his friend said, gaze lingering on the closed bedroom door.

Hawk stood and aimed for the kitchen: he had strawberries in the fridge, somewhere.

He didn't want Amala to change her habits — not for his sake. Living with him was supposed to make her feel safer, not to detach her from the life she used to have at the temple.

The bedroom door reopened and Amala stepped out, Howlite following as usual.

Hawk lifted his gaze to her, and froze.

☼

Amala expected Hawk's reaction, no matter that he tried to hide it.

His canines were instantly out, eyes wide and surprised.

"It's menstrual blood, Hawk." She simply said, one eyebrow pointedly raised, "I'm not hurt. No need to get over-protective with your mating instinct."

She had gathered some blood, smearing it across her forehead and cheeks. Amala wondered if Hawk had ever seen her like this before — he must have, she had done it with every single period since they had met. But as he gaped, fangs still out, she thought perhaps he hadn't.

She cautiously asked, "Does it gross you out?"

He studied her face, the fresh blood quickly drying on her skin. Amala never used to feel embarrassed by it, but now...

"No."

"Okay, then." She turned towards the sofa, sitting on the floor next to where Cairo sat, avoiding the carpet. She wouldn't dare stain Hawk's furniture with her blood. Amala's fingers traced her belly, massaging her swollen abdomen. "So, how are you?"

Cairo looked at her; he was handsome, skin lighter than Hawk's, with short chestnut hair. His jaw was sculpted to the edge of perfection, marked with faint stubble — eyes almost as bright as hers, though not as icy.

"I'm alright," Cairo said, then pointed a finger. "This is weird."

"Don't listen to him," Hawk's voice reached her before embarrassment could, "It's not weird, and this is not Cairo's house. It's yours."

"*Yours*," Amala countered, even as her heartbeat increased.

Hawk sneered but said nothing.

"It's weird," Cairo repeated, "But cool."

Amala chuckled. "I'm fertile only for a hundred and fifty years. I'm going to cherish every blood that I get."

It was a quick explanation of how much it meant to her: the monthly smear of blood on her face and body — a tradition, a piece of culture she loved, cherished in her temple. Her mother Kora had taught her so, as had Dhara. Amala grew up waiting for puberty, so she could finally join the other priestesses in the ritual.

Hawk approached, handing her a bowl full of freshly washed strawberries, "Here you go. For your cravings. And it's alright if you free bleed, I don't want you to change something that's important to you."

She could have sworn he refrained from touching her as he returned to the other couch. Amala picked up a strawberry, taking a small bite as her eyes rolled back with pleasure.

"Thank you," she said to Hawk, her voice a low purr.

He chuckled.

"What time are you leaving, Amala mate?"

She took another bite. "My train leaves tonight at eleven."

"Harat said Eset is having some pregnancy pain. They asked if you could visit her... can you manage to fit her in before that?"

Oh, so *now* they wanted her as a midwife, she thought, recalling the conversation with Hawk in the elevator.

Don't be bothered, Amala mate. I'm sure she'll ask you to be her midwife.

Neither Eset nor Zale Harat had contacted her, though. Not that she minded much, yet it would be such an honour to assist the Prior's mate in her pregnancy...

Amala nodded.

"I'll meditate after lunch and do some stretches to alleviate my cycle pain. You're welcome to join by the way. Then, I'm free."

"I'll drive you there, then. And to the station tonight," Hawk added. His tone sounded protective at that, and Amala knew better than complaining: the Prior had placed him in charge of her safety. Plus, she didn't mind: having Hawk around made her feel safer.

Cairo captured her attention, eyes directed to her. "Where are you going tonight?"

Amala smiled, lazily stretching her upper body; her right arm reached the floor, extended above her head, and bending to her left.

"I'm going to Ulbaros for a week."

"What for?"

"A patient of mine is due. Luckily she didn't clash with Lady Danua."

"Have you been to Ulbaros already?"

Yes, plenty of times, and she had loved it. It was a small village in the middle of the woods and was one of her favourite trips from Aglatas. It took around five hours via train to get there, and the environment reminded her of the Yonium: placid, silent, nature thriving. People with simple lives and love in their eyes.

"Several times and recently to check on her. Though her pregnancy was very smooth, and this isn't her first child. More like her sixth. They have wolf blood," she said, as it was self-explanatory.

When pure races still existed, wolves tended to reproduce the most. Their kind was predisposed to reproduction and when they mated, they could spend the first decades simply procreating, sometimes raising a whole pack.

"Have you assisted her for all of them?" Cairo asked.

Amala nodded.

"Yes. I'm very close with her, she was one of my first clients when I still had little experience — fresh from my studies."

Fatemeh was her name, and Amala loved her deeply. She was eager to see her and couldn't wait to escape Aglatas for some time. Living with Hawk, so close to his investigation, was difficult and being unable to help him was driving her crazy.

He was driving her crazy.

The idea of spending the rest of her cycle alone in the woods sounded nothing short of divine. Amala almost sighed, picturing herself walking naked between the familiar trees; she had done it so often in Mhelani Forest, but the risk of encounters with centaurs — mating or wanting to mate with her — was too high for that activity to be recurrent.

"Any success with the dagger?" Hawk now asked.

Cairo shook his head. "I'm close to something, but I can't promise it yet. I asked Blade to help, but he said Wahine was going to kick his ass if he tried to involve her again. Not so soon, at least."

"Who's Wahine?" Amala asked.

"Blade's sister, but don't even think about it. You're quite *Miss I'll Steal Your Girl*, from what I've heard."

Amala smirked. "Looks like my fame precedes me."

Wahine sounded beautiful. Amala wondered what she looked like.

"Though, I'm not so sure I believe Hawk…" Cairo's voice dropped, blue eyes fixed on her face, then sliding the rest of her body, "Maybe I'll need a demonstration?"

Her brow rose in challenge.

On a normal day, with anyone else, Amala wouldn't do it. Keeping her tone humble, she would bow her head and ignore the taunt. She had done it for so long.

But Cairo was teasing her, only to prompt a reaction from Hawk. She wouldn't stand for that. Tucking a strand of hair behind her ear, she curved her lips into a smile and replied.

"Let's arrange it for when I meet your Naressa."

Cairo started. Amala's eyes shimmered as she distinctly heard Hawk choke on his laughter. She stared back into those blue eyes and took another bite of her strawberry.

☼

Hawk needed a week away from Amala.

She had been living with him for only a couple of weeks now, but he craved a normal night's sleep — one with Howlite on Amala's side of the bed; her snoring was a thousand times better than the heady cinnamon scent of his mate.

Maybe not better, but definitely easier to get used to.

Waking up without that beautiful female by his side, regardless of how much his chest ached being apart from her, was a small blessing. At least for that day.

Hawk knew he needed a breakthrough in the case soon, otherwise he would have to tell the Prior he had zero leads. Admit he was failing his task — which wasn't true, since he *did* have a lead: a damn secret tunnel connecting the two temples on a blueprint *someone else* had access to. The more he investigated, the more the entire case seemed to complicate. At least, with Amala somewhere other than here, he could formulate logical thoughts, undistracted by those beautiful icy eyes.

It was only the thought that she would be proud of him that pushed Hawk to finally accept the fact that he needed help.

Medyr's help.

CHAPTER 24

F atemeh was due in two days, giving Amala enough time to enjoy Ulbaros' forest all by herself. She had checked on her patient already and had spent time with her as soon as she arrived.

They meditated together while Amala massaged her body, fondling her swollen womb with almost reverence. Fatemeh offered her food, following the hospitality traditions she was accustomed to back in her temple, and Amala managed to feel at home in a place far from where her heart resided.

Yes, she missed Hawk. But this time alone, she cherished.

And it was only a matter of time before Hawk and Amala would decide to take the next step and bind their souls together for eternity.

She smiled at the thought, using it to centre herself as she strolled through the dark forest. The grass was damp and Amala could barely see where her bare feet trod as she abandoned the footpath and strayed into the woods. She *really* loved Ulbaros' woods.

Every time she visited, she made sure to spend at least one night in the wilderness — leaving her belongings behind for a night outside in the forest.

Amala walked in silence until she cleared the trees and reached the stream. Even in the darkness of the night, the trees no longer concealed the moon as the water reflected pure, white light. Sitting next to the river, Amala took off her clothes.

It took a lot for Amala to feel the cold, even at night with lower temperatures. The air stilled, no breeze except the ones circulating from her own power.

Treading gently into the stream, cold water froze her feet and ankles until she grew used to it: a bath in a stream under the moonlight. Dipping her whole body in, her head plunged beneath the surface and, when she re-emerged, pure light shone on her face. She was glowing.

Amala was glowing in the moonlight, and stilled as she noticed something odd. Quietly, she listened to the silence of the night.

The regular beating of her beautiful, big heart was the only sound.

And... a whisper.

A soft whisper in her heart. That spark of divine energy that bloomed in her awoke, pulling, and keeping her on edge. The night of the earthquake she had felt it leave, concealed to the point she thought it was lost...yet now here it was. Tugging. It had never felt *this* strong before.

Amala carefully listened to each beat of her heart. Something was different.

Something was happening.

She took a breath — a deep one — and felt it.

The faint note of moonlight she would always associate with Serabel. Her Goddess' scent.

Realisation hit her, her breath stolen.

The spark inside her expanded, stretched, dilated — it *hurt*, somehow. It hurt her soul.

Then, it merged: stretching, and expanding with the rest of it.

The rest of the energy.

The Goddess' energy absorbed bit by bit in her body. Her soul.

Amala beheld the moon, and the moon glowed back, attracted by her call.

She searched for her scent trying calm her thundering heart.

Inhale.

Cinnamon, sugar, and sunlight.

Exhale.

Inhale.

Cinnamon, sugar, and sunlight.

And—

Moonlight.

Moonlight?

And as Amala glanced at the sky, gazing at the moon which glistened there, she knew.

The Goddess's energy had found her next vessel.

And it was her.

CHAPTER 25

H igh Priest Medyr was possibly the *last* person Hawk wanted to involve in his investigation. But a part of his brain reasoned with him, adopting Amala's sweet voice as it said *Give him a chance, Captain*. Of course he listened.

Medyr waited outside the temple, on the sunlit porch.

Hawk had texted before leaving but now, as he approached the High Priest, he seriously reconsidered his choice. Good thing Blade was with him, ready to punch him in the gut the moment his mate instincts took over, before Medyr was given a fair chance to help.

"Good morning, Captain." The High Priest said.

"Good morning," Hawk replied coldly.

On second thought, he realised, Medyr didn't know Hawk couldn't stand him. Especially, he had no idea that it was because *he* had his chance with Amala when Hawk hadn't.

That's a fucking stupid reason to hate someone, Blade had told him on their way there, but Hawk didn't need a reminder. He already knew that.

Hebex walked up, hips dangerously swinging with each step. Medyr's gaze lingered on her petite body: she was different from Amala, smaller and with less curves. But she was confident. *Very* confident, Hawk realised, as she stepped in and kissed the High Priest on the lips.

Amala would never do that in front of others.

"Well, well. Hello, Captain Mercurian," Hebex purred, eyes sliding from him to Blade. "Hello—what's *your* title?"

Blade met the taunt with one of his feline smiles. "Just Blade."

Hebex hummed. "Like... a blade?"

"Exactly like a blade."

Hawk didn't wish to indulge in small talk — the quicker Blade and him could make their way through the temple, the better. Medyr seemed to guess his thoughts, raising his chin high to ask, "Is there anything we can do for you?"

How much exactly did he want Medyr to know?

Zero, if it was up to him.

But he recalled Amala's words: Medyr oversaw the temple, and Hawk should show him respect if he wished for his help. It couldn't hurt. The High Priest had proven himself useful the week before during their first visit.

So Hawk decided to get straight to the point. "There's a secret tunnel under the temple and it's connected to the Yonium."

Medyr blinked in surprise. His gaze intensified as he exchanged a confused look with Hebex.

"There's a *what*?"

"You didn't know about it?"

Neither of them looked at Hawk, both wearing the same expression of stunned curiosity.

"Fuck no I didn't," Medyr finally said, raising his gaze to Hawk, "How do you know there's a tunnel?"

Hawk shook his head, "That, I can't say. But I can show you where it is if you'll allow us to check it."

"Only if I can come, too," Hebex shrugged, glancing at Medyr.

He snorted, a smile tugging on his lips as she snaked an arm around his body — utterly lost in his eyes. The High Priest held her gaze before nodding.

"Great," Hebex purred. "Lead the way, Captain."

☼

Amala had emerged from the stream only because her body would freeze otherwise. Freeze to death with no backup High Priestess to supply in her absence. Curled on the shore, her body still, she stayed there for hours: dawn came, as did sunrise, yet still she did not pray.

She barely looked at the sun as it peaked through the trees, the clear water mirroring a light that was never hers. Not ever, and definitely not now.

Because she was Goddess of the moon.

Her mind was empty, no thought important enough to form and stay, or capture any remnants of her attention.

Utter shock.

The new energy within her took its time, sensing her body, and slowly squeezing inside its new owner, as it adjusted to her soul. It had been hours, now, since the last time she allowed herself to think.

She simply didn't want to exist: beautiful, utterly empty oblivion sounded divine now.

Divine.

Fucking divine.

Fucking divine, the oblivion and... her.

Amala and her fucking soul.

She wasn't sure if she had cried. In fact, she barely noticed time pass. But when dawn settled and the moon left, there was a pull. As if a part of her whispered: *enough, my love. You had your time.*

Now stop pretending it didn't happen.

Amala lay on the grass, watching the sky painted in pink and golden hues. The colours of a new day.

She took a breath and started praying.

Though she wasn't sure *what* to pray for now, but the practice itself felt right.

Her brain gradually began processing again as Amala allowed herself to realise what had happened.

As High Priestess, she was able to feel the Goddess' energy and had been ready to embrace it for some time: always on edge, awaiting the next vessel.

Only when the energy found Amala, it didn't give her a vision.

No, it offered its whole power.

The Goddess had merged with Amala instead, making her the new living bearer of divine energy. Obtaining the balance of the world.

Why me? she thought, closing her eyes. Amala desperately tried to reach her energy — *her* energy, and not this new entity inside of her — though she couldn't. She couldn't differentiate the two beings now cohabitating inside her being.

There's no two, Amala...

A whisper in her heart, like the one from the night before.

We are one.

Amala wept then.

She couldn't possibly think that, with all the people existing on Exanthea, the Goddess would choose her. *How* was it possible?

How could she be worthy of such an honour?

How could she represent that power? Those values? Those mightiness and light and authority and serenity and love?

Amala wasn't a Goddess, nor did she *want* to be. She wanted to be High Priestess to her Goddess — uncaring of *who* the vessel was, as long as it wasn't her. A Goddess she could honour — a Goddess to devote the rest of her life to.

What would Serabel say now, to see her like this?

High Priestess turned Goddess crying on the shore.

"Please," she begged through her tears, "Please, take it back. You're wrong, I swear it! It cannot be, it cannot be me. Take it back, take it back!"

Voice shaking, Amala tried to steady herself and took a breath.

"It's not me," she repeated, sniffling. "It cannot be me."

The world around her stilled, listening.

But Amala had nothing to say.

"It cannot be me." She repeated a final time.

☼

Hebex would give a headache to whoever spent more than five minutes with her, Hawk thought.

He was pretty sure Blade, walking on his left, felt the same.

The priestess hadn't stopped talking for a second — a *single* second. Hawk had managed it before when she helped in his office, but now the situation was borderline unbearable. If Medyr had to put up with *this* every day, Hawk gave him credit.

"What do you think, Captain?" she asked.

Honest to Goddess, he had no idea what she was saying. Though it was a miracle that Hebex hadn't told anyone about him and Amala, Hawk thought, because she talked so fucking *much*—

"I think he missed your question," Blade said for him.

Hebex paused, hands on her hips as she cocked her head.

"Rude," she replied, quickly licking her lips. "I asked if you think the Yonium is better than Helioneis."

"I don't know it that well." Hawk said sincerely.

"Well, you've been there." Hebex countered. "Did you like it?"

Medyr rolled his eyes, a hand gently stroking Hebex's back. "She's asking if you think the modern vibe ruins our temple: Helioneis. The priestesses love to live in such an ancient place."

"Isn't that what hot High Priestess thinks?" Blade intervened.

Hebex nodded, "Yeah, Amala hates the idea of a modern temple."

The tunnel was quiet. They had been walking for a while now: the timer Hawk had started before their venture reached 31 minutes.

They had travelled through Helioneis, Hawk leading the way after accurately studying the blueprints. It felt good knowing how to orientate inside of the temple, rather than feel lost among the columns and altars and staircases. One of the staircases led them to a door hidden in an alcove. And then more stairs, until they reached the entrance to the tunnel. It was flat and quite ample, allowing them to stand side by side. While it wasn't narrow, it wasn't big either; the walls were lit by a thousand beacons enchanted never to extinguish. The passage extended for what felt like miles without changing once; it seemed as though they didn't alter direction at all, and it had been like this for a good while now. But when Hawk spotted something change on the walls, he halted.

"What's that?"

Blade stopped on his side; Medyr had the good sense to pause too, but Hebex kept walking as though she hadn't heard them, her eyes fixed to a spot on the wall.

"Hebs—" Medyr called.

She didn't turn. Reaching the wall, her fingers pressed against the surface, sliding them along.

A symbol.

Some sort of symbol Hawk had never seen before.

"I think this is blood."

Her voice was calm, too intrigued by the wall to betray any hint of uneasiness.

As Hawk moved closer, he realised the priestess was right. That one symbol was the first of many, as the wall travelled further with more signs painted along it: brushed with the same dark colour, and emanating a faint smell of blood.

"What is this?" Blade asked, checking the other wall. Hawk followed his gaze. There were more symbols there too: crescent moons and flowy lines, stylised scales, circles, double circles — letters and words written in an alphabet he didn't understand.

But then, Medyr cleared his throat.

Hebex gasped, startled. "What?"

They turned to him, now standing several feet away in the middle of the tunnel. His face was painfully blank, as though he couldn't believe his eyes as he pointed to the wall. Hawk noticed the trembling in his fingers.

On the wall, in big, dark letters, surrounded by all those symbols, was one word they could all read:

CHARAL

☼

"It cannot be me."

But it *was* her.

The energy had picked her and the energy was never wrong, nor would she disrespect her Goddess by telling her so.... she just couldn't believe that the *right* choice fell on *her*.

"How can it be me?" Amala said aloud, eyes still closed.

She quieted, focusing on her thoughts.

Five things you see, Amala.

Eyes open, she surveyed her surroundings: the sky. So bright and beautiful as pink gradually surrendered to the soft blue of the morning. A solitary cloud, puffy and creamy.

The peak of the trees.

Tilting her head to the left, she glimpsed the peak of a mountain.

And the sun.

Four things you hear, Amala.

The stream, clear water: placid yet constant.

A cricket somewhere close to where she lay.

The soft whisper of the wind, a familiar caress.

And her own heartbeat.

Three things you smell, Amala.

She inhaled: crispy air, fresh and pure, the air of dawn.

Flowers and the delicate smell of primrose.

Moonlight and sunlight together.

Two things you can touch, Amala.

Naked, she felt the damp, soft grass under her body.

As her hands traced the ground, she found friable sand, which crumbled in her fingertips.

One thing you taste, Amala.

She swallowed.

Cinnamon. Always cinnamon.

Amala didn't move, fixed still to her spot, though her mind slowly started to function again. Her thoughts remained, but not as loud as before. The energy...

She focused on it.

Amala had never, not for a single moment, thought Serabel was undeserving to be Goddess. And she had never seen the Goddess and the woman as two separate entities: Serabel was the Goddess and the

Goddess was Serabel. There was no way to differentiate one from the other. Even learning more about Serabel's story — before she had embodied the vessel — had never been enough for her mind to separate the two: they were *one*.

But the second that same energy entered Amala's body, she felt afraid to taint her, to contaminate Serabel's essence with her impurity. With her... unworthiness. Praying, she begged for it to leave, to not infect the divinity with her unworthy soul, but the Goddess hadn't listened.

It hadn't listened because there was no other Goddess. Not anymore.

And she had tried to find the Goddess in her... to summon her, to invoke her. But it had been vain.

There was no Goddess inside of her.

The Goddess *was* her.

She was the Goddess, and there was no way to separate the two.

Amala reached for her energy and found it the same. Nothing was different: her passion, her Love, her way of seeing the world. Her devotion, compassion, judgement, commitment, enthusiasm, courage, and kindness... it was all there.

It was all the same.

Her *Love* was the same, for Goddess' sake.

Amala.

She was still Amala.

High Priestess Amala.

And Goddess...

Amala lifted her upper body, standing fully as she turned to the sky and sun. She sensed the location of the moon and knelt in its direction.

Summoning her new, divine energy for the first time.

"Please, let me see you." She whispered.

It took a while. While she couldn't separate herself from the Goddess, she could summon the energy in its entirety. She wanted to talk to it, face it, *see* it.

Groaning with effort, she extended the power outside of her body. She didn't know it was possible until she saw it: transparent, wobbling like a beautiful, abstract bubble that reflected the sun.

Amala knelt lower.

"My Goddess, forgive me. I do not know if I am ready to take you, or if I am worthy of such power. But I am honoured that you chose me. I know we are one, but I will *never* stop worshipping you for as long as I breathe. This is what I swore when I became your High Priestess, and I still am. I still am High Priestess to the Goddess. I am your High Priestess. I swore myself to you with everything that belongs to me. No matter if we share this life, this body, this soul — as Amala, I was already yours, and I will be forever."

She couldn't hold her energy outside of her body for any longer: falling to the ground, the bubble instantly melded into Amala as though it couldn't stand to be separated. It probably couldn't, and Amala knew she shouldn't have tried.

But she meant to do it for this one time only.

She owed it to herself; it didn't matter if the Goddesses before her had never embraced the role like this. They had been sensational bearers of peace and Love, worshipped by many... but none had worshipped themselves. Not like this.

Serabel had lived in full dignity of her title, never kneeling before it. Grateful, yes, but in control of it.

But Amala didn't care that the Goddesses before her hadn't knelt.

She would.

She would kneel for her Goddess until the day she died.

She would have done it for any vessel...

She would do it for herself.

CHAPTER 26

H awk wouldn't have considered their exploration of the underground tunnel a success, but he couldn't define it a failure either. Five days later, he was missing Amala like hell, finding ways to distract himself with elements of the case.

What they found in the tunnel had been unexpected; after finding the Charal symbols, they didn't venture further. Blade took pictures of everything and they had left quickly afterwards, the air becoming heavy the longer they stared at the walls.

They couldn't use the tunnel to enter the Yonium: Amala's protective wards shielded access. Hawk knew that already, but still wished to check the tunnel — to see if anyone had used it. To see if it was lived in...

He wasn't sure what to think now; parts of it seemed untouched for years — decades, even — aside from the symbols. What the fuck did they mean, and why were they there? Hawk spent the days after trying to recover as much material as possible on the Charal tribe — Blade, unusually less stoned, had helped.

Though it didn't matter how much they tried, all the material, books, and papers regarding the Charal women seemed to have completely vanished.

Burned, he later learned, or hidden, or sold at auctions for exorbitant prices.

Rifling through articles to dig as much as he could, he figured he would never understand any of this on his own. Which was why Hebex now smiled from the opposite couch.

"I like your house."

He sighed.

"Thanks."

"I think I would have loved growing up in a house like this," she glanced around eagerly. "My parents place in Gea is nice, it has a garden and all... but I'm more of an 'apartment-with-a-view' kind of person," she explained, then turned to where Medyr currently sat by her side. "Do you like it?"

Hawk wasn't sure how Medyr had ended up in his living room. After they found the graffiti, Hawk had initially thought Blade and him could figure it out on their own. But after a few days, Cairo's help, and zero leads, he went back to the temple and asked for their help, again.

Now the High Priest cocked his head, glancing toward Hawk.

"Yeah. Nice place."

Medyr looked less at ease than him, at least.

Hebex stroked behind Howlite's ears.

"She's so cute!" she squeaked. Hawk saw the way her lips moved, ready to mention Amala, but stopped herself in time. Eyes blinking at him.

Sometimes Hawk found it hard to believe Amala shared no details of the life she had with him. Hebex had known her for much longer than he had, yet Amala had managed to keep Hawk away from this blonde, talkative priestess with sweet eyes and a scent of honey.

"So, before we start. What have you found?" she asked, eyes darting to Blade.

Blade shrugged.

"Not much, to be fair. Bits of history, some facts here and there, but that was it."

Hebex studied him for a second, considering. Her blond locks reflected the sunlight as she cocked her head, "Alright. Listen, I'm not sure my knowledge is enough, but Medyr can help fill the gaps. I don't think it will help with those symbols though."

Hawk shrugged, laptop open to quickly type his notes.

"Anything you know might be important. And there's no one else currently in possession of this information."

Hebex nodded, stroking Howlite a final time then straightening her body into a less relaxed position.

"I joined the Yonium long after the Charal business ended, but Serabel surely tried to make us outlive their traditions." She started. "But I wasn't born at the temple and the only way I picked up the culture was because Amala educated me about it. She knows more than me too."

Blade interrupted, glancing at Hawk in confirmation. "Yeah, she mentioned a paper she wrote?"

Hebex hummed in approval.

"She did. She wrote a whole study on the natural birth techniques of the Charal women, but it never published. No one would publish a study related to the Charal."

"Why did she try, then?"

"Because she had demonstrated that Charal birth techniques are a better fit for midwife training than the one she was taught at university."

"How did she learn about the techniques, if they didn't teach her?" asked Blade, eyebrows knotted with curiosity. Hebex smiled at his reaction.

"She studied a lot. There are priestesses in our temple that know more about the Charal. Dhara helped too."

"Who's Dhara?"

This time, Medyr replied before Hebex could. "The High Priestess before Amala."

"What happened to her?"

Hawk said, "Serabel sent her off to patch up the Charal. That's what Amala told me."

"Exactly," Hebex nodded, "But that's a thin line, if I'm honest, because no one even knows if they're still out there. All the records say they have *all* been slaughtered."

"But Serabel didn't think so, did she?"

"She didn't. She talked about them as if they were alive, and Dhara had clear instruction when she left..."

Hawk studied the notes in front of him, a question forming.

"When did Dhara leave?"

"Around ten years ago — longer, I think. Amala was made High Priestess soon after she left."

"So... from the year of the last persecution to ten years ago is a fucking long time," Hawk noted, writing down the exact dates. "Why would Serabel not search for them sooner?"

It didn't make any sense. If the Goddess had known for almost two hundred years that Charal women may still be out there, after *her* High Priestess had killed them — why did she wait so long before sending someone to search?

Hebex shook her head, "I don't know, Captain. I wasn't there for most of that time."

"She couldn't send Dhara right after them all those years ago," Blade observed, "If the Charal killers were still on the hunt, it would have only been suspicious, even with the other High Priestess dead. The former one — what was her name again?"

"Bresha." Medyr said.

"Bresha," repeated Blade, tasting the name on his tongue. "Sounds like a cool name. Too bad she was nuts, I guess."

Hebex tried her best not to laugh, but couldn't disguise a chuckle. If Blade noticed, he showed no sign and instead, turned to Hawk, trying to gage his opinion on the theory he had laid down.

Hawk nodded.

"Yeah, that's a good point. The Goddess couldn't send Dhara after the Charal all those years ago, but she surely waited a long time before doing it." He paused, considering. "I think when she started searching for them, it might have been too late. *If* any Charal woman had been spared by the persecution, they would be hidden again and, this time, for good. Serabel needed years to make up plans and study every chance she could to find them again."

Hebex nodded slowly, following the line of his thoughts with an admiring gaze. "According to the stories I know, if they are still alive, they are *very* hidden. Even with years of searching, there's a chance you will never find them. At this point, I'm not sure they even want to be found."

Yeah, Hawk had to agree with that. After centuries of persecution, why would any Charal woman risk ever coming out again? The pain endured throughout that time... it wasn't worth it. Not for a world so hostile to them, anyway. And with the death of the Goddess—

What would happen now with the next vessel?

If the next Goddess knew about the Charal, there was a high chance she wanted nothing to do with them. Since the last persecution, the Charal name had been cleared enough and the common opinion was now not so biased. Not anymore. Prejudice still remained of course, sometimes people's first instinct was to shut down at the mention of their name, perhaps in fear of what might happen if someone heard. But times had progressed since the persecution era.

If the vessel knew nothing of the Charal women, maybe it was better that way.

Maybe...

Hawk considered, the spark of a new idea crackling in his mind. The next vessel may have been born long after the last Charal persecution, with no idea how to continue Serabel's mission. He noted it down with a giant question mark; there was no way to confirm it until Cairo got back with some news. He sent a quick text asking for any updates, then faced Hebex and Medyr.

"Tell me about Dhara."

"Amala knows way more than us about Dhara," was Medyr's instant reply.

"But you can't ask her," Hebex countered, "Dhara was too important to her. She was like a mother figure, especially after Kora left the temple and—" she paused, "Amala didn't take it well when Dhara left, especially when she was made High Priestess in her place."

Hawk fought the urge to ask why, though his face betrayed his thoughts. Medyr didn't seem to notice, but Hebex did.

"The person she cared about the most left her. Not only did Amala have to deal with her leaving, she had to take her title too. And that's her biggest problem, isn't it?" She looked to Medyr for validation before continuing, "She never feels worthy of what she has, or who she is. Even if she deserves the world."

Medyr nodded his agreement. Hebex was good at pretending she knew nothing about Amala and Hawk being mates. Blade seemed to share Hawk's opinion, barely hiding a smirk.

"Dhara was a lovely woman," Hebex continued, "She was sweet and kind, and educated all the priestesses born at the temple. Amala was very inspired by her. But in those last years, decades even — well, Dhara got busier. She gave Amala all of her important work, so she could study — all the time. I think Serabel was giving her a hard time, encouraging Dhara to revise the Charal women as much as possible before she left."

"Was it that necessary to study them?" Blade asked, taking notes too.

"Even if she found them, the Charal would *never* have accepted her if she showed no respect or understanding of their customs. They might have even killed her before giving her the chance." Medyr said.

Hebex smacked his arm, eyes narrowing, "Medyr, that's exactly the stereotype that perpetuates the hate they receive. I would fucking kill someone too, if they approached me after I was persecuted for centuries!"

He clasped his fingers around her wrist and she gasped.

"I didn't mean it like that, Hebs. It's just really important for a non-Charal to learn of their ways before meeting them."

Hebex eyed her wrist between his fingers, a smirk playing on her lips, but Blade interrupted them before she could say what evidently was on her mind.

"Wait, so Dhara wasn't a Charal?"

Medyr and Hebex's eyes both snapped to him.

"What? No." Hebex asked, confused.

"How do you know?"

She rolled her eyes, as though it were obvious.

"Because Serabel would have fucking *loved* to have a Charal at the temple — honoured, even. She was obsessed with them."

"From what I know," Medyr added, "They had half an idea to do the opposite. To have Dhara fake herself a Charal before finding them. But that's impossible, of course."

Medyr knew. That little fucker knew Hawk and Blade had no idea why this notion was impossible. Of course, he didn't make any move to tell them either. Not until they asked. Blade was tempted to voice his irritation, only Hawk noticed and pushed aside his pride.

"Why?"

Medyr smirked, evidently satisfied with the question.

"Because," he started, "The Charal are born with a birthmark."

Hebex hummed with a nod as he continued. "The Charal symbol: the crescent moon. They are all born with a birthmark on their nape that appears only if the moonlight shines directly on it. That's how they recognize each other, and how their hunters recognize them before the kill. There's no way to hide it and no way to fake it, either."

Well, that was an interesting detail Hawk had failed to find anywhere else. He noted it down.

"Alright," he said. "So, all the crescents on the walls in the tunnel... that means Charal." He stated.

"Crescent upwards is Charal," Hebex confirmed. Eyes studying Medyr with hesitation, she continued. "I know we shouldn't have, but we went back to the tunnel to see if we could find more graffiti once you left—"

Hawk whipped his head to them.

"What?"

"That was bloody stupid." said Blade.

"I know," Hebex replied, "But I was freaking out, I needed to see the symbols again. I had no idea of the alphabet they used, but then I found one word in our letters. Medyr took a picture of it. *Kantazar*. It's what they call Charal killers."

Charal killers. Hawk had read about them before: mostly men, hired and paid incredibly high rates to go and slaughter entire Charal tribes.

They had enforced the persecutions, hunting those women through the woods and forests until none were spared. The Charal women were warriors: a warrior clan intended to protect the Goddess, powered by her moonlight. How had the Charal killers destroyed so many of them? Did someone rat them out?

Hebex went on.

"After they were slaughtered, Serabel tried her best to keep their traditions alive within the Yonium — the birth rites, our blood cycles, the dances, some of the songs... we didn't appropriate their culture, but we kept it alive in the best way we could. The Charal women were incredible warriors. We chant about them, their courage and strength, their connection with the moon and the Goddess, their stories."

"What stories?"

"Stories of when they were slaughtered. According to the chants, when they battle, they paint their bodies with their own blood. Actual blood. They cut themselves and use the blood from the wound." Hebex seemed to shiver at the thought.

"I wonder if," she added with a whisper, "With an army of Charal women by her side, Serabel would still be alive."

CHAPTER 27

H awk picked up Amala at the central Aglatas station around six in the morning. She greeted him with a small smile, though murmured something about feeling tired before she got in the car and fell asleep in the passenger seat. Hawk wanted to say how much he had missed her, but she said nothing of the sort; in fact, she didn't even seem happy to be back.

Struggling against the urge to watch her beautiful, sleepy face every passing moment, he drove around the city, wandering the streets a while longer so she could sleep some more, the movement of the car rocking her into peaceful slumber.

When Hawk parked, he finally allowed himself to observe.

Amala wasn't lying, she looked tired — more tired than usual, and even if her face bore no particular trace of exhaustion, her body told a different story. Her movements were slow and calculated, eyes wary from the moment she stepped foot off the train.

Hawk considered carrying her upstairs without waking her up but, before he could unfasten her seatbelt, Amala's body turned toward him as she opened her eyes. Barely.

"Are we home?" she whispered.

Home.

Doing his best to conceal the pounding of his heart, he nodded.

"Do you want me to carry you?" he asked.

But Amala, hearing those words, quickly straightened and shook her head.

She pinched her cheeks in an attempt to wake up and opened the car door.

"No, I'm alright."

Hawk stood, confused. One moment she was peacefully asleep, beautiful and unbothered. Now she hurried up the pavement, keys in one hand as she aimed for the main doors. She didn't look back in his direction before she entered.

☼

Amala was behaving like a bitch and she knew it.

She had missed Hawk like hell during those days spent apart.

And when she saw him at the station, a part of her wanted to run and jump into his arms, to reveal everything. Everything that had happened in Ulbaros — all of it.

But another part, a more rational one, kept her calm.

Scared.

It's Hawk. You can trust him.

That's what she whispered to her thoughts to convince herself.

But not yet — she couldn't tell him yet.

Amala wasn't used to this. They had avoided each other in public for years, limiting their interactions to the bare minimum, while knowing the second they were alone again, everything would return to normal. And now that moment — that oasis, the peace of their home and space they shared with no one else — was taunted by this secret. Her secret.

She wanted to tell him, she really wanted to... but couldn't bring herself to do it.

After the sunrise on the shore, after kneeling to her Goddess, Amala spent the rest of her time in Ulbaros devoted to Fatemeh's pregnancy. It kept her busy enough to centre her thoughts on something practical, rather than the inner mess of her brain now tainted with a trail of moonlight.

She knew nothing of her new power and didn't want to know. The only time she had reached for it was to conceal her scent.

Hawk was incredibly intuitive, picking up clues, and spotting microscopic differences — piecing it all together in a matter of minutes. That's why he was so good at his job. Another reason why Amala tried to conceal the moonlight scent which haunted her dreams.

Now she was back and with Hawk right in the middle of his investigation, the Goddess matter was a pressing issue. She felt selfish keeping it to herself, but what could she do?

She needed to understand her role, learning to accept it herself before telling anyone else.

Goddess Amala.

It sounded so, so wrong.

Not only would she have to keep it from Hawk, but from her sisters too.

Attend Helioneis and bless the Goddess' altar, the extinguished candle, and worshipping an energy now secretly alive inside of her. All the while pretending she didn't know anything more about the next vessel, and lie. Lie to her priestesses, to Medyr, to Hawk and, most of all, herself. Amala had lied to herself from the moment she woke up, praying it was all wrong, all fake, that the energy would pick someone more worthy.

Liar, you are worthy.

She ignored the wise part of her brain, as she had done so often lately.

Don't tell Hawk, she reminded herself. Anything but that.

She couldn't, *wouldn't* let it slip, whatever the cost.

☼

"Enter," Hawk said, briefly lifting his gaze from the laptop. He was at the Prior Palace that afternoon, reading all the notes gathered regarding the Charal women. Cairo entered, the door closing swiftly behind him with a twist of his wind — rain and grapefruit following.

"I got it."

Hawk's eyes snapped wide, the notes on his laptop instantly forgotten.

"How?"

Cairo was already grinning. He took the seat in front of the desk, comfortably sitting as he reached for the pocket of his leather jacket. Extracting a small hard-drive, he placed it on the desk in between them.

"Here," he nodded his chin, "It's all in here."

"I asked *how*?" Hawk repeated, picking up the hard-drive and inserting it into his laptop.

Cairo shrugged, smug.

"You know me, Captain. Ask and you shall receive."

That was true: Cairo never failed at getting the right information, regardless of where Hawk sent him. His work was neat, precise, and incredibly well done. Though Hawk wasn't sure *how* he managed it, but didn't complain as a new folder appeared on the screen. Turning the laptop so Cairo could see it too, he clicked open the file: it was several pages long, with additional pictures and reference links.

"I haven't really read into it, yet." Cairo admitted, "I thought we could give it a look together. But I can tell you the basics."

Hawk, currently skimming the first page of the report, absently nodded.

"So, this dagger the buyer was searching for, it's called the Dagger of Phule," Cairo started. "It's a Charal legendary weapon forged during the birth of the tribe and has been with them for millennia. Somehow, it survived each persecution, but it's all written there, with details, too. The story goes all the way until two persecutions ago, then it stops." A pause. "Because, since then, the Dagger has been at the Riza."

Hawk's back straightened. "At the Riza? Here in Aglatas?"

Cairo nodded. "Yes, it's under Atalman's protection and apparently incredibly well guarded." He pointed to the screen, "The Charal women use the dagger to reunite themselves. After the first persecutions, they scattered around and couldn't re-join forces. It was too dangerous, too complicated, with the risk of the — how do they say that?"

"Charal killer? *Kantazar*," Hawk answered, the name ready on his lips.

He had researched Charal symbols for days now. Thanks to Hebex and Medyr's help, he had been able to identify another one. *Kantazar*, as it was written on the tunnel walls, was a symbol of two diagonal arrows above one another, pointing upright.

"The Dagger acts as a sort of talisman. If a Charal woman invokes the clan using the Dagger, they *must* go. They must reunite and help, guarded by the Goddess. The Dagger protects them, it's like a pact enforced between them and a Goddess of the past." Cairo went on. "But two centuries ago, during the last persecution, it got stolen — or better, *kantazares* were paid to steal it, to ensure that, even if the Charal survived, they could never reunite again."

"You think this is why they haven't?" Hawk interrupted him. "They can't without the Dagger?"

"I don't think they *can't*," Cairo said. "Perhaps they can reunite in smaller clans. But to reunite the whole tribe, they would need the Dagger."

Hawk considered. This was an interesting breakthrough. He hadn't found a motive for the Charal women to link them to the case, but things were beginning to come together. Cairo's eyes studied the screen. "So, the buyer wanted the Dagger?"

"Not *the* dagger. Information on it. Do you reckon the Embers would have been able to find the same info that you did?" A moment of silence followed his words.

"Man, that hurt." Cairo pretended to touch his heart in mock outrage, "Of course not. There's no fucking way anyone but me could ever get this intel."

Hawk knew better than to ask how he had managed it. Cairo wouldn't say.

"Do you send nudes in exchange for information?"

Cairo snickered but Hawk continued, adopting a more serious tone.

"So, the dagger is at the Riza." Hawk stated, reading further down the file. Atalman would require a formal letter — personally delivered — before even remotely listening to his queries.

Cairo seemed to think the same.

"If you're about to ask me to go lick Atalman's ass—"

"Not lick," Hawk countered quickly, "More like ask him nicely for an audience."

"On your behalf?"

"Please," he said.

Cairo raised an eyebrow, amusement glittering in his eyes.

"Why can't you do it?"

"You know why. The Protectors like power games, especially with me."

He hated playing by their rules. One thing Hawk had learned in the decades spent by Harat's side, was that dealing with the Protectors was easy if one went along with their expectations. Nyla was the kindest of them; he had rarely interacted with her outside of the Round Room, but she was a gentle soul with noble intentions. Ana, her Second, was much more wicked; if it wasn't for her fortunate crush on Hawk, she would have been a pain in the ass to deal with.

Jaren was a complete asshole. He liked everything that Hawk despised, operating a policy of enslavement to those under his rule for centuries. Jaren ensured the idyllic peace of Pyramis was effectively mirrored by his neat, deep underground net of gang members. Hawk didn't allow himself to think about the Phoenix — the less he allowed the assassin in his thoughts, the better.

The Protector of Air, Raila, had always been nice to him, but only because Hawk was an air-bearer. Raila was different from the others: they cared little for politics, power, money, or honour. They simply cared for absolute order and wellbeing among their protected.

Raila and their court lived in a villa in the middle of Anemos, always ready to receive and help people, though not assisting with the chaos outside their district borders.

Atalman was probably the most approachable of the four Protectors: he didn't mind helping, and seemed to like Hawk. However, he had precise and specific customs. In order to talk to him, it was necessary to show your respect.

Which, if Cairo was ready to help, shouldn't pose much of a problem.

Except Cairo did not look inclined.

"I'm not gonna do that."

"Need I remind you that I'm your boss, Cairo? You'll do it because *I* say so, end of discussion."

Cairo opened his mouth to retort, though chose the wiser option of saying nothing at all.

Hawk didn't like to pull rank on his friends, but he desperately needed to get to the Riza, and soon. Whatever was necessary, he would do it.

"You're being a bitch, Captain."

"And you get paid to be *my* bitch," Hawk replied. "No hard feelings."

Cairo snickered as he pushed his chair back and rose.

"I'll let you know how it goes."

Once he had left, Hawk read through the report again. The Dagger of Phule had a long, miscellaneous history. Passed from tribe to tribe and place to place, it became more complicated for Charal killers to find and steal it. One detail in particular caught Hawk's attention, but he redirected it to a remote corner of his mind, only focusing on it once his thoughts were clearer.

His phone buzzed. New incoming message.

He had asked Amala to come to his office for rope-play that afternoon, as he would need to work until late. He sent her a text to ask. Amala had reluctantly agreed, the text now reading:

I'm here. What do I say downstairs?

Followed with hundreds of puppy emojis.

Right. She needed a reason to enter the palace.

Hawk quickly typed back:

Just tell them you have a meeting with me about the case I'm working on. Say that you're late and I'm waiting for you.

Her reply buzzed a second later.

I'm not late.

He chuckled, putting his phone down. The thought of tying Amala up in his office was nothing short of divine; he rarely allowed himself to fantasise about it, but sometimes couldn't help himself, desperate to tell the world she was his mate, to tie her up and fuck her on his desk, making her scream until she would forget her own name — keeping her busy before the Karale meetings and daydreaming of seeing her enter the Round Room full of rope marks.

A knock at the door.

Hawk sincerely prayed it was her, because his last thoughts had triggered quite the scent from him.

"Enter."

The door opened with a creak as Amala swiftly entered the room. Hawk sent a tendril of air to close the door behind her, while her eyes settled on him.

"Good afternoon."

"Hello, Amala mate. Everything good downstairs?"

Taking a second to look around, she sniffed once.

"Were you busy?"

Little tease.

Hawk decided to play dumb.

"What?""Why are you horny?"

Oh, she was blunt. The corners of her lips curved into a smile as she approached his desk, her anklets clinking with every step taken.

"You're here," he breathed.

Amala scoffed a little, biting her lip as she blushed.

"Stop teasing," she murmured, sitting down. Her voice sounded normal, yet Hawk detected the tension in her movements.

"Are you alright, Amala?"

She continued biting her lip, then the inside of her cheek. She didn't reply as Hawk opened one of the drawers, rifling through the equipment needed for their session.

"Just a bunch of thoughts," she said finally, her voice small. "Can we not talk?"

Something was off.

"Sure," he said reluctantly, "Is everything good, though?"

Amala nodded, but he didn't buy it. From the moment she came off the train, she had been distant. Why would she come to his office if she didn't feel like being around him?

But now he thought about it, he should have known better. Amala was a people pleaser. He had asked her to come, knowing she would do anything for him.

She leaned against his desk, a smile fixed to her lips. It wasn't a real smile, though, merely polite to protect his feelings.

"You didn't want to come here? We can stop."

"Hawk," Amala said, a hint of impatience in her voice. "I'm fine. Stop checking, stop overthinking. I'll tell you if I want to stop."

He obeyed. He started working in silence, and only spoke to give Amala basic instructions. They didn't talk much during rope-play usually, but this silence felt stiflingly oppressive.

"Hands."

Amala extended her wrists to Hawk. He wrapped the rope around them: two times. She seconded each movement, her breath steady and gaze unfazed, almost vacuous. Amala was lost in her thoughts and, no matter how desperate Hawk was to know what was going on, she didn't want him to ask. So, he didn't. Perhaps that was why she had come to his office today, to surrender to the ropes in an attempt to silence her thoughts. Hawk continued to focus, proceeding to tie her whole body without asking any more questions.

There was a knock on the door.

Amala instinctively tried to whip her head to the sound before realising she couldn't move. Losing balance, she slid dangerously close to the edge of the desk, her body twisting, while blessing Hawk with the sight of her beautiful, thick ass.

She cursed.

"Busy!" Hawk shouted in the door's direction.

Zale's voice resounded clearly a second later.

"I just need a minute," he said, but the hint of amusement in his voice revealed he knew exactly who was in the office, and why he wouldn't let him in.

"Open that door and I swear to the Goddess, I'll fucking resign."

Amala gasped at those words, but Hawk didn't look at her. He walked to the door where Zale still waited.

"Alright," the Prior's voice chuckled. "I'll be back later."

"No. I'll come to your office once I'm done."

"Once you're done doing what?"

"I'll resign, Zale."

The Prior laughed and walked away. Hawk locked the door, then returned to the desk.

And *fuck*.

He was so used to close contact with Amala during their session that he rarely took his time to observe her from a different perspective. Now he could see... what Zale would have, had he entered the office.

A beautiful woman with creamy skin and silver-white hair hogtied on his desk, red ropes tightly wrapped around her body, her arms, wrists, back and shoulders — her delicious thick thighs and decorated ankles.

Hawk might have dislocated his jaw from gaping at her, but Amala...

She didn't tease him.

She said absolutely nothing as his scent threatened to fill the whole room. She could definitely smell it, though said nothing as Hawk's raging erection got the best of him.

It confused him: happy or sad, Amala would never give up a chance to taunt him, especially in a moment like this. She loved pointing out how bad he had it for her. But she looked utterly uninterested, and Hawk felt nervous beneath her icy stare.

"Are you sure you're—"

"*Orangery*. For fuck's sake Hawk, untie me now."

She might as well have struck him.

In ten years of practice, Amala had never — *never* used their safe word like that. She would deal with the pain, the fatigue, the effort with no problem, but now — this was the first time she'd ever used it because she was *uncomfortable*. Hawk rushed to his desk, making quick work of untying the principal knots and helping her out of the ropes.

"I'm sorry," He untied her wrists and started massaging her skin like he usually did. But this time, Amala tensed under his touch and snatched her hand away.

"Fuck, sorry," Hawk repeated.

He desperately wanted her to tell him what to do, or what not to — something to help deal with this weird, unusual behaviour he had never seen before.

Amala stood too fast, dizzy from the blood rushing through her muscles. Falling over the desk with her upper body, she gripped the edges to stabilise herself.

"All good." She said, without looking at him. "I'll see you at home."

And without saying another word, she left.

CHAPTER 28

A mala cooked him dinner. It was the least she could do after the way she treated him at the Prior Palace. She had been rude, impatient: the total opposite of who she usually was. Amala had hated herself the entire time, but she was so scared of being her normal self in case the truth slipped. She couldn't risk it.

Something in her gut told her Hawk couldn't know. Not yet.

And besides, it wasn't the first secret Amala had kept from him. There was something else she hadn't told him yet: something vital, haunting her every single day... that he couldn't know. She wanted to tell him — really wanted to. She probably would soon.

She would tell this secret, and the vessel one. She could swear it.

So, she cooked him dinner, hoping he would forgive her.

Which he did; in fact, Hawk apologised too, and said she didn't need to explain herself.

Yet in the two days that followed, she kept her distance. Attending the local library, she borrowed several books on midwife techniques, manuals she had studied decades before. While she could recite page by page, she needed an excuse to avoid him. Hawk didn't complain.

Probably he was wondering what was wrong with her, but at least he had stopped asking.

Amala isolated herself, occasionally making small talk, and cuddling Howlite in her free moments. At night, she wished for nothing more than to reach for him, to sleep on his chest and breathe his scent. Instead, she stayed awake for countless hours trying to accept that her Goddess was gone, replaced by her until the last of her days.

That morning, she went to the Home of Waters, unsettled further by the clash of water energy. Praying and chanting, she knelt in front of the altar, worshipping an energy currently lodged in her own soul. Amala couldn't risk going to Helioneis.

She couldn't risk seeing her priestesses and keeping silent. To see Hebex and keep silent.

She had been normal with Seryn — or she had tried, at least — and the priestess didn't ask one question, or question her behaviour at all, which relieved some of the pressure she had been putting on herself. But when she arrived home in the early afternoon, Amala instantly knew her state of internal balance would be challenged soon.

Hawk held a letter, carefully reading each word as she approached him silently.

"Everything good?" she asked.

His gaze settled on Amala.

"Atalman summoned us."

That was all Hawk said before preparing to leave.

Amala barely had a chance to speak as she was urged to hurry, following him to the car.

Following Hawk downstairs, she hoped he would explain what was going on: why was he suddenly interested in Atalman? Had he done something wrong? Was this about the case?

Until today, Hawk had been categoric: the less she knew, the better. Why was he involving her all of a sudden?

Amala didn't like the way he asked for everyone's help but hers. He sought help from Hebex, for Goddess sake, before asking *her* — his mate, for advice!

She closed the car door and fastened her seatbelt.

"Listen," Hawk said, switching on the engine. "I wanted to keep you out of this; I was scared as fuck that if you knew something, people would have another reason to get to you. I *am* scared. But Atalman wants you to come too so I need to tell you what's going on."

And so he did.

Apparently Amala had missed a *lot* while she was away.

Hawk explained every detail: starting with the two most dangerous gangs in Aglatas who had benefited from the last unbalance. Then their visit to Pyramis, where they found out about some anonymous buyer who asked for blueprints of the Yonium.

"We managed to ask Wahine to find a copy for us. She did, but it took time. While we were waiting, we focused on whatever else the buyer had asked from the Embers."

Records, apparently, from 20031. That's why he had been studying the annals when they had talked about the Charal persecution. And an object — some sort of dagger, he said, that Cairo investigated.

Amala knew of only one famous dagger, but didn't voice it as Hawk said nothing further.

Gea was beautiful: she loved Anemos, but Gea won as her favourite district in Aglatas. It was a shame she wasn't there often, but she loved to officiate at the Riza in occasion of the Earth Games. The temple was a work of art; the scent of forest reminded her of home — of Mhelani. It was a small temple built with incredible care and exquisite skill: the circular altar room felt like the inside of a tree, the air charged with the promise of harvest.

The roof was a canopy of flowers and leaves, enchanted against bad weather, and allowing sunlight to glow upon the white stoned floor.

Amala had beautiful memories of the Riza: her sister Sinayla was born there, already a priestess before joining the Yonium.

And with Sinayla, right at the Riza, Amala shared love for the first time.

Yes, that temple held her whole heart.

She bowed to Atalman with a beautiful smile on her lips, as simply the thought of being in this space once more filled her heart with pride and joy.

He watched her carefully.

"Good morning, High Priestess."

"Thank you for letting us in," she bowed again. "It means the world to be allowed in here."

"You will always be welcome in the temple, High Priestess Amala."

Amala wasn't sure if he was being nice because Hawk was there, but minded nonetheless. She never felt at ease in front of the Protectors and, if Hawk's presence helped, she was glad.

Atalman faced Hawk then, "You want to know about the Dagger?"

"Yes, I want to know what *you* know."

Amala found herself surprised whenever she heard Hawk talk with such ease. Sometimes she forgot he was above the Protectors. But the tone he used — and the way he used it... she felt safe standing beside him.

"I'm not sure this is going to help you at all," Atalman started, "But when I read your request, I thought you might find it interesting."

"Why did you want to speak to both of us?"

"You're in charge of the investigation, so I thought you ought to know."

"No, not me." Hawk replied, a hint of annoyance in his voice. "The High Priestess."

Atalman eyed her, then. "Serabel asked about the dagger, too."

Amala stilled. It had been a while since her Goddess' name was spoken with such familiarity. Though Atalman had been Protector of Earth for centuries — he had known Serabel for far longer than Amala.

She held his gaze, deep brown eyes quietly observing the way confusion painted her face.

"What?"

The Protector nodded gravely, hesitantly searching for the right words. He knew Amala was extremely attentive to how people spoke about her Goddess.

"She was—"

You, Amala.

She ignored the mental interference, focusing only on Atalman.

"She was strange, High Priestess. I'm not saying this to disrespect her, but she *was* acting different. She came months ago, asking about the dagger, asking to *see* it."

"What did she want to know?" Hawk asked.

"Just its basic story. Though it was strange she didn't know about it, as the dagger was a gift from a former Goddess."

Amala's breath hitched as she surveyed Hawk, then Atalman.

"We're talking about the Dagger of Phule, right?"

Hawk turned to her with a mask of surprise on his face.

The Protector nodded. "I presume you know all about it."

"Not exactly," she countered, "I know it's a symbol from the Charal tribe, and Serabel mentioned it to me a few times when she was researching with Dhara."

"The Dagger of Phule is indeed a Charal symbol." Atalman explained. "It's the only way the tribe can be recollected. They will *always* answer to the Dagger of Phule. And we were to keep it, so they could not be assembled again."

Amala froze. Did Hawk know that already?

"Was Serabel planning that? To reassemble the Charal?"

"I was hoping you would know the answer to this."

Amala's heart sank. What was her Goddess doing, dealing with Protectors without telling anyone?

Reassemble the Charal *with* the Dagger? She knew Dhara had been sent to find any remaining women left in the tribe. But this? Serabel barely mentioned the Charal women to her once Dhara left.

"I'm sorry, my Lord Atalman, I do not know. Goddess Serabel lived with heart-breaking guilt from what happened to the Charal women under her rule, but she never involved me in such plans."

"And what do *you* think?"

"Me?"

The question caught her by surprise. Not only because Atalman had asked for her opinion, but for the responsibility that came with it now that *she* was Goddess. Unable to hide the tears in her eyes, she whispered.

"I don't know what to think of it. If any Charal woman are alive, I wish I could hug them and apologise on behalf of the other High Priestesses who did this. I am proud of my title, but *this* has never sat well with me. To know that some of us abused our position to commit such cruelty."

Her voice quivered as she wiped a solitary tear from her cheek. The story of those women was so heart-breaking that she couldn't bear to think about it, to realise the women who'd formerly covered her role were at fault for it.

"Did Serabel ever mention the prophecy, at least?"

Amala's head snapped up.

"What prophecy?"

Hawk tried to remember Cairo's report, a hint of confusion in his voice as he spoke, "A prophecy is bound to the Dagger of Phule. I'm not sure what it says, but—"

"It's unknown to most," Atalman explained. "What is written can be read only *on* the dagger, carved onto the blade. Serabel asked to see the dagger so she could read the prophecy."

"Did you let her?"

"I didn't. I wonder if she discovered the prophecy through other means?"

But Amala shook her head. "Not that I know of."

She had no wisdom to offer as she studied Hawk, trying to understand the thoughts behind his face. He looked troubled, and she didn't know if her own behaviour from those past days was a contributing factor, but she didn't like it. She felt troubled, too. A part of her was desperate to tell him the truth.

But she couldn't. Not yet.

"What does the prophecy say?" he asked.

"I don't know exactly," Atalman answered. "I read it a long time ago to remember it now. It's about the Charal women reuniting. That's the meaning overall."

"And Serabel wanted to read it?"

He nodded.

Hawk gritted his teeth, "Can *we* see it?"

Amala released a small gasp. *No*, a part of her said. Who was she to access something so important, something denied to her own Goddess? Was it that fundamental to read the prophecy?

But she knew Hawk was thorough and wouldn't miss the chance.

"Not now." Atalman's voice was deep, yet gentle. "When Serabel died, I couldn't help but wonder if her desire to see the Dagger was linked to what happened to her. I am sorry I denied her. I would like to help, if only to make up for it. I'll arrange for you to see it."

☆

Hawk didn't realise Amala knew more about the dagger. But after talking with Atalman, he knew the conversation about Serabel had been crucial for her. And for him too: for an instant, she was his Amala again. In an instant, he saw her grief, confusion, surprise, and her emotions the way they were before she had left for Ulbaros.

Though it didn't last long: the distance had immediately retuned and Hawk couldn't wrap his head around it.

Had he done something wrong — offended her in some way?

"How are you feeling?" He asked carefully.

Amala looked at him. "I'm alright."

"Alright or good?" he teased, the same game she'd pulled on him only days before. Fuck, it seemed a lifetime ago. Amala was only gone for a week, what could have possibly changed since then?

Did she not like Aglatas anymore? Did something go wrong with the birth?

He cursed himself for not thinking of it before. He should've asked.

"Was something wrong... with the birth?"

Amala dropped her bag on the ground, cursing under her breath as she kneeled to pick it up. Her voice was shaking when she replied.

"N—no. Everything was fine. My patient was happy and... everything went well." Though her tone said otherwise.

But she nodded repeatedly, so unconvincingly that Hawk worried, for a second, that the birth might have actually gone wrong. But she wouldn't lie about that, he realised.

"Alright." He said, trying to change topic. "How do you feel about what Atalman said?"

"What do you mean?"

"About this, Amala mate. Serabel inquiring about the Dagger or Phule... you can see why it doesn't exactly fit with our investigation."

She considered.

"How does this change your lead?"

Hawk knew Amala wouldn't like what he was about to say.

"Well, I initially thought the buyer wanted the dagger to use against Serabel."

"Maybe they found out she was interested in it and wanted to gain advantage. It's very difficult to have leverage on a Goddess."

It was his turn to consider now. That wasn't a bad idea. Hawk mentally complimented Amala's intuition, though his mind remained fixed on his original thought. "What if it was the opposite?"

Amala stilled. Quieted.

"What opposite?"

"Atalman said Serabel wanted to see the dagger, but he didn't let her. What if—" he paused, anticipating her reaction. "What if she had no one else to ask, and resorted to the last option?"

Amala bit her lip. Her energy whirled around them in restless circles.

"She went to the Embers and asked them for information she couldn't find anywhere else. What if *she* is the buyer?"

He knew he fucked up as soon as the words left his mouth. Amala flinched, taken aback by his insinuation.

"You said the buyer asked for other things, too." she murmured, and glanced behind her shoulder as if someone could hear.

"Records from the 20031st year, yes. I thought it had to do with Jaren becoming Protector, but *you* told me about the Charal persecution. And then the Charal popped up in the tunnel too. And now Atalman? It's no coincidence."

"It never was a secret that Serabel was researching the Charal, Hawk." Amala countered, voice steadier now.

"Researching, yes. But what about reassembling?"

The question left her breathless as she peered over her shoulder again. "What are you saying?"

"I think she wanted the dagger to reassemble the Charal."

"The Charal women are blessed by the Goddess. She wouldn't need the dagger to call them to her."

"Yeah, forgive me," Hawk retorted, "I'm not sure they would reassemble for the Goddess who was in command when they were all murdered."

She stiffened. Hawk sucked in a breath, regretting his word choice immediately. He opened his mouth to apologise, but Amala was faster.

"Explain the blueprints, then. If you say Serabel was the buyer, why the hell would she need blueprints of the Yonium? She owned the temple."

"She needed a cover." Hawk continued, "It would have been easy to link the buyer to her, if she spoke to someone about it. If she was stupid enough to tell Atalman, I wouldn't be surprised if—sorry," he added quickly, but it was too late.

"If she was *what?*" Amala repeated.

"I'm sorry, I didn't mean it like that-"

"Are you calling my Goddess *stupid?*"

"No. It was a mistake. What I meant is it's never wise to speak with any of the Protectors. They're wicked, you know that better than me. Serabel was a kind soul but it's never a good idea to share plans with them."

Amala opened her mouth to reply but stayed silent. Hawk regretted calling the Goddess stupid, he shouldn't have. Amala was already miles away, now seeming to get even farther from his reach.

"Explain to me, please," her small voice went on. "How is this linked to her death? Even if she was the buyer, which I genuinely don't think she was, how does this have anything to do with what happened if no one was trying to enter the temple?"

"Oh, someone *was,*" he replied. "Someone with a giant motive, with Serabel snooping in their business."

Amala brought both hands to her face, horrified. "You don't mean that."

"The Charal women killed her."

The silence that followed was so loud Hawk felt forced to lower his gaze: Amala's icy eyes sharp enough to hurt.

"No."

"No, what?"

"No, you're wrong." She said, her voice a sharp edge. "Serabel wanted to protect the Charal women; they knew that. They wouldn't kill her."

Hawk released a breath. This conversation was going to be more difficult than he originally expected.

"I'm not asking you to agree in your heart, Amala mate, but look at the evidence. Serabel was researching the tribe, wanting information so unavailable that she had to resort to crime to obtain it. She was interested in a dagger that is a pure Charal symbol and part of history. It all links back together."

"No it doesn't."

"Be fucking reasonable. I understand why you don't want to believe this, but I'm asking you to look at the facts—"

"I *am* being reasonable!"

"You aren't, Amala. Your judgement is biased, you're not being objective."

Her mouth dropped open.

"Fuck you, Hawk."

"Calm the fuck down, Amala!" he countered, "Do you think I haven't noticed? You have been so damn different since you came back!"

Her wind hit him in the face: a rush of frozen air with cinnamon undertones. There was no warmth, no sunlight. Amala relentlessly fidgeted with her hands.

"I won't stand for you disrespecting my—*your* Goddess, that's what's going on."

That's how it was going to be then. Amala keeping secrets and pretending like it wouldn't affect him in the slightest.

He huffed a forced laugh, arms thrown up.

"You know what? Do whatever the fuck you want."

"Thanks for your permission, Captain." She snarled, turning her back to him. "Go to hell."

☼

She sent him a text.

I'm staying at Helioneis tonight. See you tomorrow.

The audacity...

Hawk wasn't like that. In all the time they had spent together, not once had he disrespected the Goddess. But now he called her stupid, blaming Serabel for her own death.

Amala leaned against a pillar, watching the sunset from the outside porch.

Was she exaggerating this?

Did this feel bigger than it was because *she* was the Goddess now? Did she feel offended because Hawk had disrespected her Goddess for the first time, only after she had become the new vessel?

Amala wasn't stupid. She understood Hawk's theory, saw the thought process that brought him there.

She just didn't want to believe it.

☼

"If I had known Blade *and* Cairo bailed — and you would be moody as fuck — I would have saved myself the trip."

Naressa's red hair was a mass of fire, contrasting with the glow cast from the sunset as it trickled through the windows. It felt incredibly wrong to associate the sun to anyone but Amala, but Hawk sent the thought away — not tonight. Tonight, he was fucking mad.

"I'm not moody, I'm pissed." Hawk replied, rubbing the paper between his fingers until satisfied with the shape of the joint.

"Alright," Naressa shrugged, taking a sip from her glass of wine. "What happened?"

Hawk stormed to the opposite sofa, slumping into it with no trace of his usual decency. Holding the joint in front of her, Naressa lit it with her fingertips as fire danced across her red nails. He nodded in thanks and brought it to his lips.

"Nothing."

Naressa hummed, her brow furrowing slightly. Hawk inhaled and ignored her.

"I know you better than this, Captain."

He exhaled.

"Do you have any insight on the body, yet?"

She wiggled her eyebrows. A pure, damn vixen, she was.

"Tell me why you're so moody, then maybe I'll tell you."

Alright, Hawk thought, inhaling again. She wanted to play? He would play. If only to distract himself from the incumbent thought lodged into his brain.

"Amala and I argued. She's not coming home tonight."

Naressa immediately dropped her vixen expression, "Fuck, Hawk, I'm so sorry—"

He waved her off; he couldn't talk about Amala without exposing his true feelings, especially if he was high. That was not the best move to use with Naressa — not when he still planned to keep from her that Amala was his mate.

"Do you think she'll come around?"

He shook his head.

"Our lead... it seems like Serabel is involved more than we ever suspected. She might have been part of the same process that got her killed. I told Amala and she freaked out."

"What did you say?" Naressa inquired, tone husky and low.

"I might have called Serabel *stupid*."

"Hawk Mercurian!"

"What?"

"You insulted her Goddess! Of course she got mad!"

"I did apologise," Hawk immediately countered. "And she was mad way before that. She's unable to see the Goddess having an active role in all of this — I don't blame her, Serabel was everything to Amala, but I can't deal with her emotions while I'm on this case."

"Maybe start dealing with your own emotions, first." Naressa's lips quirked.

Hawk scoffed.

"I'm *trying*."

She took another sip of wine, then stood, strolling to his couch. Gracefully, she sat beside him.

"Well, it's not working," her beautiful red lips moved sinfully as she spoke: slow and steady. Hawk knew what she was doing.

Naressa knew him well enough. While she didn't know Amala was his mate, she could see how much he cared for her. She knew how miserable he was feeling now, and knew he needed a distraction.

Was it that wrong if he wanted it too?

He inhaled again, and she stole the joint from his lips, taking a hit.

"Any suggestions?" Hawk sneered.

Naressa pouted, then exhaled the smoke into his face. His sneer widened to a grin. She was a player. He knew that, because he was the one who taught her the game. Sliding a hand on his thigh, she halted, red nails tapping against his trousers. Amala never had red nails, they were always white. He pictured how she would look dressed in red, nails to match.

"Hawk?"

Shit. He mentally prayed to the Goddess to force Amala out of his head, so he could focus on the woman in front of him.

"What?"

Naressa stared at him through her beautiful, deep violet eyes. They weren't icy, but...

For fuck's sake, just stop.

"So..." Naressa quietly asked, sensing his doubt. "Where is she, now?"

"Temple," Hawk grunted.

He wanted to think of anything — anything or *anyone* else. Anyone but Amala and her face: a portrait of distance and a wall between their souls, right where their bond was thriving merely days before. Naressa seemed to understand.

Hawk's eyes slid to her full, red lips.

"I'll listen to your rant after you make me cum," she whispered, silvery voice a taunting caress.

His canines were out in a moment.

Naressa grinned and leaned in to kiss him: ylang-ylang and vanilla. Her mouth was felt soft as she moaned, Hawk's teeth scraped her lower lip with his canines — not enough to draw blood, but enough for her scent to engulf him completely. His hand slid to her back, reaching for her red locks; he pulled her hair back, baring her throat to him. She whimpered then tried to kiss him again, but Hawk shook his head.

"Tell me what you want," he ordered, voice so low it was barely audible.

"How many can I pick?" she managed to say, panting.

He only grinned.

"One."

Hawk brushed his lips against her neck, and Naressa cried out, "*Ice!*" so fast that he laughed against her skin. Immediately, his hands slid to her thighs as he picked her up; soon, she was locked around his waist. They kissed as he walked them to the kitchen, placing her on the island. Drawing back for a second, his grey eyes burned into hers.

"Clothes off, vixen."

Naressa moaned in his ear, her scent flooding his brain in sparks of fire and ylang-ylang. It wasn't cinnamon, but—

Fuck, not now.

Not now.

He wouldn't think of Amala now.

CHAPTER 29

Amala was too mad at Hawk to go home. This wasn't like her, to run away from problems or confrontation — perhaps confrontation, sometimes. But not with Hawk. She had never been afraid to tell him something, never been so hesitant in his regards. Maybe she should have told him about what happened in Ulbaros, instead of putting distance between them.

Amala wasn't a fan of her own behaviour recently, but her emotions were getting the better of her.

She had gone to Helioneis because she needed something different: sunlight, more sunlight and divine energy powerful enough to counterbalance hers. Aarush wouldn't be at the temple, but his energy drenched the place regardless. It was more than sufficient for Amala to sleep a dreamless night.

For the first time since she was chosen as vessel, she woke up *rested*.

Amala enjoyed a normal breakfast with Hebex, cuddling Sinayla and her beautiful pregnant belly. A normal morning, like she used to before everything happened.

Before Serabel died and she took her place.

To be in a temple after what had happened in Ulbaros, that was difficult. Not only was her energy pushing to be recognized, it reached to experiment, to play.

And when she had prayed to her Goddess with her sisters that morning, they had prayed to *her* without even knowing. All those beautiful prayers, Love and intentions directed solely to her, and she had no idea how to deal with it — or any idea of what to do or how to behave.

What did Serabel do?

By her side for more than a century, Amala observed in adoration everything she did. What did Serabel do when they prayed to her? The second she found a moment of peace, she promised herself to meditate and reflect on the matter, on how heavily it weighted on her soul.

But not now. Right now, Amala needed to go home and tell Hawk she was sorry for how she reacted. Cry her heart out to him in honesty and explain everything that haunts her. Hawk wouldn't judge her for it. He would hug her and help her and repress the need to kiss her until she felt better and teased him about it.

Goddess, she should really stop teasing him about it.

She would tell him.

Would tell him that she was the new vessel.

Would tell him sorry and wouldn't tease him for the kissing part.

She would tell him everything.

☼

It was the stupidest decision he had ever made.

After Naressa left, he tried to sleep with no success as Howlite snored beside him. Hawk wanted to take back everything that had happened in the hours before. But he couldn't sleep, so he took Howlite for a walk and, when the walk didn't calm him, went for a drive.

Driving worked.

Driving allowed him to take his mind off things, putting an end to the constant overthinking rampant in his mind. Though it was clearer now, he was an idiot and needed to go home, wait for Amala, and tell her straight away. Perhaps she would be angry and would have every right to be: he broke their celibacy pact after promising to share it with her, fucking another woman instead. He didn't know if she would forgive him, but he wouldn't keep the truth from her.

Hawk got home, taking off his jacket as Howlite trotted inside. The morning was chill, the air a soft crisp which did little to make him feel any better. But there was always breeze in Anemos.

Maybe he should make Amala breakfast. Hawk sighed, unsure of what to do or how to tell her. Breakfast seemed like a good start.

Aiming for the kitchen, the first thought in his mind was to clean the fucking mess him and Naressa had made the night before.

But Howlite was already curled on the kitchen floor, and Amala was there.

Her body stilled, facing the other way.

"Is that her scent?" she murmured. "The ylang-ylang?"

Hawk froze.

Fuck, no.

Not like that.

Anything but this.

"What?" Hawk asked.

Slowly, Amala turned towards him, her face an unreadable mask of calm and stillness.

"Naressa's scent. It's all over our—*your* kitchen. All over your house." She whispered.

Hawk's heart ached at her words — no, it didn't *ache*, it cracked.

Like a stab to the chest.

"*Our* house," he tried, but his voice was hoarse and his words wouldn't convince even himself.

"Whatever," Amala shrugged.

Hawk couldn't bear watching her shield from him like that, the wall between them reinforced as Amala encased herself in it again.

"I was going to tell you," he swore. "Literally as soon I saw you, but you got here first and—"

"Enough," she countered, raising a hand to interrupt him. "It's alright. I—I told you that you could back down from the celibacy pact at any moment. It wasn't your thing, it was mine." Biting her lip, she added, "*Is* mine."

"No," he tried, but his brain was foggy, his thoughts confusing — *fuck, fuck, fuck*, he had known it was a stupid idea from the beginning. "No, Amala, listen—"

"There's nothing to say," she refused to look at his face.

"I'm *sorry*," Hawk tried again, "I didn't mean to..." He didn't mean to what? Fuck Naressa? Betray her trust? Their pact of being celibate? Didn't mean to fuck another woman in their house? Didn't mean...

Fuck, he didn't mean any of that.

Any.

"I said it's alright," she repeated. She lingered there for a second and Hawk realised she must have only just arrived home from wherever she had been.

But she moved, walking to the door and passed him without a second glance. Hands poised around the handle, she turned a final time.

"Goodbye," Amala said. And for the third time in what seemed a damn short amount of time, she left and didn't look back.

☼

It hurt.

Amala's heart crumbled with every step taken to the Home of Waters. Hawk didn't run after her when she left attempting to patch things up and, while she thought things could be fine that morning, now she was more confused than ever.

Her mind was a constant overlap of guilt: would Hawk have slept with Naressa, if they hadn't argued? Would they have even argued if she had revealed she was the new Goddess? Did the celibacy mean anything at all, now she no longer needed to be celibate?

She knew no answers, but the strong energy of the Home of Waters steadied her restless heart. Amala sat on the floor, meditating against a pillar when her sisters came.

"What's going on, love? You look like you could use a hug." Seryn said, sitting next to her.

Amala shook her head. "Nothing. I'm fine."

"You most certainly aren't," Seryn replied, sweetly. "But it's alright. Is there anything you need?"

Amala looked into those green eyes she couldn't hide the truth from, and had never been able to.

"Can I cry a little?" Amala asked.

Seryn's eyes softened at that. "Of course."

Turning to Teleia, she asked her to fetch some tissues.

Amala let the tears slide down her face, then. Tears she had retained since scenting Naressa all over Hawk's house — *his* house, not theirs.

"Did something serious happen, High Priestess Amala?" Teleia gently asked upon returning. "Are you healthy? And safe?"

Amala nodded, a spark of gratitude in her eyes as she smiled to the priestess, reaching for her hand.

She reached for Seryn's too, then murmured, "Hawk slept with his lover."

"*What?*"

"No!"

She nodded again.

"She has a beautiful scent, it's so rich and I felt it the moment I arrived home."

"Wait, he slept with her in *your* house?" Teleia blurted, eyebrows snapping upwards.

"It's *his* house."

"It's not!" Teleia argued, "You guys are mates and live together. It's your house too."

The High Priestess sighed.

"There's just so many things... of course I'm mad that he broke his celibacy. Maybe I shouldn't have expected him to keep it, perhaps it wasn't important. But when he decided it, he was so serious. I told him he could back down whenever he wanted, but he told me there would be need, and now..."

Voicing her thoughts allowed her to rationalise the chaos in her head: Amala felt guilty for so much, including Hawk too.

"I'm not saying it's my fault." She added, "But we never said we were exclusive, we agreed we could keep seeing other people until we mated and I know if it was down to him, we would have mated already. Possibly *months* ago!" Amala bit her lip. "I've been putting this off the entire time; I keep teasing him and making him wait and — well, I could have avoided all of this."

Hawk wanted to mate her, ready to start things months ago — years perhaps — regardless of their mating bond. Amala wasn't ready. Or at least, she hadn't been. But the way she felt now made her reconsider: did she feel like this because she was ready to commit?

"I *know* he regrets it. But I'm..."

"Hurt," Teleia finished for her. "Which is completely fine and valid."

"It's just that... this, and Sinayla is about to give birth and Hawk doesn't *know* about..." Seryn instantly squeezed her hand. Her fingers were always so warm and soft.

"It's okay, Amala," she whispered, "Do you want to tell him?"

Amala shook her head.

"Yes, but not now. Not today—" A pause while she recollected her thoughts. "He'll have to know, at some point."

"You decide when, my love," Seryn said, Teleia nodding with her.

She said nothing for a while, enjoying the warmth and closure of her friends: those two beautiful women who had mated in front of Goddess Serabel and the rest of the priestesses, the Yonium shimmering in pure moonlight to celebrate.

Amala knew Seryn and Teleia were mates from the second she had seen them together. And that had been a funny moment, she recalled with a nostalgic smile, because when Teleia had moved to the Yonium, Amala had taken one look at her and called dibs, literally.

But Seryn had been faster: she had pinned Amala against a wall and bared her teeth at her, hissing, "Don't you even dare. She's *mine*."

Amala had known better than challenge her. She used to guess mates miles away and Seryn's behaviour gave it away even before the priestess herself could realise it.

And now they lived at the Home of Waters and worshipped their Goddess, loving each other deeply.

Such admiration in Amala's eyes as she watched them kiss.

Their love was so pure and real and raw and beautiful...

"I am almost tempted to ask you to make love for me," she playfully whispered.

Teleia looked back at her with a blush on her cheeks. Seryn had a mischievous smile, her deep lavender scent overpowering her mate in a second.

"Anything to cheer you up, Amala."

☼

"You are one dumb motherfucker."

It sounded like Blade had been wanting to tell him for a while now, because he looked damn smug as he judged Hawk from the other side of the desk.

"I know," Hawk replied with greeted teeth.

"No, but you *are*." Cairo added, the smugness only amplifying.

Hawk rolled his eyes. "Yeah, I know, thanks."

Cairo just stared. Blade looked thrown off by the news. Both of his friends had been *surprised,* to say the least, when he invited them to his office only to rant about his stupidity and how miserable his life was. Both were happy to tell him off.

"Why did you do it?" Blade asked now, serious.

Hawk shrugged.

"I've been asking myself the same fucking question."

But that was not the truth. He *knew* why he had done it. His brain seemed to find it a perfectly valid reason just a few hours before, even if now he only felt the dumbest male alive.

"I wanted to get her off my mind for one fucking second. I missed her like hell last week but since she's been back, she is so different. Distant. She was never like this before and I don't know what I've done to make her feel like this because she wouldn't tell me or talk to me *at all*. It was driving me crazy."

Blade blew out a breath, and Hawk knew he was considering his words, deciding if they were enough to spare him a lecture.

"Okay. So, you cheated on her?"

Hawk took the hit with his head held high — but for God's sake, it fucking hurt.

"That's a low blow, Blade. I didn't cheat, me and Amala are not together." Hawk hissed.

"She's your mate, for fuck's sake."

"We've been fucking other people for the past ten years, it never mattered that we're mates!"

Never mattered to her.

But Blade didn't seem to care, baring his teeth at him. Hawk felt the disappointment in his feline gaze, usually so bright; he didn't expect his friend to be so protective of Amala.

Cairo intervened. "So what, you didn't decide to be exclusive when she moved in with you?"

Hawk shook his head. "We never said that. We talked about our mating bond snapping soon and her celibacy for the present moment. I told her I'd share the celibacy with her; she was against it at first, but then agreed. Yeah, I fucked up."

Fuck, he had been so stupid.

"I don't get it, man." Blade said, calming somewhat. "Amala is the *best* thing that ever happened to you, you've been a totally different person since you met her, and now? You disrespect her like that?"

Hawk scowled. He didn't need to hear it, he knew Amala was the best fucking thing in his life.

"So, what did she say?" Cairo asked with a subtle note of curiosity.

"Nothing. She said she knew celibacy wasn't my thing and left."

Blade hummed, cocking back his head, and muttering something beneath his breath. Hawk let it go, deciding Blade had every reason to despise him.

"Well, she's not going to like Naressa now." Cairo commented.

"I wouldn't be so sure, she's not like that. Besides, this is Hawk's fault. Not Naressa's."

Cairo tilted his head towards Blade. "Then what? I would get it if she was jealous..."

Hawk snorted, "Amala doesn't get jealous. She's mad because I broke her trust and our pact. There's no coming back from that." He let out a breath. Idiot, he was an idiot.

"Maybe you should tell Naressa, hmm? That you and Amala are mates?" Blade casually suggested.

"Yeah, maybe. She can whip my ass and apologise to Amala, probably pulling her just to spite me."

Cairo chuckled, his next words voicing Hawk's exact thoughts.

"Probably. But you would deserve it."

☼

That was awkward, Amala thought as they waited for the elevator to reach the last floor.

She had bumped into Hawk downstairs. It was a total accident: both had attempted going home before the other in blissful avoidance, but it didn't work. Instead, they had accidentally met outside of the building without saying a single word.

And the elevator ride was the longest twenty seconds of Amala's day. Of her fucking life. When they finally entered the apartment, her energy was tingling to be released — maybe a bath would calm her.

As she moved to reach the bedroom, Hawk spoke for the first time.

"Do you—"

Amala turned to him, "Pardon?"

There was so much in his eyes, her heart couldn't take it. Intuition told her he was going to offer her the other room to sleep in, but she wasn't sure of her answer. She didn't want to sleep away from him; while the air between them felt wrong, separation felt worse. Amala wanted to run herself a bath, calm down, and clear her head.

Then he said, "Do you want *me* to sleep in the other room?"

Amala froze. He wouldn't take the sunrise away from her, wouldn't trouble her for what had been *his* mistake.

"Why?"

Hawk's eyes shot to hers: grey met ice and she refrained from sighing. He had a way of looking at her that was so intense, as though he could see all of her and loved every piece.

He opened his mouth, "I just thought—" but whatever he thought, he didn't say.

Amala couldn't bear to see him like this, or stand the expression on his face as he faced the struggle of communicating with a fucking *wall*, she knew. Amala was acting utterly unsufferable, while knowing the right thing to do would be to apologise and explain why she had been so distant.

But she couldn't bring herself to do it. Not yet.

"Don't do it, please. I still feel safer with you, Hawk."

CHAPTER 30

H e had fucked things up forever; Hawk was absolutely sure of it. The worst part was he had no idea how to resolve this mess. Even Howlite seemed to despise him, picking Amala's side of the bed for two nights in a row now.

Of course, Amala continued to sleep utterly, fucking naked as she lay mere centimetres away, waking him with her aroused cinnamon scent. Hawk knew she wasn't doing it on purpose, but it felt like a well-deserved punishment to see and live by her side without being able to tease her, touch her, or make her laugh.

Hell, they barely spoke at all.

Sitting on the couch, he checked his notes about the buyer one more time. Amala could be as mad as she liked, but it didn't make the Serabel theory any less plausible.

Hawk understood why Amala was offended by his claims, he really did. But he also knew better than letting his emotions guide the case: it never led anywhere good. Regardless of how he wanted Amala to feel, she was sworn to the Goddess — there was no impartiality on her end.

His gaze indulged on Amala sitting comfortably on the opposite sofa, Howlite's head resting in her lap. She scribbled away in her planner, a meticulous record of all her clients and appointments.

Amala lifted her gaze, meeting his grey eyes.

"Everything alright?" she asked.

He had stared for a good few minutes, if not more. Hawk quickly nodded, muttering *sorry* before returning to his notes. Then looked at her again.

"Listen, I'm sorry about the other day." He said, "I know I—"

"I don't care about you and Naressa," she lied, interrupting him.

Hawk started, weighing his words.

Carefully, he added. "I didn't mean Naressa. I meant what I said at the Riza."

She let out an *oh* of surprise, eyes wide. Hawk realised his phrasing sounded like he didn't regret fucking Naressa at all.

"I also didn't mean what happened with Naressa," he added, hoping to clarify.

"I don't care," she repeated, but avoided catching his eye.

She did. She did care.

"I'm sorry I have offended your Goddess."

Amala's eyes snapped back to him, sharp and thundering. He made an effort to hold her gaze, but damn, he had never seen Amala like that. She looked... terrifying.

"She's *your* Goddess, too." Amala hissed.

Howlite growled quietly, as if sensing the disagreement between them.

"Amala, I am not taking back my theory. It does make sense and until we get any further clues to prove otherwise, it's the best we have so far. But I'm sorry for my insensitivity when mentioning Serabel."

"She *can't* have done what you said." Amala whispered.

"She was investigating the Charal women. She wanted the Dagger of Phule to reunite them."

"It doesn't work like that! Only a Charal can wield the Dagger of Phule and reunite the tribe!" Amala countered. "Didn't you listen to what Atalman said?"

"How do you know so much about it, anyway?" Hawk asked.

"For fuck's sake, Hawk! I am High Priestess. *My* kind is at fault for the slaughter of the Charal. And for every day of my life, I have tried to be better than them, to be ready to help the Charal if the chance ever presented. I studied them too — not *as* much as Dhara perhaps — but I did my best to learn everything I could so that I could continue Dhara's work if something went wrong!"

He paused, pondering each of her words.

"I thought Serabel didn't share her research with you."

Amala scowled.

"She didn't, but Dhara did. I knew Serabel was fixed on them, but not to the point where she would deal with the *Embers*." She paused. "Serabel made Dhara study the Charal. She didn't know so much herself, but they tried their best. We kept Charal traditions, we remembered them as much as we could. I thought it was because Serabel felt guilty, but then I discovered Dhara was planning to leave to search for them. It was a few years before she left, when she told me I would be the next High Priestess."

She sighed, as though recalling the memory brought back unwanted feelings.

Hawk didn't want to pressure her into talking, but he needed her to be *present* with him — even if that meant arguing, anything was better than the radio silence from the past few days.

Amala cleared her throat.

"At the Yonium, we honour the Charal women daily. But we do it as a part of our routine, our habits. We use their chants, their traditions, and carry a part of them with us forever. Sometimes, on a Full Moon, we tell their stories. Serabel wanted us to keep them alive, but not to endanger ourselves by continuing what was forbidden, or attract Charal killers to the temple. It's a sort of habit for us, rather than intentional behaviour. We're used to it, but it's a priestess thing, not a Charal thing. Over time, everything mixed; it was the only way to keep the transmission going without risking the attention of whoever wanted them dead."

She pet Howlite behind her ears, the hound growling in approval as her body sprawled on top of Amala's. The High Priestess released a muffled moan but smiled. "Hello, love. Are you comfy?"

Hawk swallowed, his heart hurting at the sight of them so close yet so far from him. Grimacing, he forced himself to say, "When Atalman tells me I can see the Dagger, will you come with me?"

She would say no.

After last time, there was no way she would go with him.

But Amala lifted her head from the couch, pressing a kiss on top of Howlite's face, and nodded.

"Yes."

☆

Helioneis was shining under the midday light, Amala admiring its beauty.

The Yonium lit up too, but in a different way. Each temple reflected the light of its power, its source: the same way Helioneis reflected sunlight, the Yonium mirrored the moon.

Eyes running across the plane that separated the temple from the river, Amala cherished the feeling of the sun against her face, basking in the warmth and familiarity she craved and loved.

"You might as well move here forever, you know."

She gasped, turning to find Medyr beside her.

"What?"

"If you love the sun so much, I mean."

"You know I do." She chuckled.

Medyr nodded, observing her. "Do you want me to call for Hebs?"

Amala shook her head, a soft smile thanking him for the offer.

"No, I don't want her to feel sad for me," Amala shrugged. "Does she like living with you?"

"Jealous?" He grinned.

"Of course, I am. I would fuck her too, if she liked me."

Medyr burst out laughing, Amala grinning back.

"She would probably say yes, if you asked her nicely."

"Ah, I'm not going to try. I don't think I could handle the rejection."

Medyr wasn't Hawk, and he never would be. But there was a time in Amala's life where he could have been.

Just like Amala, he was born and raised at the temple. His father had been a priest and his mother a devoted follower of God Darnen. Medyr was only a few years older than Amala and they had known each other forever; building a strong, beautiful friendship as children, though drifting apart once Amala's father, Faurn, left this world, and Medyr was made High Priest in his place.

"I spent a good deal of time with Captain Mercurian when you were gone." Medyr said.

She knew about it: Hawk had told her, in his rushed explanation in the car as they drove to the Riza. Medyr and Hebex had helped him with the tunnel, and provided background on the Charal women.

Tilting her head, Amala said with nonchalance, "Yeah?"

"Yeah."

"How did it go?"

"He has this fancy house in Whisper... and a dog?"

What? Medyr had been to her house? Amala mentally cursed for viewing it as *her* house, and reminded herself that it was Hawk's house. *Hawk's*.

Though it felt wrong to call it anything but *theirs*... it also felt wrong that Medyr had been there without her knowing, like an invasion of privacy.

That was her house. Her dog. Her Howlite.

But she forced a smile, "Howlite, right? I like her."

"You've been there?"

She shrugged, "A couple times. H—" she paused. "—*Captain* Mercurian has a spare flat downstairs; he usually rents it so I'm staying there."

"Oh," Medyr said. "He didn't mention it."

Even better, she thought.

"So how was he?"

"Better than usual, I guess," he replied. "But it's strange to be a part of his case. How is he treating you?"

She repressed the urge to roll her eyes.

Breaking promises and fucking other people.

Amala felt guilty for thinking that; she told him it was fine and she didn't care.

But of course she did.

She knew it was her fault; if she hadn't been distant, if she had allowed Hawk into her mind over the last few days, weeks, months, then none of this would have happened. She could only blame herself for Hawk choosing to spend his time with someone else, even if he said it was a mistake and she had seen the truth in his eyes. The regret. How long could Amala expect him to wait for her?

Directing her anger at him was easier than feeling angry at herself for allowing the chance to escape.

"Alright," she whispered to Medyr. "He's alright, I guess."

"Then what's wrong?"

How he noticed, she had no idea. Though if there was someone she could share her thoughts with, it was him. The counterpart to the High Priestess.

Medyr.

"I miss Serabel so much." She breathed.

Medyr reached for Amala's hand, though stopped before touching her, placing his own beside hers instead.

"I am so sorry, Amala."

"Did you feel like this when your God died?"

Medyr considered. Didn't reply right away. Allowing the memories to consume him, he lingered in his mind a while longer, likely cherishing the last moments spent with God Darnen.

"Yes, I felt hopeless. Probably how you're feeling now, but..." he hesitated.

Amala remained still, peering into his amber-green eyes.

"What?"

Medyr didn't look like he wanted to finish his sentence.

His energy shifted around him, almost retreating, leaving behind a trail of cedar and eucalyptus.

Amala's voice was barely audible, a whisper broken by pain as she repeated, "What?"

"When God Darnen died, fifty years ago, it wasn't that long after you lost Faurn."

She stilled, his words slowly setting in; the mention of her father was enough to send her into a quiet, humming silence.

"I know you probably have never thought about this, Amala," Medyr said now. "And I don't blame you, I never have. But when you lost Faurn... I lost him too."

He sensed her reaction, but Amala wasn't talking. She wasn't even moving.

INGRAM EVEN THE GODDESS AND THE HAWK COPY COPY

Wasn't everything bad enough already without Medyr involving her father in this? Her Goddess was dead, with no idea of who killed her. Amala was picked to be the next vessel, Hawk had slept with another woman, Sinayla was likely hours away from giving birth and...

Amala tried to focus on what he was saying, his feelings. He was opening up to her because *she* sought his help, not the other way around.

Amala took a breath, trying to calm the rampant thoughts in her mind.

"When your father died, I felt exactly how you did when Dhara left the Yonium."

"Don't—she left because Serabel asked her to, she didn't die..." Amala countered.

"Well, Faurn did and I was devastated. He was my mentor, my role model and I had to take his place as High Priest. And then, just a decade later, Darnen died too."

Alright. So they felt... exactly the same.

Because Faurn had died and Amala had mourned. And then Kora had left her, too.

And then...

And then Dhara had left.

And now Serabel.

Tears streamed down her face.

And Hawk had slept with Naressa.

It wasn't the point, she knew, but among those thoughts, it felt so easy to cry about that too.

"I am so sorry, Medyr..." Amala whispered.

"I am sorry you're going through this now."

"Any advice?" she sniffled.

"Keep close to the ones you love the most. You already know that always works."

CHAPTER 31

Amala was slightly calmer when Hawk had picked her up from Helioneis two days ago. They didn't speak much though, and she remained set on keeping her distance. While her voice was softer, her eyes were not — mind somewhere miles away.

Asking him if she could walk back home today, Hawk had not been keen on the idea, but admittedly left her be while she wandered around Aglatas without him as an escort. He couldn't blame her for not wanting him around. According to their latest lead, Amala was slightly safer too. If the Charal held something against Serabel, they wouldn't bother Amala — not with the case still ongoing.

Hawk's phone rang.

His eyes didn't leave his laptop though. Whoever was messaging could wait.

It wasn't Amala anyway, which he knew because — damn him, she had a different ringtone. She was also still useless with her phone, forgetting how to use it, but she—

Hawk scowled, realising he was thinking of her again.

Aiming for any distraction, he picked up the phone.

Two messages appeared on the screen.

Blade Hendrix:
Get your ass here before Wahine whips mine.

Ana Sinclair:
What about having some fun, Captain?
Just sent over your info. Apàle Wharf, pier 87? Let me know.

Hawk had forgotten about Ana. Checking his emails, he found the information she had sent: the trends and tendencies of the Embers market, containing deals from the past month. No names and no faces, as they had decided. Only numbers.

He texted back:

Busy today. Case is driving me crazy, but I'll text you when I'm free. Thanks for the info.

She could wait another day — a couple of days, even — before he could think of another excuse to avoid her. Hawk had enough shit to think about, and the idea of messing things with Amala, even to save face...

No, he wouldn't risk it for the world.

Driving from Whisper to Pyramis was nice; Hawk enjoyed the way Aglatas changed around him: from the familiar soft, elegant buildings and townhouses to the opulent, lavish architecture of the Fire district. He brought Howlite with him; she liked to be driven around too. Once he had parked, she hopped from the car, wiggling her tail and sniffing the pavement.

There was no need to leash Howlite and never had been: she remained glued to Hawk's side, waiting for him to start walking before following. She was incredibly protective of him and Amala. Before rescuing her from the shelter, she had a miserable life and it took months before she warmed up to them. Once Hawk gained her trust, she gave him more love than anyone else had ever done.

Besides Amala, of course, but Hawk didn't want to think about her now.

When they reached the Den, Howlite detected Blade's scent before he did — weed, of course, clear waters and raspberries. Hawk let the hound precede him down the stairs as she hurried through the doors; Blade's surprised voice was distinct through the walls.

"Thanks for bringing Hawk's ass here, Howlite."

He snorted, closing the doors behind him. Blade raised his chin in greeting.

"Queen Howlite can be a new member of the Den," he added, nodding at the hound now curled next to him on the red leather sofa.

"She's not *that* trained against poisons," Hawk muttered, sitting on the armchair in front of him. He scanned the room for Wahine and found her at the bar, water spinning in circles mid-air between her hands.

"Hello, Captain," she purred. "I'm working. Want a drink?"

"I'll get you one," Blade stood instead, reaching for the cabinet.

Wahine twirled her fingers and the water slid into a small ceramic bowl. She kept controlling it as she added fine powder; Hawk couldn't see what it was from a distance, but she hummed carefully as she mixed, adding two drops from a tiny bottle.

Wahine took a sip from an elegant whisky glass. "What do you need my help with today?"

"First, thanks for the blueprints." Hawk replied.

"Oh, that was fun. I love reminding myself of all the power I have over the Embers." She flashed him a smile. "They don't call me Mistress for nothing."

"Yeah, I'm not gonna call you that," Blade muttered, placing another whisky glass in front of Hawk. "Considering all the orphanage kids stole our lunch, I'm proud to say they all owe you big time now. Just wait until you get leverage on the Phoenix, and you'll be queen of Pyramis."

"The Phoenix?" Wahine echoed. "I'm reckless, not stupid. I don't have a death wish, thank you."

Hawk chuckled at that, sipping from his glass. The whisky burned his throat.

"Listen, Wahine, we might have an actual lead on the buyer. I know they were anonymous, but there must be something in the archives to help us out."

"Duh," she popped her lips. "The Embers aren't complete morons. They always keep records of their clients."

"Well, that might be really useful."

"Hmm. I'm not sure," a twirl of her fingers had the water spinning again. "I have more important things to do."

"This *is* important, little drop," Blade countered.

"Don't call me that to try and get me soft," Wahine pointed her finger at him and he chuckled. Turning to Hawk, she eyed him carefully. "What's going on with you? You look miserable. Again."

"Yeah, it's not a great day."

"Why, what happened?"

"Nothing."

"C'mon."

"Nothing, Wahine. Cut it." Hawk said.

She huffed, eyeing the contents of the bowl and, after deliberating, added another drop.

"Fine," she said finally. "I'll keep an eye on that. But I'll expect compensation."

"They owe you already." Blade shrugged.

"Yeah, and now you owe me too."

☼

The Riza, again.

Hawk knew Amala loved to explore other temples, but nothing would change her mind: the Yonium was her home, it held her heart and soul.

Atalman waited for them in the altar room, face neutral.

"Good afternoon," he greeted.

Hawk nodded once; Amala bowed her head.

"Thank you for having us, my Lord."

"You don't call me that, pretty Amala."

"And you don't call *me* that, either."

She gasped, hands covering her mouth the second she realised what she had said.

Hawk, on her side, seemed to fight the urge to laugh.

"I'm so sorry," she apologised, bowing again as she blushed.

"You've grown claws, High Priestess?"

"Stop teasing her," Hawk intervened. "We have business to discuss."

Amala glanced at him, drawing a breath of relief. Though Hawk barely acknowledged her, he noticed the way her icy eyes softened. She was never as fiery as she had been over the last few days, but witnessing her words hit someone else this time was somehow pleasing.

"No time for a chat today," he added with a shrug. "Can we see the dagger, yes or no?"

It was his best attempt to sound polite, but he had work to do. No more time could be wasted playing the Protector's games.

"Very well." Atalman said. "If you will, follow me."

He turned, Hawk on his heels. Amala's phone rang — such an unusual sound: a ringtone of rain and flute melodies. It lasted all but two seconds before she picked up.

He couldn't hear what was said though, as they followed Atalman down the hallway, the Protector halting at a golden door.

Hawk turned, ensuring Amala was keeping the pace before they changed rooms.

But she wasn't there.

She stood still, twenty metres away in the atrium: body stiff, eyes wide, pale, almost shaking. Hawk had no idea what to do; was she having a panic attack or—

He quickly moved to Amala, scanning her body for any hint of uneasiness. His voice was gentle as he asked, "Are you alright, High Priestess?"

Amala lifted her gaze, breathing laboured as she fought to find the words.

"We need to leave." She said.

"What?"

"*Now.*" Her voice was harsh, anxiety coaxing through her veins.

Hawk stepped closer. "What's going on?"

"Sinayla... she's in labour."

CHAPTER 32

They arrived at the temple forty-five minutes later. Hawk had driven so fast it was a miracle she didn't throw up. She was so close to throwing up already, anyway.

No questions were asked. He saw the panic in her eyes and knew he had to drive — fast.

Amala wasn't sure of how many rules he broke as he dropped her next to the temple, to the stairs outside. Hawk had even gone off the road, trying to bring her as close as possible.

Amala didn't look back as she got out of the car, sprinting to the temple.

Some of her priestesses waited at the entrance.

One of them shouted, "*She's here!*" as they all pointed in the direction of Sinayla.

"Down on the right," someone said.

Amala ran down the hallway, reaching the last door before swinging it open without thinking. A tang of blood filled her nostrils, forcing her to pause, to consider.

"*Fuck,* thank Goddess!" Seryn cursed. Instantly, she was by Amala's side, guiding her through. The High Priestess' eyes, though, drifted to the middle of the room.

Sinayla on the ground, Caelan next to her.

And blood.

So much blood.

She held her gag.

Thoughts flooded her brain instantly and suddenly, Hebex was there.

"Hey, hey," she murmured. "It's Sinayla. It's Sinayla, my love. Your sister Sinayla and baby Xantara. And she's not—they're not going to make it unless you help them."

Amala didn't have time to think — couldn't allow herself to think of...

She wouldn't do it.

She forced herself to move.

One step at a time, Amala.

In an instant, she was beside Sinayla: the colour drained from her beautiful face, and eyes full of tears. Amala reached for her power, positioning her hands above Sinayla's belly.

"Hello, my love. It's going to be alright." She said softly, before facing Seryn. "Fill me in."

"Contractions started a couple of hours ago, and we did everything you told us. Relaxation techniques, breathing therapy, all of it. We even merged our energies to make sure Sinayla had more."

"Why didn't you call me?" Amala breathed with impatience, her hands radiating pure light.

"Because I was fine!" Sinayla moaned, the sound was strangled: *pained.*

Amala shook her head, "Don't talk."

Her energy sensed Sinayla's body, searching for the root of her pain and distress.

"Everything was fine for the first hour, but then she started bleeding and the next contraction was so, *so* painful, and then the bleeding got worse so we called you right away…" Hebex said, tamping Sinayla's brow with a damp cloth.

"The heartbeat is too slow," Amala murmured, her voice barely a whisper. Her hands started shaking. She forced herself to sit still, gesturing for Seryn to move so she could check lower.

Sinayla looked at her, face contorted by pain.

"Amala," she breathed, teeth clenched, "You'll have to make a choice. And you know what I want."

But the High Priestess met her gaze and said, "No."

Her sister hesitated at the sheer command in her tone: an order given not as her midwife, but as her High Priestess. Amala seemed to realise it too.

"Please," Sinayla said.

Amala shook her head softly, "It's not my choice, my love. It's your mate's."

She tried to look at Caelan, but failed. She couldn't bear to see his face, not while she was failing him, failing Sinayla, Xantara… all of them. Taking a deep breath, she calmed her energy. She could do this. She forced herself to face Caelan. His eyes were already on her already: sharp and worried.

"Both." He said.

Amala nodded quickly, her breath pacing.

"Both," she promised.

This wasn't the first difficult birth she had faced, nor the first haemorrhage she had dealt with. She knew what to do, knew how to save her sister and the baby.

"Here's what we're going to do, my love. Listen clearly. I'm going to heal your bleeding, but it's going to take a while and we don't have time to wait. I'll have to heal you as you push: my energy will help Xantara descend a little, and you'll be safe as long as I hold the healing. But you need to help me, alright?"

She didn't give her time to answer, beginning to steady her energy, directing it solely on Sinayla. Amala needed to keep the energy stable, targeted on her sister throughout the entire labour until Xantara was born. She could do this — wouldn't let her thoughts get in the way. Helping Sinayla into a squatting position, Amala gestured to Caelan to prop her upright, to steady her whole weight.

"Hebs," she murmured, too feeble for Sinayla to catch it, "Keep me grounded."

"I got you, Amala."

There was a spark of admiration in her eyes, as if Hebex knew exactly what was happening in her head. Seryn knew it, too. Sinayla's body tightened.

"Another contraction," Amala advised before the sharp wave of pain washed over Sinayla, her energy struggling to contain it.

Sinayla screamed pure, undiluted pain — as she clenched her fists around the blanket, nails slicing through the fabric as she dived deep into her palms.

Amala directed all her energy towards her sister's naked, aching body.

"You are doing amazing, my love."

"I'm going to die," Sinayla whispered with shaking breath, "I'm going to die and I'll never meet her — you have to save her, Amala."

Amala trembled under the power and responsibility of those words and the meaning they carried. Inhaling, tears streamed down the High Priestess' face.

Don't — don't give in.

"Listen to me, my love. You are *not* going to die, Xantara is *not* going to die, I promise you. I *promise* you."

She positioned in front of her, down between her legs, and pressed a bloodied hand gently on her abdomen, power sliding further into her body.

"Start pushing, my love."

"I'll die."

"You won't," Amala promised. "Trust me, Sinayla. I won't let you die."

Hebex reached for Sinayla's hand, Seryn by her side. Caelan was behind Sinayla, studying her face with tenderness and love. And trust.

"You've got this." Hebex whispered.

Amala knew she was referring to both of them.

And she was right. They could do this.

"Push now," Amala repeated.

A groan of pain, but her sister obeyed.

Amala's healing energy was working: it would keep her safe, allowing her to push through the bleeding. Ignoring the screaming in her head, the way her body refused to collaborate, Amala didn't let go. She needed to save her sister.

"On my count, Sinayla. Push," she breathed, hands fixed to her sister's skin.

Amala gasped on a sob as she feeling the baby's head beneath her fingers. "She's here, my love. I promise. Your next contraction is coming now, and you have to push."

Sinayla did. And again. And then again. Amala had never felt this tired as her energy fixated on Sinayla, barely remembering to breathe herself. Xantara moved beneath her mother's belly and Amala knew the time was close.

"Again, my love."

"I can't," she cried, her breath laboured as her upper body trembled in pain.

"You *can*!" Amala said. "Give me your hand." She reached for it softly, placing it beside hers, fingertips brushing the baby's head, "Can you feel her? Two more times—only two, I promise." She waited for Sinayla to nod, to show she understood. "On my count. One, two, three…"

She pushed.

Amala received the movement, hands ready — the head was so close.

Sinayla took a breath, moaning in pain, but Amala's healing power kept her grounded.

"Good job, my love. Only one more, now."

"*Now?*"

She nodded. "Now. One more, Sinayla, and Xantara is here."

But her sister couldn't do it. Sweat slid down her face, burning her eyes, and filling her nostrils. Sinayla shook her head — *no,* she cried out.

"One more."

"C'mon, beautiful. One more," Seryn whispered.

Caelan held her tightly from behind: "You are doing amazing, sweetheart. Only one more."

One more. Hebex squeezed her hand as Sinayla cried out again; Amala focused solely on the healing, on keeping her sister safe in this final effort…

And then… one more push and the head was out, the baby's body sliding right into her hands as Xantara's first cry filled the room.

And Amala almost cried herself, hearing that sound.

No, she did cry. Amala held the small, fragile body in her hands as tears slid down her face. Relief, worry, and something else — something she needed to let out.

She turned the baby, revealing Xantara to her parents.

"You are a mom," she whispered. "Congratulations."

Sinayla sobbed, exhausted, but plucked enough energy to extend her hands toward the baby.

Seryn passed her a fresh blanket as Amala quickly cleaned the baby's body, returning her to her mother. Then Sinayla picked her up and the next sob was stronger, more powerful, as Xantara cried out again and... Amala looked at Caelan.

He watched his mate and baby, utterly hypnotised as he reached one finger to touch that small, delicate baby hand.

But she cleared her throat, capturing his attention as she handed him a pair of sterilised scissors.

"The cord," she nodded with her chin.

Amala kept her energy focused on healing as Sinayla delivered her placenta, not daring to release until she was certain the danger had passed. It took her a few minutes, mentally thanking Seryn and Hebex for keeping her up. Their own energies lingered, soothing Amala's sweaty brow, taking care of her where she was failing to.

Once she was finished, Amala finally stilled: a quiet, silent calm setting in her eyes as she took into the sight of Sinayla and Xantara. The baby was beautiful: it looked more like Sinayla than Caelan, with clear eyes ready to embrace all the beauty in the world. Sinayla studied her in awe, as though she couldn't believe *she* had made that, creating such a beautiful creature which now rested in her arms.

Something in Amala's chest cracked.

Hebex saw it, instantly reaching for her.

"Amala, look at me," she whispered. "It's alright. It's *alright*. We can go outside, if you want."

But the High Priestess shook her head, refusing to turn towards her. She couldn't turn away from Sinayla and her daughter or her *mate*, Caelan, right beside them. A solitary tear slid down her face, and Amala didn't breathe, scared her breathing could break too if she tried to speak.

☼

She needed a moment.

She left them in the room, the priestesses and the priests unhurried but excited as she told them they could take turns to see enter, one or two at a time.

Sinayla was exhausted, but Amala had spent every drop of her energy to heal her, to save her.

Now she was exhausted, too. She had almost lost her best friend — her *sister* and new-born baby — all at once.

If that had happened, it would have been her fault.

Hawk waited outside the room; she gestured with her head to a different hallway, somewhere more private. She didn't feel like being around people, now.

When he lowered on the floor, she sat next to him: she was brief in her words, explaining what happened, the reason why she was so tired. As she spoke, she gave in to her negative thoughts: she had tried to force them from her mind during the labour, but now she let them consume her.

Hawk instantly noticed something was off.

"What's going on with you?" he said, eyes searching for a sign on her face. This wasn't simply exhaustion, he could tell — something else haunted her.

Amala's features remained painfully blank. She felt drained, lost in her thoughts, her mind.

"Talk to me, Amala mate. Please just talk." Hawk pleaded, worry etched into his face. He reached for Amala's hand, stroking the back of it as he tried to bring her back to reality. To him.

She breathed, closing her eyes. Once they reopened, she could see him again.

Her pupils shot back at him, searching for him, for…

"Hawk."

"Are you all right?" he asked, unable to hide his relief.

Amala nodded.

"I…" she sighed. "Sorry, I got lost in… bad thoughts."

"Do you want to talk about it?"

Yes, a part of her whispered. *Please, tell him.*

"I don't know."

"Is this something you wish to keep private?"

No, I want you to know.

Please, tell him.

Amala bit her lip, nervously wiping the tears away. She knew it was only a matter of time before she would need to do it again.

"It's not something I want to keep from you. I feel like you should know, and I feel so guilty that I haven't told you yet. And—" she paused. *And it kills me that I have to tell you now, in this moment.*

Hawk studied her, repeating, "You don't have to tell me, Amala mate."

And maybe the fact that he looked so sure — so sure that he didn't need to know the reason, as long as he could remain with her, by her side — perhaps it was that which convinced her.

"I'll tell you," she breathed, voice shaking. "But hold my hand."

CHAPTER 33

Hold my hand, she said, and Hawk did just that. He intertwined his fingers with hers, squeezing her palm, and sending gentle tendrils of air to soothe her face: so exhausted from the tears.

Not to mention the energy she expended healing Sinayla.

Her whole body looked on the verge of breaking but she stayed there, eyes low and breath steady. Hawk wanted to reach for her, hold her... but kept his distance.

Held her hand.

"Promise me..." she started, "Promise me you won't hold back, whatever I say. Please."

Amala looked so small, so fragile and defeated, he would do anything to take that away from her.

He nodded, "Promise."

"This is bad, okay?" Amala said, "I—I don't talk—I don't even *think* about this when I can avoid it, and I'm *sorry* I never told you before, but—" tears streamed down her face, breath turned uneven, as though she couldn't *bear* to think of it...

"Amala," Hawk said, "I'm here. Whatever this is, I'm here and I won't judge you. I could *never* judge you for anything, do you believe me?"

She shook her head, his heart cracking at the gesture. How could she possibly think that?

"You *will* judge me, and that's okay. I deserve it, I—" she cried, and Hawk longed to whisper in her ear, revealing he wanted nothing from this life but her. Only her.

"Listen to me." He said, repressing his need to reach for her, "Nothing, *nothing* you say will change a single thing between us, Amala mate."

Hawk prayed she believed him.

"This could change *everything*."

"I don't believe that."

She shook her head again, pursing her lips as she fought against her thoughts and spirit, and then...

"I don't think I can have children."

The words were uttered, nearly silent, as if she had never spoken them before.

Hawk's gaze met the icy, wide doe eyes of his mate, now crusted with tears and drowning in pain. So much pain.

I don't think I can have children, the words rumbled in his head; he would never forget her soft voice breaking as she murmured them.

He didn't know what to say: he felt her pain, saw it painted on her face and body, a burden kept for Goddess-knew how long.

"What makes you say that, Amala mate?" Hawk gently squeezed her hand.

She closed her eyes, hiding her pain and true feelings... Hawk couldn't stand it.

Couldn't stand to have her so near, yet so far.

They had never spoken about children, barely discussing their future together, aside from Howlite; Hawk thought back, trying to remember if their own, future kids had ever been brought up.

Amala talked about children all the time: infants, new-borns, but that was her *job*. Nothing about her own. Now looking at him, tears fell down her face as she opened her eyes again.

Hawk was there: ready to share her pain, now and forever.

"I—" she tried to say, but glanced away. "I'm not sure, I—I've always assumed I couldn't. But I've never said it out loud before."

Trust. And a will to overcome her trauma in front of him, with him. *Because* of him.

Something warmed in Hawk's chest, but he didn't allow the feeling to linger, not when his mate needed him. Gazing deep into her beautiful eyes, he carefully said, "Would you like to tell me why you think so?"

Amala nodded. Barely.

She took a breath. Then another, squeezing his hand.

"This happened many years ago."

"How many?"

"Fifty-three," she said. Another breath.

Fifty-three years.

Whatever her trauma or pain, she dealt with it alone, single-handedly for fifty-three damn years. Hawk ignored the rage rising in his veins, the instinct to claim and protect and...

He inhaled. Pacified the fury in his blood.

"What happened, Amala mate?"

A while passed as he waited patiently for her answer. Hawk knew then that once she started, she would tell him everything. And if she needed more time, he would give her that.

He would give her anything.

Amala searched for the courage to speak, but found it in his eyes.

Thoughts exposed: *I will always be here for you. With you.* Amala fought her own demons, her own fear, and then began.

"Fifty-three years ago, I had... one of God Darnen's priests was my lover. I didn't *Love* him, but we were stable. We liked to be together. Though we knew we weren't mates, and never discussed our future. And..." She paused. "I got pregnant."

Hawk froze.

His head emptying, while all other thoughts instantly vanished.

Pregnant.

Amala had been pregnant.

Hawk didn't let the feelings hit him — the claim, the jealousy, the primal need to *be* the one for her — he repressed the instincts, regaining control. His Amala had been pregnant and suffered because of it. That was all that mattered.

Sensing his thoughts, a proud sparkle glinted in her bloodshot eyes, knowing Hawk fought an internal battle of his own, and won.

"It was an accident, Hawk. The pregnancy was an accident and I... well, you know me: I wouldn't judge anyone who chooses differently, but I would *always* choose to keep the soul that chooses my womb." Amala bit her lip, her voice breaking. "Of course he didn't agree, but I suspected that already. I decided to keep it anyway. I didn't need his support, I had Serabel and Dhara, and the other priestesses. But as time went on, he grew used to the idea." A steady calm took control of her words, "Sometimes, he checked how I was doing and be *nice*, but I didn't hope for him to change his mind. I wasn't in love with him, not like that. I was okay with the idea of raising my daughter or son by myself. *Daughter*," she corrected, pain washed her face once more. "It would have been a daughter."

Amala looked up at him.

"I lost her."

Hawk's heart sank. If he thought his head was empty before, it was hollow now. Nothing existed anymore. Life itself had lost all fucking meaning, and Amala...

"I miscarried in my fourth month, and I—" she paused.

Hawk waited.

She closed her eyes, "I'm not sure I want to relive what happened. I just... lost her. A soul chose me and I failed it. She *died* within me because I wasn't able to carry her," her voice trembled, "I already was a midwife, and I was planning to give birth by myself — with some helping hands in case — but that never happened. I found it all so ironic: I'm such a good midwife and everyone praises me for my work, but my *own* baby, I couldn't keep. I felt dishonest, untrusting, and unworthy of Love, of anything..." she couldn't finish the sentence.

Hawk stilled in utter silence; he knew she wasn't done.

"And the *father* of the baby — you would think he was relieved as he didn't want the baby in the first place. But no, he blamed me. For not being able to carry her, and—"

His head was screaming, mind urging him to fucking do something, *anything*... Once again, he kept those thoughts at bay. It was about *her*, not him.

Her, his mate and her pain that she had decided to finally share with him.

A burden she had carried for a lifetime, a secret only now voiced aloud.

"Hawk, I wished so many times that I had died, on that day."

Enough. Enough pain — enough, enough, *enough*.

When would it stop?

Every damn sentence was worse than the last; how had she survived every day since?

I wished so many times that I had died, on that day...

Amala sniffled, "That's it. I couldn't keep the baby, so I don't think I'll ever be able to keep one, to... not miscarry. I'm not sure if I will ever be ready to risk it all again."

When she paused this time, Hawk knew she was finished.

Amala squeezed his hand, the small movement enough to ground him.

"Amala mate," Hawk whispered, "I am so sorry."

He didn't move, no idea what to do, but she didn't give him a chance to decide. She quietly slid into his arms, resting her head against his chest. Hawk leaned in, kissing her brow.

"Thank you for listening to me," Amala murmured.

"Thank you for telling me."

Hawk didn't know what to think: he needed to process everything she had said and relive every moment with Amala, to detect any sign she had felt this way without him ever realising.

But not now. Now she needed him, his mind lucid and there for her.

"I never allow myself to feel like this," Amala admitted, face buried in his chest. "I know most of my fear is irrational, but those memories are the worst moments of my life. And today... Sinayla's birth was too much."

Yes, because she had miscarried, and had still kept doing her job for the rest of her life. Amala was the best midwife in Aglatas and had set her pain aside to help others, reliving her trauma in the process.

Hawk kissed her forehead again, "You've been a midwife your whole life, Amala mate. Do you feel like this every time you assist someone's delivery?"

Pulling away from his chest to look at him, she nodded.

"At first, it was terrible. I would need *days* after one birth to recover, I could barely stand to look at myself in the mirror. But time helped me heal. I thought I had forgiven myself, but now I don't think I have."

The way her voice threatened to break again as her eyes glanced elsewhere — Hawk *knew* there was something else. Something she hadn't told him yet.

"Was today different?" he asked, fearing her answer.

"Sinayla..." she started, "She didn't live at the temple, back then. And, fifty-three years ago, my lover was Caelan."

She let the words sink in.

Hawk could barely breathe.

Caelan. Sinayla's mate — her sister's mate — had been her lover.

Had got her pregnant.

Had blamed her when she had miscarried, traumatising her for the rest of her life. Yet Amala still accepted to be Sinayla's midwife, saving her life and the baby's.

And...

Not now, a part of him reminded.

Not now, because now she needed him to listen.

Just listen.

Amala exhaled, "I haven't allowed myself to say this out loud yet," she admitted, "But I have loved Xantara from the moment she was conceived. But today, as she was born, I saw in her the daughter I couldn't give Caelan. Sinayla is my sister, but her baby is alive. And I know it sounds horrible, but she is alive because of me. And my daughter — mine died *because* of me."

Hawk's arms tightened around her small waist.

"I am so sorry you're feeling like this, Amala mate." He whispered as her eyes found his, lips attempting an unsuccessful smile.

"I am happy I finally told you. I was afraid you'd be angry, because this means we cannot have children and—"

Hawk interrupted her instantly.

That was the last thought on his mind. How could *that* be her fear?

"Amala, don't you even dare. This changes nothing, *nothing* between us."

When he felt her body relax, her face easing as a breath of relief escaped her lips, he thought he would cry too. For what his mate had experienced, for how all of it had caused her such fear.

"Are you certain?" Amala whispered, a hint of surprise as if she couldn't believe his words.

"I promise you."

"Oh, Hawk," she threw her small arms around him, pulling him to her.

Gently, he brushed her hair, "Does Sinayla know about this? And she still asked you to be her midwife?"

Amala nodded.

"Yes, but it's not like that. Sinayla knows, the priestesses know. Most of them were there that day, helping me get through it... And Sinayla checked a million times, to make sure I was sure. I *was*, or so I thought," she sighed. "I know they are *mates* and it's different, but as I gave her Xantara, I saw Caelan watching them and, suddenly, I was reliving all the things he said to me that day."

Hawk finally allowed a segment of his rage to rise to the surface. His knuckles tightened against Amala's skin and she gasped, sensing the sudden shift in his behaviour.

"What did he tell you?"

Amala placed her index on his mouth.

"I'll tell you, but only if you promise that, after this, we'll never speak of it again. Any of it."

Hawk nodded.

"Never." He swore.

Amala was so small in his arms, yet her soft voice was steady as she said.

"He rushed to the temple as soon as he knew, finding me in a puddle of blood. I had refused to move; I couldn't leave, couldn't bring myself to accept what had happened. I wouldn't allow anyone to touch me, but I would have allowed *him*. When he saw me..." she bit her lip, "He called me useless. Said it was my fault for losing her. Told me it was bullshit that I was ready to raise her by myself, when I couldn't even keep her in my body. He said I would never be a mother and deserved to lose her, because I wished to keep the baby against his will."

She shook her head, sending the thoughts away, forbidding them to return.

"Every single day, I still hear his voice yelling at me that I'll never be a mother."

Hawk understood, then, why Amala was so convinced she couldn't have children simply because *Caelan* had told her so. Because in the most painful moment of her life, she had searched for him and instead of support, he had hit her with that instead.

"The trauma I have from Caelan," she added quietly, "Is also the reason why I haven't been with any males after him. Besides that one time with Medyr."

Hawk just squeezed her tighter, grateful for every word she told him, for every feeling she trusted him with. "And Sinayla? How can she—" Amala pressed her finger against his mouth, halting his words.

"They're mates, Hawk. Of course she loves him, and I can't blame her for that. A mate is a mate... You would lov—" she froze, eyes widening in realisation. "You would feel the same for me regardless of what I said or did."

At her mistake, the truth neither were ready to say out loud, Hawk's heart started beating again.

CHAPTER 34

Curled up against Hawk's chest, Amala woke at dawn, breathing in his scent of midnight wind and lemon. He moved behind her, sensing her energy. His hands rested on her waist.

"Morning," he grunted, voice deliciously hoarse.

Amala shivered feeling his breath on her nape.

"Good morning," she replied.

She didn't move, afraid to break whatever spell made this moment so perfect. He blew on her neck softly.

"Did you sleep well?"

She hummed, fighting the urge to stretch against him and his beautiful body.

"Did *you?*"

He tensed behind her and she knew the spell was broken. Quickly sliding away, Amala turned to him, after creating a good amount of distance between them.

"Hawk," she murmured, "Did you sleep at all?"

Hawk turned, lying face up now, bare chest and golden skin exposed.

"Not really."

Fuck.

It had felt so good sleeping in his arms after yesterday, but not once had she questioned his feelings after their conversation. After what they had discussed, it was no wonder that Hawk had struggled to sleep. Yet for the first time in her life, she was surprised the pain — the unimaginable pain burdening her life for years — hurt somewhat *less*, when she had woken beside him today.

"I'm sorry," she whispered. "I didn't realise it would be so much to process."

"No," he interrupted, "Don't even think that, Amala. I just can't believe you've felt so much pain all this time and I've never known."

Her face softened as she extended a hand to him. He took it, stroking her palm.

"I would've wanted to know that you felt like that. You wished to die, Amala mate. I understand why you didn't tell me before but I can't believe I've been close to losing you without even realising."

He paused, his fingers a soft caress against her skin.

"You are the most important thing in my life. I am so sorry you felt that pain, and I'm sorry you had no one to share it with."

Amala blushed and thanked the Goddess he wasn't looking at her. She didn't think she deserved his sweet words, but appreciated it nonetheless.

"And I—" Hawk added, indecisiveness in his voice.

"Yes?"

He exhaled. "I spent the whole night remembering every single time someone mentioned babies to you, in these last ten years. I know it's your job and you must have those conversations all the time, but we could have avoided it—"

Oh, she didn't deserve him.

It was an effort to contain her tears as she said, "Hawk, you have *never* mentioned children. I know that for a fact. I notice these things a lot, you said it yourself."

"Okay, maybe I haven't, but what about other people? Like fucking Blade the other day…" he cursed, "At Helioneis, when he asked you—"

"—How many births I have assisted?" Amala finished.

Hawk's reply was resolute, "No"

She waited as he turned to face her.

"He didn't ask how many births you assisted. He asked how many babies you have given birth to."

Mate.

This was her mate. This beautiful male who had spent his whole night unable to sleep, reliving details in an attempt to understand how she felt — her mate. Utterly hers.

"And he said it in front of Caelan…" Hawk added, voice still hoarse.

"Yes, he did." Amala said simply.

When Blade had asked the question, Hebex was horrified, Sinayla had the common sense to not react at all. Amala had just wished to die.

"I don't deserve you, Hawk." She murmured, turning her head into the pillow.

He snorted, "I'd say it's quite the opposite, Amala mate."

She tilted her body again, eyes appearing from the corner of the pillow to watch him.

"Thank you. For everything. You have no idea how much it means to me — all of this, honestly. I should have told you a long time ago."

"You should have told me when you felt ready to. I would have waited my whole life."

☼

A couple of days passed and things had returned to normal.

Or as normal as it could be with two mates sleeping half naked in the same bed without mating or being together. Properly together. But yeah, that was *their* normal, Hawk supposed.

Pouring some juice into a glass, he handed it to Amala sitting next to him on the kitchen counter. She lifted her gorgeous icy gaze from her planner to take it, watching him.

"Why do you have the fancy glass and I don't?" Amala pouted.

Bite. Those. Lips. Now.

"You're right," he said quickly, swapping the glass with his. "Here you go."

Her pout twisted into a smile.

"Thanks."

Hawk observed her as she took a small sip, beautiful lips parting slightly, her throat bobbing as she swallowed...

He should really get a grip before *she* noticed and started teasing him about it. Though, given her behaviour over the past week, it would be a blessing to have Amala tease him again. He still had no idea why she had been so distant coming back from Ulbaros but, after everything that had happened since, he had no intention of prying.

Amala swallowed again, sensing his eyes on her.

"What?"

"Nothing," he answered, far too quickly, looking away.

Hawk swore he glimpsed a smirk.

"You got a busy week?" he asked, nodding to her planner.

Amala picked up a piece of mango from her fruit bowl. "Nothing today, but I'll need to go back to Mhelani Forest soon."

Hawk cocked his head, confused. "You miss the centaurs?"

Amala snorted. "I have two centaur patients. One of them isn't even in her second trimester, while the other is further ahead."

A bead of juice drooled on her chin as she bit into the mango; he repressed the urge to lean forward and lick it. He really needed to get his dick out of his brain.

His phone buzzed, a needed distraction from his lust-filled mind. The sound reminded him to reach out to Atalman again, to see the Dagger of Phule on a different day. After Sinayla's call, they left in a rush, but Amala was set on going with him. However, when he unlocked his phone, he discovered he didn't need to speak with Atalman at all.

"What is it?" Amala asked, eyes worried as she sensed his energy shift.

Hawk looked up from his phone.

"Atalman, he—" Hawk paused, trying to process this new information and what to make of it. "Someone tried to steal the Dagger of Phule. And died."

☼

Naressa's beautiful flame of red hair was well distinguishable among the forensic team. Conversing with one of her colleagues, she spotted him under the archway and offered a smile. With a nod of her chin, she gestured for Hawk to wait as she removed her gloves, tossing them into a plastic bag. Naressa was unapologetically confident in each of her movements, as if murder scenes unfazed her. She had been on the forensic team longer than anyone else and her skills were commended across Exanthea.

"Hello," she purred, reaching him.

"Hi, Naressa." Hawk mirrored her smile. "What happened here?"

"Is that what Cairo was looking into? The Dagger?" Naressa asked instead, voice lowered.

"You should stop snooping around when you're at his place. That's classified information."

"I didn't *snoop*. I never do, even if he does leave his laptop lying around." Naressa snickered. "He mentioned something about a dagger — nothing else but when I saw this one, I mean, it was easy maths."

"You've seen it?" Hawk asked, curiosity getting the better of him.

This was the third time in a week Hawk had attended the Riza. His whole life he had never set foot in the temple yet, somehow, it had become the main site of his investigation.

"No, I couldn't see it. It's *very* well guarded. This guy surpassed one of the obstacles before the protection mechanisms killed him. But his energy was still around, projected in the next room's direction." Hawk tried to talk again, but she raised a hand. "I already registered the evidence, the notes are ready for you."

Hawk couldn't help but grin; she knew him so well.

Not as well as Amala, but well enough to know that he'd ask for evidence the second he'd step foot on a crime scene. "What happened here?"

"I'm not really sure. I think it's a male, but he was burned alive by some fire spells. Your report has everything I was able to gather, but the biggest lead we have is one tenth of a fingerprint — maybe less... I'll ask Cairo to cross reference as much as he can while I run tests."

"He'll make something out of it. In the meantime, it's not like we can play guess who."

Hawk sighed. He would have to talk with Atalman too.

"Thanks, Naressa."

A spark flicked in her violet eyes, red eyebrows arching as she assessed him.

"You alright, Captain?"

Hawk realised this was the first time they had spoken since sleeping together a few days before. And Naressa was clueless as to everything that had happened after — no idea of the fallout with Amala, unless Cairo or Blade had told her.

"Yeah, I'm fine."

"Everything good with your High Priestess?"

She's not mine. Not yet.

"Yeah."

"Cairo mentioned that you argued."

Of course he had. Hawk gritted his teeth.

"We're fine now," he said, deeming it enough explanation.

Naressa's eyes narrowed, checking if he was telling the truth. This was more awkward than he intended; after many casual hook-ups throughout the years, things had never been weird like this. Naressa was his *friend* first. Then, an occasional booty call. And she thought the same of him. Well, and Blade and Cairo.

"Cool," she said in the end, violet eyes sparkling.

Hawk hesitated. He should...

"Listen," he said quickly. "I'm out."

Naressa licked her lips, smugness oozing from her body as she crossed her arms. "I knew it."

She looked more vixen than ever as Hawk sneered, "Yeah, whatever."

"Leaving me with *only* two choices," she smacked his shoulder in mock betrayal.

"Two very good choices, though."

Naressa chuckled. She really was a vixen, Hawk thought, and Amala would absolutely love her.

Loved her, decided to hit on her, and pull her with minimum effort, taking her to her bed.

Which currently was his bed.

He sent away the thought before he could even allow it to form. No way. No fucking way he'll ever allow himself to fantasize on that.

No.

No, no, and no.

CHAPTER 35

E very time he suspected a possible breakthrough in the case, something weird happened. Hawk had been in a bad mood for several days now, unsure about which direction to go in whilst he waited for Naressa to finish the autopsy. She was supposed to call him any minute downstairs, at her lab in the precinct.

As he rifled through his notes, Blade strolled in with a cheeky grin on his face.

"Captain," he mocked.

Hawk raised his eyes to him: he looked smug, even more so than usual.

Before he could ask what was going on, he stilled; a delicious scent filled his office — a scent he instantly recognised. Hawk didn't have time to raise his eyebrow at Blade's feigned innocence before Amala entered the room. She looked different.

Her hair was tied up in a small bun, but that was the least surprising thing about her. She wore *clothes*. Actual clothes. Hawk gaped: dressed in a pair of denim shorts, Amala wore a cropped, stretchy white t-shirt, nipples peaking against the fabric. Her heeled boots clicked against the floor as she stood before him, smiling.

"Hello."

Hawk suddenly found it difficult to speak, forgetting how to. Amala dressed like a normal person very rarely. It was odd to see her like this, yet she continued to emulate her usual light, her irresistible energy wrapping him in a warm — and incredibly sensual — hug.

"I retrieved our hot High Priestess," Blade said with pure smugness and a feline grin that Hawk imagined punching his fist through.

"You look good, Amala mate. Have you been shopping?"

She giggled.

"No, I just went to Kora's house after my visits this morning. I had some clothes there." She explained, "I would've gone shopping but... alone? I wouldn't trust myself at all."

Blade snickered, flashing his teeth at her.

"I'm down to shop with you, if you ever need help choosing lingerie."

Amala playfully smacked his shoulder.

"I'm not spending money on that." She shifted closer to the desk, sending a gentle whirl of air around his tattooed neck. "Are you worried, Hawk?"

He met her eyes and instantly calmed.

"The last murder doesn't exactly help our case."

She tried to sense his energy, examining the look on his face.

"Is there anything I can do for you? Do you want brownies?"

He chuckled at the offer.

"We can bake brownies when we get home, but now I'm waiting for Naressa to finish the autopsy."

Amala gasped, uncontained excitement on her face. "Am I meeting her too?"

Blade barely contained his laugh. Turning to him, Amala's eyes suggested she knew exactly why he found it so funny. Hawk sighed. He couldn't keep putting this off, could he?

Nodding to Amala, Hawk glanced at Blade. "Yeah, about that — why did you bring her here?"

Amala popped her lips, "Blade came home and said you looked gloomy and needed a hug. Now that I'm here, I can confirm that you do look sad."

"Enough for a hug?" Hawk suggested, gloom suddenly gone. Amala was there, surrounding him with tendrils of cinnamon-fuelled air.

She smiled back.

"Sure."

☼

Halting in front of a metal door, Hawk stepped in and knocked twice.

"Come on in." A silvery, female voice said.

Hawk held the door open for Blade and Amala as they entered before him.

"Ooh, did you bring guests?"

Naressa sounded delighted. Amala offered Hawk a shy smile as she strode in front of him, then gaped. The female before her was utterly beautiful.

"I—wow," she said, words escaping her. Naressa glanced up, spotting Amala's blush. Those violet eyes sharpened as they looked right through her; there was no trace of malice though, but she studied her with a clarity that only amplified her beauty.

Naressa had golden skin and long, voluminous red hair that draped all the way to her hips. She was not too tall, but not short either. Standing in the middle of the room, Naressa crossed her arms as her breasts slightly heaved from the neckline. Her scent was a sweet caress of ylang-ylang and undertones of vanilla.

Amala's mouth fell open. "Wow. You truly are stunning."

Silence fell for a second, Naressa contemplating the new guest with a subtle look. Hawk knew Naressa's inner reaction was very similar to the one Amala displayed. The High Priestess looked magnificent, her pale skin gleaming, while the hoops adorned to her ears added to her attractiveness. Her cinnamon scent waved towards them, and Naressa felt that, too.

"Are *you* Amala?"

She didn't wait for confirmation as she turned to Hawk, eyes sparkling, "Well, it's about time! Why didn't you tell me she was coming today?"

He shrugged, but his expression softened at Naressa's excitement.

"I had no idea Blade would bring her in."

Truth be told, he was happy they could finally meet. Hawk had always wanted to bring Amala further into his world — the people he knew, his friends, his life outside of being Harat's Second. Amala shifted closer to the beautiful redhead, extending a hand.

"It's a pleasure to meet you. Hawk has told me a bit about you. I wished I knew more but he's always very secretive of what goes on here..."

Amala gestured to the room and Naressa shook her hand, holding it for a moment as she appreciated Amala's facial features.

"The pleasure is mine, High Priestess Amala."

She winced.

"Oh, God and Goddess," Amala gestured to her clothes, "Amala is fine."

Hawk refrained from expressing his confusion; this was the first time since knowing Amala he saw her refusing her title. Naressa looked surprised too, and Amala felt their three gazes on her.

"Next time you see me, I'll be in my usual clothes and you can call me that if you wish," Amala explained. "I'll make an exception for today."

Naressa couldn't avoid another look at Hawk. Then she fixed her gaze on Amala, sensing her.

Amala's lips curled upwards with a hint of amusement and curiosity as she let Naressa assess her, understand her, piecing the clues together. Hawk anticipated it and patiently waited too.

Naressa's brows narrowed, puzzled. As if there was a jigsaw in front of her and she was moments away from solving it all. Violet vixen eyes surveyed Amala's body the same way she observed the thousands of bodies in her life, attempting to understand the story behind them.

The story was quite different this time.

Her eyes widened.

"Hawk Mercurian, I'm going to fucking *kill* you."

Hawk didn't even try to hide his grin; Blade, on his side, looked equally amused, as if he had been waiting for this moment a long time.

"She's your *mate!*" Naressa blurted, "High Priestess Amala is your *mate* and you never told me." She paused, turning to Amala. "How long have you known?"

"Since we met." Amala smiled politely.

"Ten years ago?"

Amala nodded, amused as she subtly watched Hawk. His grin was broad now, savouring the moment of messing with Naressa's head. Raising an eyebrow, Naressa repressed the urge to go for Hawk's throat.

"That's why you didn't want me to meet her. If I had—fuck, if I had known..." Her voice dropped, slightly less confident as she redirected her attention to Amala once more, "I am so sorry."

It was Amala's turn to be confused.

"What for?"

Naressa whipped her head in Hawk's direction, disoriented. "She *doesn't* know?"

A primal fury shimmered in her eyes as she looked ready to rip Hawk's head from his body.

Amala understood then, and quickly intervened.

"No, wait! I know you're his lover."

"You know?"

She nodded.

"I'm sorry," Naressa repeated. "I didn't know you were his mate."

Amala's eyes softened in an attempt to reassure her. "We're mates, but we are not mated."

"Yeah, but... wait, what?"

She chuckled. "Me and Hawk are not mated. Our bond hasn't snapped yet."

Naressa checked her expression; made sure she told the truth.

"Why didn't you tell me?" She asked Hawk.

"Would it have changed anything?" Amala inquired.

"Well, we fucked for years,"

"And what would have changed knowing he had a mate?"

As Naressa, Blade, and Hawk gawked at her, she explained.

"Everyone has a mate. You have a mate, Blade has a mate, and Cairo has a mate too. They just haven't found theirs yet... you can still have fun together. What changes knowing who your mate is or not, when your bond still hasn't snapped?"

Naressa quieted, her brain reasoning with Amala's logic. Amala smiled at Hawk and, for a moment, the room disappeared as he lost himself in her icy eyes. He would never understand the forgiveness in her heart, but would devote every day to earning it back.

Then he met Naressa's gaze: he owed her an explanation.

"When me and Amala met, we knew right away." Hawk started, "But our bond wasn't really pulling; it was just... *there*. We wanted to be in each other's lives, but there was no need to mate just yet. And we barely knew each other, so we decided to wait."

Amala waited for him to pause, then added.

"We have waited for years, but it was the best choice because we got to know each other. Hawk is my best friend; it will be worth it, when the moment comes and we swear our souls to one another forever."

Naressa's eyes softened, resting a hand on her chest, violet eyes sparkling with happiness, as if she couldn't believe Hawk had found his person in someone so incredible:

"I'm so glad I met you." She said sincerely, "I have seen you, of course, but you look even more beautiful in person."

Amala's face widened into a beautiful, bright smile.

"Thank you, love. I don't recall seeing you at the Yonium, though. I definitely would have remembered."

Naressa chuckled, a quick glance in Hawk's direction. "Oh, no. I didn't mean there. I saw you because you're Hawk's phone background."

CHAPTER 36

"**S**o you forgave him?" Hebex hummed, unspoken disagreement in her tone.

Amala glanced to her right where Sinayla and Caelan sat, the former breastfeeding Xantara while he observed with pure love in his eyes. She didn't look at Hebex as she replied, "Yes."

"And you are truly fine?"

Yes. She was fine. Meeting Naressa had steadied her heart; that beautiful female had kept her mate happy, satisfied, and content for so many years and she was grateful to her, not angry. Naressa had been on Hawk's side, allowing Amala's friendship with him to blossom with no romantic feelings in the way.

Now Amala studied Caelan as he stood, placing a kiss on Sinayla's brow. She waited until he left and was out of ear's reach.

"I told him." Amala whispered. "I told Hawk about... my miscarriage."

Hebex's eyes widened in horror, conveying nothing except surprise. The priestess had been by her side every second of that day, and an immense help with her recovery. Amala knew what Hebex's eyes conveyed: the miscarriage was not only the worst day of Amala's life, but hers too.

Holding out her hand, a daisy bloomed on her palm; she didn't hesitate to tuck it into Amala's hair. "What did he say?" She asked slowly.

Amala bit her lower lip.

"He was amazing," she admitted, "He said... all the right things. I felt so safe, Hebs."

Her sister pondered, cocking her head.

"I might forgive him too, then."

Hebex didn't respond well to Hawk breaking the celibacy pact. As the most protective of Amala's sisters, she would fiercely defend the High Priestess without even blinking. Amala had chosen not to tell Hebex right away, when the memory was still fresh and painful: her reaction often varied depending on the level of hurt caused to her friends, and seeing Amala right after she'd found out would have ensured Hebex hating Hawk forever.

Now she nudged her, chin nodding to Sinayla: the priestess slowly approached, a silky white scarf wrapped around her body to hold Xantara.

"She wants to talk to you," Hebex whispered. "Find me later?"

She didn't wait for an answer before vanishing. Sinayla looked nervous, stopping before her. The High Priestess gestured to the space now free on the cushioned bench, then helped her sister to sit.

"Are you alright, my love?"

Sinayla took an unsteady breath, fingers delicately stroking Xantara's forehead.

"You suffered, didn't you?" Sinayla didn't look at her as she spoke. Amala frowned.

"You were dying, Sinayla. Of course I suffered."

"*You* saved me. *Us,*" Sinayla countered, eyes wary. "But that's not what I meant, and you know it. Tell me the truth."

Amala braced herself. It didn't matter that Sinayla almost *died* — her baby with her — she still planned to scold her for pushing aside her pain, no matter if that meant saving her life.

"I may have had a small breakdown afterwards." Amala admitted.

Sinayla scowled.

"*Amala!*"

"Listen, it was fine, Hawk was there..."

"What if he wasn't?" There was a serious edge to Sinayla's voice. "We talked about this. You should have stopped assisting the moment you felt that way! It was our only deal—you would only do it if you were not reliving—"

"You would have *died*, and Xantara too, and I couldn't make it happen *again*!"

She startled, covering her lips with a hand. Sinayla gaped too. The silence between them became thick, stretching for what felt like minutes.

"I—I'm so sorry," Amala murmured, "I didn't mean it like that. It's— "

"Is that why you did it? So you wouldn't fail him again? Caelan?" Her voice was almost harsh, and Amala couldn't bear it. She shook her head, fighting the tears.

She didn't want to cry, not again. She hadn't been able not to cry even *once*, in her life, when talking about this.

"It's not," she whispered, silently pleading for Sinayla to believe her, "It's not, I swear it."

"Amala, you don't owe him anything," she said, a hand reaching for hers. "I don't care if Caelan is my mate, he was terrible to you. You don't *owe* him a baby." Noticing the harshness in her tone, her face softened. "My love, I am sorry this happened."

"No. I am grateful I could assist your birth. I am grateful I could help you bring Xantara into this world. I thought I could do it without a problem," she admitted. "I prepared for months."

She had. Since Sinayla confided that she was expecting, Amala had exercised, reliving her miscarriage over and over, reliving Caelan's words so that she wouldn't break if they came to mind during the labour. Sometimes, she relived it without breaking. But not always.

"I thought I could do it," she repeated. "But when things got complicated, it suddenly felt very difficult. Sinayla, I know he would never act like that — not to you, he's your mate and he loves you. But I didn't want, not even for a second, him saying those things to you. Or blaming me again."

Sinayla tilted her head, cautiously. "Blaming you again?"

Amala closed her eyes, exhaling.

She felt stupid for thinking that, but... "I was afraid that, if anything went wrong, Caelan would say I did it on purpose in... *vengeance* for all those years ago." It felt even more stupid to voice it and immediately she wished to take it all back.

But Sinayla shook her head, understanding in her eyes.

"My love, if he had done that, I would have killed him with my own hands."

☼

The ropes were so tight, and Amala loved it. The ropes and the way Hawk was able to drag her to the edge of pain — the delicious edge she found so attractive. Pleasurable.

"Does it hurt?" he teased.

Amala wanted to reply, but the ties were too tight, the chances of moaning too high.

"I missed this," she gasped.

They hadn't indulged in their sessions since the last time at the Prior Palace; even now, she felt guilty for how she had treated him, the wall she built between them. She should have been honest rather than using their safe word as a weapon against him. Hawk halted behind her, momentarily letting go of the rope.

"I missed this too, Amala mate."

Both were not merely referencing the rope-play, they knew it. No, it was the familiarity, the safety and comfort of something so theirs that every other thought vanished. Amala had missed this. Them. The way they usually were together — not High Priestess Amala or Captain Mercurian.

Just them.

Amala and Hawk.

She felt him pick up the rope once more, beginning to slide it between her legs. The rope needed to drift on her crotch, connecting to the one already wrapped around her chest. But the *way* he moved, so skilled and precise, without a single second of hesitation — oh, she loved his confidence.

Amala held her breath as he kept moving: Hawk working in silence, eyes focused on the ropes. Out of all those times he became distracted by the thought of her body — she knew it, catching him so many times before — their sessions were when it happened the least. They were both equally determined to do a good job rather than enjoying the sight and feel of each other. However, he was making it painfully difficult for her, right now, to focus on anything except his hands. The coldness of his rings against her skin, his fingertips brushing against her back from time to time...

She tried to move, the pressure on her intimacy felt so deliciously painful: sinfully good.

"What do you think you're doing?"

Amala's knees went weak at the sound of his voice, the sheer dominance in his words.

Oh, he knew.

"Nothing," she managed to say.

Hawk clicked his tongue, "Nothing?"

Amala hummed unconvincingly, whelping when she felt a tendril of air snake across her body. "Hawk—" she warned, but he just chuckled. She caught a glimpse of his canines and couldn't help fantasising of how good it would feel if he were to reach out and bite her.

Amala wasn't celibate anymore, she could kiss him and be done with it. Kiss him, taste him, bite him, finally telling him how much she—

"Whatever you're thinking about, get a grip. I can't focus on what I'm doing if I'm breathing in your scent."

☼

"This is worse than I expected."

Hawk exhaled in agreement while Zale scrolled on his tablet, wincing at the close-up pictures of the corpse.

"That's disgusting."

Hawk didn't need to look again at the man whose eyes had been carved from his skull: another victim to gang violence, the ultimate example of how the death of the Goddess kept things constantly on edge.

"We'll take extra measures to prevent it from happening again," Zale was saying now. "I'll have to talk to Jaren again."

"It's not the Phoenix," Hawk quickly said. It couldn't be — the Phoenix liked to torture victims, yes, but had a different style of execution. Carved eyes came only after the rest of the body was slaughtered too.

"The Embers are under Jaren's control for a reason," the Prior countered. "He needs to regulate them better than this. He can order the Phoenix to do it for all I care, but this cannot happen again."

"This is plain gang violence, Zale. It may not be linked to our case at all."

"That's not a good reason to let it go."

Hawk shrugged.

"Agent Vesper is still busy with the last autopsy, but—"

"Let Naressa do her work. I'll put someone else on this." Zale replied. "Any news on the Goddess?"

"Former or next?"

He wouldn't say something like that if Amala was there; currently, he waited outside the Home of Waters for her. Zale had joined the drive so they could recap any progress in the case.

"Both."

"No news about the vessel. But Serabel was in deeper shit than we thought. Something about her plans seem off — either I'm missing a giant link, or she was far cleverer than she wanted us to suspect."

The Prior sighed, "You need to finish this, Hawk. As soon as you can."

"I'm trying, boss." Hawk gritted his teeth, gaze drawn to the temple's entrance as Amala stepped out, hand raised to cover her face while she searched for him and once her eyes found their mark, a bright smile painted her face. Amala walked down the steps with quiet grace, white robes swinging and — somehow — never failing to cover *that* part of her body. Hawk forced himself to stay still, focused on keeping his canines retracted.

Not in front of Zale.

To be forced to watch that white robe swaying, but *never* revealing Amala's body was pure torture — as was sharing a bed while she slept naked beside him, knowing he was unable to touch her.

Zale sensed his discomfort, shooting him an amused glance.

The High Priestess bowed before the Prior, beautiful light in her icy eyes.

"I'm honoured by your presence, Prior Harat."

He offered her a smile, "Good evening, High Priestess."

Hawk surveyed her for a moment.

"Everything good?"

Amala nodded with a quiet smirk as she grabbed her wrist with the other hand, rubbing the skin on a faint rope mark.

"Good," she replied, "We had a small ritual for a priestess. It's her birthday. What's going on?"

He wasn't sure how she sensed it so quickly. Hawk watched her face change as he told her about the gang violence, the light trembling in her gaze as she flicked her fingers, holding back the restless wind brewing inside of her.

She said nothing.

He finished his conversation with Zale, while Amala remained subdued.

When the Prior left, she bowed her head, but kept silent, too.

Only once they were alone she spoke again.

"Hawk?" Her lips pressed together as she drew a long, shuddering breath.

"I need to tell you something."

CHAPTER 37

"Are you alright, Amala mate?"

A gentle tendril of air circled towards her, stopping an inch from her body as if waiting for permission. Amala stepped closer, releasing a small sigh as she enjoyed the cool breeze. She sat next to Hawk, crossing her legs in the lotus position.

"I am fine, but this cannot wait. I've been keeping this to myself — I know it's wrong but I'm confused. I need to—" Amala paused, rearranging her thoughts.

Straight to the point, Amala.

"Whatever it is, I'm here for you." Hawk said.

Amala's doe eyes fixed on his lips before studying his expression, sensing his honesty. Hawk looked back, his whole soul bared — as it had been from the first day they met.

She could tell him. She *should* tell him. If anyone could help her figure this out, it was him. It felt right to tell him: Hawk. Her mate.

Amala began.

"When I was away in Ulbaros, something happened. It's the reason why I've been so distant since I've been back. I *know* I have been — it's why I couldn't blame you for sleeping with Naressa. I understand you felt the difference in me and it's true, I was different. I am," she said, but he interrupted her.

"If this is about Naressa, I don't want you to excuse me. I shouldn't have—"

"It's not about that. I have..."

Tell him.

Tell him.

Tell Hawk.

She took another breath as she thought of the best way to word the truth.

"When I told you about my... *past*, I warned you that it may change everything between us."

Hawk silently nodded, unsure of where she was going with this.

"Well, this is unrelated, but I am afraid this may truly ruin things." Amala continued, voice cracking.

Gentle air soothed her skin, face, neck, and shoulders; Amala relaxed in Hawk's power, grateful for his attention, almost resting in it.

The attention he should give you, a part of her whispered.

Yes, because she was his mate, and his—

Amala waved the thought away; she was afraid. Afraid this was different to her past, afraid there was no coming back. Never.

And if he rejected her... that would be forever, too.

Amala couldn't stand the thought of losing him, but felt guilty for thinking so lowly of his character.

Steadying herself, Amala nervously bit her lip before going all in. Hawk gave her time, eyes never leaving her face. Waiting. He would wait forever until she assembled the courage to voice her fears aloud.

"While I was in Ulbaros, something changed."

Amala paused, unsure if she had the confidence to keep going: a silent question to her soul met by utter silence.

She could do this.

Eyes locked with his, Amala said, "The Goddess' energy has found the next vessel."

It took Hawk less than a second. His eyes widened in realisation; his intuition was formidable and rarely failed. Sometimes all he needed was half a clue to piece the puzzle together. Eyes interlocked, she didn't dare to breathe: afraid to break the delicate balance.

Mates, mates, *mates*.

"Who is it?" Hawk asked, his voice hoarse. Dry. As though he had summoned a great deal of will power to speak those three words. As if, even though he knew already, he still wished to hear it.

Amala couldn't believe she was saying it aloud as she finally whispered—

"Me."

☼

Hawk was stunned. It required a good five minutes before his breath returned to normal. Amala could sense the hammering of his heart in his chest, but he didn't care.

Goddess. Amala, his mate Amala, was the next Goddess.

"Say something," she whispered, eyes wary.

Amala had stared at him the entire time, those icy eyes never leaving his face. She was afraid he would run, if she lost sight of him for even a moment.

But Hawk wouldn't run. He was shocked, yes, but mostly...

He was mesmerised. To him, Amala being Goddess made complete sense.

She was perfect: a Goddess of Love, which was what she had always been.

The way she Loved and cared for the world around her — even those she knew and those she didn't — pouring Love into every gesture, every action. He was so used to Serabel as Goddess, he never paused to think of who a better option could be. Wasn't it obvious? Amala always gave Love — to him and everyone else.

"How do you feel about it?"

Amala bit her lip, "Unworthy, mainly. I know the energy chose me for a reason. But it still feels crazy. Wrong."

She was fidgeting, shifting position countless times to avoid looking into his eyes. Crossing her legs, their knees touched and Amala held back a breath as neither moved.

"How many things are you Goddess of, then?"

Finally allowing herself to meet his gaze, she chuckled.

"I can't believe you don't know already."

"There's like an infinite list. And I don't have a priestess exam to pass, so I'm not required to know."

"There's no such thing as a priestess exam," she scoffed, "C'mon, tell me."

"Alright, but don't get mad if I mess up," he raised his hands in a defensive gesture. Amala mocked him by sending a gust of air directly to his face.

"I'm waiting."

"Goddess of the Moon," Hawk started.

Amala nodded

"Goddess of Love."

Another nod.

"Of... beauty?" he asked, uncertain.

"Not *beauty*." She corrected. "Goddess of all things that are beautiful."

"Alright," he said, licking his lips. "Goddess of everything that's female."

She wrinkled her nose as she nodded. "I never agreed with the way that's phrased. We all have feminine and masculine so... that just sounds wrong."

"Maybe you'll change it," he suggested.

"Maybe," Amala said, but she didn't sound convinced. "Keep going."

Hawk licked his lips, "Goddess of creativity."

Her eyes widened, smiling.

"Look at you, nailing the priestess exam."

"Sometimes I listen to you boasting about being High Priestess." Hawk winked, and she laughed, tilting her head in silent expectancy.

"I'm out of ideas."

"Alright," Amala said, her voice soft and blissfully inviting. "Goddess of Birth and Fertility."

A pause, her face was bright now.

"Goddess of Water and Air, and Things that are Cold."

Her cheeks blushed, fluttering her beautiful, thick lashes as she continued, "Goddess of Sex."

"*You*'re Goddess of Sex?" he blurted, pushing aside the mental picture instantly forming in his mind: Amala, naked in her temple, basking in the adoration and worship of thousands of followers, when she was his. Utterly his.

She chuckled. "The Goddess has always been protectress of Sex. What did you think?"

"I thought..." he hesitated. Pondered if what he was about to say would sound like blasphemy to her. "I thought Aarush was God of Sex."

"Oh, he *wishes...*"

"He owns a sex club, for Goddess' sake," Hawk continued. Amala raised an eyebrow, and he froze. Had he just...

Curling her lips, she cocked her head and studied him. Waited.

"Did I just curse on you?"

A slow nod.

"Yeah," Amala said. "Yeah, you did."

CHAPTER 38

A mala's smile vanished as soon as Hawk announced Medyr was coming to their house. Moving closer to the couch, Hawk handed her a glass of juice.

"What, are you bribing me?" she huffed, but the corners of her lips tugged upwards.

"It's the fancy glass," Hawk tried.

She laughed, taking a lengthy sip.

"Should we tell him?"

"*No.*"

"It just feels weird to pretend while we're at home. This is the place where we can always be us." Amala grunted, Hawk's heart warming at her words. He knew what she meant: he felt the same way.

"I'm not sure I can hold it in for much longer, Hawk." She added. "I can't be around you in our home and pretend you mean nothing to me." She said it with such nonchalance, but he knew what each word meant to her. His beautiful Goddess.

He could not imagine how hard it had been for her to keep this secret. To deal with the pain and the surprise, the shame and fear. Now, he brushed his tattooed fingers against her cheek.

Amala smiled at him. "How do we remove my scent from here?"

Hawk grinned; the last time had taken hours to remove every trace of her, spending the remaining days missing her cinnamon scent like crazy.

"Maybe we can pull it off if he finds you're already here. I'll keep the bedroom door closed anyway."

"I will have to tell him at some point. Medyr knows me well enough to figure it out on his own, if he sees us in here."

"He told me a little about you," Hawk confessed. "While we checked the tunnel under Helioneis."

She hummed in surprise, "What did he say?"

"He seemed a little nostalgic of your friendship."

Amala sighed.

"We were close when I was younger, then drifted apart after my father died. I mean, *I* drifted apart from him — it was my choice, my fault. And he doesn't know about..." she paused, and Hawk knew she needed a breath before mentioning her miscarriage. "*That*."

Promptly focusing on anything else except that last statement, he introduced a lighter tone to the topic.

"Okay, I'm not buying the best-friend-Medyr bullshit."

Amala giggled, "You are my best friend, Hawk. But Medyr is *also* my friend."

"He didn't even make you come."

"You haven't, either!"

"Because you have never given me a chance."

Amala scoffed, unable to hide the blush creeping up her cheeks.

"Is that what you think about? Every time you see Medyr?"

Her tone wasn't accusatory. It was amused, possibly with a hint of curiosity.

Hawk shrugged.

"Yeah." That, and how much *he* wanted to make her come, to give her what she deserved.

His scent thickened and even though he said nothing, Amala noticed.

"Stop picturing making me come, Hawk."

☼

Hebex was visiting a couple of stores in the neighbourhood, but would join them shortly. That's what Medyr had said before falling into a casual conversation with Blade. He looked vaguely surprised to find Amala there, but she had opened the door and greeted him with a smile.

Now, she sat next to Howlite, trying not to slump down on the couch like usual. She wore proper clothes too.

It felt so uncomfortable to pretend Hawk was a stranger in their own house, but she knew it was for the best: until they were mated, she wouldn't risk it yet. The door opened as Hebex's lovely scent of rose and honey filled the room. Cairo's grapefruit and rain was there too.

"Found this one downstairs," he said, eyes falling on Amala. "Friend of yours?"

"*Best* friend," Hebex corrected, waving her hair over a shoulder, and glancing in Hawk's direction. He could not contradict her with Medyr here, so she would enjoy the title for as long as possible.

"So?" Cairo asked, sitting on the couch behind Amala. "Did they join our case for good?"

Hawk exhaled.

"Listen, I've tried to get around it for the past month. But there's too much stuff we can't do without them. Medyr can act on behalf of

Aarush — who is an asshole and refuses to talk — and Hebex and High Priestess Amala knew Serabel personally."

Cairo surveyed each of them, his clear blue eyes indulging on Amala.

"I agree," Blade said from the kitchen counter, rolling a joint. "Looking back, I think we lost a bunch of details because we didn't have any insight from a priestess. Things started making more sense once you told us all that shit about the Charal." He pointed at Hebex and Medyr.

The latter acknowledged the words with a nod of his chin. "What do you need help with, today?"

"Just a checkpoint. Too many things are happening at once and I'm not sure which direction to take." Hawk paused, "I'm pretty sure Aarush is keeping something big from us."

Amala pursed her lips, icy eyes wide as they settled on his face.

He ignored her piercing gaze and refocused on his words. "I went to see him a month ago, before the Goddess' funeral. I asked him about Serabel, if he could tell me more about her, and give his perspective on things..."

"Did you ask *nicely*?" Medyr asked with a note of mocking.

"I did."

"What did he tell you?" Amala breathed.

Hawk sighed. "Nothing. He implied to know something, but gave me a deal that I couldn't take. Of course he might be lying, but I think it's worth a try to figure out what he's hiding."

"But he's willing to talk? Why didn't he—" Amala asked, considering. Then her eyes widened in realisation, "What was his price?"

"That you dance for him."

Hawk had never told Amala about it, not even hinting of the God's request. Aarush had a thing for making her uncomfortable, he had witnessed it too many fucking times. When proposing the deal, Hawk had gathered all of his self-restraint not to reveal that Amala was his mate. Now she blushed, exchanging a brief yet eloquent look with Hebex.

"Don't you even *dare*." The blonde priestess whispered, eyebrows bunching.

Cairo hummed as he exchanged a look with Blade. Hawk knew she was pondering her options as he watched her mind weigh the pros and cons. There was no way he would let her do that.

"So, me dancing for him will give us what you need?" She asked.

"Amala, shut up." Hebex snapped, turning to Medyr for help. "Tell her she shouldn't do it."

"Hebs, I'm no one to tell Amala what she should and shouldn't do," he replied. "You know that a deal with Aarush will always include something like this. That's why you *don't* make a deal with him."

For perhaps the fifth time in a short — too short period of time, Hawk found himself no longer disliking Medyr. Amala gazed at the High Priest, colour staining her cheeks. "But what if it can help?"

"You know better than sacrificing yourself for this, Amala. You've *never* given in all those years he's been messing with you. Why consider it now?"

"For Serabel," she whispered. "What if he knows something important?"

Cairo cleared his throat and her attention switched to him, sat behind her.

"We'll find another way, High Priestess. I agree with your companions: we won't jeopardise your position in this case for the sake of a clue."

When she opened her mouth to counter, he added, "I'm sure Captain Mercurian agrees with me."

Hawk nodded, more than glad for Cairo's intervention: Amala had enough of him telling her what to do, but maybe she would listen to the others.

"Aarush and Serabel were messing around, everyone knows that. I think it started a few years after he was made God." Medyr said.

"I wouldn't know," Amala shrugged. "I never interrupted my Goddess' personal time."

"Which she would've loved for you to do," Hebex added. Amala blushed and shook her head.

Hawk ignored the innuendo. "Do you think hooking up with Serabel meant he knew some of her plans?"

"Knowing those two, I wouldn't be surprised if she told him about this business with the Charal women. You see, initially, she was helping him out — me too, trying to teach him everything he needed in time for his initiation ceremony. And that was a pain in the ass, let's just say he wasn't the fastest learner." Medyr reconsidered his words, remembering the respect a God deserved. Nodding to Amala, he added, "Just get ready for the next vessel's ceremony. It's your duty to make sure the New Goddess knows everything."

Amala nodded with interest, eyes wide. Hawk knew she was trying not to blush, fighting against the feeling of unworthiness within her.

"We'll do it together," Hebex promised, squeezing her hand. "Any news?"

Amala shook her head. She was good at pretending: pretending she didn't know Hawk, pretending to be fine despite her past trauma. Now, she pretended she had no idea who the next vessel was, acting as though it wasn't her who harboured the vessel. Hawk asked himself if there might be anything else she was pretending about. He would have no way to know about it.

"Anyway," Medyr continued. "With time, she started confiding in him too. They became close. I thought it couldn't be possible for Serabel to be as close as she was with God Darnen, but I think their bond was even greater than that."

"Oh, Serabel and God Darnen were absolutely incredible," Amala whispered, eyes shimmering. "But yes, she was close to Aarush." She looked at Hawk, nervously biting her lip. "If you think Serabel was the buyer, he might know about it."

Hawk nodded slowly, knowing how much acknowledging his theory meant to her.

"Did Aarush ever mention anything about that?" He asked the High Priest.

"A buyer?"

"We call them the buyer, but it's not an official name. Did he mention anything about the Embers?"

"What, the gang?"

Hawk nodded in confirmation.

Medyr shook his head. "I mean, I know from time to time he gets drugs from them — he's sent me to get them before. Otherwise, he hasn't mentioned them."

"He sent *you* to deal with the *Embers*?" Hebex exclaimed, whipping her head to him.

"It was fine, Hebs." He chuckled. "The Embers won't kill you as long as you bring them money."

The earthy smell of weed spread across the room and Hawk intuitively turned to Blade, who wiggled his eyebrows while taking a hit from the joint between his fingers.

"You want?"

Hawk shook his head. "I'll make mine."

He almost asked Amala if she wanted one too, before realising that would've looked way too intimate for what they were trying to display. As he lay on the kitchen counter what he needed, he heard Hebex saying: "Did they tell you about the tunnel?"

"Yes," Amala said. "Did you go with them?"

"I did," She answered, gesturing to Medyr. "We went a second time too. We tried to help them decipher some of the Charal symbols, but... maybe you can help?"

Amala hummed. While she had told Hawk everything she could, he supposed inspecting the symbols wouldn't hurt.

"Blade?" Hebex called. "Do you have any pictures?"

Hawk finished laying the weed into the paper, then tucked it underneath the filter. Blade handed his tablet to Amala, a picture of the tunnel's walls on display. She observed it for a while, eyes narrowed on the figure.

"What did you find?" she asked Hebex.

Pointing at the screen, Hebex said, "*Kantazar* means Charal killer, right?"

"Yes. It's this symbol here, I think."

"It is?"

Amala nodded. Hawk couldn't see the symbol they referred to, but Blade quickly noted it down. She stared at the screen some more, zooming in on the picture.

"This one with the round sides is *kuris*, which means blood. I can't read all the symbols, but blood is mentioned in their birthing techniques, so I know a bit about that." Her gaze narrowed on the photo. "That circle is a full moon. It means Goddess."

"Really?"

"Charal women are connected to the moon. The moon *is* the Goddess," Amala explained plainly.

Hawk made a mental note to study the pictures again with this newest information: perhaps he could connect it to the *Goddess'* death, now he knew more meanings. He gestured to Blade to hand him the lighter. He threw it with precision, and Hawk caught it immediately: usually, Naressa just snapped her fingers to light up their joints. As he breathed out, the smell of cinnamon spread all around him, whirling to the living room.

Hebex subtly turned to Amala: "Are you... alright?"

She hummed, confused. "Yeah?"

"Your scent is all out, babe."

Amala sniffed. Her eyes widened and she quickly shook her head, gaze searching for Hawk.

"It's not me," she said, a soft blush on her cheeks.

But her eyes quickly found him. Narrowed on the joint that was half between his lips.

"That's Hawk. He only smokes weed if he puts cinnamon in it," Blade explained, taking another hit.

Amala's mouth quirked upwards, as in saying *gotcha*. She mastered it well, but there was something sparkling in her eyes as he inhaled again.

"Why cinnamon?" Hebex inquired.

Why cinnamon?

Because he was a total simp. He'd been smoking like that since he'd met Amala, always careful not to do it around her. Now he shrugged, "It makes you higher."

But from the way Amala looked at him, he could tell she knew that wasn't the only reason.

Hawk turned to Medyr, avoiding her gaze. "I think it would be safer if you didn't check the tunnel anymore. I can't forbid you from going, but I don't want to draw attention to you or Helioneis."

"Thanks for the interest, Captain, but I have no intention to die in a tunnel," Hebex winked, "I'd be second on the murder priority list then, it would take you ages to solve my case."

He chuckled at the words, but his eyes soon fell on Amala, who wasn't laughing. Shooting Hebex a reprimanding look, a flash of pain lit up her face as she likely recalled the memory of Serabel's body. Hawk summoned the memory too.

His gaze caught Amala's again: the other Goddess. The Goddess he wanted, currently sitting on the floor: humbleness in each of her words, convincing herself she wasn't worthy of the divine energy that had chosen her forever.

CHAPTER 39

T he Yonium did not shine in the sunlight, but the sight of the midday rays reverberating from the marble walls was still utterly beautiful. Amala allowed herself ten minutes to get lost in contemplation.

She missed the temple.

She missed waking up in her room, having her self-love ritual as the first remnants of sunlight peeked through the window; she missed walking in the hallways while Serabel's energy surrounded her.

She missed the daily prayers, the moon rituals, the meals with her priestesses.

She missed taking care of the animals and the plants.

She missed all of it.

But getting used to life outside of the temple was not as difficult as she had feared. Maybe it was because Hawk always ensured she felt comfortable in her new home. He gave her space when she needed it and was there when she didn't. Hawk cooked for her, allowing her an opportunity to try all that food she never would have at the temple. Most of all, he understood her: no one else knew her the way he did, and he seemed to understand her even *more* now that he knew she was the next Goddess.

Sparing another glance at the Yonium, realisation hit her like a wave of cold, utterly freezing water.

That was her temple. *Hers.*

That was the Goddess' Temple of Yonium, and *she* was the Goddess.

If she were to go back in there now, she would take Serabel's space: the Goddess' quarters. The rooms Amala had visited every day to wake her up and get her ready. To worship Serabel: her beautiful body and soul.

Would someone do that for her?

Amala sent away the thought of a new High Priestess. *She* was the High Priestess.

Being High Priestess was the main, most precious thing in her life: something she had always wanted and worked for. Being a midwife was her whole life too, of course, but... being High Priestess somehow supplied for what she had lost as a mother — a mother she was unable to be, as Caelan's words reminded her daily.

Amala would keep her High Priestess title with her own claws and teeth, if need be.

Plus, the idea of undoing the wards on the temple, and move back there, in the rooms where the Goddess had been murdered...

Moving quickly among the trees, Amala's hands touched trunks and branches as her wind twirled through the leaves and flowers. It didn't take her long to reach the border of the Centaur kingdom. While there was no true separation from the rest of Mhelani, the vegetation grew more vivid, the fruit more juicy. Amala spotted a pair of centaurs and stepped onto the footpath, signalling to one of them.

"It's me," she said quietly, "High Priestess Amala."

The centaur closest to her left recognized her with a bow of his head. Amala returned the gesture, knowing better than to spite centaurs in their own kingdom. She was accustomed to them, and they tended to like her. Amala followed them through a pathway of Qelcenae drifting to the inner part of the forest, until she reached a small clearing and recognised Aries' familiar dark braids.

"Show me around?" She asked.

He held her stare with a smile: "It's quite nice to see you, High Priestess."

"I hope my priestesses are well?"

Aries nodded. "They have been a great addition to our tribe. We are indeed grateful for their presence."

"And I'm grateful they have your protection here."

"I'll take you to Palana," he offered as they strode side by side. "Are you in a rush to leave, after your visit?"

"Why?" she dared to ask.

Aries threw her an amused side glance. "Kanaan misses you."

"And you don't?"

"I know better than searching for trouble. The Captain who picked you up from the temple — does he have a claim on you?"

"Not one he has fulfilled." Amala said, even as her soul screamed to say *yes* — to claim herself as *his*: Hawk's only.

"But one he might fulfil?"

"That's between me and him," she smiled politely.

"If his claim is stronger than mere desire," Aries continued. "I'll wish you happiness and leave you be."

"Did you tell Kanaan this?"

The centaur chuckled.

"I'll let him figure that out for himself."

☼

Palana was still in her first trimester: her pregnancy would last for eight more months, though she was doing fine — pain sometimes, and body sensitivity, but the cramps had improved since last time.

Amala devoted a good hour working around her with some crystal therapy. She disposed unakite stones over her swollen belly, rose quartz on her chest, and carnelian on the ground, planting the crystals deep into the surrounding earth.

They focused on breathing as Amala taught her some relaxing techniques she should practice for the rest of her pregnancy. Whirling around them, her energy was a soft breeze as she sensed the foetus. It was healthy and growing steadily.

Palana thanked her profusely and Keneti, her mate, seemed more than relieved. Amala knew they both felt guilty, somehow, to have accidentally lured her outside the temple that night, away from Serabel. But when Palana tried to apologise, the High Priestess shook her head.

"For all we know, you might have saved me. My energy was still protecting the temple, and it wasn't enough. You have nothing to blame yourself for."

Her other patient, a beautiful, black-skinned centaur named Helerai, was due in a couple of months.

She had some trouble walking long distance and was resting below an oak tree when Amala reached her, guided by Aries.

"Good afternoon, my lovely soul." Amala greeted, kneeling beside her.

Helerai offered her a smile, "I'm honoured by your presence, High Priestess Amala."

Amala's gaze wandered, searching for any sign of a male centaur.

"Won't your mate be joining us, my love? Am I allowed to visit you without his presence?"

Centaurs had strict rules: their pairings meant more than anything to their tribe, crucial for their hierarchy. Mates were traditionally bound to spend all their time together — *wanted* to spend their time together. Amala always admired the deep love that secured a mating bond between centaurs.

Helerai nodded to Aries.

"My mate is hunting, but Aries shall be present for the rest of the visit. If you don't mind, of course." Amala reassured her it was all fine as she opened the small bag she carried and prepared the space around them.

"Do you happen to have amethyst with you?" she asked. "A big geode, perhaps."

"I'll bring some," Aries said.

Amala lit up a stick of incense.

"Turn around," she gently asked Helerai, "And tell me how you're feeling."

The centaur obeyed, slowly moving her body so that her swollen middle faced Amala.

"Lots of emotions, lately. But I am excited. This shall be my biggest adventure yet and I'm impatient to meet the creature now growing within me."

The High Priestess' hands trembled. Her own pregnancy had lately come to mind more often than she usually allowed it to. Sometimes, she still needed to take a steadying breath during her visits, sending the pain away to give her patients the most beautiful experience.

She called to her energy, hands splayed upon Helerai's belly: white, pure white light drifted from her fingertips and into her soft brown skin. She closed her eyes, allowing her power to guide her.

She could see all of it: her womb, the vital organs. She could see the foetus' position and sensed its breathing. Could see its energy starting to blossom. Amala smiled at Helerai, tears stinging her eyes. "It's... beautiful. Perfectly healthy and stable. Oh, you will have a beautiful labour."

"Is it in the right position?"

She nodded.

"It is. It may still change as time passes. We will know nearer the time."

The sound of hooves on the ground disrupted their moment, as they turned in the direction of Aries, now carrying a big chunk of amethyst. Behind him, another piece was carried by Kanaan.

Amala stood and reached for them.

"Thank you."

She observed the crystal: it was utterly beautiful, a natural pattern of drusy gemstones that glimmered under the sparks of sunlight, creating delicious flashes of pink and purple. Some of her admiration must have shown, because Aries said, "These pieces were a gift to our tribe from Goddess Serabel."

Amala's eyes widened in surprise: her Goddess had been generous, but she didn't tend to deal much with centaurs.

"When?"

She planted the amethyst on the ground, tilting and pressing the bottom of it into the soil.

"It was payment after we swore to protect her priestesses," Aries explained. "We didn't need payment, however, as we would have served her regardless of any prize... but she wished to reward us with these amethysts. We have an entire collection. Quartzes too." He glanced at Kanaan to confirm.

"Yes," he said. "Pink and Clear quartzes. Another gift for another pact."

Amala stilled.

Sinking the second amethyst into the ground, she looked up and assessed Kanaan closely.

"What do you mean, another pact?"

"The same way the Goddess asked us to protect her priestesses, she made another deal with our king, some decades ago." Helerai answered.

Decades?

Amala said nothing, her brain working quickly, mind suddenly questioning everything.

It couldn't be. It *couldn't* be, and she shouldn't ask questions. Or pry in a business that wasn't hers.

Only that... it was hers, wasn't it? As the new Goddess, wasn't she entitled to know what kind of pact lived between Serabel and the centaurs?

But if her intuition was right...

If she dared to ask the question, she was accepting Hawk's theory — acknowledging it, perhaps even supporting it.

Was it worth it? To think such a thing of her Goddess? She had trusted Serabel with her soul, devoting every aspect of her being to the Goddess, but where had it brought her?

Amala trusted Hawk with all of herself, too, despite not always agreeing with him.

So she asked, "What manner of deal, if I'm allowed to know?"

Kanaan observed her carefully.

"I thought you knew already. Aren't you supposed to know your Goddess' wishes?"

"Believe me," she replied, voice quivering. "I thought so too, but I fear she may have kept a couple of secrets to herself."

Please, please, tell me, she silently begged.

She wouldn't seduce Kanaan to get her answer, would she?

There was a time where she wouldn't have hesitated. But now it felt wrong to even try, her thoughts drifting to Hawk. Kanaan exchanged a brief look with Aries, but it was Helerai who said, "The Goddess made us swear to protect the women you call Charal."

Amala held her breath.

What?

To hell with coincidences.

What was Serabel doing? Was this her plan all along?

She exhaled. "Here?"

"None ever came. The Goddess didn't seem to think it would happen anytime soon. But she made us swear to protect them, to hide and care for them — like we are doing with your priestesses."

"But *would* you protect them?"

"We swore so," Aries intervened. "All of us. If a Charal woman ever enters Mhelani Forest, she will be safe."

CHAPTER 40

V isiting Mhelani Forest had utterly drained Amala. Returning home with a pounding headache, she lay on the floor with an amethyst placed to her forehead as she summoned a cool breeze all around her. She waited for Hawk to come back, then updated him on everything the centaurs had revealed — which was not much, to be honest.

Hawk listened intently, his own power whirling to soothe and relax his Goddess. He chose not to speculate about Serabel; instead, he just picked Amala up and brought her to bed.

In the morning, Amala woke up before dawn with a clear head and a full heart. Full of Love, to grow and to give, to nurture and blossom and share. She had that Love in her heart always, and wasn't afraid of it.

Had never been afraid of it — almost never.

The only person she was afraid to share it with lay right beside her. Hawk.

Amala knew no one deserved her Love more than he did.

Yet she was terrified: to receive part of her Love was one thing, but to receive it all at once?

Love, passion, hunger, devotion, admiration, light and intensity... would he be able to return it the same?

She had known the answer for a while now.

Most people wouldn't. But he would. Hawk would without hesitation.

Amala extended her arm toward him, gently stroking his arm.

He opened his eyes, as if her touch alone was a call he could never ignore.

"Hi," she whispered.

He smiled, tenderness melting his features. "Hi."

She ignored the way his husky voice triggered a shiver through her spine. She shifted closer to him, careful not to hurt Howlite.

"Watch the sunrise with me?"

Hawk was unable to hide the hint of surprise on his face, grey eyes lighting before he nodded, pulling the covers aside to stand. She rose too and reached for the glass door that took her outside, glancing at him. He was beside her: his tall, muscular frame so inviting as she surveyed his bare, muscled chest, golden skin exposed for her to admire; the grey sweatpants fell right on the delicious V of his abs, hypnotising her. He tensed under her gaze, his tattooed hands raising to his hair as he tucked it up into his usual bun.

Amala cracked a smile but said nothing, nodding to the glass door as she stepped outside: she was unbothered by the cold as a chill breeze hit her bare skin. She just sat on the floor, crawling to the end of the balcony, then elegantly leaned against it as she stretched her legs towards the glass railing.

Hawk followed, sitting next to her. The silence thickened as seconds passed; Amala didn't look at him, eyes fixed on the horizon instead as she released a breath. She summoned no energy, yet felt a soft breeze around her, as if the air had started whirling in circles between them.

The quiet allowed her thoughts to grow louder: she was sharing the sunrise with Hawk.

Her mind wandered back to the only other sunrise they had watched together, all those years ago. Nothing but friends, Amala had invited him to join her. Never would she have imagined being this close to him now, sharing their second sunrise. Hawk loosed a breath by her side. Subtly, she looked at him and knew he was recalling the same memory.

The first glimpse of sun hit the horizon, and Amala stilled, eyes fixed on the thin ray that gradually lit the surroundings. Every day of her life this was her favourite moment. What better way to practice gratitude than watch the sunrise? Blessed by every single ray that approached the sky.

Amala breathed again, hypnotised by the light, then started her daily prayer. Though it was in fact quite different to a prayer; she set her intentions, affirming her own energy as she committed to the day. Shifting closer to the railing, she pressed her hands against the glass and tried to claim more of the sun, welcoming the view.

"I am Amala," she murmured, "And I beg you, beautiful Sun, to shine on me. Shine on me, and take my energy with you, and I swear, it's full of Love and Love only; take my energy with you and let it go whenever someone needs it, let it be helpful and let it bring Love to people. To anyone and everyone. Thank you for being so beautiful, and bright; I am grateful for my happiness," she whispered "And today I Love so deeply, so strongly. My heart is beaming and I feel blessed by your light. And I feel..." she paused. Breathed.

Rising, eyes on the sun, Amala felt tears run down her cheeks as she braced herself.

As low as she could, she whispered, "I feel loved. So loved. I don't know if I deserve it — perhaps I do, or maybe I don't, but *he* loves me and that is so special. He's special," she hoped he couldn't hear, but Amala could no longer hold back. To the sun, she would reveal her deepest secrets.

It was the only being that wouldn't judge her as she whispered in the silence of the dawn. While it started as a prayer, Amala told the sun everything.

And at last it came out.

"I know Hawk loves me."

Never had she spoken the words aloud, but she knew. And she told herself it was okay to pretend it wasn't true, because one day she would feel honest enough to embrace that feeling, and that day she would make things right.

The sun fully appeared in the sky as she murmured her thoughts to the wind, voice so low in fear of regretting Hawk's presence — regretting that she invited him here. She stilled, waiting for the feeling: she didn't want to feel regret, but it was better to embrace the sensation as soon as it came true...

Yet the feeling never came.

As she waited for that unpleasant sense of remorse to pierce her heart, to remind her why she kept sunrises a private moment... she felt nothing. There was no regret at the thought of Hawk being with her, even if he heard her words. It still felt right.

As she slowly turned to face him, she was surprised to find him standing, leaning against the wall behind her. Maybe, she thought as she shifted closer, that moment was all she needed. Hawk's eyes were fixed to Amala's, the sun reflecting in his dark pupils, as if it whispered: *here. I am here.* The sun and Hawk. Together. She had already decided that was her favourite thing.

To see that now, the sun and Hawk before her — so close and so real...

Amala kissed him, and a small part of her whispered that perhaps the day she would make things right could be today.

CHAPTER 41

Hawk wasn't sure exactly what had happened; he was there but he wasn't there, and Amala—

Fuck, Amala was kissing him.

One moment, he was lost in her icy eyes, the sun rising behind her: gaze so magnetic he couldn't risk blinking, almost afraid that if he did, this bubble around them would pop.

Then Amala's lips were pressed against his. Her heady scent swirled around him as if the wind itself controlled it. And her lips were soft — so damn soft — how had he spent all these years without tasting them?

Cinnamon, sugar, sunlight: the taste melted on his tongue and drove him wild.

If he sharpened his senses ever so slightly... yes, he could taste the faint, sweet note of moonlight too.

The taste was subtle, but it was there.

Moonlight, because Amala was the new Goddess.

His Goddess.

And his mate.

He was kissing his Goddess and his mate.

Hawk inhaled a sharp breath, causing Amala to quickly pull away. Cheeks rosy and eyes bright, she looked at him with no shame or fear. She curved her lips upwards — those sinful, soft lips pressed against his mouth only moments before.

Hawk couldn't breathe.

His Goddess looked at him with icy doe eyes, sunlight surrounding her as if she was made of it.

Then she whispered, "Sunrise is my favourite."

☼

On her way to the Home of Waters, Amala relived the scene in her head on repeat.

They kissed. Hawk and Amala had kissed.

Technically, she had kissed him but... that was beyond the point. They had kissed.

They had been friends for ten years, never sharing a moment like that until this morning.

Amala had often wondered what his lips tasted like. Whether they were soft or rough, how it would feel to have his mouth pressed against hers.

Countless times — so many more than she cared to admit — she imagined how their first kiss would be and how it would happen. Before, she would have sworn to her Goddess that Hawk would eventually be the one to initiate it.

But no. She had done it.

Amala had looked into his eyes, saw the sun reflected there and went all in.

And she regretted absolutely nothing.

For Hawk to see her at her most vulnerable — so real and raw before the sunrise, meant the world to her. She needed to be her truest self before kissing him, and she would only be when watching the sun.

She was grateful Hawk didn't insist on accompanying her: he was likely to grow protective — even more so — soon, and she needed to be alone to replay the kiss in her head over and over.

Searching for the golden thread beaming in her soul, the one connecting her to him, Amala found it painfully tight, but not different from before. Some sort of realisation set in her head then: their mating bond hadn't snapped.

They didn't kiss *because* of their mating bond.

They kissed because Amala wanted to.

A smile rippled on her lips as she released a laugh of relief, but before she could relish into it, another thought pulled her attention away.

Her celibacy.

Had she broken it?

She took a few seconds before blinking in realisation. No, she hadn't. She wasn't bound to it, not anymore: there was no vessel to find.

She could be with Hawk. But how would she explain it to her sisters? They knew about her abstinence: how could she justify it now, if she wished to hide the truth?

Perhaps she should just tell them. Not today, but soon.

Yes, she would tell them soon, though the thought terrified her. The sole fact Hawk already knew was enough, somehow, to steady her heart.

Amala arrived at the Home of Waters with the silent promise to focus on her role as priestess and nothing else. The shiny temple reflected the beautiful sunlight that had just witnessed her kiss with Hawk. Of all the ways she had dreamed of it, nothing could ever beat a kiss in front of the sunrise.

☼

"What's going on with you?" Naressa scolded, smacking his shoulder.

Hawk barely heard her. His brain wasn't there, still unable to process. He couldn't *believe* what had happened.

After Amala went back inside, he had lingered on the balcony a moment longer, giving her space but most of all, giving space to *himself*. To breathe, deal with his thoughts, emotions, *instinct* and most of all, repressing the urge to go inside and fuck her, marking her skin so everyone would know the truth.

When he thought he could finally face Amala, she was gone. She must have gotten ready and left without saying goodbye. Howlite's water and breakfast bowl was full and, when he got to their bedroom, her scent was everywhere. As if she had touched herself in every single spot of the room. Thoughts instantly drifting to his cock, he pictured her delicate frame writhing in pleasure with the soft moans he heard every morning coming from her swollen lips. Swollen because *he* had kissed them.

There was a note on his pillow.

Best orgasm I had since I moved in with you. I loved to picture something real, this time. Think of me if you make love to yourself. See you later, mate. – A

He turned up late to work, but didn't fucking care. Not when Amala had touched herself, thinking of him, and implied he did the same. So, he did it too. Twice.

And now...

Hawk lifted his head, meeting Naressa's gaze.

"What?"

She couldn't hold back the laughter.

"I haven't spoken in five minutes."

Shit. "What did you say?"

"I asked what's going on with you! You've been late and unfocused all morning."

"That's not true."

It was.

He couldn't stop thinking of Amala, of their incredible moment shared on the balcony.

But he nodded to himself and then Naressa, gathering his thoughts. "What's up, then?"

"About what?"

He was in deep shit. Having Blade around, constantly high, made Hawk look like the serious one; but today Blade was missing, and there was no buffer to his utter lack of attention.

"I have no idea what you've been saying." He admitted.

"Hawk!" Naressa scolded again, throwing an exasperated glance in Cairo's direction. Cairo was amused, but Hawk didn't look at him, knowing better than asking for a taunt.

"Sorry. I'm focused."

Like hell he was. On Amala's lips, he was focused.

Indeed, Cairo cocked his head. "What happened with hot High Priestess?"

"What about her?"

"Is she... responsible for whatever got you so bad?"

"No," Hawk said. Too fast.

Naressa hummed and shared another glance with Cairo. "Atalman is not gonna let you see the dagger. We asked him twice, formally and all, but after the stealing attempt, he won't open that door for anyone. Not even you."

Fuck. That was bad.

Whatever was written on that dagger must have been the reason why Serabel wanted it so badly.

Serabel, or whoever the buyer was.

Hawk never relied on only one theory, not until he could prove it.

"What's new from our friend who tried to steal it?"

Naressa sighed, shaking her head. "There was almost nothing I could do. There's only one portion of the fingerprint I could salvage, and it matched ten thousand people. Cairo got it down to fifty."

"That's impressive."

"It was just cross-referencing, trying to sort out who was in Aglatas and who wasn't, who possibly had a reason for this and who could have been in the Riza perimeter by that hour and who couldn't."

"That's still brilliant," Hawk observed. "Thanks man."

Cairo shrugged. "Fifty is still a lot of people. We can't check them all."

"Anyone interesting that might be missing?"

"Two of the fingerprints belong to two guys from the Embers. One's a man and one's a woman." Naressa explained.

"But the guy who died was a dude, right?" Cairo asked.

"Yeah, I wasn't able to see much more, but he was definitely male. The whole thing is weird, especially how he simply burned alive in the Riza."

"I searched those spells," Hawk said. "The ones that killed him. The only person who can do them is Jaren, but it doesn't make sense asking him. If he is behind this, he would have told them how to avoid being burned alive." He turned to Cairo. "Anyone from the Dragons?"

"No matches."

"But he passed the water spells, so perhaps it's worth chatting with Nyla."

"Do you need me to reach out?" Cairo asked, "I'm getting good at this formal shit."

402   CHIARA GALA

"Yeah, I would hate to waste those skills."

Naressa chuckled. "It's not about the spells, though. It's about the motive. If only a Charal woman can wield the dagger, why would anyone else try to steal it?"

☼

Amala couldn't hide her surprise when she saw Naressa waiting outside. She walked quickly toward the beautiful redhead, who surveyed her movements from where she leaned against her car. Amala had decided she liked the female. Despite only meeting her once, it had been enough to set aside any doubts, and any jealousy or resentment. Naressa was Hawk's friend, and she was beautiful, smart, cunning, ingenious, attentive, and loyal. She had love to give, and Amala would always appreciate a soul like hers.

"Good evening," she said politely.

Naressa took one look at her clothes and said with eyebrows arched, "Good evening, High Priestess."

Amala lifted her chin at the mention of her title.

Goddess, a part of her whispered.

Not yet. She replied.

"What do I give the honour?"

"Captain was kept back at the office. He'll be home by the time we get there, but he asked me to retrieve you."

Amala arched an eyebrow.

"Why?"

"What do you mean, *why*?"

"He's been fine with me going back on my own, lately."

Naressa cocked her head, "Well, I won't lie, he seemed particularly protective today. I wouldn't cross him if I were you. Shall we?"

Hawk and home.

She couldn't wait to see him again, to *kiss* him again. To tell him all the things she had kept in her heart for too long.

The redhead opened the car door for her and gestured with her chin to hop in.

Amala sighed. With one last glance at the temple, she followed her inside.

CHAPTER 42

A mala followed Naressa upstairs as there was no need to guide her, seeming as she had visited Hawk countless times before. *Too* many.

Forcing the thought away, Amala focused instead on how much she *liked* the woman.

"I love how your scent is everywhere," Naressa said, stepping out of the elevator, and aiming for the apartment door. Indeed, Amala's cinnamon scent coated the entire space outside the apartment. The High Priestess lingered by the elevator, amused that Naressa's words resembled her own after finding *her* scent all over the house only weeks before.

"Do we ring or you got keys?"

Amala handed her the keys in response: a small heart shaped keychain hanging between her fingers. She didn't hide the smirk blooming on her lips as she realised Naressa didn't have Hawk's keys — Blade had them, and Cairo did too. On any other day, Amala wouldn't have done it, smirking merely to prove a point. Usually, she wouldn't allow jealousy to have such control over her actions.

But today was different.

"Did he give you that, too?" Naressa nodded at the keychain.

Amala shrugged, "I've had Hawk's keys for years now. He gave them to me four years ago. The keychain was only so I would accept them. I don't own much."

She assessed Naressa's confused gaze, and rephrased: "I don't *like* to own much, I guess. Life at the Yonium isn't very materialistic: I had my clothes, my crystals, and my books. Everything else I do in my day — my rituals, and my energy connecting to the ground and the Goddess and the world... it is so much more important to me."

As she explained, Naressa opened the door and Amala's scent became stronger as they stepped into the apartment.

"Do you have a favourite possession?" Naressa asked, "What's the most precious thing you have? The one thing you would never give up?"

Amala turned towards her, cheeks flushing as she understood the question and the answer—

Naressa read the expression on her face.

"Too personal?" She joked in a quiet attempt to correct her aim, but Amala shook her head. Refusing to reply.

Hawk, behind her, looked up and answered for her. "It's the sun."

Amala hadn't dared to look at him yet, but she did now.

God and Goddess, he was handsome. It was as though, during the day spent apart, he had become even *more* attractive. Her eyes took in his grey gaze, and the man bun she loved so much. And what he had just said... Amala barely nodded at his words, embarrassed to say the least. She had never revealed it aloud to Hawk, or anyone, but it was true. The sun. She would never give up the sun.

Naressa shifted closer, "You alright?"

No response, but Amala's face reddened again. In an instant, Hawk's arms were around her, bringing her closer.

"It's okay, Amala mate." He glanced at Naressa, "She loves the sun. As long as she can watch sunrise and sunset, she doesn't care about anything else. But," he stopped, stroking Amala's hair. "She feels a bit guilty when people address it."

Naressa raised an eyebrow, confused.

"Why? It's beautiful—"

"I'm High Priestess to the Goddess, and the Goddess is the moon." Amala interrupted, voice bitter.

"I've always felt selfish to admit I like the sun *more*." Her face still burned, unable to conceal the embarrassment. Hiding her face behind her small hands, Amala turned away.

The guilt was eating her alive. And not only for what she just said — that the High Priestess shouldn't like the sun more, but because she wasn't High Priestess anymore.

Not *just* High Priestess, at least. She was Goddess of the moon, and the sun could never be hers.

Swallowing the groan of frustration that rose in her throat, she banished those thoughts away. Finding a new High Priestess would have to wait too; Amala sure as hell wouldn't give up the title yet.

"It's okay, Amala," Hawk tried, "There's nothing wrong with preferring the sun. Serabel was fine with it, wasn't she?" he paused, sensing her energy. "And I'm sure the next Goddess will be too."

Oh, that fucker.

He knew her so well — too well, probably. Amala shot him a deadly glare, and he chuckled.

Naressa said, "It's beautiful that you love the sun so much you're willing to claim it as your dearest possession. It *is* yours, in some way."

Amala nodded in appreciation of her words, but didn't feel like replying. The question weighed on her; to admit in front of others that she loved the sun more than the moon — even if it was obvious — felt wrong.

"I'm gonna get changed," she said, and strode for the bedroom.

☼

Hawk trailed her figure leaving the room, eyes insistently pinned to her back. Naressa studied him, eyes wary.

"I'm sorry if I offended her." she cautiously said, in case the High Priestess could still hear.

Hawk shook his head. "You didn't. She just never forgives herself for that, but we're working on it."

There was pride in his voice — pride, as though he was an integral part of that growth. Naressa realised it too and smiled.

"I know what the sun means to her." Hawk added, "It's everything she wants... and she makes sure to claim it every morning. A couple times, she asked me to join her."

He paused, the memory of that morning too strong for him to fight it. Naressa didn't feel like interrupting the smile now growing on his face, simply waiting for him to return to their conversation. But he didn't. He grinned, eyes widening as he thought of him and Amala on the balcony: the way she whispered to the sun as it appeared in the horizon, shining upon her delicate skin. Watching Hawk with eyes full of pure Love. And then...

Amala had kissed him.

"What's going on?" Amala's sweet voice tethered him to reality.

Naressa snickered.

"Must have been a good sunrise, Hawk."

Amala flushed. She wore a pair of loose, large white trousers, and a single strap of silky white fabric wrapped around her breasts. Recently, she had made more of an effort to cover up, not that he minded when she vibed naked around the house. Reaching the kitchen, Hawk followed after, unable to keep his distance.

"I can cook." she offered.

"Blade and Cairo are getting takeaway, they'll be here soon. Naressa needs lots of chips to work overnight and we need to do a checkpoint of the whole case. I'm sorry, it's probably going to be a boring night." Hawk didn't bother to hide how much he would have preferred spending the evening with her.

Amala didn't seem to mind. "Can I stay? Next to you?"

He cocked his head, confused.

"What?"

"Next to you," she repeated softly. "I'd like to help, if I can. I need you close to me and I don't care if there's other people, I *need* to be *us*."

Her words were everything. Having Amala by his side, unashamedly touching her body and stroking her hair in front of his friends made him realise how Amala was sharing his exact feelings. They needed each other.

He couldn't help it, then. Some part of him told him to stop before it was too late, but he had already opened his mouth.

"If I manage to work with you by my side," he started, "Can I have another kiss?"

A second of silence stretched between them. Amala blinked, lips parting in surprise, before offering him a dazzling smile.

"Yes."

☼

"The Goddess was found dead."

"I really don't need a reminder," Amala muttered, covering her eyes as Blade showed the pictures from the crime scene.

He chuckled.

"Gang crime started rising. We expected that though, and when we checked the Embers, we found that a buyer had been in contact about temple blueprints and other stuff."

"Records, dagger, blueprints," Cairo added.

"Each of them turned out to be connected to the Charal tribe. The records were from the year of the last persecution. The Dagger of Phule is one of their symbols and that tunnel on the blueprints is absolutely full of them. A whole damn alphabet of symbols." Blade continued. "If only we had any idea of what it means."

"Aarush knows something but won't say what it is. We have confirmation that Serabel *was* researching the Charal women and spoke to several people about it — Atalman, too, which means she may have told other Protectors as well." Hawk said, checking the notes on his laptop. "And then, there's the centaurs."

Amala hummed at that. She was curled on the sofa with her head on Hawk's lap, his fingers stroking her hair. For once, she didn't care that someone watched them like this: she needed him more than her own soul cared to admit.

"She made them swear to protect the Charal women if they ever set foot in Mhelani forest." She explained, summing up what Kanaan told her.

"Could Serabel hide the Charal *in* the Yonium?" Naressa asked, "We know for a fact they must have been in the tunnel at some point."

"She couldn't hide them without us knowing," Amala countered. "There's too many of us and we all share the same spaces. Mhelani would be much safer for them: people don't go there."

Hawk approved her words and rewarded her by gently stroking her neck: she shuddered.

"Plus," he said, brushing her soft skin. "We checked the temple. I thought the Charal symbols from the tunnel could match something in the Yonium, but nothing corresponds."

Amala exhaled, eyes blinking as though banishing a bad memory away.

"There's no Charal symbols at the Yonium because they burned them all. High Priestess Bresha made sure that *nothing* Charal was left in the temple. We honour them with some of their customs, but it's mostly that: oral tradition. Serabel never risked bringing back symbols that could be recognised."

It took her some courage to voice her next thoughts.

"At first," she murmured, "I didn't agree with Hawk. Serabel *being* the buyer made no sense to me, and even less that the Charal themselves might have killed her. I knew my Goddess, and she only wanted the best for their tribe: she was trying to give them that, to make up for her past mistakes." Amala took a breath.

"But it cannot be a coincidence that the centaurs know about it, too. It sounds like she was actually *planning* something. And they were ready to obey her." Amala didn't like the sound of it, but knew she needed to stop fearing answers and start searching for them instead.

"What's next, then?" Blade asked.

Hawk's hand slid to Amala's spine and caressed it slowly. He lifted his head to Blade.

"Mhelani next, I'd say. I want to know more about this pact Serabel made with the centaurs."

He rested his hand on Amala's naked back.

Right. *There.*

Amala's eyes widened instantly, her scent escaping in a moment and intoxicating the entire room. She bit down on her lip to avoid the release of a soft moan.

"Fuck," Hawk muttered, lifting his hand right away. "I'm sorry, Amala mate. I didn't mean to—"

"It's fine," she said, her entire face red with embarrassment. Raising her upper body, she moved away from Hawk and onto the other side of the sofa. She gestured to Howlite, patting the middle cushion to secure further distance between them.

"Sorry," Hawk said again.

Fuck, her scent was *everywhere*. She should have known being close to Hawk while her body so desperately craved his was a bad idea. Now though, distance secured, she raised her gaze to the others, hiding her face behind her small hands. But Hawk must have shot them a look of warning because, when she peeked between her fingers, she found them all utterly disinterested. Amala exhaled in relief, happy to play pretend.

Even if now she was so wet it was a miracle she wasn't dripping onto the couch.

Cairo cleared his throat.

"I'll gather more files on Bresha," he slid his gaze to Amala. "Can hot High Priestess help fill the gaps?"

"I wasn't there when she did all of that," Amala replied, ignoring the nickname. "But yeah, I'll try my best."

She threw a side glance at Hawk: he wore a face of guilt for touching her back like that in front of his friends. Amala knew he hadn't done it on purpose, but now...

Oh, she was *so* aroused.

The cuddling had been a shitty idea, but the promise of a kiss lingered in the air between them for the rest of the evening.

☼

When everyone finally left, the silence was thick, barely interrupted by Howlite's growling. Amala prepared for bed, taking off her soaked underwear and tossing it into the laundry basket before Hawk could see. She'd rather him seeing her utterly naked than finding out how wet she had been that whole time and what her thong looked like after that evening. No fucking way she'd live with the risk of him knowing.

Sitting on the edge of the mattress, she pet the beautiful hound at her feet.

"You really shouldn't move from the middle of the bed tonight," she whispered to her. "That, or you should really leave now."

Howlite yawned.

Yeah, Amala thought. *I wish I was feeling sleepy.*

The door opened.

Amala lifted her gaze to Hawk and found his eyes already on her.

All of her.

This time, he didn't try to hide it. Closing the door behind him, he leaned against it. His eyes roved across her beautiful body with no holding back. Amala didn't hold back either and sat there for him, utterly still. For him to watch, survey, observe, and savour.

She would wait hours if it meant he would explore her whole body with his eyes.

His grey eyes lit with pure fire, burning with desire and passion and love and the primal need to claim her right *now*. Amala waited, icy stare settled on his face.

Hawk cleared his throat. "How did you find it? The whole investigation talking."

Amala raised an eyebrow, confusion on her face as he spoke. Though his eyes never left her body, regardless of what he was saying.

She shrugged.

"Honestly, it wasn't boring at all. Is that why you like mystery movies?"

Hawk sneered, "Crime movies give you the same investigation thrill but leave out the boring parts. I always try to solve the mystery before they do."

He enjoyed the smile on her face as she asked, "Do you actually solve it?"

A single nod.

"Every time."

Amala took that glimpse of normal conversation as her opportunity to turn the other way, peering at the moon through the window, the bright glow glistening through the glass and creating shadows on the wall.

"Full Moon tomorrow," she said. "Big feminine energy. Look at her... she's so fierce." Lost in contemplation of her Goddess, she stood still a moment.

Her thoughts were loud as she tried to calm, looking at the moon until the only sound was her heartbeat, and Hawk's behind her.

Twisting to face him, she find Hawk still leaning against the door. Then she was in front of him, rising on her toes to reach his level.

"You stayed focused the whole time," Amala simply said as she leaned forward and kissed him on the lips. Again.

She had wanted to kiss him for the whole damn day, fantasising on the moment she would see him again.

Hawk.

His lips were softer than she remembered as he moved them against hers, kissing her back. He bit her lower lip, Amala gasping softly at the unexpected contact. Barely, she opened her lips to gently invite his tongue in. It brushed against hers, savouring the taste of her as he had dreamed of doing for weeks. Months. *Maybe* years.

Then his hands were on her body and she sighed under his touch. Hawk had touched her body plenty of times, but never like this. Before, his touch had always been soft, and gentle, and loving, and *cuddling*, but now it was different.

Not rough, but assured and steady: firm and not possessive — not that much, at least — yet it claimed her. *Mine.* He grabbed her bare thighs, pulling her up into a straddle as he turned and pushed her body against the wall. He kept kissing her, teasing her lips with his own, only stopping to whisper in her ear: "Can I bite you, Amala mate?"

She knew what he meant. Nodding, she managed to pant an answer.

"No marks," she gasped as his canines traced her neck. He grunted his approval as he teasingly grazed her soft skin with his teeth. Repeatedly. Again and again, he bit her neck with his canines, never strong enough to cut her skin, but not gently either.

He wanted to bite her so badly, but didn't dare — not the way he wanted to.

Amala's hands cupped his face as she moved him in front of hers.

"Now you kiss me." She whispered.

Hawk didn't wait another second: his grip on her thighs only tightened as he pressed his body against her, further into the wall. On her mouth again, his tongue licked her lips and lapped at her soft skin. He teased her tongue, sucking and biting, tasting her as she moaned softly, sliding her hands through his locks. She loved his hair and gripped his strands, pulling so hard his head moved. Amala had dreamed of doing that endless times and Hawk groaned as his delicious scent merged with hers, and nothing, *nothing* had ever felt better than Hawk's lips...

It required all his mental strength to break their kiss — not abruptly, but slowly as he parted from her, their brows touching as he stared into her eyes. She pulled his hair again, but said nothing as he put her down. They both could scent each other's arousal but neither mentioned it. Amala stared at him as he grinned, then aimed for the bathroom. His voice came a second later: husky with the hint of a groan.

"You better go to sleep or you'll never wake up in time for sunrise, Amala mate."

She didn't move, still against the wall as she relived the kiss they had just shared: she was burning, aching for him, but understood what he didn't say. Until she said the words out loud, Hawk would never make a move on her. And right now, his self-control pathetically hung by a thread. There was no way he could keep kissing her like that, not without going further.

Finally, she stepped away and aimed for the bed: wrapping the sheets around her naked body, trying to ignore the aching, throbbing feeling between her legs. Inhaling Hawk's scent, she fought the urge to touch herself, her thighs burning from where his fingers had been.

CHAPTER 43

I t took him forever to fall asleep. After saying goodnight, no more words were shared. He didn't dare venture to her side of the bed: even Howlite sensed the tension between them as she jumped to the floor in the middle of the night. Hawk didn't blame her.

He woke up before Amala and thanked the Goddess for that; he didn't want to interact with her before her personal moment in the morning. No sunrise yet as dawn peered inside the bedroom as he stood, trying not to disturb her.

But her voice, slightly hoarse, reached him from the other side of the bed.

"Are you in a rush?" she murmured.

He stilled, wondering how he hadn't realised she was awake. Hawk shook his head, then realised she couldn't see him. "No, just... your morning ritual," he said, opening the door for Howlite. He heard a rustle of bedsheets, turning to find Amala leaning on her side, watching him. The blue ice of her eyes glistened beneath the dawn light, cinnamon wrapped around him.

"Care to join?"

His jaw dropped, and he didn't bother to hide the evidence of what her words were doing to him. Amala's gaze fell on his pants, and she smirked.

"You don't have to say yes if you don't feel like it," she added.

His reaction said enough, and she *knew* how bad he wanted this. Hawk stared, still in shock, as she stretched her body, squirming between the bedsheets. Exposing a glimpse of her beautiful, naked skin. Teasing him.

Hawk took his time; Amala's eyes never left him, trailing his body as he closed the door, then strode for the bed. Slowly, he pulled down his sweatpants — not because he wanted to tease her, but because he was so focused on Amala he barely noticed his own movements.

Amala knew Hawk's body: she was perfectly aware of him. His muscular chest, his incredibly defined abdominal muscles, his strong arms that made her drool. She kept her gaze on his muscled thighs, biting her lower lip, but couldn't keep her mouth shut as he finally stood naked before her. Amala's lips parted as her breath turned uneven.

"You're drooling," he teased, the same way she always did with him.

But to watch Amala lying down, looking at him with that hunger in her eyes...fuck, she was looking at him in the same exact way he looked at her — it was too good to be true.

"You simp on me on a daily basis, Hawk. Allow me a single moment, at least." Amala said, her eyes moving to his face. Then, her gaze dropped right to where he was now hard for her.

He took his cock into his hand and stroked once.

"You have no idea how much I want to choke on that piercing," Amala whispered.

Oh, yeah. That.

The piercing.

Amala flashed a smile, nodding to the bed.

"Aren't you gonna come here?"

Hawk stopped holding back. Leaning on the bed, she shifted closer to meet him, grabbing his arms and rubbing his biceps. Touching his muscles the way she had dreamed of, Amala blushed as if she felt compelled to say something — anything to justify her craving for him.

"I've been wanting you for so long, don't be surprised if I rub myself on those abs. I want you, I *need* you the exact same way you need me, Hawk. I was just much better at hiding it."

Those words... something clicked in him.

Snapped.

And something snapped in Amala too.

That was all it took.

Hawk grinned, grabbing her thighs and pulling her body on top of his, so she would straddle him. He patted his abs.

"Rub away."

"For real?" she murmured, incredulous.

She had said it as a joke, but Hawk had heard what her voice wasn't saying. And he didn't want to deprive her of such a fantasy. So, he nodded.

"Sure."

She released a breath, then crawled up until she was on top of him. Sitting on his abs, her legs straddled his torso. She was so fucking wet — so damn wet that it dripped onto his skin, even more so when she sat down completely. Utterly drenched. She blushed, well aware of it, and aware he felt it too.

The thought only contributed to turning her on, however, as her scent thickened around them. Hawk groaned, inhaling her delicious cinnamon. He grinned when she placed her hands on his pectorals, holding herself up as she began rubbing herself against him. Her first moan was a blessing to his ears: his cock hardened even more, though he didn't dare move, completely hypnotised as he watched Amala move on top of him. Her little body squirmed as she panted, rubbing her clit on his abs as Hawk tried to distract the rising pleasure in him — he was fairly sure he could come just by looking at her writhe upon him. But it was difficult to think of anything else, especially as Amala's moans grew louder.

"Fuck, Hawk," she whimpered and he groaned, grabbing her ass and squeezing hard, eliciting a moan again.

"You like that, Amala mate?" he said, enjoying the sight of her utterly devoured by pleasure.

Barely nodding, he clenched his abs as she continued rubbing against him; she cried his name once more.

Amala panted, making an effort to speak, desperately needing to say the words.

"This, rubbing myself on your perfect abs," she murmured as she kept moving, "I've been dreaming about it for *years*, Hawk. Since the first fucking time I saw you without a t-shirt." His grip on her ass intensified.

"You want to come on my abs?" He growled.

Amala gasped in surprise but kept her pace, not daring to interrupt the constant friction and risk losing the climax building between her legs. Her clit was throbbing and nothing had ever felt better than that, than *them*. Then she nodded, unable to speak as her eyes rolled in the back of her head in pleasure. A moment later, she felt Hawk's hand on her back.

He didn't linger there: his fingers aimed for her weak spot as he started stroking her utterly sensitive skin. Grazing lightly, she arched moaning. He did it again: Hawk knew her body so well — he wanted to see her completely undone.

"Hawk," Amala cried out, she sounded so close. "*Hawk,* fuck, I'm going to come if you do that again."

He grinned, making sure she didn't alter her own pace as he fondled her sweet spot again: fingers barely grazing her skin. The idea of having her at his complete mercy, rubbing herself against him as he tortured her most erogenous spot over and over and over...

Amala squirmed, and when he touched her again — right *there* — she came, screaming his name.

She didn't stop her movements, grinding against him for the entire duration of her climax. Hawk didn't halt either, his fingers stroking her skin as she slowed. Amala's pants echoed in the room, and then he felt... her wetness on his abs. Hawk could barely control himself as Amala sat on him again, splaying it on his skin.

And then, it hit him.

His mate, Amala — *Goddess Amala* — had just come all over him. *Goddess of Sex Amala.*

Hawk took in the sight of her, her chest rising with laboured breath. She met his gaze, eyes glimmering.

"That was..." she started, her voice hoarse, "A thousand times better than how I imagined it. And I touched myself thinking about it every fucking day of my life."

She leaned closer and kissed him on the lips, laughing in relief, and it was pure bliss. Crawling backwards, still on top of him, Amala lowered her head to lick his abs. Licking *herself* off him.

Hawk stared, unable to even process what she was doing as her tongue lapped, tasting her own cum on his skin.

Fuck. *Fuck.* He wasn't even entirely sure he hadn't come, by that point.

Amala raised her body once again, a smile on her lips, now glistening with her own release.

"Fucking delicious," she muttered.

He was hypnotised, certain the vision of Amala licking her cum off his abs would haunt him forever. Passing a finger over her bottom lip to gather what was left of her release, she sucked. Her finger was still in her mouth as she watched him.

"Want a kiss?"

"In a second," he muttered.

She yelped because he grabbed her thighs, pulling her until she sat on his face. He didn't let her say anything as he tasted her, hands pinning her right above his mouth. Hawk refused to let Amala move an inch as he lapped his tongue between her flesh, dipping it inside of her and savouring every drop.

She tasted like... Hawk could not describe it. It was the most feminine thing he had ever known. Pure lust, luxury, and sweetness, and he didn't know which words to use to say it any better: it was pure woman.

Enjoying her soft moans, he dragged his tongue over her sensitised clit. Amala pulled his hair.

"Fuck yes, Hawk," she muttered, her scent whirling towards him once more.

He couldn't hold back anymore and flipped them over. Amala was sprawled on the bed, ass up in the air as she looked at him over her shoulder. Grabbing her ass from behind, he run his hands on her cheeks, and gently slapped her skin.

When he moved away, he glimpsed her pout. Little tease.

Amala's eyes hungrily followed him as he reached for his nightstand, gaping when she saw what he pulled from his drawer. Amala bit her lip, feeling him move behind her once again.

He groaned at the sight of her glistening sex.

"Aren't you a little bunny, getting wet just because you saw the ropes?"

He teased her sex with a finger, dipping it inside and splaying her wetness around her sensitive flesh. She writhed around him.

"I am *not*."

Hawk grinned. He liked when she behaved like a brat. Binding her wrists to her calves, Hawk wrapped the rope around her thighs, making it impossible for her to move. Amala tilted her head as she leaned on the bed, breasts rubbing against the sheets and ass up in the air.

"Are you really tying me up the *first* time we have sex?" she breathed.

Hawk nodded, gesturing for her to try moving her arms. Amala pulled, but couldn't move: she had to spread her knees a bit more to avoid falling on a side, since she couldn't use her arms to keep her body still.

"Yeah," he replied. "I'll tie you up, worship the shit out of you, and fuck you until you beg to touch me." Her breath caught and he grinned. "And don't even try to be bratty. If you open that pretty mouth of yours, it will be only to scream my name, Amala bunny." Hawk slapped her ass.

She whimpered when his hands hit her skin, but protested, "Don't call me that."

"Why not?" he inquired, slapping her ass again. Harder.

"*Hawk*," she warned, trying to retain a kernel of sanity.

But she couldn't. And Hawk knew it.

He could see every drop of her, becoming more wet each time he touched or teased her. There was no way of hiding it.

"Why not, Amala bunny?"

Amala panted. *Fuck.* She couldn't even try to pretend she wasn't loving it. His fingers teased her drenched sex again.

"Because it makes you so wet, you're dripping on my bed?" his husky voice moved dangerously close to that spot on her back.

"*Please*," she said, wiggling her ass, offering herself entirely to him.

"Please what?"

"Fuck me." she muttered, tugging at her restrained arms.

"Admit you like that and maybe I will." Hawk stroked his cock once, twice, then aligned it right in front of her wet opening, teasing her with his tip, and the piercing he had there. Amala writhed.

"Please," she begged. Her soft voice hardened his cock even more. There was nothing he wanted more than to push himself into her and fuck her so hard she would pray the Goddess before she could remember *she* was one, now. But he waited one more agonising moment, enjoying this relentless torment.

"Fuck, Hawk — *fine,* I love it when you call me that." She admitted.

Before she could protest further, she screamed as Hawk thrust his cock inside her, legs spreading her knees apart even further. Keeping her body still as she squirmed, Amala clenched around him. Hawk swore as he felt her for the first time. She was *so* tight — he had fantasised about her tightness for years. And she hadn't allowed anyone else to *take* her, not the way he was doing now. Hawk slowly tried to fit himself inside of her and Amala moaned again, louder this time.

"Fuck, I can feel it *so* well."

He pulled out, almost completely, then thrust into her again.

"Hawk," she moaned.

"How does it feel?" He whispered in her ear, husky voice masking the attention he put in the question. He would always check in with her, ready to stop as soon as she said the word. He traced her spine with his finger, tattoos contrasting with her creamy skin.

"Fucking *good*," Amala panted, "It hurts just so right..."

Oh. *Oh.*

It took Hawk a moment to understand as he slowly thrust into her again. She *was* in pain. She only... fucking loved it.

His little Amala bunny was a big, big masochist.

"*Please,*" her body writhed, as much movement as she could manage, "More, *more.*"

Hawk's tattooed hands tightened on her waist as he finally managed to fit all his cock inside of her. She moaned, so deliciously stretched that her whole body trembled. Thighs shaking, she clenched her fingers. Hawk knew she would have gripped the sheets, if only she had been able to reach them... Such a shame she couldn't move.

He lowered his face to her ass to bite her soft skin. *Hard.*

Amala screamed in pain, pleasure — probably both.

"Fucking *move*," she seethed.

Hawk intensified his grip on her hips and started thrusting inside of her, retreating each time to push harder the next.

Yes yes yes, she whimpered.

"Please." Her anklets clinked at the sheer power moving her with each thrust, and she cried out once more.

"Such a good bunny, my pretty Amala mate." She was so damn tight. Mind meltingly tight.

The feeling of her warmth wrapped around him — clenching so much there wasn't any space left — threatened to melt Hawk's brain, becoming the only thing he would think of for the rest of his life. He welcomed the idea with open arms though. Amala was everything he had ever wanted and she was his, his, *his*. Hawk made love to her like he had dreamed of doing from the moment they met, and she loved it — pain and pleasure mixing and driving her crazy.

"Don't hold back," she pleaded, "Hawk—"

He pounded, feeling her wetness against him.

"Fuck, Amala," he groaned, his grip on her ass intensifying as he started thrusting harder. She tried to move her body towards him, meeting his thrusts as she moaned louder.

"More, please!" She begged, trying to move her arms. Hawk loved when she tried to pull herself free.

"No moving around for you, Amala bunny," he growled, thrusting harder, "My *pretty* Amala bunny all tied up for me..."

She couldn't resist as he teased with those words.

"*Fuck*, Hawk," Amala whimpered as she came again, her delicate flesh clenching around him and moving with him as he continued thrusting. Hearing his name on her lips drove him absolutely crazy.

"Fuck, that's it, Amala," he groaned as he spilled himself into her. His hands still squeezed her ass as he pounded steadily, not stopping until he had pumped every single drop.

Their pants fused together as they slowly halted, and Hawk stilled inside of her.

Her muffled voice came a second later, her head still tilted between the spilled sheets.

"I need to kiss you. Now."

Amala tried to stretch a little bit as he pulled out, then began to untie her: he barely pulled the final rope away and she was already on him, small hands clenching around his jaw as she kissed him furiously. With what energy, he didn't know. She looked utterly spent.

"I loved it." She murmured, biting his lower lip.

Hawk smiled back, "I loved it too. I didn't know you liked that pet name so much,"

He started massaging her skin, where the ropes had left their mark.

"I didn't know either," she admitted, enjoying the soothing touch of his hands rubbing at her arms and wrists. "That was hot."

"You're hot, Amala mate." He leaned on her, pressing a kiss on her neck.

Amala felt his canines instinctively trace her skin, though he held back.

For now.

She caught his gaze as he massaged her calf, the spot where the rope mark was well visible.

"Mated mates, then."

Hawk's mouth dropped open for a split second, before he reconquered his usual smugness. He rubbed his fingers against her soft skin.

"Mated mates, indeed."

Amala smiled, "What now, then?"

He pressed a kiss on her calf, a dark chuckle against her skin.

"Now you're mine forever."

CHAPTER 44

"Nyla agreed to talk with us later today," Hawk said, wearing his leather jacket. He grabbed his sunglasses, then glanced in the mirror, Amala's figure reflected before him.

She smiled.

"Do you want me to come with you, then?"

"She agreed to talk only if you were there. She told me to come at four, but I told her two so you can head straight to the Home of Waters after, and be on time for Full Moon. I can pick you up from the temple after lunch."

Her smile said enough. When Hawk showed interest and care in her High Priestess life... she couldn't help it, it meant the world to her.

"Thanks," she said. "But I can meet you there. I have a patient on my way back to the city, it's her first visit. I'll walk to Nyla's palace." She angled her body, checking herself out in the mirror. Amala's stunning figure beamed, white tight dress wrapped around her curves as her beautiful bare hips undulated with every step she took. "What are you doing this morning?"

"Looking up the centaurs, Blade's gonna help. You down to accompany one of us to Mhelani Forest?"

Amala looked at him carefully.

"You or Blade?"

"Does it make a difference?"

"Blade would likely make a stupid joke and offend them, but you're my mate, which might piss them off. Not all, just..." she cracked her neck to the side, "Kanaan is the one who told me about Serabel. If you want answers from him, I suggest not telling him we're together."

Hawk considered. Did he want to face Kanaan — his own scent merged with cinnamon in a not so subtle indicator that *he* was the one who mated Amala? Yes. Did he think it was a stupid move? Also yes. Amala was right: if he was to speak to the centaurs, it was wiser to hide their relationship.

They had showered separately — to get rid of each other's scent, although the urge of a quick fuck under the water felt tempting. But both agreed: right now, it wasn't the time to broadcast the news.

"We're mated now, huh?" She absently asked, tracing his tattooed hands. Her nails grazed his left ring finger, the word written there. "Weren't you gonna tell me what this meant?"

Hawk scoffed: his clever, cunning mate. Always trying to trick him.

"Who, me?" A flash of his canines, "I'll tell you when you finally accept to be the next Goddess." Amala giggled, hopelessly shaking her head. "That's going to take longer than all the other times you've found an excuse."

"I don't mind. I have a whole life to spend with you."

Hawk was hopelessly in love with Amala. With one last goodbye as she walked down the street, he strode for his car. They had parted like that every day for weeks now, but to know he would kiss her next time in greeting made his heart thump in his chest. Their bond had snapped and he was madly in love.

There was no need to hurry things though. It had taken them ten years to kiss, he could only imagine how long it would take for her to say she loved him, even though he knew she did: it was all that mattered.

The drive to his office felt shorter than usual, probably because he couldn't stop thinking of Amala's creamy skin rubbing against his, her tightness wrapped around him as he pounded into her...fuck, no.

Hawk forced himself to think of something other than her — anything else — he couldn't afford any distractions today. He just hoped Blade wouldn't taunt him when he entered the office fifteen minutes later. Blade was sitting at *his* desk, going through something on his laptop as he sipped coffee from a paper cup.

"Hey," he gestured, "I got one for you too."

Hawk thanked him as he grabbed the cup and sipped the coffee: lukewarm.

"Anything new?" he said, checking the laptop's screen.

"Not really. I got a bunch of stuff on the centaurs, but it's still a..." his voice trailed, gaze quickly checking him out. "Did you fuck hot High Priestess?"

Hawk grinned. "Yeah."

Blade grinned back. "Sick."

Then the moment was gone and he nodded to the screen, "Do you know any of these guys?"

"You got anything on them?"

"Well, we know they know *something*, that's for sure." Blade shrugged, "Their whole kingdom has been relying on the Goddess' energy for centuries. I refuse to believe they're not affected by the lack of it, right now."

Hawk frowned, his brow wrinkling as he read the information Blade had gathered on the centaurs. "If you wanna talk to them, Amala's down to come with you."

"Me?" Blade asked, "What the fuck am I gonna do? Say some shit and get myself killed? No, thank you. Tell your girlfriend you can go with her." He paused, considering. "Is she your girlfriend, tho? Or did you just fuck?"

For how much he didn't like the sound of it, that was a legitimate question.

Before he could reply, Naressa entered the office, Cairo behind her. They both took one look at Hawk and grinned. He seethed, bracing himself for whatever was coming. There was little to do with his friends: to look at details and figure out the bigger picture was their job, and needless to say, they were all damn good at it.

Naressa arched an eyebrow. "How was it?"

"How was what?"

She gasped, fire dancing at her fingertips as she let out a bright laugh. "Is this how it's gonna be?"

"It depends," Hawk replied, "On how much you can mind your business."

She was in front of him in a second, fiery fingertips mere inches from his face. To his credit, Hawk didn't back down, didn't even blink as he stood firm.

"Don't play scary bitch with me."

"Just tell me how it went," she pleaded, fluttering her lashes.

He finally cracked, revealing a half smile.

"My pride is intact, and my mate is satisfied."

She frowned.

"What's that supposed to mean?"

"That he didn't cum before she did," Blade explained.

Hawk approved with a nod as Cairo taunted, "That was a possibility?"

"Absolutely yes."

Cairo howled at Hawk's words, but it was only happiness on his face. And admiration. Since he had met Amala, he kept telling Hawk how much she was meant for him. *She completes you. More than anything else has ever done,* he had said — and he had been right, even after meeting her for a mere hour.

Naressa pulled Hawk into a hug. The scent of vanilla and ylang-ylang was sweet, his mind trailing to the sugary cinnamon he had washed off his body earlier today. It felt almost frustrating not to bask in her scent for the rest of the day, but he planned to ask her to coat him again very soon.

"Back to business."

Blade grimaced.

Cairo snorted.

Naressa rolled her eyes.

He was in for a long day.

☼

It was Amala's turn to guide Hawk around Aglatas.

Her knowledge of the city was limited to temples, hospitals and her patients' homes, but she had been to the Home of Waters many times, especially for Lady Danua's pregnancy. Hawk had texted, agreeing to meet in a café next to the Apàle. They walked together from there.

Amala's eyes were bright when she spotted him waiting, but she hadn't done as much as smiling at him. Neither of them would risk a kiss in another Protector's territory. It offered too much leverage, especially when they were in search of information.

Aquar, where the Home of Waters resided, was probably the most beautiful district of Aglatas. Pyramis was the most opulent, Anemos a shiny realm, whereas Gea was a blooming urban forest. But Aquar? It was incredible.

CHIARA GALA

On the way to Nyla's palace, they spotted more fountains than they could count. Streams of clear water flowed next to the pavements, small canals creating a maze of marble bridges and creeks filled with fish and cobblestones, all drifting from the Apàle's clear, humming waters. The palace itself was glorious: waterfalls cascading from tall, elegant windows, and the sound of running water a constant background layer as they entered through the silver gates.

Such beautiful, utter luxury, surrounded by a sheer layer of sobriety. It was not tacky or preposterous or too much, like Jaren's court. The Water court was beautiful and that was the only way to describe it.

Lady Nyla sat on a throne too. But differently from the other Protectors, she guided and ruled her people — refusing to flaunt her power before them. On her left sat her sister Danua, who acknowledged Amala with a bow of her head. In her arms, a new-born baby.

Amala knelt. It wasn't a big deal to her, kneeling for others. She had worshipped Serabel since the day she was born and manifestations of respect came to her naturally.

Hawk couldn't help but think they should have knelt for Amala, instead. Their Goddess.

"It is an honour to be invited to your beautiful palace, my Lady." Amala said.

Nyla smiled: she had always been the nicest in the Karale. The one who treated Amala with kindness and quiet admiration, the one who saw her Love not as a weakness, but a strength.

"The honour is mine, High Priestess Amala. You are always welcome here."

Amala turned to Danua, "How is everything?"

"So well, High Priestess. I never knew I could feel such joy every day." A glimmer of gratitude shone in her eyes. Amala held that gaze without blinking.

Hawk glimpsed the spark of pain hiding behind that façade and wished he could take that away — all the pain from her past. He knew it wasn't up to him, though. It was up to Amala, and only Amala, to forgive herself and move on. He could only be by her side as she did so.

Nyla stood. She didn't speak to her court as she descended the steps from the throne, striding with regal grace.

"Thank you for coming." Amala greeted Hawk with a curtsy of her head. "If you will follow me."

He fell into step behind her, Amala by his side. They spotted a flash of Ana's green cat eyes as they left the throne room. Walking through corridors surrounded by the sound of flowing water, they reached a smaller, quieter room, with décor much like the throne hall. Nyla gestured to a cushioned blue sofa, as she sat on the one adjacent.

Hawk waited for Amala to sit before doing so himself.

She adjusted her robe, trying to cover her thighs as they splayed on the soft blue fabric. Hawk appreciated the attempt, but couldn't keep his eyes off her. Amala glared: a silent order for him to stop. But how could he pretend to keep his attention on *anything* else when their mating bond had finally snapped?

Amala looked at Nyla before Hawk's behaviour could cause any further damage.

"Why did you want me to come here, my Lady?" She asked.

Nyla dipped her chin, apprehension painting her face.

"I got notice that you wished for a meeting," she started. "So, I thought I'd take my chance. I would have summoned you myself, sooner or later." Nyla glanced at Hawk, though her eyes quickly returned to Amala, as if *she* was the real focus of their conversation. "Perhaps you are here to ask the same question."

"That would depend on your answer, Nyla." Hawk said.

"Serabel came to me some months ago."

Amala stilled. This time, though, her face didn't betray surprise, rather... something like defeat. Once more, her Goddess had hid something else from Amala. It wasn't like she knew everything the Goddess did or planned but, as her Second, she thought Serabel would involve her in *some* of her plans — especially the ones involving other Protectors.

Hawk saw Amala flinch, so assumed control of the conversation.

"When was this exactly?"

"Almost a year ago," Nyla said. "In the fifth month she came to visit me for the first time. But it happened other times too, after the first. She was searching for something."

Amala held her breath, icy eyes widening in surprise. Something like fear or anticipation flickered in her gaze, as though she *knew* the truth but genuinely didn't wish for it to be confirmed.

"What did she want?" he asked.

Nyla focused on him.

"She wanted manuscripts. Ancient texts on the Goddess' energy that my court has protected for centuries. They were a gift from the former Goddesses to the former Protectors. Not only that but she wanted more texts on the flow of energy, of life and reincarnation. I believe she wanted to study the subject."

"Why would she? Serabel already knew all of that..." Amala whispered.

"I do not know. But she seemed eager to learn of it again. She—" A hint of fear marked her scent of river waters and seafoam. "She mentioned something odd. About some power greater than any other I'd known."

Hawk let the information settle in his brain. Power. In every scenario analysed since Serabel's death, power had never been in the picture.

"I don't think she wanted to *scare* me," Nyla continued. "But she looked different when she said it. Eager to know more. I let her borrow the texts and wondered about this power for a while and, barely a month later, she came back."

"More texts?" Hawk mused.

Nyla's lips curved upward, "No. She wanted to know about the Charal women."

The silence stretched for several seconds. Then—

"Fuck this."

Hawk's head snapped to Amala whose teeth were gritted, white hair floating around her shoulders as she didn't bother keeping her air under control. Hawk would have sent his own wind to calm her, but refrained from doing so. It would give away too much, more than they could afford now.

"Fuck this," Amala muttered again. "I can't believe she had this whole thing going on and didn't speak to me about it even *once*," her voice broke on the last word, holding back her tears.

Nyla threw her an apologetic look as her regal face appeared worried.

"I am so sorry, High Priestess. She never mentioned you, but I assumed you knew. It was only after Atalman told me about your visit that I realised you weren't part of Serabel's schemes."

"You know about Atalman?" Hawk intervened with a huff of annoyance.

"He hinted you might want to talk to me."

He scowled. "Not about this, though."

He told her about the Riza and how the water spells had been the only ones the thief had successfully passed, before failing Jaren's task and burning alive.

Nyla listened carefully, face betraying no hint of emotion.

"I cast those spells centuries ago, Captain. I myself barely remember which ones. But regardless of enchantment skills, you are not considering a key point: the Riza is Atalman's territory. I would never send someone from my court to *steal*."

Amala released a breath, almost in relief. Hawk knew she couldn't stand the idea of Nyla siding against them. She tried to steady her voice.

"Please, would you tell me more about the books she borrowed? Goddess Serabel?"

"She wanted to study the genealogy of power. How divine energy flows and why. My libraries have vast collections of manuscripts, and I let her borrow some. She returned them, though."

"And the great power she mentioned," Amala continued. "You think she meant the Charal women?"

Nyla nodded gravely. "I am sure of that, High Priestess. Serabel was always interested in them after the last persecution, but during this past year she became obsessed. I don't know if it was guilt, but it was odd. She already did so much to preserve the Charal traditions, yet it was like nothing she had done had ever been enough."

"It's not enough if it can't bring them back," Amala said softly.

Nyla's gaze indulged on her face, seeming to realise what she had said.

"My apologies, Amala. I didn't mean it lightly."

"It's alright, my Lady. My heart breaks at the thought of those women, but I am proud of my Goddess for trying to make things right."

The Protector offered her a smile. "I don't know what matter of power Serabel was talking about. But from what I gathered, she seemed sure the Charal women would rise again."

CHAPTER 45

A mala opened the door into their home, finally pleased to be back. Her thoughts had been messy and confusing after leaving Nyla's palace, and the Full Moon ritual had drained the rest of her energy.

It had been the longest day, and she couldn't wait to enjoy the comfort of her space once again. And her mate.

She heard Howlite rushing to the foyer and discarded her bag on the floor, reaching out first.

"Hello, love," she greeted, petting her head, "Did you have a nice day? Do you want to take a nap together?"

Hawk closed the door behind them; he had picked Amala up, finding her exhausted by the end of her rite, though there was a glimpse of mischief in her eyes as he drove back home. He had no idea how he made it to the end of the day, his brain permanently reliving that morning, and the way Amala had made Love to him so fiercely.

Standing up from the floor, she now walked to the living room with the clear intention — she'd told him in the car — to slouch on the sofa for at least half an hour.

But as he followed her, he was confused to find her stood in the middle of the room, and the sofa already occupied.

Cairo greeted them with a nod of his chin, Blade waving. On his side, Naressa beamed.

"Hello, lovebirds."

"Are we having a mating party?" Amala muttered, but she didn't seem enthusiastic.

"We aren't," Hawk replied, amused. "I have no idea what they're doing here."

Cairo chuckled, "That's bullshit. We always have recap dinner on Thursdays when we're on a case. It's not my fault if you have other stuff on your mind." He glanced not too subtly at Amala.

"Don't call me *stuff*, thank you," she said with a smile, then turned to Hawk: "Alright. I'll shower as you work."

"No," he replied instantly. "They're leaving."

Amala shook her head. "Don't be rude. I'll be quick."

"They're leaving," he seethed, but Amala was already on her way to their bedroom. She threw a glance over her shoulder to ensure Howlite followed, then closed the door behind them. Hawk kept his gaze fixed to her back until she was out of reach, eyeing her beautiful bare hips swaying with each damn step she took. Then, he turned to his friends.

"Don't you *even* start—"

Blade burst out laughing.

"You are hopeless."

"I've never seen you *simping* so hard..."

He made a point to ignore each of those comments and made his way to the kitchen.

Grabbing a beer from the fridge, he clarified, "Your time here ends the second she comes out of that room. What's going on?"

"We were waiting for your updates. How did it go with Nyla?" Cairo snickered.

"I could have fucking texted you, if you wanted an update."

"You can calm down, man." Blade suggested, "You mated, it's done. Wasn't she celibate, by the way?"

Hawk's eyes snapped in direction of the door. Too fast.

"She had some kind of vision, but it was blurry." He said, going for the version Amala and him had agreed on. "The energy found someone, but she hasn't been able to fully see who. But technically, she's not celibate anymore."

"That's dope," Blade shrugged. "Why are you moody, then?"

"Because you're all here."

Now Naressa chuckled too. Hawk gave up on his forced scowl, allowing himself to grin, just a little. He quickly summed up how things had gone in Aquar: Nyla's newest information, mainly, and orders to research the manuscripts mentioned. Though he didn't how the Protector's information had sparked a new idea in his mind: he would need to reflect before he could rationalise it. He definitely wasn't in the mood to overthink right now.

Cairo agreed to search up the texts, Naressa promising to help while she had a few days off forensic duty. The autopsy conducted on Serabel's corpse had been inconclusive, but she was eager to help in other ways, making herself useful. Hawk was about to ask if Wahine had reached out again, but Amala emerged from their bedroom, wrapped in a white towel, hair still wet from the shower. She ignored how everyone's gaze instantly fell on her, as the towel hugged her curves, leaving all of her thighs exposed. Hawk's eyes fell on her delicious breasts, and he temporarily stopped listening. His head emptied, filled only by the memory of Amala's little body riding on top of his abs, her thick, beautiful, creamy thighs shaking under the power of her orgasm. Hawk still couldn't believe he had touched her, tasted her, *fucked* her.

"I want an apple."

Her icy eyes gazed into his as she reached for the kitchen counter, hand snaking into the fruit basket to grab a red, crispy apple. She halted when she saw his bottle.

"Are you drinking?"

"Just passing time."

Amala glanced at his friends, then back at him. "Time's up."

☼

Hawk didn't even wait for Blade to close the door before picking Amala up and placing her on the kitchen counter. The apple fell on the floor as she giggled, placing both hands on his face.

"I thought about you all day." Amala whispered. He grabbed her thighs as she pressed a kiss against his lips.

The first kiss they shared since that morning.

Amala had struggled to have him by her side while unable to touch him, but she let him feel all the desire and tension she had accumulated during the day as she fiercely explored his mouth, her tongue scraping against his teeth, licking his lips and stealing his breath.

When she licked his canines, Hawk pulled her hair to expose her neck.

"Don't play."

"I'm not playing." She breathed.

He lifted her again, his grip on her thighs tightening as he headed for their bedroom.

"I have ideas for our new life together," Amala said as she stroked his hair, lips kissing his neck. "Let's start with: your friends are *not* allowed in here when I come home horny?"

When he laughed, she stilled: serious.

"I mean it. It's happened two days in a *row*."

She kissed him again — neck and then lips — and he flipped them, pinning her against the wall. She gasped, unsettled by how fast he had changed their positions.

"You are such a little tease, Amala mate," he softly groaned in her ear, feeling her small body squirming beneath his.

"I'm *not*," she protested, a moan escaping her lips as she felt his teeth graze against the sensitive skin of her neck.

"You are," he stated. "But I don't mind."

Amala purred softly as he grasped her neck, eyes rolling to the back of her head.

"Bite me."

Holy fucking Goddess.

Hawk's own *soul* groaned at those words, and he needed all of his self-control to wait for her to finish the sentence, to double check. His grip on her neck only intensified as he asked, "You mean it?"

Amala nodded, icy eyes so wide and pure and beautiful.

"Voice, Amala mate..." Hawk growled in her ear.

"Yes!" she gasped.

Hawk would have thanked the Goddess had she not been standing in front of him. Moaning for him to bite her neck. *Begging.*

"*Please*," she panted. "Bite me. *Mark* me."

He lost any form of control at those words.

Amala cried out in pure ecstasy at the feeling of his canines sinking into her skin. She was mind-blowingly soft, her cinnamon scent so sugary and intoxicating and absolutely delicious. He tasted all of her — the sunlight and moonlight — and decided he would never have enough: of her, her delicious scent and her delicious *blood* and anything she would give him.

Hawk stopped to catch his breath, blood trickling on his chin.

Amala licked it, lips turning red.

"Sweet," she whispered.

"You are in for a long night, Amala mate."

"I fucking hope so."

Her fingers trembled as she undid whatever miracle had kept her towel on until now, letting it fall on the floor at her feet. She grasped the edge of his t-shirt, pulling up and, once his chest was bare, pressed her bare breasts against him. Amala groaned at the feeling of her nipples against his skin.

Hawk's hands lifted her against the wall, and she gasped when she felt his fingers trailing up her inner thigh. His bite had made her so wet it had trickled down her soft skin. He seemed to realise too as his grip tightened, one steady hand below her ass, as his other hand clasped in between her legs, cupping her whole.

"Hawk," she pleaded. "Bite me again."

Hawk pulled away for a brief second, his canines sticking out as he licked his lips.

"Bite or claim?"

Amala shamelessly panted. "What's the difference?"

He pressed his fingers against her neck, on the spot he had bitten mere moments before. She winced at the pain, a soft moan escaping her lips.

"This," he pressed harder. Amala's eyes rolled back in pleasure. "Is a bite mark. It goes away. But I can give you one claiming mark, too — only one."

"A mating mark?"

"A mating mark," he repeated. "And it's forever."

"*Oh*," she writhed under his touch. "I thought that's what that bite was."

But he shook his head.

"I wouldn't give you a permanent mark without asking where you want it. *If* you want it—"

"Of course I want it, Hawk," Amala whispered, fingers tracing his lips.

He grinned. "Choose a spot on that beautiful body of yours, then."

Putting her down, Amala leaned against the wall, steadying herself on shaking legs. With shaky steps towards the bed, her hips dangerously swung so, *so* sensually — oh, she was well aware of how her body drove Hawk completely, utterly crazy.

"And where would *you* like to mark me?" she asked in her innocent, sweet voice.

Hawk's gaze was fixed on her face, grey eyes merging with cunning ice.

"I'll take whatever you want to give me, Goddess Amala."

She silently climbed on the bed until she was on all fours, her beautiful naked body glowing under the Full Moon, her wetness gleaming between her folds now totally exposed to him. Amala looked at him over her shoulder, a shaky hand grazing the sweet skin of her thigh, that spot just below her full, juicy ass. "What about here?"

She knew Hawk would go feral. Absolutely feral.

She *knew* he had a thing for her thighs.

Hawk was on her in a second. She instantly lost control of her body: she was his — *his*, and his hands were everywhere, holding her in place as he lowered his head to the spot she pointed to.

"You're fucking mine, Amala mate."

Yes, yes, she moaned.

His fingers trailed to graze her back, right on that sweet spot that drove her to absolute madness.

Then Hawk's teeth sank into her as he marked Amala forever.

☼

Hawk would have loved to focus on his work. Instead, he was was struggling to process the paper he was reading — or was supposed to be — busy reliving biting Amala again and again and again, her thighs shaking under his mouth. He had been staring at the document for the past thirty minutes. Not that he had any news from the case.

Nyla had only given him more questions and still zero fucking answers. He was supposed to go to Mhelani forest soon too, but he wondered if that was going to be another waste of time.

Hawk sighed: everywhere he looked for clues, only more doubts popped up. The only pattern until now had been the constant correlation between Serabel and the Charal women, wherever lead he had followed. It didn't really help catch who had killed her.

Hawk was waiting for Amala to text him she was finished for the day when his phone buzzed.

But it wasn't Amala.

And in that exact moment, the only thing he considered certain became another unanswered question.

Blade:
Wahine texted.
The buyer reached out again.

CHAPTER 46

B lade didn't look as worried as Cairo.

Which might have been because Blade had smoked three joints before meeting up, or he was just irrationally calm about very serious matters. But here they were: Blade still and calm, while Cairo nervously checked his phone.

"Alright," Blade spoke first. "Wahine was very brief but very clear. The buyer is *still* out there. The Embers got a call and a new request. She still doesn't know what it is, just that it's not urgent and that she'll get new info soon."

"What debt did she collect this time?"

Blade shrugged. "Whatever it was, I bet that guy already owes her again."

"Wahine is smart as fuck."

"Yeah. She's got all the brains."

"Your brain is fine, dude. Just maybe... don't smoke so much?" Hawk suggested, though he knew it was a lost cause. Blade would never give up on being a stoner.

He glanced up at both his friends, his stare conveying what they avoided to say.

"You can say it, you know," Hawk advised, taking a hit from his joint. *Hypocrite*, he thought to himself, after just scolding Blade for the exact same thing. "The buyer can't be Serabel, and I was wrong. My whole theory was wrong."

Cairo smirked, "It wasn't a stupid theory."

"I never said it was stupid," Hawk replied, inhaling the smell of cinnamon, "Only incorrect."

"What now, then?" Cairo asked after a moment of silence.

"Wahine will keep me posted, it's only a matter of time before we figure out who this guy is. And once we do, hopefully we can finish this shit."

Blade's fingers raised to where he kept another joint tucked on top of his ear.

"*Seriously*?" Cairo snorted as Blade lit it up and inhaled. "You've got some apologising to do too." He pointed a finger to Hawk.

Hawk raised his hands in defence. "I already said I was wrong. I'm sorry."

"Oh, not to us." Cairo smirked, "If we had listened to your girlfriend instead of you, we wouldn't be in this situation now."

Hawk refrained from grimacing. Amala was opposed to his theory from the beginning. And she had been right: if Serabel was trying to reunite the Charal tribe, it wasn't by dealing with gangs or paying for information. It meant only one thing: someone else was interested in exactly the same things the Goddess had been researching. Whoever it was could very much be her killer.

☼

Amala looked at the baby, heart full at the sight of the beautiful creature in the arms of her mother. Sinayla smiled, her eyes lovingly admiring Xantara.

"I can't stop looking at her," she murmured, mesmerised. "She's just perfect. She's perfect, Amala."

Her gaze moved to the High Priestess, adding in a whisper, "I'll never stop being grateful for what you did for me."

Amala whipped her head to look at her, eyes filled with surprise.

"Don't say it like that, my love," she whispered back. "I'm so happy for you, and beautiful baby X is having the time of her life feeding from mommy," her gentle voice was like a soothing caress as she stroke one finger against the baby's forehead.

"I know what this means to you, Amala. You are a special soul. You are..." she paused, trying to find the words.

For a moment, Amala considered sharing with her everything that was going on with her lately — the vessel and everything else, but...

"Fuck, fuck, *fuck*!"

They both turned to the sound of Hebex's voice.

"Are you alright, beautiful?" Amala said.

The priestess shook her head, gaze wandering on the porch outside the temple's main entrance.

"Captain Mercurian is here," she breathed, looking at Amala. Her gaze moved to Sinayla, "And he's walking to Caelan."

Fuck.

Amala instantly stood, heart thumping in her chest.

"*Shit*," she cursed, gesturing to Sinayla to stay down and finish breastfeeding in peace.

Hebex swiftly aimed for them, worry in her eyes.

"What do we do?" she whispered.

"What is he doing here?" Sinayla said, worried. "Do you *want* him to speak to Caelan?"

"What? *No!*" Amala blurted, "I think he's just here to pick me up, but I—he didn't know about... the last time he saw him. And now—" Shit.

Hawk was going to kill Caelan if they ever crossed paths. Hebex seemed inclined to agree, but neither of them voicing their fears in front of Sinayla. Though Sinayla seemed pretty sure of it too.

"Hawk is going to kill him." She hissed.

Amala hadn't touched the topic of her celibacy, yet. While her sisters had saw her marks, she told them they had mated, but nothing sexual had happened besides the marking. Which was a blatant lie, of course, given they hadn't been able to stop making love to each other for days now. Hawk had fucked her on every surface of their house: their bed, shower, bathtub, floor, bathroom floor, even the goddamn balcony.

Yeah, he just marked me, she had told her sisters. She almost laughed now, thinking about it, before realising Caelan had reached Sinayla, and Hawk entered the altar room.

Caelan looked like he knew what was going on; Amala wasn't sure whether her sister had told him, but everyone at the temple had seen those mating marks. And the Captain who was always around her.

The same Captain now walking to her, gaze fixed on her beautiful body.

She let out a tendril of air to sneak to him in greeting. Part of her hoped he would punch Caelan in the face, though she knew she didn't wish for it. Not truly. Hawk glanced at Hebex, then blinked in the priest's direction, eyes narrowing before his gaze fell on Amala again.

"Good morning, High Priestess."

Amala sighed with relief.

He wouldn't make a scene, she should have known. Hawk wouldn't make a scene, even if he *really* wanted to kill Caelan. Instead, he would play pretend, imagining a thousand ways to beat the shit out of him if he ever had the chance, while not doing so much as baring his teeth in

Caelan's direction. Not in the middle of the God's temple in front of his mate.

Or Sinayla.

"I didn't know you were here," Hawk said.

She frowned, confused.

"You told me you had a visit at the temple and I thought you meant the Home of Waters. So, I went there." Hawk added.

Amala chuckled in realisation. "Oh, I'm sorry. I meant Sinayla. Today was her postpartum check," she explained, nodding to the priestess with her chin. She turned to Caelan, nervously biting her lower lip before saying, "And she's doing great. Everything is perfectly healthy."

He assessed her words with a nod.

"How's Xantara?" he asked.

Amala dared to look into his eyes for a short second. She swallowed, forcing herself — *commanding* her brain to think of anything but the words he had told her all those years ago.

Focusing her thoughts on Xantara: the beautiful, healthy, joyful Xantara whom she loved so much.

"She's..."

Alive.

Not dead like mine — dead, and it's my fault.

It's all my fault.

She breathed, resolute. She wouldn't allow those thoughts to get the better of her. Not in front of Caelan and not in front of Sinayla. She didn't deserve that.

Swallowing her tears, Amala looked up to Caelan again.

"She's perfect. Healthy, eating enough, and growing stronger every day. I'm very glad she gets to live full time with the both of you, here."

And that I'm not here, she wanted to add.

Goddess knew that leaving the Yonium had been life changing, but at least she didn't have to live with Sinayla and Caelan and their new-born child.

"Thank you, Am—" he started, but Sinayla nudged him, not at all discretely. "High Priestess Amala," Caelan corrected, earning an approving nod from his mate.

Amala turned to Hawk, whose eyes were already on her, not daring to leave her for a single second. She met his gaze, her lips automatically tugging upwards when she realised the look he was giving her: those beautiful dark grey eyes staring at her face as if she was the most beautiful thing in the world.

He dropped the formalities for a second.

"Wanna go home?" he asked.

She nodded.

"I'm hungry, though."

"We'll stop for strawberries and cinnamon rolls."

"Deal." Amala chuckled, eyes shimmering with gratitude at his promise to take care of her. She turned to her sisters, holding out a hand to pull both of them into a hug.

"Have the best day," she whispered.

"Have the best sex," Hebex said back, not bothering to lower her voice.

Amala didn't bother to correct her.

✡

There hadn't been sex.

Amala was too astounded by Hawk's words.

Serabel wasn't the buyer.

The buyer wasn't Serabel.

The buyer *couldn't* be Serabel because they had reached out again.

Which meant that...

"What the hell was she doing, then?" Amala muttered, eyes wandering outside the car window. "If she wasn't the buyer, why all the business with Atalman and Nyla and the centaurs, and..." She couldn't stop the tears streaming down her beautiful face: relief, yes, but anger too. Anger because of all the secrets she hadn't known about, and all the secrets she had to keep.

"I'm sorry for what I said, Amala mate."

"I fucking knew it was wrong."

"You were right."

"I don't care... I just wish she wasn't dead, and that I wasn't Goddess."

She ignored the sting of guilt at her own words, as if a needle had pierced her heart for a split second.

I know, Amala apologised to herself as her soul merged with that divine energy. *I know there's a reason. I just wish my Goddess was here with me.*

Hawk's finger gently brushed her cheek, wiping her tears away with such tenderness, such care.

And then he said, "Don't cry, my Goddess of Love."

Amala released a small gasp of surprise. When she looked up at him, her eyes were full of tears, but bright.

"Say that again," she whispered.

"My Goddess of Love."

"What happened to Amala mate?"

"Can't I call you both?"

She sniffled, her lips tugging upwards, then closed the distance between them with a soft kiss to his lips.

"What now, then?" she murmured, brow against brow.

"Now there's two people, at least, that wanted to know more about the Charal, and we have no clue why."

"Well, Serabel *wanted* to find them," Amala corrected. "That I know."

"Do you think that she did?"

"No. She was waiting for Dhara to come back."

"But she never talked about it, right?"

"She didn't." She exhaled. "Believe me, Hawk. I might know nothing about Serabel's plans, but anything about Dhara... I would have known. Serabel would have told me, or I would've found out myself."

He brushed her cheekbone, using his thumb to play with her lower lip.

"Alright. So, Serabel wanted the Charal but someone else wanted them too."

"The question is: was it to protect them or kill them?"

"I don't want to argue again, but *kill them* sounds the most reasonable option, given their history."

Amala scoffed at the implication that his claim would offend her.

"I know," she said. "I don't like it, but I know. But Hawk, all this business with the Charal, do you still think it is the reason Serabel died?"

He considered it.

"Well, she wasn't the buyer, but she was snooping around enough for someone else to figure it out — Charal included. There might also be a conflict of interests: she wanted to protect them, the buyer wanted to kill them — perhaps Serabel was murdered before she could become a bigger problem."

"What a mess." Amala exhaled.

"Yeah."

Amala touched his forehead with her cold, small fingers. "Thank you for not killing Caelan today."

Hawk snorted; he could use a change of topic, even if it was about someone he despised.

"I was tempted. But I'm not going to kill him. Not before he apologises to you."

"He has apologised already. Multiple times, I told you. I just don't forgive him."

"Yeah, well, he should apologise for another thousand years."

She huffed a laugh. "I don't blame you, though. For being tempted. It must be weird when you suddenly look at someone under a different light."

At those words, Hawk decided to remain uncomfortably silent. Amala raised an eyebrow.

"What?"

He shook his head, repressing a laugh, but she smacked his shoulder forcefully.

"Hawk!"

"Don't take this wrong, but I have been wondering about Caelan for a while — him and you, I mean."

Amala didn't hide her surprise and Hawk snickered.

"What do you mean?"

"You know what I mean, don't you?"

Play dumb.

Dumb.

She knew damn well what he was talking about. Her sisters had mocked her enough already, but there was no way she would admit it to him.

"What?" she said again.

Hawk grinned. "That we look alike."

Amala reddened. "No, you don't."

"We do."

They did.

"You don't."

"Amala, we really do."

"You are much more handsome than he is."

Hawk only scoffed, shaking his head. "I knew I was right."

"Fine, I have a type. I like people who look like you."

"How didn't you hate me when we met? Didn't I remind you of him?"

"What? No," she shrugged. "You are *similar*, but... no."

Amala paused, then placed her head on his shoulder, her hand reaching for his and her small fingers squeezing tight. "No one is like you, Hawk."

CHAPTER 47

T oday wasn't particularly sunny, which made Amala incredibly moody.

Hawk thought she looked funny. After spending half an hour meditating on the balcony, she came back in and sipped her apple juice with a pout.

"There were too many clouds for a good sunrise." She muttered.

She hadn't even touched herself today and Hawk wondered if it was due to her heart broken by the absence of the sun, or because he had devotedly gone down on her the night before.

He had been solely focused on her since they had mated: his main goal now seemed to be pleasuring Amala at *least* all the times he had pictured it in his head. Innumerable times, then.

She had tried to return the favour, but he didn't care. He only cared about her.

"We're here, Amala mate."

She let out a groan, cracking her neck as she awoke. She had dozed off during the drive.

"It's your fault I fell asleep," she was saying now, unfastening her seatbelt. "You kept me up all night."

"What, are you sore?"

"*And* tired. But like, deliciously sore."

He let Amala take the lead. Besides the path leading from the parking lot to the temple, Hawk had never been in Mhelani forest before. He listened to Amala's stories about it — its beauty and energy, its quiet, humming wilderness — but he had never seen it with his own eyes.

He shoved aside the mental image of Amala and a centaur-partner having fun against a tree.

Amala didn't go for the temple, but strode off the footpath, following a narrower one almost fully covered by the trees. She moved with ease and confidence, never missing a step and never faltering. Hawk took in the thick vegetation, the tall trees and green, giant leaves that covered the ground. Flowers bloomed and a soft, humming breeze twirled at every turn on his path, as if the forest was alive. Amala turned to him, ensuring he kept the pace.

"Keep it together, please. Aries suspects that you have a thing for me, and—"

"I imagine you absolutely denied it."

"Of course I didn't."

He huffed a laugh, following her through the woods. She moved swiftly, pointing to the ground whenever she needed to indicate the path.

"Kanaan doesn't know about us, though, and we'll have to talk to him. He's..." she hesitated. "Please, let me lead this. He'll get very annoyed if *you* look in charge. And whatever he says to me, Hawk," she looked him dead in the eye. "Just suck it up and do *not* intervene. Promise me."

He snorted.

"Yeah, fine. But it's the last time I meet a lover of yours and pretend you are not mine."

Hawk had already seen the first centaur they met. Male, tall and broad, with dark long braided hair. He recognised him from the day outside the Yonium a couple of months ago, before Amala moved in with him. A part of him now wondered if Amala had ever braided his hair herself.

"Aries," Amala greeted with a smile. He offered a smile back, then his eyes wandered to Hawk.

After a moment of internal debate, he bowed his head. Amala glanced at Hawk, raising an eyebrow.

"Bow back, Captain. Be nice."

In all honesty, bowing to Aries felt easier now Hawk had mated Amala; he knew several of her past lovers, but had never needed to *bow* to any of them.

Aries guided them through the forest as they trailed behind. Thankfully, no one seemed to comment that hopping on his back was perhaps a faster way to travel. Or, if Aries thought to offer Amala a ride, he had the common sense not to ask in front of Hawk. Amala seemed to think the same thing as she subtly glanced at him with a smirk.

Kanaan was busy when they found him. He was with a female centaur, sat in a small clearing, the trees around it blooming into a canopy of flowers. A small fire crept on the ground, confined between stones, and big chunks of crystals Hawk didn't know were pinned into the soil.

The centaurs spotted them but didn't move. Amala murmured a silent greeting as she knelt next to the fire, mesmerised: she sent her wind all around, easing the energy among them, soothing the space. The tension simmered.

"I'm so tempted to steal one of these for Seryn," she said.

Kanaan chuckled, "Seryn has more crystals than our entire kingdom, and surely she doesn't need any more."

"She'll never have enough carnelians," Amala extended her fingers to the red stone. "Can I touch?"

At Kanaan's nod, her fingertips brushed the carnelian's sharp point: her eyes lit up, as if she could feel the very energy of that... rock.

Hawk didn't say it aloud, though. He knew crystals were among the practices Amala studied, but he also knew she had studied traditional and modern medicine for this exact reason: healing was a mixture of both, and one couldn't find relief in the former without accepting the latter could also be an option.

"Why are we grounding?" She asked quietly.

The female centaur next to Kanaan replied instead.

"Just some monthly cleansing, High Priestess. We miss the Full Moon rituals at the temple."

Oh, Amala missed them too. The Home of Waters wasn't nearly as beautiful as the Yonium.

"Mind if we join?"

Kanaan raised an eyebrow. "What are you here for?"

"Answers, if you can give me them." Amala replied. "But I'd never say no to energy circles. Can the Captain join, too?"

Hawk blinked. Him?

With the rocks?

He did his best not to look sceptical. Amala must be mocking him; she *knew* he had zero crystal interest or knowledge. Kanaan looked doubtful too, but more at the idea of Hawk joining their meditation. Nonetheless, he nodded.

Amala handed him a flame shaped, tumbled, red crystal. He frowned.

"Which one is this?"

"Carnelian," she smiled, tugging at her lower crystal waist-chain, the slightly darker one. "Like this."

"Seryn likes carnelians, I take."

"Seryn *is* a carnelian."

The female centaur emitted an interested sound.

"What crystal are you, High Priestess?"

This, Hawk knew.

"A sunstone."

The only correct answer he'd ever give in terms of crystals. He extended a hand to Amala's waist, touching the other crystal chain, the upper one. That was sunstone, he remembered. She gave him another smile, a broader one, but Hawk didn't miss Kaanan's eyes, or the way they paused on his hand touching Amala's waist.

Suddenly, he remembered he was supposed to keep distance and quickly retreated, but glimpsed Amala's face darken from the sudden lack of touch. Hawk focused on their... meditation. Or whatever it was.

Each of them called to their power. The centaurs were mostly blessed with Earth gifts and let it spark between them with a thought of gratitude. He expected some talking — perhaps a prayer — but nothing. Their energies were loud, yet the clearing was silent. Whatever was going on, it was fully in their heads, which was likely a blessing, since Hawk had no idea what to say aloud or how to say grace to some rocks.

Amala was perfectly relaxed, wind humming softly around her as she pressed into the soil. He sent a tendril of his own air to snake under the robe of her skirt. Amala opened her eyes, shooting him a pointed look.

"Don't you dare," she mouthed.

He had to give it to her; while he might not be into the rock stuff, he couldn't deny the lighter atmosphere in the air afterwards. Cleansed. Amala gently waited for Kanaan to reassess himself, almost prompting him to start the conversation by saying nothing. Indeed, it worked soon: he turned to her with curiosity.

"What answers do you want?"

Amala stretched her arms above her head. "You mentioned something about Serabel that I had never known. Please Kanaan, I really need to know what she said. Anything that you know, it might be crucial."

He brushed a hand against the carnelian point.

"The Goddess didn't speak with us much. I told you, Amala: we had two agreements. To always protect the Yonium's priestesses, and to host and protect the Charal women, if their tribe ever found themselves in these woods. If they ever step foot in Mhelani, we are bound to protect them. Our king swore it."

"That's a colossal deal," Hawk couldn't help but observe. "A colossally stupid one too, given the Charal history."

"Hawk," Amala glared at him. "Watch your mouth."

Kanaan briefly assessed her cold tone.

"I only mean that I doubt *kantazares* would stop their hunt. Regardless of how high your protection might be."

"It's not a matter of physical defence, that's not what the Goddess asked from us." Kanaan replied. "Our kingdom shall hide them."

A short, deep silence followed his words. Amala bit her lip, puzzled as Hawk's eyes conveyed the question he wanted her to ask. She gave him a pointed look: *no.*

Amala faced Kanaan again and exhaled, her cinnamon wind suddenly stronger.

A subtle, slow blink. "Are you?"

"Am I what?"

"Hiding them? Is your kingdom hiding Charal women?" She blinked again, "Kanaan."

Hawk hated the way she said his name. A part of him wondered how many times she'd said it. Had she said it more times than his own? Had she said it with that same sweet voice?

"Tell me the truth. Please."

Kanaan kept his eyes fixed on her, almost unable to look away. In the end, he breathed, "No, Amala. There have never been Charal women in Mhelani."

Oh.

She didn't say it, but her disappointment was clear. For the rest of the their time spent in the clearing, her gaze drifted to Hawk, eyes wide and apologetic.

Sorry for wasting your time coming here, they seemed to say. He knew she really had thought they were onto something; Hawk had thought the same.

He shared her disappointment, but didn't blame her at all.

When they stood after, as Amala murmured an excuse to leave, Kanaan walked them back onto the footpath.

"It's a shame you're leaving so soon," he commented.

"I'm afraid I'm expected at the God's temple," Amala said, making an effort to look regretful.

"What about a little distraction before you go?"

She shook her head.

"I can't. But thank you for meeting me. It was nice to see you again."

Then she turned, making to leave, but finding Hawk's eyes locked to where Kanaan placed a hand on her shoulder.

"Amala."

"Kanaan, I must go."

His hand trailed off her shoulder, fingers tracing her bare spine. Amala shivered.

"Don't—*oh*," she bit her lip before any other sound could escape as Kanaan's fingers circled that sweet spot on her back.

"Are you sure you want to leave?"

This couldn't be happening. Her brain and body threatened to turn to jelly the second her skin was stimulated, but she tried to focus. Eyes widening in alarm, she looked at Hawk: he was impassable, but his eyes darkened, fists clenched by his sides.

"Kanaan, don't touch me."

He circled that spot again. Amala was barely holding it together.

"Just a quick one, Amala."

She managed to step away and quickly turned to face him, cheeks red with embarrassment.

"I said *stop*."

Kanaan opened his mouth to reply, but Hawk was quicker.

"You heard the High Priestess." He said, voice harsh.

He moved his gaze to her.

"We're leaving."

CHAPTER 48

H awk sunk in the driver's seat: the whole trip to the forest had been a complete failure, and he radiated a mild fury that he wished to take out on that damn centaur.

Amala seemed to share the same thought as she stretched on the passenger seat next to him. She waited for him to say something, but he didn't.

"I'm sorry, that was useless." She said after a while, breaking the silence.

"It's not your fault. I thought we were onto something so I'm just pissed it was another dead end. Listen—" he started, and Amala instantly faced him, as though expecting his next words. "You asked me to say nothing and I did. But I don't want you to think that I was okay with what he did, are we clear? The only reason I didn't beat the shit out of Kanaan is because you asked me not to."

Amala slowly nodded, a chill breeze of air sliding from her hands towards him, cooling the rage in his eyes as he remembered the way the centaur spoke to her.

"I know, Hawk. Thank you for respecting me," she murmured. "And I'm sorry for... taking so long to tell him no." The admission made her blush as she hid her eyes from him.

Hawk's own eyes were wary, noticing the slight tensing of her body. As if she was recalling something unpleasant. His blood began thrumming in his veins, but he pushed it down, summoning a tendril of air to swirl around Amala's neck. She shivered in response.

"Did..." he started, cautiously, "Did Kanaan do that because he knew you would give in?"

Amala said nothing, raising her legs to her chest as she rested her head above her knees. She refused to look at him, but her body language... Hawk blinked in realisation — she was *embarrassed* to look at him, embarrassed for him to read the expression on her face because her answer to his question was...yes.

He took a deep breath, trying not to expose the rage silently building.

"Did Kanaan ever touch you *there* so that you would consent to... do whatever you and him did?"

Amala slowly turned her head towards him, cheeks still blushing as she pursed her lips together, then nodded. Barely, but still.

Taking her time, she murmured, "He did that all the time. To get me in the mood."

"What do you mean?" Hawk said, forcing himself not to reach for her, not to touch her.

She finally dared to meet his eyes.

"Kanaan was my lover for some years. He was always very respectful of my wishes, as I made clear from the start that I wouldn't interact with *him* as—" she paused. "You know what I mean. He always seemed content to focus on me, and that was it. But I wasn't always in the mood. Sometimes I just wasn't. And," she paused, thinking about her words. "And if I said no, he would do something like—like touch me there until I said yes. You know me, that spot is a game changer, so I always ended up saying yes. I'm not very good at saying no."

She looked so small, curled in the passenger seat with her big doe-like eyes. This time, he didn't stop his hand from reaching for her. He touched her cheek and she let him stroke her skin, caressing her face.

"Would you say that Kanaan forced you to say yes, Amala mate?"

She stiffened and he opened his mouth to apologise, but her nod was more convincing this time.

"Maybe," she whispered.

Their eyes met again.

"Yes," she admitted, "Yes, he did that. But I've never realised how *bad* it was until today. And when I said yes to him all the other times, I meant it. I gave my consent." She tried to say, as if that made things better.

"Amala mate," Hawk said, voice was low and reassuring as he gently stroked her cheek. "I am perfectly aware of how sensitive your sweet spot is and of how much it drives you crazy when I touch it. But I would never use it like that. If you say no, it's *no*. I'm not going to make you say yes — if you wanted to say yes, you would have."

She shivered under his touch, and innocently shifted closer to his seat.

"Thank you for telling him to stop. I would have never given in today, but that's because I am with *you*. If I was still... available," she shrugged, not finding any better way to say it. "I would have probably given in. I'm not good at holding my point."

Her body arched as Hawk's fingers drifted to her neck, now stroking the sensitive skin below her ear. "And you don't need to tell me how much you respect me. I know, I know that you are... something else." she whispered.

"Something else, huh?" Hawk chuckled.

Amala's lips curved into a smile. "I had a half idea to tell Kanaan that I suck your dick. I never sucked *his*, so it would stop him from teasing — now, I'm kind of regretting I didn't say it."

He grinned. "I'm sure you would have gotten the reaction you wanted. But you don't lie, Amala mate."

She rolled her eyes, her scent thickening as she frowned at him. Hawk stared back and Amala groaned.

"Do you want me to write a formal enquiry, Captain Mercurian? Or can I suck your dick?"

Hawk looked thoroughly stunned as she lifted her eyebrows with a small smile, satisfied with his reaction. Her eyes tracked his face, then his upper body, pausing at his pants and lingering there. She *really* wanted him to say yes.

But...

"No," he said and she pouted, ready to protest. "There's no way I'd let you do that if I don't make you come first."

She blushed again, without any trace of embarrassment this time.

"Not fair. We don't have to always be even, Hawk."

"I don't care if we're even. I care about worshipping you the way you deserve first and if you still want to suck my dick by the time I'm done, then you're more than welcome to." He knew his words had found their mark as Amala's scent whirled towards him — cinnamon and sugar and sunlight as she shifted even closer, her small hand reaching for his arm. Hawk grabbed her wrist and pulled her towards him.

"What if *I* want to worship you?" she purred, fingers clasping — or at least trying to clasp — his biceps. He held her face with one hand, fingers slightly pressing against her throat.

"We'll never know, since you do what *I* say."

Amala's body tensed, then relaxed under his touch; he gently lowered her face until she rested on his lap, her head nested in her arms.

Hawk paused. "Come here, Amala mate."

He tugged at her, and she slowly stripped out of her long skirt, untying the white robe clung around her waist before curling her legs into his lap. Hawk reclined his seat, then moved her body, grabbing her thighs and placing each either side of his lap. She straddled him, but faced the other way. He helped her balance herself on the steering wheel, tucking a strand of hair behind her ear as he whispered, voice low.

"Careful, now. If you hit the horn, everyone will know what I'm doing to you".

Amala writhed as Hawk pulled her waist towards him. Carefully, she rested her arms against the steering wheel, and lowered her body as much as she could without risking the press of the horn or any other sounds. Hawk's fingers lazily traced her spine and she shivered.

"Isn't it interesting," he purred against her skin, "That your weak spot would make things *very* difficult for you if anyone knew about it... yet you never cover it?" One finger drifted towards her most sensitive area, circling around — but not close enough — as she shivered in anticipation. He brushed her skin and she squirmed.

"Always so exposed, Amala mate," he growled, quickly untying the knot that held her top in place. He gently removed the white fabric, making sure to stroke it against her breasts as he pulled it away, chucking it onto the passenger seat.

"Not fair," she murmured, arching under his touch.

"What's not fair, Amala mate?"

She made a small sound of approval when his fingers grazed the skin on her back, drifting closer her weak spot. *Yes,* she let out, "It's always exposed so that you can play with me whenever you want," she managed to say. Arching, her body begged for his touch — right where she wanted.

Not yet, his touch seemed to say, as he stroked away and up towards her shoulders, prompting a muffled protest from her lips.

"I could play with your sweet spot all day, Amala mate. It's so *easy* to get you completely undone for me—" Hawk teased.

"Do you like it?" she challenged, voice slightly louder as she tried to face him, to show she wasn't *that* undone. He sneered, amused with her reaction and decided to tease some more, to prove he was right.

"Yeah, I like when you're a soaked little bunny, Amala mate. Even more when I don't even need to touch you cause you're already fucking *drenched*. Look at you," he said, fingers sliding to her sweet spot, and stroking lightly on the utterly sensitive flesh there. Amala couldn't help the moan that escaped her lips, and Hawk grinned.

"See? I barely touched you *once* and you're a mess already."

Her body squirmed, leaning into his touch as he withdrew his hand, leaving her unsatisfied before he grabbed her ass and squeezed hard.

"More," she hissed, "Please, touch me *there* again."

"There where?"

Amala groaned.

"On my back," she whispered, "Please."

Hawk brushed his fingers against her ass cheeks, enjoying the sight of her body writhing under his hands.

"What would you do for me to touch you there, Amala mate?"

Anything, she breathed, her scent so thick and aroused it threatened to drive him mad. His cock throbbed in his pants. She could probably feel all of it, but he wanted to focus on her: worshipping her like she deserved until she begged to return the favour.

She was begging him already anyway.

"Very well, then" he managed to say, keeping up the pretence, "Say that you're my soaked little bunny."

She whimpered as he dug his fingers into her skin, becoming more aroused upon hearing those words, what he had called her. Hawk seemed to understand her thoughts, moving closer to whisper.

"Don't pretend you don't like it, Amala mate. I know you love when I call you names."

It was true. She absolutely loved it and this time she did nothing to hide it.

"Please," she repeated, grinding against him.

"I already told you what to do."

Another plea. She liked playing this game, and Hawk was the master at it. There was no way he would let her win. He teased around her weak spot one more time and she yelped, trying to resist—

"I am your soaked little bunny."

He was so close to losing it then: not only was he hard as stone, but when Amala gave in to his demands — it was his favourite moment. He didn't hide his satisfaction and decided to play with her a little more.

"What?"

Amala groaned in frustration, and lost it first.

"Soaked little bunny," she repeated, "I am your soaked little bunny, Hawk. *Please* touch me," she whimpered when he finally grazed her sweet spot, fingers steady on her skin: twirling and stroking and teasing.

"Keep saying it," Hawk said, lazily continuing his movements, "And if you stop saying it, I'll stop touching you."

Soaked little bunny, Amala moaned in response, now utterly undone as she repeated it — softer or louder, she didn't care, so long as Hawk kept touching her.

His other hand resting on her waist now slid between her thighs, playfully stroking the inner part of her ass, near to her butthole — he halted his fingers, swearing under his breath.

"You are so fucking wet, Amala bunny." He said, brushing his fingers against her butthole, "I can feel it from *here*." He pressed on it again, the touch emphasising his words.

He slid his fingers down against her sex, growling as he found the wetness there.

He knew touching her skin would cause this reaction from her body, but *feeling* it was completely different. Knowing he couldn't hold back for much longer without exploding, he decided to speed things up.

"Are you so close that you could come only after a few strokes right here?" He teased her, the sensitive skin of her back tested by his expert, steady fingers.

"Soaked little bunny," Amala muttered in response, body arching under his touch — both of his touches.

Soaked, indeed, Hawk thought with no small amount of satisfaction.

The fingers he brushed against her sex slid up to the apex of her thighs, and he slowly circled her clit. Amala moaned so loudly that he halted. Devoured by pleasure, the only sounds escaping her lips were whimpers of *soaked little bunny*. Hawk touched her clit again, two fingers now prodding the bundle of nerves.

"My soaked little bunny is all ready to come, huh?" His husky voice breathed in her ear.

She moaned his name, so he waited no longer. Hawk's fingers softly pinched her clit, gently pulling as he rolled it between his fingers so *so* carefully...

Amala came so hard he was sure anyone in the parking lot would hear her scream his name, body tensing as her thighs shook under the power of her orgasm. Her body arched as Hawk continued relentlessly stroking her sweet spot and the steady touch on her clit. She screamed and screamed.

When she finally relaxed, she rested against his chest, panting as she tried to catch her breath.

Amala chuckled softly as he kissed her neck, now glistening with sweat, and sent a gentle chill to cool her down. She slowly turned towards him, taking her time to move her body with her and reposition her shaking thighs until she was straddling him, facing forward.

"I just wanted to suck your dick." Amala panted, looking into his eyes.

Hawk snickered, "I told you. Worshipping my Goddess is my main priority."

Amala blushed under his gaze.

"You are amazing, Captain Mercurian. I can't believe I *purposefully* avoided that for ten years. I am a dumb little bunny," she winked as he intensified the grip on her waist, sneering. Amala nested her head in between his neck and shoulder, kissing his tattoos.

"Will you let your Goddess suck your dick now?"

One of her hands slid on top of his cock, stroking against his pants.

"Please," she added.

"Not if you're too tired," Hawk said, letting out a low breath as she squeezed him, praying that she wasn't. He hoped he hadn't done his part *too* well.

"You're *so* hard," Amala moaned, "I *really* want to. Can I be your soaked little bunny Goddess? *Please* let me taste you."

"Alright, soaked little bunny Goddess," Hawk stroked her hair, groaning as she rubbed her own body against his cock, "Do you want me to call you that?"

"I like soaked little bunny," she admitted, "And I like Goddess, if *you* say it. But only this first time... call me Amala mate."

Hawk grinned as Amala swiftly moved back onto the passenger seat and kneeled, leaning towards him with her upper body. Her hands were already on the edge of his pants when Hawk pulled her hair to gently yank her back.

"Not like this," he grunted. As her big icy eyes widened in surprise, he added, "I need to see your face as you swallow me."

Amala licked her lips, then looked around in the car.

"Let's move outside, I don't think I can kneel here."

She didn't wait for an answer before opening the door, and Hawk hesitated: was he really about to let her do this? Suck his dick in the middle of a parking lot, right next to her temple?

Though Amala didn't seem to think twice as she reached his door and playfully knocked on the glass, gesturing with her head to come outside. He opened the door and got out, taking in the sight of her fully naked figure standing in front of him. His eyes darkened and she blushed under his gaze, slowly moving towards him as if bound to him by gravity.

"Please," she breathed as they locked glances. "Let me do this. I need you so much, Hawk."

Amala had been aching for him for days, desperate to take him in her mouth and taste him, to show him that whatever he felt for her — whatever urge or desire — she felt it too. And she couldn't wait to satiate her need for him.

Hawk read it in her eyes too, shimmering with the silent promise to give him the best head of his life, if only he'd let her. She pressed a kiss to his mouth; he closed the door behind him and leaned against the car. Amala kissed him again, her hands playing with his hair and bare breasts rubbing against his chest. Kneeling before him and peering up through her lashes, she reached to unbutton and pull down his pants, not completely but enough that he would be comfortable. Hawk studied her movements: the beautiful Goddess stooping before him, naked and eager to play. He gently pulled her hair, a quiet reminder that he was *letting* her do this — that he was still the one in charge. Amala nodded softly, a whimper escaping her lips as he yanked on her hair slightly harder.

Groaning, she felt the hardness of him against her hand, and her desire to please him grew with every passing second. Her fingers moved swiftly; she didn't dare look at his face until she finally pulled him free, biting her lower lip as she took in the sight of his length. Amala barely was able to admire it the way she wished to over the last week, yet now she planned to take her sweet time: worshipping the shit out of him.

Hawk wasn't sure he was breathing, eyes locked on Amala. Her silver-white hair swirled around her perfect face as she gaped, moving closer, her mouth so close to his cock he had to restrain from prematurely closing the distance between them. She was moving slowly, *so* slowly... as if she was pondering all the filthy things she wanted to do but couldn't decide where to start. Then she lifted a small hand, and Hawk could swear the anticipation was fucking *killing* him but he didn't dare move, questioning her next move.

The first contact almost brought him to his knees. Amala's fingers ran across the proud length, nails gently tracing the shape and size of him, then lingering on his piercing, her breath soft against his skin. Hawk's hips bucked but she didn't seem to notice: absolutely hypnotised as she absorbed every single detail of his cock, exploring it bit by bit. She inhaled his scent, now thick with his arousal: midnight wind and that delicious note of lemon that drove her crazy. Her small hand grasped him. Hawk groaned and as she blushed under his darkening eyes — her stare fell onto his cock again, slowly moving her hand up and down.

Hawk sucked in a breath, the feeling of Amala's small fingers prevented him from thinking properly: Goddess, he had wanted this to happen for — how long? Fucking *years*. Years of daydreaming about her full, pouty lips wrapped around him, aching for her soft touch. Hawk never thought Amala wanted him, unsure if this moment would ever come. But as he watched her now, eyes sparkling in wonder and intoxication — almost in adoration as she touched him, he realised she had wanted this just as much as him.

Amala licked her lips, unable to take her eyes off his cock.

"You are so *big*," she murmured, her cheeks flushing. Face moving closer, Amala's hands now rested against his muscled thighs, and she licked the metal of his piercing once, twice. Gently placing her lips around the tip, she sucked, letting out a small sound of approval as she tasted his skin. Amala didn't dare to take all of it, not yet, but she allowed her tongue to linger there, stroking his soft, marble-like skin.

Hawk's eyes rolled back into his head, panting, and then he heard *her* moan and knew he would come right now, if she did it again. He looked down: Amala moaned again as she sucked on his tip, her tongue teasing his slit as she tasted the small drop of precum gathered there. Her throat bobbed as she swallowed it and she shuddered in pleasure and approval, eyes sliding to his to make sure he'd seen her — building anticipation of what she would do later, when he actually came in her mouth.

Eyes locked to his, she opened her mouth to suck on the full, big head of his cock.

Fuck.

"Fuck, Amala mate." Hawk groaned, hips bucking towards her. She received his movement, and her mouth slid further on his length, taking more of him. Her sweet saliva coated every inch of his skin, drool coming out of her soft lips; she moaned against him, the sound shooting through his body and threatening to melt every thought in his brain.

She didn't interrupt their stare, hands reaching for her aching breasts and grazing against her peaked, hard nipples. She moaned again, shuddering under her own touch, as she kept sucking on him with lethal precision. Taking more and *more* into her mouth, covering the full length of his cock until he felt it bump against the back of her throat. Amala rolled her eyes in pleasure to feel him so deep.

Hers.

Hawk was hers and when she looked up at him again, she felt the urge to tell him. To see his face change as he heard the words. Hawk panted, the feeling of her mouth warm and tight against him, her tongue caressing every inch, and her teeth gently squeezed from time to time: his mate. His Amala. She looked fucking perfect as she enjoyed the taste of him, sucking on his cock as though she was starving. Swollen lips sliding on her own saliva, she withdrew until only the head remained in her small mouth and licked his slit again, *loving* the sight of him undone before her. But it wasn't enough. And she wanted him to know.

Pinching her nipples one more time as whimpers escaped her lips, her hands reached for his cock again, fingers tracing across his skin, teasing and squeezing. She released his tip with a gentle pop of her lips, holding his gaze as she whispered, voice low against his cock.

"You are mine, Hawk."

And Hawk had no idea how he had managed not to come yet at the sight of the Goddess kneeling in front of him. *Fuck*. Her eyes were bright and innocent, yet somehow matched those sinful lips as she said again, "*Mine.*"

She pressed a kiss to his tip, her hand moving up and down on his length.

"Mine, Hawk. And I am yours," she squeezed him, now moving faster. "Your bunny."

He let out a low breath, struggling to hold back.

"*Your* Goddess," she continued, pressing another kiss.

Then another. She licked his piercing again.

Hawk growled, his hands grasping fists full of silver-white strands. Amala soothed as she felt his fingers brush against her scalp, but she wasn't done.

"Your Amala mate."

He couldn't hold back, then. Fists clenching on her hair, he thrust his hips towards her as she opened her mouth for him, sliding her lips down the entirety of his length until he hit the back of her throat again. She gagged, clenching around him. Hawk grunted with pleasure, withdrew, and repeated the motion. Amala moaned as she met every thrust, hands grabbing his thighs, nails digging and slicing into his skin.

Hawk fucked her mouth, rough and hard, pulling her hair so much it hurt, and she loved it.

"You are fucking mine, Amala mate." He thrust harder, voice unsteady, and she knew he was close.

As he kept the pace, she dared to look at him again, her big, beautiful, ice doe eyes meeting his stare... When he thrust, she clenched her throat, lips clasping on him as she sucked harder than before, not allowing him to withdraw as her head moved steadily. The feeling shot through his whole body and nothing could stop his orgasm then: her beautiful face, those incredible eyes locked with his, her lips wrapped around him, filled with him...

Hawk came with a groan, spilling himself in her mouth so much that it dripped from her swollen lips, trickling onto the visible section of his cock. He kept his pace, throbbing inside her mouth as she didn't release him, waiting until she was sure he had finished. Hawk fucked her mouth even through his orgasm, hands clenching on her hair as she moaned her pleasure, the sound driving him crazy.

Amala was a drooly mess by the time she popped her lips off him, his cum glistening on her chin as she swallowed. Her eyes rolled in the back of her head as she tasted him down her throat.

"*Fuck*," she moaned softly, "You taste so good."

Hungry eyes shot back to his cock, now glistening with what she couldn't take in his mouth. She grabbed him, licking all over his length, making sure to clean every drop. "*Mine*," she said again, gasping when she felt Hawk's fingers stroking on her hair.

"You've got such a pretty mouth, Amala mate." He breathed.

She gracefully stood and stretched her body. Hawk smirked, his hands making quick work of fastening his pants again, then moving onto her waist, holding her as he pressed a kiss to her forehead. Then kissed her lips.

Amala swiftly parted her mouth for him to swipe his tongue inside, tasting himself on her. She loved that they were on the same wavelength when it came to sex: they reasoned the same way, trusted each other more than anything, and *felt* things the same... everything between them was deafening yet silent, they didn't need to say it to *know* — mates, and more.

Hawk stroked her nipples, just lightly, as he finally dared to look at their surroundings. With Amala kneeling in front of him, he barely had any time to think, but now he took his time to realise Amala had just sucked his dick in the middle of a parking lot.

"You afraid someone saw us?" She asked, following his gaze.

Hawk grunted, "If that's the case, it would be incredibly rude of them not to thank you for the free show."

Amala blushed, eyes sparkling.

"Told you I was good," she aimed for the car door, Hawk smiling behind her as he entered the car on the other side.

CHAPTER 49

She found Hebex and Medyr together in the internal yard, sitting on the ground and sharing a kiss.

Amala smiled as she approached them, waiting for them to finish. Hebex straddled Medyr's lap and their kiss grew more passionate. Amala considered that perhaps it was the wrong time to intrude.

But that part of her that loved to watch people in love wouldn't allow her to move away. It wasn't the voyeurism, though she did like to watch people, it was the *love* of watching their energies merge together. It didn't fulfil her lust, it nurtured her soul.

Hebex spotted her and wiped a bead of sweat from her brow, golden hair falling in messy strands around her beautiful face.

"Amala!" She called, lips parting in a big smile.

Medyr didn't look as happy to see her. Amala couldn't blame him.

"I can come back later," she said in greeting, throwing him an apologetic glance.

"You said you wanted to talk," Hebex insisted, stroking Medyr's hair.

Amala had sent a text a few hours ago after finishing her morning meditation. She was bleeding today, bearing the sign of it clear on her face. Hebex had a phone, she had always had one. It was far more difficult for those who weren't born at the temple to stop using technology after joining the Yonium.

While she couldn't use her phone there, she could keep one.

"Yes, but it's fine if we wait."

"No, it's not."

Amala held back a laugh. Hebex was... Hebex.

Naturally too curious to procrastinate a good chat, even if it meant sacrificing good sex.

"Didn't you say you needed Medyr, too?" her sister added.

She did. Her text had been brief, but she really needed to talk to both of them.

Hebex sat up straight, Medyr following her movements until they both faced Amala.

"Sit with us?"

Amala nodded, lifting her robe to sit on the fresh grass: small, fresh daisies bloomed all around as Hebex's energy lingered in twirls of honey and roses. Amala took a deep breath. She had thought about it for hours after returning from Mhelani forest. Serabel's secrets were a stab in her chest every time she uncovered one more truth. The Love for her Goddess wasn't faltering, and yet she couldn't Love with a heavy heart.

Couldn't keep her own heart heavy for the sake of fear.

When she spoke, her voice was feeble but with no hesitation.

"I found the next vessel."

☼

It hadn't been a great choice.

Hebex was unable to contain her excitement on a normal day while dealing with regular news — *this* news, however, resulted in overwhelming babbling for at least ten minutes, until she finally quieted and placed her head on Medyr's shoulder.

"I don't know what to say," she finished.

Medyr looked absolutely astonished, briefly glancing at Hebex before returning his attention to Amala, as if he was expecting to find some hidden truth in her icy eyes.

"I really don't know what to do," she admitted.

"What—" Hebex started, now whispering. "What are you going to tell Hawk?"

Amala flushed. She felt somehow guilty, knowing she had told Hawk *before* telling them: *they* were involved, they cared. They *needed* the information, Hawk didn't. But Hawk had always treated her like a Goddess: vessel or no vessel.

My Goddess of Love, he called her. Amala couldn't think of that without smiling.

"Hawk knows. I told him weeks ago."

Hebex gaped, shocked at the revelation. Perhaps it was because Amala rarely revealed what Hawk meant to her and never mentioned how much she shared with him.

"So you guys had sex."

Amala winced, confused, then remembered her pretend act of celibacy.

"God and Goddess, you *totally* have!" Hebex chirped. "I knew it, there was no way you'd mate without giving in to..." she met her gaze and quieted, recalling the original topic of their conversation. "What did he say?"

What had Hawk said? All the right things. All the things she was too fearful to tell herself, that he had voiced instead. Voiced with such kindness and care and tenderness, she had ended up believing his every word.

"I've seen him with you," Medyr intervened before she could speak. "He already thinks of you as a goddess."

He wasn't surprised at the news of her mating after finding the marks on her a week earlier. *The cinnamon weed gave it away*, he had grinned.

Amala blushed now, realising the silent praise Medyr had given Hawk. He was right.

"He does," she conceded, lips tugging upwards.

She paused, taking in their expressions, the way their eyes now surveyed her. Were they looking at her under a different light? She hoped not.

"Please," Amala started. "Don't tell anyone. I really need to figure this out by myself. I don't..."

She couldn't seem to make sense of her own thoughts, but how could she tell her priestesses when, still, she felt unworthy of the role? How could she ask her *sisters* to swear themselves to... her?

A small part of Amala — the rational one which tended to become more inconsequential during her moments of overthinking — whispered that some of her sisters would probably love to serve her as Goddess. Sinayla would, and Seryn and Teleia.

But another part of her, the overthinking one that must have spent too much time with Hawk's brain, asked *how?*

Amala shook her head. How could she ever tell her sisters?

It wasn't going to happen anytime soon.

"I don't want to accept it until we figure out what happened to Serabel. I want—I *need* to mourn her."

She hoped they would understand — one of them, at least. She wasn't sure who could relate more. Hebex mourned Serabel with her, but Medyr was High Priest and both shared so much with Amala. It was the main reason she had decided to tell them.

She couldn't keep living with the guilt of doing nothing about it: someone *had* to know. Someone who was possibly close to her and could understand how she felt. But now, even with the weight of the truth finally off her chest, her divinity felt overwhelming.

Had it been the right choice, to share her secret?

She couldn't stop the tears, of pain and guilt, grief and regret.

But then Hebex hugged her, holding her tight: while Amala doubted it was the best choice, it definitely hadn't been the worst.

☼

Amala twisted in the bedsheets and Hawk's arms wrapped around her waist.

"How are you feeling?"

She relaxed in his touch, head leaning back against his shoulder; he took it as his cue to bury his face into her neck, his hands running up her hips and grazing the underside of her breasts. Swallowing a laugh at the ticklish sensation, she raised a small hand to wrap around his wrist, halting his movements.

"Sore."

Hawk couldn't hide his smugness at that. While she couldn't see his face, she guessed as much and elbowed him in the ribs.

"Yes, congratulations. You're a great lover. Now quit that."

"I meant it, though." He said. "How are you feeling about Hebex and Medyr?"

"I don't know what I expected," Amala admitted, cracking her neck. "A part of me hoped they would tell me I was absolutely crazy and wrong. But..."

She hesitated.

Hawk already knew what was left unspoken.

"But?" He prompted.

Amala scoffed.

"Stop, I know you already know what I'm going to say."

"Are you still going to say it?"

She groaned in frustration, hiding her face in the pillow. Her muffled voice emerged a moment later.

"They *love* it. They agree with you — all that stuff about me being absolute pure love and blah blah blah..." She moved against the pillow, squeezing it. "Why don't I feel like that?"

Hawk considered what she wanted to hear and balanced it with what he wanted to tell her.

Although Amala acted more conscious of her role every day, she still struggled to grasp the reality of it, and the meaning of her divinity.

"No person aware of the sacredness of the vessel process would ever doubt this choice, Amala mate. I think that's why you are so scared, too. Because you know how official it is, the same as Hebex and Medyr. You know what it means."

She exhaled, trying not to relent to his words, "What does it mean?"

"That you are a Goddess until the last of your days."

☼

A few days after their adventure in Mhelani forest, Amala knew Hawk had formulated a new theory he wasn't willing to share. Hawk wasn't secretive, still discussing many elements of the investigation with her while omitting any hints of his newest intuition. The night before, Blade and Cairo joined them for dinner to recap the situation. Naressa couldn't come, but had called them for an update, and to make sure — she said — that both males left early so that Hawk could spend the rest of his night worshipping Amala.

Which, by the way, he had done.

After letting her 'win' in the parking lot, he made very clear that he didn't care one bit about being even. He would focus on her and her only, and just when she could barely move anymore, limp with pleasure, he would let her return the favour.

And Amala would never tire of him.

Madakahiri was now approaching and Amala was busy rehearsing all the ritualistic elements she would officiate instead of Serabel. She had partaken in the festivities from the moment she was born, but hadn't officiated until becoming High Priestess. After that, she would join Medyr in the celebration, sharing his role and guiding the first part of the day: the one with the prayers, ritualistic dances, and well wishes to the God and the Goddess.

Studying Serabel's exact role during Madakahiri was taking longer than expected — perhaps because she couldn't think clearly when memories of her Goddess flooded her consciousness, or maybe because she wouldn't accept that she was now Goddess herself. Amala found she was quite exhausted as she sat on the floor, an ancient text from Helioneis' library placed in front of her.

"I'm surprised you have a physical library," she admitted. "I thought Aarush changed it all to digital."

"He doesn't care about the books," Medyr replied. Howlite groused as he shifted his position, prompting her to move from his lap. "Serabel told him to keep them, so he did. He never crossed her."

Amala nodded in agreement. That was true. Aarush was many things, but disrespectful of the Goddess he had never been. He had always carefully valued the guidance Serabel gave him.

"C'mon, read it again." Hebex sighed as she rested her head on Medyr's shoulder.

Amala smiled at the sight of them: Hebex and Medyr had been amazing since she had revealed the truth. They had stood by her side, calming her when she was overwhelmed, and sharing their energy when she was drained. They were ready to support her whichever her choice would be, and had promised not to tell a soul until Amala feel ready to share the news herself.

She cleared her throat.

"*Mighty Sun, and merciful—*"

"Amala mate?"

Howlite jumped off the couch, making her way to the foyer. Amala lifted her eyes from the parchment.

"Hawk?"

"I'm back early. Did you take Howlite out?"

She nodded, then realised he couldn't see her yet. "Yeah, a couple of hours ago. Medyr and Hebs are here."

Hawk appeared in the living room, Howlite jumping around him in search of attention. He undid his bun, long dark strands falling around his handsome face and brushing his jaw; Amala smiled as she absorbed those details.

"Did you have a good day?" she asked.

Hawk nodded, eyes quickly scanning her body. She knew he loved to do it now that he could. Now he didn't have to hide it anymore. Only a week before, when they were laying in bed, he had grasped her waist and whispered in her ear: "I could look at you for days, Amala mate."

She pointed to the kitchen, hiding a squeal of excitement in her voice as she said, "I made brownies. Normal, and weed brownies since Blade is coming later."

Hawk snorted, giving in to temptation and brushing a finger across Amala's collarbones.

"Blade is coming later?"

She nodded, grabbing her phone from the coffee table.

"I think so. He texted me, see?" She pointed at the screen, then read. "*Hawk's phone is dead but Wahine's got news for us. See you later HHP.* Took me a while to realise what it meant — Hot High Priestess, I mean."

Hawk strode for the kitchen and washed his hands in the sink.

"I put a sprinkle of cinnamon in your brownies," Amala teased as he aimed for the tray.

Chuckling, he picked up a couple and returned to the sofa, plugging the charger cable into his phone and leaving it on the cushioned arm.

"How's studying?"

"Tiring. I need to stretch," she groaned, cracking her neck. Amala brought her fingers to her shoulders and applied slight pressure.

"Do you want to smoke?"

"I'd love that," she admitted, stretching one arm above her head, then down on the opposite side of her body. She threw an apologetic glance at Medyr, who shrugged. "Maybe if you're high you'll stop overthinking the ritual so much."

"That, for sure. She'd fall asleep on the floor after she smokes." Hawk said, handing her the joint. She put it in her mouth and waited for him to light it up. He couldn't help but stroke one finger across her cheek.

"Can I be honest and say I don't feel ready *at all* to replace Serabel for Madakahiri?"

"I said stop overthinking, Amala," Medyr replied, though his face was full of understanding. He knew what she meant and how she felt. "We can ask Aarush for some variations, if you like. It's not like he cares that much."

"Serabel cared *way* more," Hebex hummed her agreement, stealing the joint from Amala's mouth with deft fingers, and taking a hit. "Oh, this is *fucking* good, Captain!"

Hawk chuckled as she passed the joint to Medyr, who took a hit and muttered his approval in turn.

"Who's your dealer?" Hebex inquired, her clear eyes surveying Amala's lips as the joint got back to her.

He shrugged. "Blade."

"*Blade?*"

Amala exhaled, a small cloud coming out of her lips. "Blade is a great dealer. All the stuff I brought back to the temple, I got from him."

Hebex gasped, bringing her hands to her mouth. "Even the one from my birthday?"

She nodded. "Oh, that one was good. We can ask him later, he can bring some tomorrow."

Amala's eyes studied the parchment, and she groaned in frustration. "*Merciful Sun* — no, *Mighty Sun, and merciful light. Heal, warm, shine. Bless us with your heat and intensity, for what you are is born to be worshipped and we are born to bask in your power. We* — wait, am I supposed to sing this part?"

Medyr extended a hand, grabbing the parchment roll. He studied it for a second, then nodded.

"Not this sentence, but beginning from the next."

"I have to *sing?*" Amala repeated, a trace of horror in her voice.

"Well, Serabel did. But it doesn't need to be the High Priestess, according to tradition. Anyone can sing."

She raised an eyebrow at him. "Is Caelan doing most of the chants?"

Hebex's eyes widened in alarm, but Medyr didn't seem to notice. He nodded, and Amala blew out a breath.

"Then Sinayla can do it. They're mates who just had a baby, I can't see a better way to open the ritual. I can join your prayer after that?"

Sinayla had the most beautiful voice among them. She always sung, back to when she lived at the Riza, and now often led the Yonium priestesses' chants.

Blade arrived unannounced, but the smell of weed sang the moment he stepped foot into the apartment.

"How did it go with the centaurs?" he asked in greeting, pulling a napkin from his pocket. He opened it, throwing a piece of beef jerky to an exultant Howlite.

"One must pay homage to the queen of the house," Blade shrugged in explanation, catching Hebex's gaze. He made his way to the couch and sat, not gracefully at all.

Hawk opened his mouth to answer the question, but Amala replied in his stead.

"Not very well," she admitted. "Serabel had a deal with them to protect the Charal women *always* and *no matter what*. I'm not sure they knew the extent of *kantazares'* hunger for blood when they swore it, but they are definitely bound to their promise now."

"Which sounds a lot like Serabel wanted the Charal to come to Aglatas so they could be protected in the forest." Blade observed. Amala nodded.

He countered, "Wouldn't the temple offer *more* protection?"

"Not really," Medyr answered, "Not in the case of the Yonium, anyway. I can see why after Bresha's betrayal, Serabel wouldn't offer the Charal refugee *in* the temple. But the forest is close enough, and with the centaurs sworn to her..."

"She'd have the tribe right under control, but distant enough for them to feel safer," Hebex concluded.

Hawk glanced at Amala, lips curled in a slight pout: the expression she usually wore when she disagreed with something, but didn't wish to contradict anyone's opinion.

When she caught his gaze, he said, "I don't think *control* is the right word here. From everything we've gathered, Serabel wanted to offer the Charal the chance to reunite and start anew, giving them a safer place to live. Her influence and power would merely protect them from further persecution, that's why she wanted them close."

This time, Amala hummed her agreement.

"Hate to tell you this," Hebex intervened, reaching for the High Priestess' hand, "But it seems like a bloody good reason for the Charal to kill Serabel. Why would they want to be bothered, when their slaughter was ordered from the Yonium, from *here* in the first place?"

Amala didn't reply to that. Hawk knew she disagreed, but Hebex's words made sense. For how much she disliked the theory, they still hadn't found any evidence to contradict it. Yes, the former Goddess couldn't be the buyer, but she had tried in several ways to contact the Charal, or what remained of them. Hawk knew Serabel had only good intentions, but he wouldn't blame the crumbs of a secluded, broken, and hidden tribe — survivors of mass slaughter — to seek vengeance on a prying Goddess who hadn't done enough to protect them.

It sounded like a perfectly valid reason to make a countermove.

Which could only mean one thing. If the buyer wasn't Serabel then *two* people, at least, were concerned about the Charal tribe. Another reason for them to strike first on the defensive, even risking catching the wrong opponent.

"Hate to leave the party," Medyr said, "But I have to get back to the temple. Hebs, you coming?"

Hebex hugged Amala tightly before leaving, the hug conveying everything she couldn't say, words she had said numerous times already. *You are worthy, my love. I can't wait for the day you realise it, too.* There was a small part of Amala where the words took root: she wasn't going to let them bloom now, but she might allow it one day. Hebex's blond hair caught a glimpse of sunlight as she left.

She turned to Blade. "Hebex wants some of that weed you gave me for her birthday."

"I'm honoured that you think so highly of my memory, hot High Priestess. But I can't remember today's breakfast, and that was this morning. When was her birthday?"

"And I made you brownies. Weed brownies."

Blade's lips curved into his familiar feline smile. "I'll bring you the weed tomorrow."

Amala stood up, reaching for the kitchen counter to hand over the brownies. "You're the best."

"I'm flattered," he replied, chugging down on a piece of brownie. "Listen, Wahine called."

Hawk snapped his head to him.

"When?"

"A couple of hours ago, but she just sent me more info now. She said the buyer was supposed to meet the Embers today and that she'd try and get us the location of their meetup." He pulled his phone out of his pocket, scrolling down the screen.

"How do you know the buyer is going to show up?" Amala asked.

Blade shrugged.

"The buyer or anyone connected, it doesn't really matter as long as we catch *someone*. We'll find a way to make them talk, whoever they are." He tossed his phone at Hawk, screen unblocked on Wahine's message.

His eyes narrowed reading the text.

Three minutes after sunset.
Apàle Wharf, pier 87.

The location wasn't far from the Meads, he thought. He wasn't sure he had been there, yet something about the name sounded—

"Wait," Hawk said, eyes fixed on the screen.

"What?"

He made to grab his phone from his pocket, then realised it was still charging on the couch. Battery now at 20%, he frantically scrolled down his messages until he found the one he was looking for.

"Shit."

"What?" Amala repeated.

Hawk didn't waste any time.

"Call Cairo." He ordered, standing up and reaching for his jacket. Blade didn't question the tone in his voice and quickly rose, phone against his ear as he made the call.

"Amala."

She tilted her head, confused.

"What?"

Hawk offered a hand, helping her to get up. "You're coming, too."

"You know who they are." Amala blinked in realisation, surprise filling her face. It wasn't a question. "Hawk."

"I have a hunch. We need to get there as soon as possible, Amala mate. I'll tell you in the car."

She didn't question him. With a quick goodbye to Howlite, she followed him downstairs, and thanked the Goddess for her seatbelt as Hawk drove recklessly to the pier — so fast she barely had time to concentrate. Amala felt a rush of adrenaline through her body, the thrill so unfamiliar yet so addictive — she wondered if this was how Hawk felt every time he was close to uncovering the truth.

How did he feel when the moment of truth came near, when he was about to find out if his intuition had been correct, or failed him miserably? She was too overwhelmed to understand the logical sequence of what Hawk now explained. Blade probably understood every word as he hummed from the backseat, but Amala was dumbfounded, her brain unable to piece the puzzle together as she focused on one name. That name. *The* name.

And as they approached Pier 87, she knew Hawk was right once again.

For at the end of the pier, summoning cold water between her fingers, stood Ana.

CHAPTER 50

H er cat eyes shimmered in the dim light of the harbour.

A rivulet of water made its way to the floor, sliding toward where Amala and Hawk stood frozen on the spot. They were alone — Blade and Cairo ready to intervene if needed.

Ana cleared her throat.

"Captain," she said. "High Priestess Amala."

Hawk's eyes didn't falter for a moment, but Amala felt dizzy, unstable.

Ana was the buyer. Ana Sinclair, Second to the Water Protector, was the buyer.

Which meant she was complicit in Serabel's murder.

"So what, you finally accepted my offer to meet? You could have texted and told me you were bringing company."

Hawk bristled.

"I'll tell you only once. Don't fucking move, or you'll get a bullet in your head, and I'll prevent High Priestess Amala from saving you. And I'm pretty sure you have no backup; I doubt you have the balls to tell your Dragons you've been dealing with the Embers."

Ana's pupils dilated in the dark, gaze quickly searching in an unsuccessful attempt to spot Cairo. She instantly dropped her act.

"Please don't tell Nyla you busted me."

Hawk stifled a laugh. "I can't believe you would hook up and make deals in the same spot."

"*That's* what gave me away? I thought the fucking Embers sold me out."

"That's none of your business," Hawk said, choosing not to mention that none of the Embers knew who she was, yet.

But Amala shifted on her feet uncomfortably, glancing at Hawk before directing her icy gaze to Ana. "Why did you need blueprints of my temple?"

Hawk's jaw dropped — just slightly, but enough to betray his surprise hearing Amala use that tone and the power in her voice... a Goddess' power. *My temple*, she had said.

The Yonium was her home, her temple, not only as priestess — as Ana would understand — but as Goddess. Ana wasn't expecting it either as she gaped, eyes alternating between the two of them while deciding who to address.

When Amala repeated the question again, something seemed to sparkle in her.

Ana brought both hands to her mouth, horrified.

"You don't think *I*'ve got anything to do with her death, do you?"

"Just answer the fucking question, Ana."

"I don't!" she blurted, shaking her head. "The blueprint was leverage, just leverage in case something bad happened, I promise!"

"Well, something bad *did* happen. *You* put your hands on the Yonium blueprints exactly a month before Serabel's murder." Hawk shrugged. "I don't have to tell you how it looks."

Ana shook her head again, eyes darting to Amala, pleading.

"Please," she whispered. "You *have* to believe me. I had nothing to do with that. I've been dealing with the Embers for much longer and yes, it started because of Serabel, but it's not like that!"

It was so dark on the pier that Amala wished she could summon fire. Just a spark of it, so she could look at Ana's face and see if those bright emerald eyes told the truth. She threw a side glance at Hawk as if to ask: *what now?*

He sighed.

"Start talking. If you miss out any information, I'll know, and what happens next won't be nice for you."

"I have nothing to say," she countered. "And it's none of your fucking business."

"Fine. I'll let Harat explain Nyla why her Second was found dead, I hope he won't mind—"

"You can't be serious."

"Try me," Hawk shrugged, lifting a hand to signal Cairo. Ana's eyes widened as she followed his movements.

Amala marvelled at the confidence in Hawk's voice, though it was painfully obvious that he wouldn't murder in cold blood. He couldn't; Harat would never approve and Hawk wouldn't be able to do it.

"Wait!"

Hawk halted.

"Yes?"

"D—don't shoot." Ana nodded, drawing a breath as she adjusted the sleeves of her coat.

The breeze from the Apàle grew stronger as Hawk directed his power in Amala's direction, to protect her from the cold evening air. She huffed a laugh at the casual intimacy, the hint of a blush on her cheeks barely visible in the darkness. If Ana noticed Hawk's gesture, she showed no sign.

Instead, she took another breath, and propped her elbows on the railing.

"Fine," she gave in. "You've talked to Nyla already, so you must know how weird Serabel was acting. She was always so sweet, so lovely, but she turned crazy by the end."

"Careful," Amala murmured, her own power heightening a fraction as she sent a cold tendril of air in Ana's direction. The woman shivered as the cool breeze snaked around her face and neck.

"Well, I'm not making this up — she *was* different." Ana continued, "Serabel and Nyla used to meet up regularly; they were friends, of sorts. Until something changed. She became obsessed with the Charal women: what happened to them, what *we* were doing and if we played a part in their persecution — which, by the way," she added, noticing Amala's eyebrows bunching. "We never did. She wanted information, secrets, and promises. Nyla complied at first, but then it became *too much*. Serabel preached about the biggest-power-ever — do you know anything about that?"

She nodded to Amala, hoping for some clarity.

"You don't have the luxury of asking questions, Ana. Leave Amala out of this." Hawk said, voice low and lethal.

But Amala turned her head toward him, her lips imperceptibly parting. He cleared his throat. She was right, he knew better than protecting her like this. Ana was vicious and would take advantage of Amala any day. While Hawk would do anything to prevent that from happening, he could not take from his mate the chance to talk back. Not after all the times she had stayed silent already.

Hawk nodded, and Amala settled her attention on Ana.

"Lady Nyla told us that she borrowed texts, but my Goddess never mentioned this to me. I knew of the research she conducted on the Charal women, but the *power* you speak about... I know nothing of it."

"Likewise," Ana replied. "Because I still have no clue what she meant. Anyway," she threw a glance at Hawk. "Nyla and I didn't feel safe anymore. Serabel *threatened* us, speaking so openly of a source of power stronger than all. Perhaps she meant the Charal women and the idea that, if they rose again, their power would be like none other. So, I was sent to gain leverage on her. Anything to give us an advantage if things went south."

She quieted, her breath the only audible sound on the pier.

"Then what?" Hawk probed.

Ana may have rolled her eyes.

"Then I spent a month researching the Charal with every source I had and ended up with a whole bunch of nothing. Absolutely nothing. It wasn't great for my pride but when the Dragons failed me, I realised the Embers might have a better chance to give me information. Nyla didn't care that I was dealing with them, as long as I got the info she wanted."

"Why the annals?"

She flinched in surprise, as if she didn't expect him to know that much.

"If I find the jackass who ratted me out, he's a dead man."

"Well, you won't. And *you'll* be dead if you don't keep talking."

Amala had never heard Hawk's voice adopt such a lethal tone and wondered if he was always like this in these situations. When he only had one shot at the truth and needed to make the most of it.

"Nyla and I knew nothing of the Charal's history, so we began from their last persecution. The last time Serabel was involved with them."

"She *wasn't* involved with them," Amala hissed, but Ana ignored it.

"What else do you know?"

"Stop asking, keep talking." Hawk replied with a hint of annoyance. "Tell me about the Dagger of Phule and why the fuck you sent someone to retrieve it."

Ana blinked. "I—what?"

"Keep playing dumb, and I'll stop playing nice."

"I *swear*—"

"The man who died at the Riza, Ana. He was burned alive for trying to steal the Dagger of Phule, after successfully passing Nyla's water spells."

"Nyla told you it wasn't sent from—"

"I'm not asking Nyla, now. I'm asking you."

Ana snarled.

"Well, put me on fucking trial, Captain! I know nothing of it. Whoever tried to steal the Dagger, it wasn't us! I would be less surprised to know it was Serabel herself!"

"Did Serabel mention the Dagger to you?" Amala inquired.

"She did. And she spoke about the prophecy carved on it. I'll swear it on my life, High Priestess, we were sure she was going to retrieve that dagger one way or another. We didn't feel safe. That's why I asked for blueprints of the temple. I wanted to have something on her — something more *real*, in case things turned bad."

Hawk hummed silently, possibly thinking of his next question.

Amala continued, "What do you mean if things turned bad?"

"The damn power she was talking about," Ana snapped, "She spoke of it like it was something we should all fear. Excuse me, if I didn't really like the idea."

Silence fell on the pier and the wind rising from the Apàle was once again the only sound in their surroundings. Amala's heart was crumbling under the weight of all the new revelations: what was even going on? Had they got it all wrong? Did the buyer never intend to kill the Goddess in the first place?

She didn't dare look at Hawk, afraid of what she would find in his eyes and not ready to take the risk. Instead, she focused her energy on Ana.

"So you *didn't* kill her?" she whispered.

Ana's voice was surprisingly soft when she replied.

"No, Amala. I didn't. Me and Nyla—our court has nothing to do with it. You can check our alibis, if you need."

"Yeah, sure," Hawk replied impatiently. "Because in the two months since the murder, there was no way you could come up with any cover."

Amala sensed he was nervous because Ana was telling the truth. She might have been the buyer, but she wasn't involved in Serabel's death. Amala craved his touch, some physical contact. She was in desperate need of him and his warmth. Her body language told him enough; Amala's fingers shook slightly, accidentally sending more tendrils of tepid air around the pier.

But he looked at her for a second too long, and Ana didn't miss it.

"You're mates?"

Hawk had always known they were going to get busted today, but he'd thought it a worthy price for catching Serabel's killer. Still, when Ana's gaze narrowed on them, even anticipating her words couldn't stop the feeling of a cold shower.

Amala whirled toward her, icy eyes wide and full of worry.

"What?"

Her voice was so soft, and Hawk barely repressed a smile.

"You are *mates*," Ana repeated, realisation hitting her like a tidal wave. "You are mates and have been hiding it *all* along!" She brought a hand to her mouth, eyes wide in confusion and surprise. "Have you been together this whole time?"

Neither of them dared to speak a word. Amala subtly tried to catch Hawk's eye, and, this time, couldn't help herself from searching for his hand.

He let her do it. There was no point in hiding anymore.

Hawk felt Amala's immediate relief when she finally touched his skin, mentally cursing himself for not scooping her into his arms sooner. Fuck Ana and fuck all of them. It didn't matter one bit, not anymore. The secret wasn't worth it if it made Amala uncomfortable even for a moment.

He fixed his gaze on the female across the pier.

"You keep it shut, Ana." Hawk ordered, voice low.

Her mouth gaped, surprise fixed to her face. "You can't really assume I won't tell my Lady."

"I really don't care if she tells Nyla," Amala told him. "It's a miracle she didn't figure out the other day."

He wholeheartedly agreed. It had been an incredible effort to focus on the conversation with Nyla when the only thing on his brain was the memory of Amala's thighs on his face. He was half inclined to get her out of there, now, just to ask her to sit on his face again.

"*Hawk*," she scolded him, eyebrows bunching in her classical *Stop Thinking About Making Me Cum* look. Which suggested he'd been inadvertently showing his *I Really Want To Make Amala Cum* face.

He looked at Ana again. "Tell Nyla if you must. But this is not your information to share."

Ana didn't look inclined to agree, but her expression betrayed something else, as though stuck on a memory she couldn't quite place.

"That day, at the Home of Waters..." she murmured, eyes falling on Amala: regretful and full of respect. The respect she had always given, despite their differences. "I didn't know Captain Mercurian was your mate. I'm sorry."

Amala tilted her head, confused. She was expecting anything but an apology.

"Whatever for?"

"That day, when you... found us." Amala swore Ana was blushing. "You *both* tricked me, but I would have never done it if I had known he was your mate. I apologise for that."

"It's quite alright, my beautiful Lady." Amala said.

Ana took in the sight of the pair, now closer to one other: cinnamon and midnight wind merging together in a faint breeze that crept along the end of the pier.

"You guys aren't half bad at pretending," she admitted.

"You better have told us the truth now though," Hawk said between gritted teeth. "And I swear to the Goddess, Ana, if I find out you didn't, I'll call the damn Phoenix on you."

Amala couldn't name the underwhelming feeling taking control of her heart: she had felt so close to finding out what had happened to her Goddess, merely to realise it had never been related in the first place. And not simply that: it was just another confirmation that Serabel had entrusted the truth to everyone but her.

CHAPTER 51

A mala extended her arm, brushed the marble floor once, then stretched her fingertips to the air.

I want to feel you.

When she started, some weeks ago now, she had no idea where to begin. So, in the utter silence of her mind, she began with what felt most familiar.

Feeling the air whirl between her fingers calmed her, *gave* her something. Then, she started thinking.

Serabel could do wonders with her power: touch the soil and make it bloom, sway the clouds from the moon, slow down the dripping of water. Her power as a Goddess enhanced her birth power of Earth but gave her the ability to control the other elements, too.

Mostly, she was able to bring quiet — instil utter calm and admiration in every room she stepped into, making you beautiful with a brush of her fingertip, fertile with a gentle caress to the womb.

Create art from a fraction of thought.

And, as Amala had seen many times, make you orgasm from a mere look.

She was still unsure of why she had refused her Goddess' attention for so long. Perhaps, if she'd given in to Serabel's wishes, her Goddess wouldn't have left her so soon.

She would never forget the feeling of Serabel's power on *her*.

Every time her Goddess blessed her blood, her womb — when she still thought she could have children — her hands and midwifery work. Every time Serabel kissed her forehead or interlaced their fingers... the sparks of divine power were strong, full of delicious lust and love. Amala didn't know if she'd ever become like that, though she didn't mind the love part.

If there was any part of her power she *wanted* to explore, that was it: the ability to show her Love with every breath of her being. When she told Hawk this some days before, he stroked her hair and said.

"I don't think you need to be Goddess to do that, Amala mate."

"What do you mean?"

"I mean that you've been doing that your whole life. No need for special powers."

She had blushed while Hawk grinned, then proceeded to fuck her on the floor. Twice.

And when she pointed out, panting, that it was almost sunset, he had picked her up, carried her outside, and fucked her on the balcony too.

If she was honest, the only thing that eased her anxiety about the whole Goddess situation was the way Hawk behaved about it. He had explained her already: to him, knowing that she was a Goddess or wasn't didn't change a thing — she was a Goddess *to him*, always had been.

I want to feel you, she said again.

It was a habit now, to talk to that divine energy as if it was an influence that didn't belong to her: the only way she would allow herself to accept the divinity living inside of her.

That was *her*.

She closed her hand into a fist, then opened it again. This time, she directed her focus to her power: a soothing, gentle tendril of air hummed around her fingers. It wasn't like the breeze so easily summoned during the day. This one carried something else: a faint heartbeat, the promise of a love beating so strong that nothing could stop it.

I am Goddess of Love, Amala thought, reminding herself to breathe. With every breath, she summoned more tendrils. Glancing around, she lost herself in the quiet of the night as she let the power whirl around her.

It wasn't something to be afraid of: that power had been a constant in her life since the day she was born. She couldn't remember a day where she had woke without the feeling of Serabel's power and love aligning her soul.

One of the tendrils sneaked under her hair, brushing against her neck, then the shell of her ear.

It felt warm — if not the air, what the air carried within: pure, undiluted love — so much and so strong that Amala blinked, almost unprepared.

Do I Love like this?

Is this my *Love? The Love I give?* As if she didn't know the answer already.

Her Love felt like the softness of clouds mixed with the force of an earthquake. It was deep, strong, centred and immensely powerful and, at the same time, gentle, careful — caring. Not invasive, but still overwhelming; not unsettling, but strong like the heartbeat of a storm.

She looked up, scanning the clouds. Where was the Moon tonight?

After Serabel's death, she had found herself searching for the moon less and less. Sometimes she had to for rituals and prayers, but other times she prayed to the Sun, instead — much more than she liked to admit. Not only during sunrise and sunset, like she'd always done. Now she did it all the time.

Her eyes pierced the sky, searching for a moon that had never belonged to her.

Amala felt her power whirl, the breeze feeling like the arms of a lover.

She hoped her lovers felt like this when she was around them. But then, a faint ray of moon peered from the clouds and beamed onto her. Then another and one more until half the moon was visible in the sky, and Amala realised that her lovers *did* feel like this because that fierce, passionate energy which embraced her... was hers.

Do I love like this? She asked again, peering at the moon.

But the moon wouldn't tell her something she already knew.

☼

With Madakahiri just a couple weeks away, the Prior saw fit to call another Karale meeting.

It shouldn't have been a surprise: it was common for the council to reunite more often before Madakahiri and Verbamadeni, the Goddess' festivities... but Amala didn't want to go. Maybe because now both Medyr *and* Ana knew about her and Hawk. Nyla, too. And Harat. The thought of being in the middle of the room with *all* of them knowing felt too uncomfortable.

She should have been relieved to finally stop pretending and yet, she couldn't scratch the feeling: Hawk was *hers* and she didn't want to share her beautiful Love for him in front of people who didn't deserve it. Or maybe it was because she hated to be in Serabel's place, especially without them knowing that she *was* the next Goddess. However, some of those heavy feelings lifted when Hawk announced he couldn't make it to the Karale.

"Zale was busy with Eset's pregnancy, so there's a couple things he left behind. I'm supposed to catch up while he's at the meeting," Hawk had explained.

"Why can't he do that while you're at the meeting in his stead?"

"Oh, because I *hate* Madakahiri's meetings. I asked him to drop me out of this one."

It was fine. More than fine. Amala didn't want any trouble and spent the whole meeting in silence, only talking when it was her turn to answer questions, and when someone required her opinion on a prayer, a ritual, or something. She politely bowed to Nyla, acknowledging Ana with a nod, and tried to focus on what Medyr was saying for the rest of the meeting.

Which she had succeeded in, until Jaren arrived.

He was late today, which was quite unusual, but that wasn't what captured Amala's attention. It was... him. A glance in his direction and she knew something was wrong.

Not the wrong she felt that night at the temple, when the Yonium had crumbled as she felt like she was dying. Not a bad wrong.

Not wrong, wrong, *wrong*.

Just... wrong.

Weird, unusual, and irreversibly wrong.

Amala barely focused on the meeting, throwing subtle glances at the Protector of Fire as if he could help her understand this mystery. Distinctly, she heard Medyr repeat the schedule of Madakahiri — already imprinted in her brain — as the Prior now wrapped up the council. Her brain refused to focus on anything else.

Anything that wasn't the delicious scent that melted all of her senses.

That scent.

Jaren's scent wasn't usually like that: it was musky, flickering fire and embers, and a drizzle of maple syrup. But now she sensed wood and blackberries.

And...

Fuck. Strawberries?

It was different. *Way* too different. Yet it was a call, one she couldn't ignore.

As the Karale left the Round Room, Amala gave Jaren all but thirty seconds before storming after him, following his scent through endless corridors. She tried to be quiet, but her brain was so goddamn loud she feared he could hear her thoughts screaming.

Something was off.

Jaren didn't seem to notice her presence and, when he finally halted, Amala stopped too, keeping her distance as she hid behind the corner, not daring to make that final turn, to face whatever was going on in her head. Amala's heart begged her to step forward, to see, but she didn't dare.

And then she heard Jaren's voice.

"Finally."

"Don't piss me off," another voice replied.

A female voice.

Modulated, yet harsh. The voice of a person who didn't like wasting time and could hardly stand the sight of the Protector before her.

"You took your damn sweet time, and I was late because of you. I think I'm entitled to return the favour."

"Oh, *fuck off*, Jaren," the voice groaned, but there was something else now: the trace of a faint sigh, as if she didn't really mean it.

That delicious scent — it grew deeper, more intense, and the smell of strawberries was now intoxicating. Amala waited for them to talk, for anything at all.

But found only silence. A muffled sound, but too faint to catch her attention.

Curiosity was eating her alive — that and something else — something she couldn't quite place but was determined to figure out. Amala's soul screamed to go, to *see* — to follow him and find out.

What was going on?

Amala trusted her gut and turned the corridor.

Jaren and a beautiful, stunning woman were kissing. Her dark skin reflected the soft sunlight peeking through the windows, and her long, long braids swinged by her back as Jaren pushed her body against the wall. She was quite tall, athletic, her bare arms clenching as her hands pressed against his chest and kissed him back.

Something primal sparked in Amala's own chest, then. She contained it, confused, but was unable to stop looking at them.

And then it hit her: wood, strawberry, and blackberry, that delicious scent that she had felt in the Round Room — it wasn't Jaren's scent. It was *on* him.

It was *her* scent on him.

So many thoughts in her mind, one after the other: so many yet so difficult to process. Trying to calm down, she sent gentle tendrils of air around her, and...

One of them swirled out of range, swiping towards them and brushing against the neck of the stunning female.

The woman immediately halted, pushing Jaren's body away. Then as she slowly turned, Amala felt her own knees go weak, threatening to melt. Her whole body threatened to when *those* eyes peered into hers: beautiful, dark brown eyes that melted with her ice.

"I—" Amala tried to say, her throat dry. She dared to move her gaze to Jaren, who now stared back.

"I am so sorry." She murmured. "I didn't mean to interrupt you."

The Protector of Fire had a weird grin on his face, as if he was pleased to have been caught in the act. The female's eyes, on the other hand... her glare proclaimed death.

"Don't apologise, hot High Priestess. I believe you haven't met the Phoenix."

The world stopped.

Amala's breathing, thinking, reasoning, halted as her eyes zoned on *her*. One single, piercing thought settled in her mind: screaming.

The Phoenix was a woman.

And she was her mate.

CHAPTER 52

A mala had felt like this only once in her life.

When she had met Hawk, and her soul whispered the word *mate*. Hawk's soul had said it too.

A thin thread connecting their souls forever but not pulling, not yet. Not on the night of the Full Moon outside the temple, nor for the ten years that followed. Now things were different: she felt that thread tugging her to him, and she loved it.

She loved *him*. Her mate.

Hawk was her mate, *Hawk*.

But the female in front of her...

She couldn't be wrong. A mating bond didn't lie... and this one, *this* thread pulled hard.

A thread binding her to the *Phoenix*.

Aglatas' most feared killer, torturer, assassin.

Jaren's Second — almost a mythological figure — as many had never seen her, never even guessed that she could be a woman. Amala mentally cursed herself for considering such a thing. There must have been a reason: someone must have told her, must have led her to believe so.

But the more she thought about it, she began to realise no one had ever referred to the Phoenix as a male. Amala had been so convinced of it the her brain now struggled to accept the truth.

It wasn't a man.

It was *her*. The beautiful female in front of her.

Fear or realisation hit at the same time the Phoenix's scent grew stronger — almost harsh as the thread pulled: the wood, strawberries and blackberries intoxicating her mind.

She couldn't help it — couldn't prevent her own scent from escaping.

The Phoenix's scent met hers.

Cinnamon, sugar, sunlight and the moon.

Her expression changed. Those brown, deep eyes that looked like they wanted her *dead* now narrowed, eyebrows softening for a fraction of an instant before her face tightened again.

Mate.

The word surged to Amala's lips and required all of her self-control to repress it. Her mind, soul, and body screamed it.

Mate, mate, mate.

But she quieted, keeping her silence and biting her lips until she felt a tang of blood pool on her tongue. The Phoenix bared her teeth: elongated canines, just like Hawk's, instantly emerging at the smell of blood.

Amala knew then that whatever she was feeling, the Phoenix felt it too.

She knew they were mates.

Mate.

It lingered in the air between them — a silent, secret thread that knotted around Amala's soul. Maybe it had always been there. But how could it be? How could she have more than one thread and have never known?

Amala already had a mate: an incredible, brilliant male who had waited ten years to simply gain a kiss from her.

A small part of her considered, just for a second, that she had never loved only one person. That her heart was too big for that and she had always known. But she sent the thought away.

She had two.

Two.

Hawk Mercurian, the love of her life.

And... the Phoenix.

Who was definitely *not* a man.

Amala couldn't stop her gaze from surveying her figure: the Phoenix was made of fire and it was obvious with every step she took — every time her arms moved, fingers flickered, or eyes blinked.

Such dark eyes.

Amala always thought Hawk's eyes were deep, a warm depth that melted her soul and made her feel safe. The Phoenix's eyes only said: *I'm going to fucking kill you, and enjoy every damn second of it.* Each braid was impeccably plaited and Amala's heart pained at the memory of caring daily for Serabel's beautiful hair.

"Well, aren't you gonna leave?"

That voice.

She thought it was harsh when directed at Jaren, but it was unyieldingly cold when directed at her. A sharp blade cutting right through Amala's soul and the blazing thread they shared. A thread she couldn't break.

A woman made of fire should not have such a cold voice.

Jaren gave a disapproving look, the silent scoldingly clear: a look worn whenever someone spoiled his fun.

"Our hot High Priestess doesn't deserve such rudeness," he said with a pointed look at Amala. "Maybe we should ask her to join."

His words were wrong for so many reasons, but he couldn't possibly know, could he?

He couldn't know the Phoenix was her mate.

Amala wondered what her true name was. Wondered if she was supposed to introduce herself — not as her mate, but as another member of the Karale. How was it possible that, for more than a decade, she had attended the Round Room meetings, along with the rest of Aglatas' official events, yet had never met this woman before?

Maybe she didn't even know who Amala was. Why would she?

Then she remembered Jaren had called her hot High Priestess. Amala still hadn't replied to his advances. God and Goddess, he'd made advances to her in front of her *mate* and his lover.

A spark of jealousy rushed through her at the thought of them together and the fresh memory of the kiss she interrupted. The Phoenix, her mate, was Jaren's lover. And she knew her heart shouldn't have crumbled, but it crumbled anyway.

"I—" her voice sounded strained. The Phoenix's head made a small, involuntary movement, as if she didn't expect to hear her voice again. But Amala didn't let any more disruptive thoughts in her way, "I'll leave you to it."

She left, steps quick as she paced back to the Round Room.

Then out.

Out, away from there, as far away as she could.

CHAPTER 53

"We *might* be at a dead end."

Hawk closed his eyes. He didn't want to hear that.

He had soon understood that Nyla and Ana's involvement with the buyer would lead to a change in his investigation, but no breakthrough. There was no way they had killed her. Serabel didn't die from a weapon wound, Naressa was sure of it. And Hawk had sent Cairo to check for any hints that the Water court were responsible for what had been done to the Goddess, but he always knew it was a long shot.

"Alright." He sighed. "Spill."

Cairo offered his laptop.

"This was all I could find, Hawk. Nothing ever recorded from *any* Water tribe, nothing under Nyla's Protectorate, nor *before* that. The way Serabel died, it cannot be them."

Naressa offered him an apologetic glance, "I have been studying her body for a month, Hawk. I've run all the possible tests, and I have *no* idea."

"Well, that's just shit. Because if the buyer isn't connected to the murder, then only the Charal can be. That, or there's someone else in this city good enough that we haven't found *a thing* on them."

"So what? The Charal wanted to kill Serabel, they *all* entered the temple from the tunnel, and then killed her, leaving before the priestesses could find them? A *group* of them?"

"Should we go back *on* the priestesses, then?"

"If that's the only option." Naressa admitted.

The priestesses. Oh, Amala would hate any more investigation on her sisters. But if they had no other leads, and there was no way the Charal women—

"Wait." Hawk said as a spark of a new possibility rushed through his mind, unfolding. "Wait a moment. We never considered—what if some priestesses *are* Charal?"

A moment of stunned silence followed his affirmation. Hawk exhaled, the thrill of a new thread filling his body with adrenaline. He didn't know why he didn't think of it before but... it was something.

"But—" Cairo stumbled on his words, "We looked into all of them."

"What if we didn't pick up on something important? I don't think they would broadcast the information," he countered, the idea beginning to formulate. "The priestesses cannot harm the Goddess. But if some of them are Charal, they could have helped the tribe to get inside the Yonium."

"Through that damn tunnel."

His gaze bounced to Cairo, a glow in his eyes.

"Which makes sense. It's fucking full of their symbols. The priestesses could let someone *else* harm the Goddess."

Naressa hummed. They both turned to her, but she nodded quickly. "I don't hate it."

"Amala will." Cairo said.

Hawk avoided his eyes, but knew his friend was right. Amala would give him *hell* for this new theory; when the time would come for Hawk to tell her what he actually thought, he didn't want to picture her reaction. No amount of sex would ensure her forgiveness.

☼

The house was quiet when Hawk arrived home.

Amala was outside on the balcony, the glass door left ajar with a piece of raw amethyst preventing it from closing. Howlite was outside too, the pair lying on the marble floor together. He gently knocked on the glass.

Howlite raised her head instantly, then her body as she saw him. Amala followed her movements, smiling when she met his eyes. She opened the door for Howlite, letting her back inside before bending down to pick up the amethyst. Hawk held the door open, closing it once she entered. Amala pressed a light kiss on his lips.

"Hi," she said, reaching for the coffee table and placing the crystal atop of it.

"Hi."

He allowed his gaze to indulge on her body: she was completely naked, aside from her sunstone and carnelian waist chains, her skin a red hue as she had likely fallen asleep on the floor outside. Amala sat on the sofa, extending her legs to the side and laying her head on the cushioned arm. She looked impatient, as if the nap was only a brief break from a restless afternoon. A quick tendril of cold air hit Hawk in the face, snaking up his nostrils until he coughed.

"Sorry!" Amala gasped. "I have had trouble controlling it all day."

He looked at her and she nervously bit her lip. Something was off.

"Can we talk?" They asked together.

A brief moment of silence followed their outburst. Amala broke it first with a nervous chuckle while Hawk surveyed her attentively, trying to understand the hidden words concealed in her body language.

"Do you want to go first?" he offered.

"No," she instantly said. "You go. Sit closer?"

He obeyed, sitting on the adjacent couch. He didn't think she would want him any closer as he delivered the news of their latest lead. Hawk wasn't sure how or where to start. Since his conversation with Cairo and Naressa, he promised himself to not beat around the bush. Yet after seeing her so on edge, he wondered if it was the right call. He didn't want to make things worse.

Dubiously, she studied his face and tried to read his expression.

"Don't you dare give me the parental guidance version. What is it you have to tell me?"

He had to give it to her, Amala was undeniably good at reading him.

"Alright." Hawk sighed, "Do you trust all of your priestesses?"

He allowed a moment for the question to sink in. Amala pursed her lips, eyebrows furrowing suspiciously.

"None of them ever gave me reason not to."

Her voice wasn't defensive — not yet at least, which was a good sign. Judging from her reaction, he decided to take the long route.

"You know that we have zero suspects now, right?"

"Right."

"And you agree that it's not completely foolish to think the Charal women *may* have something to do with it?"

Her nostrils flared slightly but, slowly, she nodded.

"And Serabel was murdered in the temple."

"What is your point, Hawk?" her voice trembled, trying to stay calm.

"Have you ever considered that some of the priestesses might be Charal?"

Complete silence followed his words. Amala's breath caught and her body tensed. She cracked her knuckles in a desperate try to relieve tension.

"My *sisters*?"

"I'm sorry to upset you, Amala mate," Hawk countered quickly. "It's just that—"

"We cannot harm our Goddess, Hawk. We are sworn to her, it's physically impossible. And *even* if we could, we wouldn't." Her voice cracked, but he shook his head.

"That's not what I asked you. If the Charal tribe is behind this, any incognito Charal woman in the temple could have helped them enter without harming Serabel directly."

Amala exhaled, icy eyes now crusted with tears.

"I don't *know* if my sisters are Charal women." She seemed inclined to say something else, lowering her head instead.

"Tell me."

"No, Hawk..."

"I know you want to protect them, Amala mate."

"It's not that!" she snapped.

Hawk's eyebrows bunched up. "What is it, then?"

More tendrils of cool air whirled around him. Amala didn't apologise this time.

"I find it very hard to think that some of my sisters are Charal and I don't know about it. My priestesses tell me *everything* and, with Serabel's protection, they would feel safe enough at the Yonium to be honest about it."

He waited for her to continue.

"And if Serabel had known, she would have told me. I know she didn't tell me shit about her other plans," Amala's nostrils flared again. "But something like *this*... she wouldn't have kept it from me."

Hawk took a moment to consider.

"What if some of them are Charal, but never told her because they were plotting this entire scheme?"

Amala almost snorted at that.

"If you think Hebex can keep a secret for more than five minutes..."

"I don't mean Hebex. I don't even know *who*, I just—"

"If you want my permission to do some research on them, just say it."

"I know it requires a giant motive — and an even bigger plan — to wait two hundred years before acting, but I can't ignore the possibility."

He observed the way her face tightened, then how it relaxed when she forced herself to breathe.

"Listen, Hawk..." Amala murmured. She hesitated again. "There aren't Charal women at the temple. I might not know what you need, but you have to believe me when I say that *none* of us would have ever harmed Serabel. I don't like this idea, but I understand why you have to follow the lead: you may research all of us, but I won't help you. I can't bring myself to doubt my sisters like that."

Hawk couldn't hide the breath of relief that escaped his lips.

"I know you mean well. It's just too much for me." Amala added weakly.

"Thank you, Amala mate. And thank you for not getting mad."

Amala shrugged, a bit hopelessly.

"Maybe you can try the same when it's my turn to talk?"

He owed her that, at least.

Leaning back on the couch into a more comfortable position, Hawk decided to think about the investigation later. Cairo was already looking into the priestesses one more time and Hawk trusted him to pick up any additional threads he might have missed. Still, there was a chance Amala was right but he needed to try.

"Tell me everything."

"No, you..." Amala shook her head. "Come here. Please."

She didn't need to ask him twice. Hawk rose and sat beside her as she curled up on her side to give him more space. Amala was too tense; Hawk could feel her restless energy pulsate, restless — what could have shocked her to cause such a reaction?

"Are you okay?"

Timidly, she shook her head.

"You took me by surprise, with this new lead about my priestesses. And I had a difficult day."

"Why didn't you talk before me?"

"Believe it or not, what I have to tell you is *more* important than Serabel's murder — more important to us, at least."

His curiosity pitched, unable to understand what could be triggering Amala like this.

It couldn't be worse than what she had revealed after Sinayla's birth. Could it?

His hand snaked to capture her ankle, lifting her bare legs to place her feet into his lap.

"It's okay, Amala mate. Talk to me."

But when she didn't move, didn't even try to talk, Hawk knew it was more complicated than she wanted him to think.

"Come here, my Goddess of Love?" he offered.

Amala instantly obeyed, crawling up on the couch and sliding in his lap. Her cinnamon scent whirled with those uncontrollable tendrils of air, her warmth a feeling that easily propagated throughout his whole body. She savoured his closeness and admitted, "Something happened."

Hawk traced imaginary lines along her arm.

"Do you want to talk about it?"

A single nod.

He said nothing, giving her time to collect her thoughts. With no idea what to expect, he continued cuddling her, ensuring she felt safe within his embrace. Hoping it was enough to ease her tension.

Amala took a breath, eyes still closed.

"Do you think I could have two mates?"

Hawk's body went rigid. He was unable to stop himself before it was too late. She felt the change instantly and stiffened too.

"Did you meet someone, Amala mate?"

Amala nodded again, swallowing back tears, or at least trying to. Raising her upper body, she brought her face closer to his, and looked into those eyes. Her beautiful icy eyes, now the portrait of absolute guilt and despair.

"I am *so* sorry, Hawk..." she breathed.

He tried to relax, wiping away her tears with one finger.

"Why are you sorry?"

Amala swallowed.

Her voice was barely a whisper as she said, "I think I mated someone else."

Hawk half expected his heart to crack. Maybe it did, but he was too focused on Amala and *her* feelings to realise.

Hawk had been in love with Amala for a while now. More than a while. He knew she Loved — Loved so deeply that he couldn't possibly be the *only* one on the receiving end. Often he had wondered if she would find another mate before accepting him. Yet here they were, finally mated, and none of his fears had materialised. After watching her with multiple partners for years, he understood Amala. She never neglected any of them and her Love never faltered. Amala loving or giving herself to somebody else would never mean she wasn't his.

Because she was.

High Priestess Amala, *Goddess* Amala was his mate and nothing would change that. Ever. And yet he guilt in her face was unbearable and so sincere, Hawk suddenly blinked in realisation.

"Wait—you didn't think you could have more than one mate?"

He tried to keep his voice soft and gentle, but there was some sort of eagerness there — disbelief.

"What do you mean?"

Amala titled her head, confused. A warm breeze of rich cinnamon invaded the room as she closed her eyes, relinquishing control. "What do you mean?" she asked again.

Reaching for her hand, Hawk interlaced their fingers.

"Have you never thought that you could have more than one mate? Since your heart is so big?"

Amala shook her head, confused.

"Did you already know?"

"Of course I didn't, Amala mate. But I'd be lying if I said I had never suspected it. It wouldn't be fair to you or your beautiful heart to be bound to a single person forever."

"No!" She quickly said. "That's not true. That's why I never thought about it. I *wanted* it to be just you. For the rest of my life."

Hawk's face softened, his heartrate increasing while hearing those words. He squeezed her hand.

"That's very sweet, my Goddess of Love, but you would never be happy with only me by your side."

"That's not true."

"Amala."

She looked at him and released a breath.

"Hawk?"

"You have the biggest heart I have ever seen and I'd be incredibly selfish to be the only one blessed by your Love." He felt like letting go of something heavy then. As if he had wished to tell her for so long, never finding the right moment.

Hawk would love her no matter what. He had always suspected he may not be the only one for Amala but none of it mattered. Hawk was still hers. And she was his. As long as she was by his side, he didn't care if she was by someone else's.

He loved *all* of her. Mostly, the incredible amount of Love she had to give. And that included loving more than one person.

His expression softened as he brushed his fingers against her neck. "You *are* Love, Amala. Someone with your heart and soul would be wasted loving only one person for the rest of their life."

But Amala shook her head, wiping her tears, icy eyes now resolute and confident.

"I'm not wasted loving *you*, Hawk Mercurian."

She pressed her lips against his, her energy so strong it rushed between them, burning like sunlight. Amala kissed him like the fierce lover she was, capturing his breath, his very soul, her words resonating in the cinnamon air that whirled with ferocious pace.

"I love you, Hawk."

The whole world ceased to exist.

I love you, Hawk.

I love you, Hawk.

I love you, Hawk.

There was nothing else, nothing but those beautiful words — words he never thought he'd hear from her lips. At least, not before he said them first.

And yet, Amala was the one who said it. And now she was kissing him as if she'd never let him go, *never* spending another moment without him.

"I love you, Amala."

She made a small sound of surprise at the words and he thought she might cry. He thought he would too. Amala's small hand reached his jaw and she kissed him again, now slower. When she finally retreated, her beautiful eyes glimmered in a new light.

"So you're not mad?" She whispered.

"I love all of you, Amala. And the way you Love is probably the thing I love the most."

Her body melted in his arms, as if she couldn't believe his words. The relief oozing from her was almost heart-breaking.

She sighed.

"I don't deserve you, Hawk."

"Shut up."

Amala chuckled, kissing him again while Hawk held her waist, fingers hooking the carnelian waist chain.

"So are you going to tell me who your other mate is?"

"Maybe," she teased. "Do you have a prediction? Since you have thought about it so much already?"

"It's not like it was my favourite thought," he replied. "But I don't care. You have me, Amala mate, and I am with you whatever happens next. Whoever your mate is and whatever they decide to do."

Amala left her worries aside for a second, lips curving upwards in a mischievous smile.

"What if it's a male that wants to fuck me relentlessly for days and days, pleasuring me for the rest of my life?"

"Then you'll have two."

There was nothing except clear honesty on his face as he raised an eyebrow and added, "But I'd feel sorry for him, as one of us will clearly be better at his job."

She playfully smacked his shoulder.

"It's not a male."

"I know it's not a male."

"How do you know?"

"You asked for my prediction. I've always known you couldn't stand more than one male in your life, everyone knows you prefer women."

"It's not my fault women are delicious."

He agreed with a gesture of his hand, gently brushing her spine with his fingers. One of them slid dangerously close to her sweet spot.

"So? Aren't you gonna tell me?"

"Make me," Amala breathed, enjoying his touch.

"Dangerous words, my Goddess." Hawk said, playing with the spot on her back. He grazed his fingers against her soft skin, causing her to moan. He asked again, "Tell me."

"Turns out," she slowly said, "That I have a thing for Aglatas' Seconds."

Hawk paused. He stopped brushing her skin, hand falling down to hold her waist as he collected his thoughts.

"You didn't mate Ana," he reasoned out loud. "You couldn't have."

Amala could see his brain working and her lips quivered.

"It's not her."

It couldn't be. It *couldn't* be.

In all those years Amala had never known, and now...

If he was right, that explained why she was acting so restless. Not only because she discovered another mate... but because of *who* her mate was.

"You didn't know the Phoenix was a woman, did you?"

CHAPTER 54

A mala gaped.

"You *knew*?"

Hawk burst out laughing, and his laugh was so sincere it melted Amala's heart.

She loved him. She loved him so fucking much.

"How could you let me think it was a man?"

He intensified the grip on her waist.

"You were so fucking scared every time her name was brought up! I barely mentioned her. I didn't realise you didn't know."

"Is that a thing many people know?"

"Not really, no. But in the Karale... I'd say yes? Was she in *today*?"

Amala swallowed, then shook her head.

"I thought something was off with Jaren. His scent was different today, and it felt so good. It called to my soul. So, I followed him after the meeting and I found him with *her*." She paused. "She is so beautiful, Hawk. I've never met a woman more beautiful than her."

Hawk snickered, one hand stroking her back. Amala rolled her eyes in pleasure, pausing for a second to sooth in his touch.

"So you smelled her scent on Jaren?"

"They were kissing when I found them. I guess she's his lover."

He halted.

"Jaren is *fucking* the Phoenix?"

"So there *is* something you don't know," she teased, arching her back to give him better access. When he didn't get the hint, she hissed, "Touch me."

She must have looked comical because he couldn't hold back his laughter.

"I knew Jaren had a death wish," Hawk replied, resuming his ministrations on her sensitive skin. "But I didn't know he planned to risk his life daily. In the worst way possible."

Amala knotted her eyebrows, confused.

"Is she that bad?"

"I've never had a proper conversation with her. She hasn't attended the Karale in decades, that's why you have never met her before."

"She's beautiful. And terrifying."

"How did she look, when she saw you?"

Amala sighed, reliving the bittersweet moment when the most beautiful woman she had ever seen had stared at her like garbage in the street.

"She knows we're mates. She felt it, too. I was biting my lip trying not to say it and she smelled my blood. But..." she paused. "She didn't say anything. She... I thought she wanted to kill me."

"Thank Goddess she didn't, or I would have to kill *her* now, and I'm not sure I'd win."

"I believe in you."

"Well, I would also have to explain Harat why I've been keeping from him that my mate is the new Goddess. But at least we'd know who killed *you*," he shrugged. "We still have no idea for Serabel."

Amala snorted. "Okay, this isn't funny anymore."

But her smile lingered as she kissed Hawk a final time; she couldn't get enough of him today. Gently caressing her face, Hawk moved to get up.

"Where are you going?" She protested.

"Now that you admitted your love for me, I have something for you."

Amala's head tilted, curious.

"What is it?"

He left for a minute, returning with a small, white box.

She fixed her gaze on his movements, a smile curling her lips.

"So… how long have you been waiting for me to say that I love you?"

"I don't know. Ten years?"

"Oh."

He laughed at the expression on her face. "Relax, Amala mate. I'm just messing."

"Hmm. Is this a way to mark your territory? Because we found out I have another mate?"

"It's not my fault if you chose that moment to tell me you love me." He replied. "You have shitty timing."

She giggled, nodding in agreement. Fingers trembling, her hands gently picked up the box.

"Is this another vibrator?"

"You wish."

She was *excited*. This male meant the world to her, and finally she admitted her Love for him. Regardless of what else happened, it was that love which filled her heart and soul. The lid came off and Amala held her breath as she peered inside.

A little gasp came out of her lips, eyes widening in surprise.

Her fingers swiftly reached inside as she picked up a golden anklet cuff.

"*Oh*," she whispered, eyes shimmering in contemplation.

It was absolutely mesmerising: the hard, yet smooth metal perfectly glided into a circular shape, reflecting sparks of sunlight, and emitting flashes so bright Amala thought she could never pry her eyes away. Her gaze searched for him.

"Hawk," she murmured, "It's... *beautiful*."

"I'm glad you like it, Amala mate."

She bit her lip.

"Come here."

This time, she kissed him tenderly, with gratitude and a hint of incredulousness. She inhaled Hawk's rich scent of midnight wind and lemon, suppressing a smile.

"So, anklets... are they a thing you like?"

"You know damn well they are."

She chuckled. Snaking her hand in between his hair, she clamped around a single lock and pulled. His handsome face moved closer, mirroring the movement.

"I'm sorry if I find it difficult to keep track of all the things you're into."

Hawk's hands slid to her bare thighs; the grip so strong it made her gasp as he lowered his mouth to her ear.

"I'm into *you*, Amala."

He nipped at her creamy skin, and she squirmed beneath him, instantly turning molten at the feeling of his canines as they scraped against her neck. Tugging his hair again, she moved both hands onto his face, staring right into his grey eyes.

"Would you put it on me, then?"

Oh, she loved that smug smile. Amala observed each of his movements as he turned to pick up the box, extracting the beautiful, golden anklet. He held it on two fingers while devouring her body with his gaze, paying special attention to her legs.

"Which one?"

How did he manage to turn her brain to complete jelly every single time? Amala didn't notice she was holding her breath, only wanting to look at him — to take in the way he rubbed his jaw or tied his hair up into the bun that made her feral, or when he clenched his fists, or adjusted his rings or...

She sighed.

Hers. Hawk was utterly hers. Amala could admire him for the whole day if she wished.

Extending her right leg, her anklets clinked together as she did so.

Hawk grabbed her ankle, "I fucking love that sound."

She blushed, then made the jewels clink again.

"Yeah?"

He raised an eyebrow.

"What's so funny about it?"

"I like when I discover new things about you. I didn't know you liked jewellery so much."

"I don't." Hawk shrugged, "I just love anklets on you. I love to hear them clinking when I fuck you and that beautiful body of yours is squirming uncontrollably."

"*Hawk!*" Amala brought a hand to her mouth, blushing.

He merely grinned as he slid the anklet down her foot, then her ankle. As he did, it clinked with the others, his grin widening at the sound.

Amala couldn't take her eyes off him. Releasing her leg, she kept it up as sunlight hit the new jewel — that shiny sparkle capturing her attention.

"It's beautiful," she murmured, dangling her leg. "Oh, it's too beautiful, Hawk. I never want to take it off."

"Good thing you won't have too, then." Hawk replied, grabbing her ankle again and kissing it.

Amala considered, eyes rolling back in her head as she basked in his adoration.

"When I shower. Or bathe. I really don't want to ruin it."

He shrugged, the grip of his fingers only intensifying.

"It won't get ruined. It's pure gold."

Her jaw dropped.

"*What?*"

"You heard me."

Amala scoffed.

"You're crazy. And don't bullshit me saying 'I'm crazy about you' because I know that already. You are *crazy*, Hawk."

It was his turn to laugh.

"Need I remind you that you are a *Goddess*, Amala?"

She threw her arms around his neck and claimed him in a possessive kiss. All of her kisses were like that today.

Mine, mine, mine.

Hawk picked her up and grabbed her thighs, fingers digging into her skin, almost hurting. Rolling her eyes in pleasure, Amala continued kissing him; she had no idea how he didn't bump into a wall or doorframe but, a few seconds later, he tossed her body onto the bed.

She fell onto the soft mattress and he hovered above in an instant.

Her lips found his, fingers pulling his hair. Hawk groaned into her mouth, flipping their bodies so she was on top. Amala licked his canines, anticipation building in her lower stomach.

"I fucking love you." She said.

Hawk couldn't stop looking at her — the way her beautiful body bounced when she slowly lowered herself onto the bed, one hand tracing her hip... oh, she had him in a chokehold.

Amala turned, straddling his lap as she faced the opposite way, her skin jiggling at the sudden movements. She playfully shook her beautiful thighs.

"Claim me again."

And he did, sinking his teeth into her skin.

CHAPTER 55

T he sun was shining on Helioneis, but the sun always shined around the temple. Amala had always loved to stay over as a kid, when Faurn was still alive. Kora spent the night too sometimes. It was the only memory she had of her family as a whole.

Kora and Faurn were together until he died, but things had been so different after. When Amala's mother had met Kyne, her actual mate, things became even more different.

And Ayan — Amala didn't want to think about it.

There was so much of her family story she *couldn't* think of, but she didn't mind the memory of peace and quiet as she watched the sunrise in her mother's arms, her father a steady presence by their side. Amala's parents loved each other and their love was real, pure, and full of respect. Often, Amala had wondered what it would be like to love someone before loving your mate.

She had loved before. More than one person. She had said "I love you" to more than one person.

She had loved from the day she was born, and never would she take that Love back, not even when the relationships didn't work out. But she loved none of them like she loved Hawk.

Hawk was — Amala didn't even know. Her Love for Hawk was deep and raw — more so than any other person she had loved. At first, she couldn't tell why. But, deep down, she had always known what made him so different from whoever held a place in her heart before. It wasn't because Hawk was her mate.

It was because Hawk had never feared the way she loved.

She recalled the words he told her the night after they said it aloud: beautiful, powerful words.

"I'm grateful for the Love you give because I've felt it since the day we met and I have done my best ever since to give you just as much, if not more. You deserve all the love in this world and in any other world beyond this. I don't know anyone else that Loves the way you do, but I will be that person for you. I've always been that person for you, Amala mate." Hawk had kissed her, his midnight wind brushing her skin. A memory she would never forget: for how long she had dreamed to hear those words said to her instead of saying them first. The thread made of light linking their souls seemed to sing. Amala pulled it and, when Hawk pulled back, she was overwhelmed by *his* love.

He loved her and he loved her the same.

"Shine for me, my love."

☼

The words Amala whispered to him would be forever engraved in his brain.

I'm not wasted loving you, Hawk Mercurian.

It had been the best moment of his life and of all the lives he could ever live. He found it difficult to remember how his heart felt before meeting Amala: alone, probably. Empty.

He thought he had fallen in love before. He was three hundred and nine years old, God and Goddess, it would be strange if he hadn't shared his heart with anyone else, questioning if they could be the one. But those memories hadn't lasted a second the moment he met Amala.

The Goddess of the Moon was the sun of his life.

His Goddess of Love.

Amala had been scared to Love him too much, while Hawk was scared she would never Love him at all.

I'm not wasted loving you, Hawk Mercurian.

He felt the thread in his soul spark at the memory, the sound of her soft voice playing in his mind on repeat. And then his phone buzzed and the spell broke. Reminding him of all the things that still were not going according to plan, all the unanswered questions and the clues leading to dead ends.

Oh well, at least Amala loved him.

One message appeared on the screen as he unlocked his phone: the coordinates of some location in Pyramis and two brief lines.

Naressa Vesper:
Come here NOW! Don't tell Amala.

CHAPTER 56

W hen Hawk got into the room, he found himself unusually surprised.

A body lay on the ground: sliced through its middle as blood drenched the floor. It looked like the skin had been ripped — by what, he didn't know. Ripped and destroyed, along with the ribcage and every organ contained within it. Naressa stood next to the body, gloves and everything. Right beside her forensic team, stood Jaren and the Phoenix.

Amala had been right, he thought. The Phoenix *was* beautiful. Her hair was plaited in several long braids, her dark skin glowing as the sun marked it from the window.

Hawk had never spoken with her much; she was the kind of person that didn't like conversation. In the few times he had seen her, she talked to Jaren about her hits or reported anything unusual. He gave her more orders and she would leave right away.

She never attracted too much attention which was probably why everyone feared the Phoenix, yet no one knew who the Phoenix was. Still, it wasn't a secret. More like a warning. No one was ever certain of who it was as everyone she had ever taken died. No survivor to tell the tale. Hawk had to give it to her, the Phoenix was great at her job.

Which made him quite uncomfortable, finding her so close to Naressa. While his friend was fearless, he wouldn't have chosen to stand so close to the Phoenix, if he could avoid it.

Naressa spotted him and gestured him closer.

He obeyed, ignoring every suggestion from his brain: he wanted absolutely nothing to do with Jaren, even less with the Phoenix, but if Naressa had called him on the murder scene, there was probably a damn good reason. Still, it was his job.

Hawk greeted them with a single, simple nod.

"Captain," Jaren said. This time, there was no trace of mockery in his voice.

The Phoenix nodded back, dark eyes dangerously deep.

"Thanks for coming so quickly." Naressa said.

After sending the text, Naressa had called him to tell him about the corpse, though failed to mention that the Protector and his Second would be there. Hawk snaked a hand around her waist in greeting as she continued.

"I didn't know who to call, but I think you might find this very interesting."

He looked down at the corpse: it looked like painful work.

"What happened here?"

Naressa shrugged, pointing to Jaren and the Phoenix. "*They* called me."

Hawk's gaze indulged on them, his brain working fast.

"Care to enlighten me?"

The Protector of Fire glanced sideways, catching the Phoenix's eye.

"Tell him." He ordered.

The Phoenix sighed, keeping a snarky comment to herself as she shot a final look at the corpse. When she met Hawk's eyes, her features seemed to tighten.

"I was supposed to kidnap this guy. When I got here, I found him like this."

Her voice was softer than he remembered — harsh, but like she was trying to talk like that, to modulate the sound in a way that was less gentle than her natural tone.

"I believe it's not the first time this has happened to you? To find one of your victims already dead?"

"It's not," she confirmed. "But it's the first time I found them like this. I can usually trace back to who did it in my stead and catch them to finish the job. But this is... different."

Hawk had to admit she was right: he had found several of the Phoenix's victims during his past investigations, and whilst gore was her style of torture, it was not her style of murder.

"And you said none of this is your doing, right?" Naressa asked.

The Phoenix raised a defiant brow.

"I wanted to stab him, just for fun — he was worth a lot of money but since he died before I could kill him, it ruined the whole thing. What does this have to do with your investigation?"

Harat glared.

"Don't question Agent Vesper. I believe you know what she's doing, if *you* called her."

She pursed her lips in a thin line but said nothing else. Naressa nudged him playfully, a small smile of gratitude on her lips. There was no need to thank him, Hawk wanted to say: he was perfectly aware of how good an agent Naressa was.

"Who is this guy, anyway?" Hawk asked, nodding in Jaren's direction.

Jaren didn't like talking about his victims: all the people he sent to the Phoenix either owed him something or had broken too many rules of his Protectorate for him to ignore any longer. For minor offences, he sent the Embers. But if he sent the Phoenix — whoever was going to die had deserved it, according to him. He opened his mouth, but their attention was caught by loud footsteps in the hallway before he could start explaining.

There was no knocking on the door as Cairo entered, eyes searching for Hawk. His face was confused and his expression urgent, as though he was dealing with something outside his usual job description.

Hawk's heart sank: he could read in his eyes what was wrong.

"What's going on?"

"Your mate is here, Captain." Cairo replied, "And I don't think she's doing good."

Fuck. She *wasn't* supposed to know about this, not until he could figure out a way to tell her. Amala couldn't deal with another death in this case, not when she would likely accept the blame for it, cursing herself for not healing the unbalance by accepting her role as Goddess.

Hawk ignored the way Jaren's eyes lit up at the word *mate*.

"*Cairo*," Naressa scolded, eyebrows darting up.

Cairo seemed to realise his mistake as he turned to Hawk again, lips gaping in regret. There was no time for it, Hawk decided.

Jaren could go fuck himself.

Instead, he asked, "Who told her?"

"She overheard Blade on the phone with me. I didn't know she shouldn't know and—"

"She *can* know. I just wanted to wait before…"

He paused, because Amala was at the door.

Eyes red as though she had just finished crying, tears remained on Amala's face. Naressa was instantly by her side, shooting Hawk a worried look. Then his Goddess looked at him, icy eyes meeting his and voice breaking as she murmured.

"Who died again?"

Amala thought it was her fault, for not accepting her role of vessel sooner — perhaps for not seconding some of his leads, or giving full contribution to the case. But before he could reply, Jaren's voice interrupted.

"Thanks for blessing us with your presence, High Priestess."

That was another reason Hawk wished she wasn't here. Not only did she have to deal with a murder terribly similar to Serabel's, but the audience wasn't exactly her preferred choice. Amala turned to the voice, visibly gawping when she saw Jaren.

And when she saw *her*, Amala halted.

Too distracted by crying to scent her, Hawk realized. Or perhaps it was the smell of the corpse, the stench of his blood absorbed in the walls and that of every other room.

Amala's eyes darted from one person to another, and Hawk couldn't help to look at the Phoenix, to see *her* face.

While she wore her usual mask of intimidation, her eyes were fixed on Amala. Though her expression was blank, the Phoenix betrayed herself by glancing at Hawk. Immediately, she looked down as their eyes met, but now her thoughts were clear.

High Priestess Amala had *another* mate — *him*. And *he* knew about her.

Amala herself seemed to realise what was going on in their heads as she turned to Hawk and muttered: "I didn't think so many things could go to absolute shit in less than one minute."

Ah, he surely couldn't blame her. He opened his mouth to reply, but then several things happened at the same time.

Jaren said something but Hawk couldn't hear him distinctively. Though from the tone, it was evidently another of his unpleasant remarks that Amala couldn't stand. And as Amala, Naressa, Cairo, *and* Hawk looked at him, Jaren seemed to realise: Hawk had been there, present every time Jaren had made Amala uncomfortable over the past ten years, just as he was doing now.

But Amala was impassable today.

"Can you not?" She asked, politely. "There's a corpse on the floor, a corpse that died exactly the way my Goddess did."

Cairo and Naressa simultaneously hummed at her words. Amala turned to them, raising a brow.

"What? I imagine this is why you didn't want me here."

Naressa raised her hands in front of her chest apologetically.

"I'm sorry, Amala. I didn't mean you couldn't come. I just didn't want to trigger you."

Amala had stared at Serabel's corpse for days after her death, transfixed on the images on Hawk's laptop.

"I'd like to know what happened." The High Priestess turned to Jaren, hopeful.

He glanced one more time in Hawk's direction before turning to Amala.

"He blew up a big deal for the Embers. He knew the Phoenix was going to get him."

"Wait, *you* did this?" Amala gasped, eyes darting to the Phoenix.

She regretted it instantly, covering her mouth.

"I'm sorry," she murmured, "Sorry. I didn't mean it like..."

"I didn't do this." The Phoenix interrupted, her tone and attitude like trying to rid a particularly annoying fly. "You would know if you bothered showing up on time."

Hawk fought every instinct yelling at him to rip out the Phoenix's throat. How *dare* she speak to Amala like that, using that tone with a Goddess... But Hawk couldn't act like a possessive mate in front of them — especially not in front of Amala's *other* mate. Firstly, she would have every right to challenge him. Secondly, Amala would never forgive him if he blew her chances with the Phoenix.

But those unpleasant words didn't find their mark as Amala raised her head like the High Priestess she was, the hint of a smile blooming on her perfect lips.

"I wasn't invited," she replied, then lowered her voice as in revealing a secret. "They think I'm a cry-baby."

Cairo snorted but didn't contradict her. The Phoenix's expression didn't change, not a fraction.

"I haven't seen Serabel's body, but if you say this is how your Goddess died—"

"She was *your* Goddess too, Jaren." Amala snapped, icy eyes pinning him to the spot. "You do not get to disrespect her just because she's dead." She looked back at Naressa, glancing at the corpse. "I know they're similar, but this isn't *exactly* the same. She was completely devastated. There wasn't a single organ in place."

A moment of tense silence followed her words, as if each of them could remember the scene vividly.

"I'm an idiot." Naressa mumbled, kneeling again and touching the corpse's arm through her gloves. Amala knelt with her, ignoring Hawk and Cairo's flinch of disgust.

She turned to them, huffing.

"You guys remember I'm a healer, right?"

"I'm pretty sure making someone give birth is a little different than an autopsy?" Cairo countered.

Amala's eyebrows quirked upwards.

"I know getting paid to fist women sounds like a dream, but I can assure you my job has its great deal of blood and umbilical cords to deal with." She turned to Naressa, "And you're not an idiot."

"I mean it, Amala. This is no normal murder scene." Naressa's eyes glanced in Hawk's direction as she shook her head. "This is a blood pact."

He froze. The whole atmosphere in the room shifted as an uncomfortable quietness took over, each of their glimpses bearing the same frown. Naressa exhaled.

"I should have seen it. I *fucking* should have seen it sooner! This is a blood pact because that's how it works, an organ per organ and so on, but Serabel — she was absolutely torn apart. I have *never* seen a blood pact breaking to the point of something like *that*. That's why I would have never guessed..." she trailed off, assessing the corpse again.

"Serabel died because of a blood pact?" Cairo repeated, voicing the question that lingered in the air.

"Because she didn't fulfil one," Hawk said, a nod of his chin to the floor. "That's what happens when you don't. But..." his gaze snapped to Amala who shook her head before he could ask.

"I don't know," she whispered. "I swear it. I didn't know she had made a blood pact, she always said that blood pacts were a stupid way to make a bargain. Why risk your soul if you were sure you'd fulfil your part of the promise?" Amala paused, biting her lower lip. "I'm not even sure she knew how to make a blood pact."

"It's easy knowledge," Jaren intervened. "Blood pacts are quite common among fire bearers."

"Yeah, we know you have your army of slaves," Cairo remarked.

The Phoenix flinched at that, and Hawk didn't fail to notice. But everyone's attention was now back on Naressa.

"A fire bearer is more likely to initiate a blood pact because it's part of their culture, yes." She approved. "But Serabel's body... the punishment is more severe depending on the power of the being who did the pact. And judging by *her* wounds, it must have been the blood pact between the two biggest powers I've ever seen. A Goddess and..."

Amala's eyes snapped open as realisation hit.

"A God."

Aarush.

CHAPTER 57

"I haven't been here since before I was made High Priestess." Amala commented.

The Raging Heart waited for them on the other side of the street. The club looked almost inviting, glowing under the warm sunlight. Sunlight followed Aarush everywhere.

"What happened after?" Hawk asked.

He probably knew already, or could definitely piece things together, but would still rather get an answer from her to keep her brain busy.

"He knew me. Aarush. I don't think he ever paid attention to who I was before he saw me at the Karale. I didn't want to give him a reason to bother me."

Smart choice, he thought.

They had decided Amala would lead this. She knew Aarush better; he would be more inclined to talk to her than Hawk. She *knew* the God's secrets would have a price and, a day before, she would never have accepted — but the blood pact, this latest breakthrough... it was too important for her pride to get in the way.

Aarush wanted her to dance for him?

She would dance.

Coaxing from him all the answers she needed.

So, Amala took the lead and Hawk followed. It had been a while since she had used her charm with someone else, especially in front of him. Years before when they were only friends, they attended clubs together, betting on who could get the most numbers. She would go all in, charming her way through every bartender, dancer or performer. Now it took her time to flash a smile at the bouncer.

She wasn't out of practice, at least she didn't think so. No, she felt awkward to charm someone else in front of her mate, the same way she had done with Kanaan that day in the forest.

"High Priestess Amala," she introduced herself with a smile, handing her ID.

Hawk just showed his Priory badge.

"Show-off," she muttered as they passed the glass doors.

A rich, heady, and sensual scent wrapped their bodies the second they stepped inside. It whirled around the onyx pillars and through the crowd of people. People. So *many* people and it wasn't even night-time. But it didn't matter: the Raging Heart was open at every time of the day, blasting music through the sweaty rhythm of hundreds of bodies.

Amala glanced at Hawk as they made their way through the crowd: they *had* a plan. Aarush had no idea they were there, and the only way to get him was to capture his attention. He saw everything. They just needed to be seen.

"Dance with me?" She asked.

Hawk took her hand and tucked her body closer to his, placing his other hand on her waist.

"Play it cool?"

"Nonsense. We'll never catch his attention if we don't look like two horny teenagers."

Lips parting in a seductive smile, she started moving on time with the music. Amala was such a good dancer; she had grown up at the Yonium and danced every day of her life, or perhaps it was her title as Goddess which instilled her movements with such innate grace. She loved to move her body and creating shapes through it. Hawk danced with his mate; the music was addictive. Amala's body was too. *My Amala,* he thought as he spun her.

Her lips found his. Midnight wind and lemon crashed with her sugary cinnamon, as her fingers grasped his locks and pulled his hair. His canines came out to bite her lower lip, so abruptly that she gasped, then moaned at the familiar, delicious pain. She felt the tang of her own blood, rolling her eyes in pleasure as Hawk sucked on her lip. It was wicked and she knew it, but she couldn't stop.

"I fucking love you," she groaned in his ear.

Hawk tightened the hold on her hips. His canines lined with her neck and she shivered in anticipation, but the bite never came. Instead, Hawk's hand clasped her wrist and he pulled her with him. Amala turned to see him nodding to one of the girls in golden robes — typical Raging Heart attire.

She should have been happy that their plan worked, but couldn't shake the feeling of Hawk's teeth on her neck. She *needed* Hawk to claim her.

Following the girl away from the dance floor, the volume of the music declined as they entered a new set of rooms. The tunes changed completely from the common, well-known hits to a sensual, decadent melody instead. Amala felt bliss at hearing such music, it was like honey dripping on skin, candle wax pouring into a golden, shining bowl and melting every known sense.

And there he was: God Aarush sitting on his throne. A petite girl sat in his lap, another was perched on the arm, and one more sat behind him, the back of his head leaning just between her legs.

Hawk exchanged a glance with Amala, expecting to find her contemplating the females but she seemed sturdily dubious: he wondered if her eyes didn't see women the same way now she had met the Phoenix.

Amala stepped forward, kneeling down to her God. Hawk admired how she didn't allow her pride to sway her. Never would Hawk have knelt for Aarush, but Amala was used to it. Showing adoration and worshipping her deities was something she had done her whole life.

Perhaps Hawk understood her a little: he wouldn't kneel for Aarush, but he had been pretty busy worshipping his Goddess himself, and he actually quite enjoyed kneeling in front of her.

"Did you two put on that show just for me?"

Amala just shook her head, eyes surveying each woman on Aarush's sides before replying: the portrait of innocence.

"What can you mean? Your people interrupted us just when my mate was about to mark me."

Aarush gaped, eyes shimmering in what he considered a delicious challenge.

"Mark you? He hasn't *claimed* you yet?"

Amala chuckled sensually, shaking her head with amusement.

"Of course he has," she turned, her thighs bouncing as she pointed at that spot below her backside. "See?"

She took a breath to steady herself; she hadn't played this game in a while. But Amala had always been a great player, unable to recall a time she had used her sensuality to obtain something without ever achieving it.

"Actually, now that you say it." She added, fingers absently touching her lips. "There was a thing we wanted to ask you. Right?" She glanced to Hawk, eyebrows raising in a hopeful expression.

"I told Captain Mercurian my price for talking a couple of months ago." Aarush said with a shrug of his shoulders. "So, I gather that you know?"

Amala shook her head innocently, playing dumb. A part of her hoped he would not make her dance, but she couldn't afford to second guess her confidence right now. Keeping up her precarious facade.

"Dance for me, pretty Amala."

Her lips popped open, her face a portrait of surprise and embarrassment.

"Dance?" She repeated, breathlessly.

"Dance."

Amala glanced at Hawk with feigned shock and guilt, as if she couldn't believe it.

"Dance for you? For how long?"

"However long it takes to please me."

"*Oh.*"

It took her so much restraint not to release a smug smile. It was working. She turned to Hawk, nodding to the door, and said in her most innocent voice, "W—would you mind waiting outside?"

They had talked about this: Amala felt safer with Hawk around, but she didn't want to trigger his instincts by dancing for someone else right in front of him. It was a short-lived wish, though.

"No," Aarush ordered. "Your mate watches."

☼

Amala danced for Aarush as if she wanted to steal his attention — his eyes, his mind, his God damn soul. He watched her raptly as she moved in time with the most sensual music Aarush ordered to play; her hips beautifully bounced as she isolated her upper and lower body and danced, danced, danced.

She gave her best: one moment she was up, on the floor, and then on her knees. She belly danced, fingers hooked in her waist chains, moving swiftly and sensually as her thighs shook, ass bouncing, arms creating patterns and lines as her chest heaved. As Amala's head fell back, her eyes *glowed*. Amala looked at the God the whole time, but her body betrayed her: she hoped Aarush didn't notice. She wasn't dancing for him.

She was dancing for Hawk.

She never caught his gaze, but knew he was watching her. Hypnotised, probably. Very close to losing it and marking her right in the centre of the room. When the last song ended, her movements ceased with it but she remained on the floor, awaiting the God's next move.

"Leave us," he ordered, gesturing to the women around him.

They obeyed, but each of them left the room with their eyes fixed on Amala. She didn't have time to bask in their attention, no time for her Ego to be fulfilled. Aarush watched her, and she held his stare. "I must say, you dance—"

"I hope you enjoyed because no fucking way I'll do that again," Amala sighed, dropping her act the moment only the three of them remained in the room.

She quickly got up, nodding at Hawk to come closer.

"Told you I'd get him to talk."

"You would get anyone to talk dancing like that, Amala mate."

She smiled at him, a genuine smile this time. Then Amala faced Aarush.

"You'll be happy to know I hated every second of that. Besides when your concubines realised I would be a much better lover than you, that was my favourite part. Now, own up to yours."

Aarush had a weird spark on his face, as if he had never believed Amala's game in the first place, yet let her dance for him anyway. He slightly spread his legs, assuming a more comfortable position.

"A deal is a deal," he gave in, a hint of amusement in his voice. "Ask your questions."

Amala nudged Hawk, but he shook his head. She could lead this. She had done it so well, delivering exactly what she promised to.

"I think you know how Serabel died." Amala started slowly.

"Do you, now?"

Aarush liked games. He would be straightforward to fulfil a deal; they risked losing momentum if they kept playing. Hawk said she needed to be straight to the point.

"You made a blood pact with Serabel."

Amala's voice was clear and unequivocal. Aarush's eyebrows quirked upwards, gaze intensifying on her figure. Amala held his gaze without blinking.

"You didn't know about it." It wasn't a question, but a statement.

"I didn't."

"I thought she'd tell you at some point." He admitted. "I didn't think she would keep this from you."

"Well, she kept this and more," Amala said with a hint of reluctance, "Why? Did you tell Medyr?"

"Of course not," Aarush snorted, "Me and Serabel agreed to keep it secret, but she always had a soft spot for you, so I often wondered. I know she didn't tell you *some* things," he added, and Amala wondered what he meant. "But this... I always thought you deserved to know. For how much you cared about her."

"She *died* because of it." Amala went on. "All her wounds match what happens when someone doesn't respect a blood pact."

Aarush fell silent. His eyes fell on Hawk for the first time, and there was something else in them now — worry? Realisation?

"When—" he started, his voice hoarse. Strained. "When did Serabel die?"

"You're kidding," Amala breathed. "You are—"

"When?"

His demanding tone made her flinch. Hawk intervened.

"It was the 17th night of the second month. But you already know this: she couldn't have died *because* of the pact without you knowing."

Aarush was silent for a long time. His gaze stretched between Hawk and Amala as they both felt his divine energy wander the room in incomprehensible swirls. A spark of fire beamed on his fingertips as he clenched his fist.

"Fuck," he muttered. "I didn't know."

"How could you not know? To die for a blood pact implies to break a deal. You should *feel* it."

"I couldn't feel it," he snapped, a pointed look at Hawk. "It wasn't... I didn't know it was on that day. One night, I called for our pact but Serabel didn't answer. I hadn't realised—"

"That it was on the same day?" Hawk replied, very much unconvinced.

"No. I—that night, I forgot everything that happened. I—" Aarush hesitated again, no semblance of smugness remaining.

"Serabel was killed by a blood pact." Amala whispered. "What happened for her to not fulfil it?"

She thought he wouldn't answer. On a normal day, he surely wouldn't but something was different now. Aarush wanted to answer their questions because he craved the answers too.

"We made our blood pact right after I became God. It wasn't my idea, believe it or not. I knew nothing about being a God and Serabel was eager to teach me but I didn't know how to protect myself and she wanted to make sure we were each other's collateral, just in case things ever went south on my side. That's the pact we made: if one of us was ever about to die, our energy would call to the other and we would transfer our powers to keep each other alive."

Hawk hummed. Amala blinked in confusion.

"So how did she... not fulfil her part? Did you—"

"I was poisoned."

Aarush's voice was even more strained as he said the words.

"I got tested and apparently, I ingested some anyeth. I felt normal all day but at night things got bad. I puked my guts up for an hour before starting to feel a pain so terrible, I thought I would die. I remember nothing but agony and confusion. That's when I called for my pact with Serabel, but nothing came back. It was like she never heard me." He took a breath, adjusting himself on the throne. "I felt like shit for weeks after. Even after my test results came back, I could barely place the pieces together. I knew Serabel had died but I remembered *nothing* of that night for so long that I never — I didn't even know it was on the same day. Hell, it took me a long time to even realise what had happened to me and when, and how many days I had lost. The anyeth fucked me up for real."

Shit. Anyeth was a powerful poison: a powder made from the sharp teeth of northern gryphons, inducing paralysis to whoever ingested it and, in some cases, quickly leading to fatality. Aarush must have taken an incredibly small dose, brought to the threshold of death without passing through it: one of the main reasons anyeth was used as a drug for those wishing to experience how it felt to be a blink away from death. Hawk blew out a breath in realisation.

"That's why you looked like shit when I came here, after Serabel's death."

Aarush nodded, certainly not amused by his choice of words.

"You may blame it on me, if you must, but I had nothing to do with her death. It was her *choice* not to answer my energy's call. Though I don't think she did it on purpose, it's not like her. She knew she would die if she didn't fulfil her part of the oath."

"It's not your fault, my God," Amala intervened. "I know you cared about Serabel. I would never imagine you could wish her such illness."

Hawk rolled his eyes at her sweet words.

"That's not how we do our job, Amala mate. It's not based on how much you trust someone."

"You trust *me*," she replied. He didn't contradict her, but still looked *very* unconvinced.

She took her head between her hands, confused.

"What does this mean, though? She just didn't answer and *died?*" Amala groaned: it didn't make any sense. "What if she *couldn't* answer, instead? What if she tried and couldn't, what if—" she blinked, thoughts rushing in frantic search of an explanation. "She would have never let you die."

"I'm pretty confident she wouldn't," Aarush replied, "And yet..."

"So, this is it?" Amala breathed, incredulous. "You ask for her help through the blood pact bond, she doesn't answer and she *dies*? Just like that?"

Hawk's hand grasped her shoulder, a not-so-vague attempt of steadying her through the storm unfolding in her head.

"We still have to figure out why it happened."

"How? She's *dead*, Hawk."

She shut her eyes, surrendering to the feeling of failure she so desperately tried to keep away. Panic rushed through her, the underwhelming sensation of discovering something she now wished to forget. It thumped in every corner of her mind faster than any heartbeat.

Their last stretch — their last *hope* — was another dead end. Amala turned to the doors, taking a cautious step. She didn't even know where to go.

But Aarush's voice sounded from behind her before she walked away.

"So, *this* was what you wanted to know?"

She turned to him with a scoff, crossing her arms on her chest.

"What else should I want from you?"

"I thought you wanted to ask me more about *you*, Goddess Amala."

CHAPTER 58

A mala froze. Completely: body, brain, and soul. Frozen on the spot, her eyes went unnaturally wide. Hawk looked equally shocked.

"*What?*"

This time, her voice sounded breathless, as though she was talking while gasping for air. Her biggest secret, what Amala had so desperately tried to protect — to feel worthy of — so flippantly raised by Aarush.

"You thought I didn't know?"

Aarush's face was a mask of smugness.

"How... how?" She said. "How long have you known?"

Amala's mind went blank; moments before, thoughts about Serabel's death pounded on her temples like hammers — now there was nothing but blissful silence.

"I thought *that* was what you wanted to know," the God said, amusement in his tone. "I've been waiting for you to come here for a long time now."

"Since when?"

"Since Serabel died, of course."

Why did Aarush know her secrets? Did he knew about—

"I don't understand," she said. "Why haven't you told me?"

Aarush studied her and, for the first time, *really* seemed to see her.

"I thought Serabel told you."

"Told me what?"

"That you were going to be the next Goddess."

Her jaw dropped and, for a moment, she stopped breathing. Hawk threw her a worried glance, though didn't look as surprised as her.

Aarush went on. "She seemed quite inclined to tell you the last time I saw her."

Amala's icy eyes glowed of some dark light now as she stepped closer to the throne.

"Please, my God," she begged. "Tell me what you know. I'll dance for you again if I must, or kneel or beg, I don't care. Please tell me what you mean."

She made to kneel, but Aarush halted her before she could.

"Amala, don't."

She halted.

"You're my equal. You shall not kneel."

"Why did you make me dance, then?"

"I *really* thought you knew. I was certain Serabel had told you." He glanced at Hawk, as if to ensure the Captain wouldn't kill him while he was distracted. "Serabel has always thought *you* should have been the next Goddess. If she had known for sure, she would have left this world just so you could own the role and embrace being the next vessel. But she couldn't know, how could she? So, she started researching it and looking for evidence."

"The texts," Amala breathed. "She asked Nyla for texts about the genealogy of power."

"She did," Aarush confirmed. "Serabel always thought that you and your pure Love would make the perfect Goddess. A kind of power that—"

"No one had ever witnessed before."

That was Hawk's voice. Amala jerked her head to him so fast that she might have pulled a muscle.

Her eyes trailed his face: pure, undiluted terror in her stare.

"What?"

Hawk exhaled, clearly conflicted.

"You know the theory I wouldn't tell you about? Well—after you told me you were Goddess, when Nyla said Serabel was researching the genealogy of divine power, things started to make sense. I'm sorry I didn't tell you, but I didn't want to risk hurting you without knowing for sure."

Amala instinctively reached for his hand. "We agreed with Nyla. The power Serabel mentioned were the Charal women."

"It was never the Charal, Amala. It was you."

She shook her head, blinked, then focused on breathing as her body trembled. She shook her head. "No."

"It was," Aarush said. "It is."

"How long have you known?"

"Serabel suspected it for years — she explained to me this whole parallel with the prophecy—"

"What prophecy?" Amala interrupted, mind rushing to the Dagger of Phule.

"The chant. The Goddess' chant. It's a prophecy for a future Goddess." Aarush explained, as though it were obvious.

"It's *not*. It's a blessing and a well-wish for every vessel that came and that will come." Amala countered.

"It's very much a prophecy, Amala. Serabel explained to me every verse, all relating to you."

It couldn't be. It just, simply *couldn't*.

Her wind started breezing around the room in hurried twirls, the cinnamon and sunlight growing stronger as the *moonlight* joined too. Amala gasped for breath, panic rushing through her veins.

"I can't—" *Breathe*, she wanted to say, only the words died on her tongue. Hawk was by her side in an instant, using his weight to steady her as his hand rested firmly on her lower back. Uncaring of Aarush's presence, she buried her head in Hawk's chest and started crying.

"W—why wouldn't she tell me? If she thought I... *deserved*," she spat the word like a curse, sobbing, "To be Goddess. Why wouldn't she—"

Hawk held her in silence, glancing at Aarush as he frowned. Prompting him to answer.

For several moments, Amala's weeping was the only noise in the room. Then, the God opened his mouth.

"Amala... Serabel was in love with you. Completely and utterly in love with you."

She turned to him hesitantly, shaking her head.

"It's not possible. She couldn't be, not with *me*."

"How many times did she ask you to be her lover?"

"Many, but you did too, and it's not like you love me."

"Well, Serabel did. She was in love with you for years. Decades, probably."

Amala kept shaking her head. She didn't believe him, didn't *want* to believe him.

"How do you even know?"

Please say you don't. Say that you made it up. Please.

"She told me. She talked about you all the damn time." Aarush said.

It had to be a nightmare. Every word he said was a stab to Amala's heart. Serabel in love with *her*?

Why *ever* would that be? Hawk's grip on her waist tightened, as though sensing the darkness which suddenly consumed her thoughts.

She felt his breeze a second later, whirling around her and drying her tears.

"Why wouldn't she do something?" Amala murmured, confused. "She was Goddess of Love: she could have made things easier, if she really was in love with me."

Her tone implied disbelief, but she knew Aarush wasn't lying. Amala had avoided Serabel's loving gaze for too long, hiding behind excuses and thoughts of her traumatic past.

"She knew you weren't ready to commit to Love for a long time. I don't know why, she wouldn't tell me—" Amala breathed a sigh of relief at that. "But she was hesitant. And then you met your mate, and she wouldn't dare step in after that."

Hawk's head snapped toward him on alert.

"You knew Amala and I were mates?"

The God readily shook his head.

"Serabel only told me the High Priestess had a mate and it was a male. I didn't know it was you before today. He shrugged, eyes falling on Amala again, a spark of fire in his gaze. "I'm sorry you found out like this. But Serabel loved you more than anything, she would have given up her life to make you the next Goddess."

☼

Mistress of the Night,
Lady of Water flow,
Surge when lovers fight,
Stand when shadows grow.

Goddess. That was plain, easy, with no double meaning. Or maybe...

The fight between lovers: lovemaking. Amala had always found it so beautiful.

"It's also because of your ritual as High Priestess," Hawk murmured. "You stood in the shadow that night of New Moon. There was no other light in the temple."

Amala sighed, tears sliding down her cheeks.

Bringer of life,
She's both and she's neither.
Holding the knife,
That makes her moon-breather.

Bringer of life.

"I've been a midwife my whole life, Hawk..." she murmured incredulously with a sob. "A goddamn life-bringer. But both and neither?"

The Goddess was both: herself, her soul, and the divine energy merged within. Both and neither as she couldn't be one without being the other.

But Amala was High Priestess *and* Goddess. She couldn't be either of them at once, she had to choose. But right now, she *was* both but she was neither.

"What about the knife?" Hawk asked.

"Aarush said Serabel wouldn't explain this verse," she shuddered. "There *is* a knife. A relic that the High Priestess uses during Verbamadeni. It's just on the altar at the Yonium, next to the Goddess' flame." She murmured the words, as though refusing to believe it.

For carrying a secret,
So deep in her soul.
For her heart beats so strong,
That two make her whole.

She carried a secret. *Many*.

Amala couldn't stop crying.

"I should tell the rest of the world that I miscarried, then at least this fucking passage would be wrong."

Hawk snorted, pulling Amala toward him and holding her tight. They were sitting on their bed, piecing together everything said at the Raging Heart.

"And your heart beats strong, my Goddess of Love. I've always known." He told her.

She nodded, biting her lip.

"I know I have a big heart…" she exhaled, "But two… two—"

Amala gaped, overwhelmed with surprise as she met Hawk's gaze in a hurry.

"Two mates."

Two make her whole.

Hawk and the Phoenix. For her heart was too big to Love one person only, and she would have two threads in her soul forever: one made of light, and one made of fire.

Amala cried for hours. She couldn't and wouldn't stop.

After all, Aarush had been right.

Goddess, keep shining,
Let the story be told,
Let the light be blinding,
Let the power unfold.

CHAPTER 59

After talking with Aarush, Hawk and Amala had barely seen each other for a week.

Madakahiri was close and Amala was busy with rituals, prayers, and rehearsals. Hawk was busy too. It felt almost surreal to drop the main lead on their case. But there was nothing else they could do: Serabel was dead because of a blood pact, and she had decided her own doom by ignoring Aarush's call for help.

Despite Hawk's insistence on never letting emotions cloud his judgement, he believed Amala when she said Serabel would never do that *willingly*. Serabel was an amazing Goddess, she had fulfilled her role for centuries: a present, caring, and loving vessel. The idea that she had simply *refused* to help Aarush, especially when bound by a blood pact, didn't add up.

He asked Naressa to run additional tests over the corpse, or whatever was left of it; he was still waiting for her report. Though now, all he wanted was to return home and focus on his Goddess.

Hawk couldn't imagine how hard this had been for her, settling into her new reality after their conversation with Aarush. Neither had spoken much about it, Amala probably preferred to figure it out on her own.

Their own commitments had started consuming so much of their time that they barely saw each other at all. Amala was far too tired from the Madakahiri preparation — dealing with Aarush's revelations too — and was usually asleep the moment her head hit the pillow. Hawk felt mentally exhausted from all the recent breakthroughs on the case.

There were still so many questions, only he didn't have the luxury to ponder them, not when he had reports to file, meetings to attend and a mate to worship, always ensuring she felt like the true Goddess she was. Amala laid on the bed when Hawk entered. It was only afternoon, but she must have been completely drained to fall asleep so early. Howlite jumped from the bed and stalked towards him, but Hawk was prepared and managed to avoid being pinned to the floor. He observed the way Amala's hair spilled onto the pillows, white on white with flashes of silver. She mumbled something in her sleep then blinked, gradually opening her eyes.

She took a minute to realise he was in front of her. Alarmed, she spun to the window.

"W—"

Amala paused, swallowed once. Turning to the nightstand, she reached for a drinking jar filled with water with an orange straw poking from the lid. Amala cracked her neck as she took a big sip, then exhaled.

"I thought..." her eyes trailed outside again. "I didn't mean to fall asleep. What time is it?"

Hawk flashed her the screen of his phone. Amala yawned, absently stretching her body while Hawk pet Howlite.

"How are you?" she asked as he strode for the bathroom.

She distinctly heard the sink running as he washed his hands.

"I'm alright. How was your day?"

"I missed you," she admitted, her body crawling closer to the edge of the bed. To him.

Hawk let his gaze linger over her skin, eyes burning with hot, passionate love. She felt the shift in his scent, that irresistible note of lemon reaching her, tempting her, compelling her body to ache for him. "Not fair," she muttered, inhaling deeply, but she didn't mean it. She would bathe in his scent, if she had the chance.

"I missed you too," Hawk replied, lying down beside her. "I've been thinking about you all damn day."

Amala bit her lip.

"Yeah? What did you think of?"

Hawk grinned: handsome. He was so handsome, and Amala thought her heart would burst for all the Love she felt for him.

"I was thinking..." he started, then looked at her. Teasing.

"What?" She insisted, breathless.

He shrugged.

"Nothing, really,"

"Hawk," she panted.

Wicked. She couldn't stand when he did this... except she absolutely loved it. She tried again.

"What were you thinking of?"

That damn grin. Again.

"You almost got me in trouble today, Amala bunny," he said.

That. Fucking. Name.

She couldn't even describe the way her body turned molten when Hawk used it.

"I wasn't even there!" She protested.

"You were in my mind all the damn time, and I almost got distracted because of you."

"Must have been some deep thoughts then," she replied innocently.

Hawk bit his lip, eyes darkening. "Yeah," he said, "Of all the ways I could tie you up and eat you out for days."

☼

Amala's mouth gaped at the sheer honesty in his words, intoxicating her thoughts... A blush crept up her cheeks as she leaned back into the pillows, covering her burning face with small hands. Hawk smirked as he sensed her cinnamon scent warm the room.

Of all the ways I could tie you up and eat you out for days.

"I'm not sure we have *days*," she breathed, "But I'm yours until sunset."

She didn't need to tell him twice.

Hawk was on her in a second, canines scraping against her skin as he kissed her deeply. Amala basked in the love from his kiss: such undiluted care, and a tenderness that felt like a claim. She was his and Hawk was hers. Amala pulled away to catch a breath, and then she didn't know how, but Hawk was tying her wrists to her ankles. She sat on the bed: naked and exposed with her thighs spread as she balanced on her knees, arms behind her back and hands tied. Her fingers played with her anklets, making them clink.

Hawk groaned, eyes meeting hers. He knew exactly what she was doing but Amala merely studied him, tugging at the ropes. She couldn't move an inch and her arousal only grew: defenceless and vulnerable.

"Can you move?"

Such a *tease*. Of course she couldn't move and he knew it. Grunting, she shook her head. Hawk raised a disapproving eyebrow.

"Voice, Amala bunny."

"No, I can't move."

He stroked her neck with his fingers.

"Good. If you don't want to talk, just ask for a gag."

She gasped, "No moaning your name?"

"I like your moans, Amala, I don't care if they're loud or muffled."

Her eyes shimmered in challenge. She nodded with her chin — the only part of her body that could still move.

"Gag me, then."

Hawk met her gaze, slowly shaking his head. As if he had known already what she was about to say but was, somehow, always a step ahead. Or ten. "I said *ask* for it."

Oh, Goddess. She would come right now if he kept teasing her like that. How? How did he know exactly what to say to drive her so cruelly crazy? To torment her just the right amount, every single time?

"Please," she licked her lips, "Could you gag me?"

The anticipation was killing her, cinnamon scent so thick she doubted it would ever fade. Hawk brought a smaller piece of rope to her lips.

"Open," he ordered.

The hard material met her tongue as he slid it into her mouth. She realised too late that there was a knot, forming a smaller ball her teeth now clamped.

Amala was so wet, she was certain the bed sheets were soaked already.

"Look at you," Hawk said, his voice a taunting caress, "You are such a pretty bunny, Amala."

She tried to protest — to pretend she wanted to, at least — but only muffled sounds emerged from her lips. Amala could only watch as Hawk gave a hungry glare, lying down in front of her.

"You look delicious," he said, and licked his lips, "Now sit on my face."

☼

Hawk found it difficult, sometimes, to realise Amala was a part of his life, and was here to *stay*.

There were moments where he couldn't believe it. He had probably spent hours simply basking in the memories of the two of them, reliving every single detail as though it was the first time. He would have done it now too, had he not left the room to grab Amala some orange juice — just to find Blade and Cairo in his living room. On the sofa. Right outside the bedroom.

Amala had returned from the balcony after watching the sunset, halting in surprise at the sight of them.

"When did you arrive?" She asked.

"Too long ago." Cairo replied.

Amala had blushed but said nothing. Her body still bore faint rope marks as she sat beside Hawk, Howlite quick to slouch her head in Amala's lap.

"Are you coming every day of Madakahiri?" She was asking now, stealing Hawk's joint to take a hit herself.

"Don't get high," he mused, "Or you'll fall asleep in a second."

Blade shrugged.

"I guess. Maybe I'll skip the day of the Water, since Wahine isn't coming."

"Oh," Amala said, "Madakahiri's day of the Water can be one of the hardest days of the year for me. Lots of women are pregnant, giving birth in the middle of the water energy during the God's celebration at Helioneis. It used to keep me very busy."

"I'm definitely not coming now, then." Blade chuckled.

"No, it's different now." She quickly explained, "Aarush forbade giving birth at Madakahiri. God Darnen allowed it and many women planned their pregnancies so their due date aligned with the festivities. Even more do it for Verbamadeni."

"Did you like that? Assisting births during Madakahiri?"

"I love that," Amala said with a smile. "It's a bit overwhelming, sometimes. I used to raid Mhelani's trees for Qelcena leaves to make loads of hibiscus tea."

"Hibiscus tea?" Cairo repeated.

She nodded.

"You know, to calm them down. Qelcena leaves are an energy inhibitor. Madakahiri asks for a great part of your energy and if you're there, you want to give it. I make sure they have energy to spare after they have given birth so that..." but Amala's voice trailed off, the sentence unfinished. Her eyes widened.

"Amala?"

Something clicked and she turned to Hawk, her face a mask of utter dread.

"Serabel was drinking hibiscus tea."

Hawk's head snapped on her. "What?"

Amala tried to concentrate. Serabel had been sick with the arrival of the rain. She often was and Amala was used to it, accustomed to all the little things she needed to do to make her Goddess feel better again: a warm bath every morning and one every night; fresh coconut in a white ceramic bowl; an infusion of hibiscus tea and Qelcena leaves three times a day. Realisation hit her, a whip slicing her brain just like she had felt the night of the earthquake. The night her Goddess had died. "She had been sick, so I made her hibiscus tea."

"*With* the leaves?" Hawk's voice echoed. "What—"

"Yes," Amala breathed, voice barely audible.

"How often did she drink it?"

"Thrice a day. Every day. Including the day of her death..."

It couldn't be. *She* had made her tea.

"Her energy was weakened. It was *totally* inhibited. That's why she didn't answer Aarush's call."

Hawk was silent. Blade hummed.

"Can it work like that?" Cairo asked.

"It does. It inhibits women's energy enough that they don't answer the call from the God's energy on Madakahiri."

Strong enough not to answer the call of a God.

Strong enough to prevent Serabel from doing the same.

CHAPTER 60

T he sun always shone on Madakahiri.

Amala wouldn't admit it to herself, but she always preferred the God's festivities to Verbamadeni.

Verbamadeni happened at night, from dusk to dawn with bonfires and firelights. They lit up lanterns, danced in circles around the fire, chanted aloud, danced some more, drank wine, and ate fruit from the Yonium's orchard.

Madakahiri was quite the same, only celebrated during the day, beneath the mighty sun that never failed to shine on Helioneis.

The first days passed in a blur: Amala slept at Helioneis, settling for a small cot on the eastern balcony. She didn't mind the breeze and used her own power to shield the gusts of wind when it became too insistent. Amala hadn't slept alone since leaving the Yonium.

Before Hawk, she had her own High Priestess rooms.

But before that, eleven years ago, she always shared with someone else. Seryn, first and — once Teleia joined the temple — Hebex. Now Hebex slept with Medyr, Seryn and Teleia had claimed a room where no

one could bother them, and Sinayla, Caelan, and Xantara spent most
of their time together, adjusting to their new family dynamic.

So, Amala had slept alone, away from the rest, spending her time
reliving Aarush's words and what they meant to her.

Serabel had known she would be the next Goddess. Suspecting it for
years, she had been willing to give up her *life* and power so Amala could
embrace the role she was called to.

Why had her Goddess never told her the truth?

Amala had an answer, but she didn't want to believe it.

Was she really that humble? Did she really feel that unworthy that
Serabel considered it a waste of time to reveal her plans? If Serabel had
ever revealed she was intended to be the next vessel, Amala would have
just shrugged it off, choosing to forget it had ever happened.

She didn't feel remotely worthy of such a position.

Yes, Madakahiri certainly provided enough time to bask in her own
anxiety and fears.

The first day was the most exhausting. Both festivities began
the same, as the starting ceremony ensured each Protector received
individual blessings from the God or the Goddess — occasionally, their
Seconds would receive blessings too.

Amala stood in place of Serabel, observing the scene as the Prior,
Nyla, Jaren, Atalman, and Raila received their blessings. Their Seconds
waited behind them, but the Phoenix was nowhere to be seen.

Though no matter how much Amala would have liked to see her
again, she had too much on her mind to deal with that too. It was
difficult enough to take over Serabel's role, assisting Aarush in the
sunrise opening ceremony under the gaze of all Aglatians. Not to
mention how nervous she felt now that more people knew about her
and Hawk.

But Aarush had been kinder to her, which was unexpected. As if,
after their conversation at the Raging Heart, he now finally understood

what she was going through. She wasn't sure *why* he would keep her secret, knowing that now she was his equal, but she didn't mind this change of heart.

Amala danced, prayed, laughed, and loved for the rest of Madakahiri: the weight in her chest had lightened during the day, returning heavier than ever at night. It was easy to pretend everything was fine during the rituals; her friends were with her: all the priestesses and priests she knew from when she was a girl. She *belonged* there and it felt great to belong again.

Each day brought its own blessing and happiness. On Water's, Nyla and Ana gifted the temple a smaller stream, departing from the Apàle to bring its pure waters closer to the temple. On the day of Fire, Aarush's birth power, the rituals were beautiful, and the dances more so.

On Air day, Hawk was there. He made love to her on the balcony under the sun, and Amala had asked herself how long she had waited for a Love so strong and deep.

On the day dedicated to Earth, she watched Hebex and Medyr honour the God by joining their bodies and souls under the mighty Sun.

Today, on the sixth day of Madakahiri, everyone would join the festivities once more.

The plane was starting to fill at dawn before the sunrise would signal the start of the celebration. Hawk met Amala under the pomegranate trees. She picked one, opened it, and offered him half as he approached.

"Morning," he said.

She plucked a single seed and placed it in her mouth. Biting into it, a rivulet of red juice drooled from her lower lip. Hawk lowered his head to lick it. Amala shivered under his tongue, then smiled.

"Morning."

"How was yesterday?"

"It was beautiful." Amala replied said, but her expression was unmatched to the sincerity of her words. She looked troubled and unable to disguise it.

"But?"

Amala bit another seed of pomegranate.

"But my head is so loud. I haven't been so restless since..." her voice trailed off, eyebrows knotting, but he knew what she meant. Her miscarriage.

Hawk reached for her hand and Amala's body relaxed somewhat.

"I just want this to be over so I can... think. I can forget it during the day, but it just comes back louder at night."

Hawk pulled her into his arms. "Do you want to be alone, when it's time to think?"

He would be there for her, with her. She just needed to say the word.

"Maybe you could hug me. Help me think." She was quiet for a while, hesitant as she chewed more pomegranate. Then murmured, "I love to see myself the way you do."

"I love to show you why you're so worthy of everything that you have." He said back, words laced with beautiful promise. "I'll never stop convincing you of it, Amala mate."

When Amala returned to the temple to prepare for the first ceremony of the day, Hawk reached the rest of his friends in the middle of the plane. It took him a while to find them among the multitude of people, until finally he recognised Naressa's flaming hair.

"Drinking before sunrise?"

He noticed Blade drinking beside her.

"A new record," she replied, chugging down the rest of her glass. "How's Amala doing?"

"She's coping."

Naressa hummed, glancing over her shoulder. "Blood results came back an hour ago. There *was* Qelcena in the hibiscus tea. It didn't make any sense without the blood pact, but now—fuck, Hawk. Did she die without facing her killer?"

"*If* she had a killer," Blade added. "Aarush called for her and she didn't answer. The blood pact cursed her and she died. It's not like someone killed her *directly*."

The way Blade summed it up so quickly gave him chills: all the work they had done, leading to nothing. Serabel's secrets — her deals and promises of a restored Charal tribe — made no sense in the end, though Hawk sent the thought away: something still felt abnormally out of place.

"Where's Wahine?" He asked.

"She's not here yet. She was excited, though." Blade replied. "She couldn't come on the Water day because of different shifts at the orphanage, but today she's bringing the grown-ups: the ones finally old enough to attend." He half-yawned. "Everyone wants to do drugs on Madakahiri, so we've been working through a ton of orders this past week."

Hawk sneered, but his face betrayed a hint of worry at the feeling brewing in his gut. Naressa probably noticed, shifting closer to him.

"You've got this, Hawk."

"I don't," he gritted his teeth. "Not yet. I can't scratch the feeling away."

He hated how defeated his voice sounded. It was supposed to be Amala's day, he knew how hard this was going to be for her, and yet all he could do was obsess over a case he hadn't solved.

"We should try to keep our eyes open."

When they started walking to the temple, the plane in front of Helioneis was packed with people from every element, district, town and village. Hawk's brain merely repeated a single thought.

Eyes open.

☼

Amala finished her prayer and nodded to Sinayla. It was her turn.

The priestess stepped forward, taking her place in front of the altar, and began to chant.

Mighty Sun,
And merciful light.
Heal, warm, shine,
bless us with your heat and your intensity,
for you are born to be worshipped
and we are born to bask in your power.

Caelan joined her, their voices fusing together. Amala had never heard anything more beautiful.

Two mates in love.

Two mates who had started a family together — created *life* together.

Something she may never be able to do.

Her chest ached at the thought but she sent the thought away and searched for Hawk in the audience. She spotted the Prior and his beautiful mate, Eset, whose pregnant womb was growing day by day.

Hawk wasn't near them, though.

Amala searched again, but no luck.

She sighed, eyes settling on Sinayla and Caelan. Her sister's face glowed in the sun, pure love in her eyes: the will to remember that moment forever.

The chant ended and applause erupted. Sinayla bowed solemnly, a grin in the direction of the priestesses. And then it was their turn. Amala's eyes trailed outside of the window as though she could procrastinate this one second, stretching it as much as she could to avoid what came next.

But the second passed.

Mistress of the Night,
Lady of Water flow,
Surge when lovers fight,
Stand when shadows grow.

Bringer of life,
She's both and she's neither.
Holding the knife,
That makes her moon-breather.

Amala gasped for air, searching the crowd for Hawk again. He wasn't there.

Hebex glanced at her mid-song, knowing what was going through her head yet unable to do anything about it. Well, she couldn't.

It wasn't like Amala could ask them to stop worshipping their Goddess just because *she* was the next vessel. It didn't work that way. The priestesses were sworn to the Goddess, *whoever* she was.

For carrying a secret,
So deep in her soul.
For her heart beats so strong,
That two make her whole.

She needed to leave.

Amala winced as the song unfolded: her sisters chanting for a Goddess that *was* there, was one of them. She didn't deserve them, or any of this. The small part of her convinced that perhaps there was a chance that she could be Goddess vanished in a whisper.

Silently, she slipped away.

There were too many priestesses in the front row for anyone to notice, managing to leave the altar without catching their eye. Once she was out of reach, Amala ran.

Helioneis' corridors were empty; she was out of breath, but kept running anyway.

Running from the ceremony, running from her priestesses.

Running from reality — a reality she couldn't make real.

She chose an alcove at the end of a hallway, slumping against the wall and bringing her knees to her chest. No longer could she repress the tears.

It cannot be me, she sobbed.

Please, anyone but me.

She recalled the other day, playing with her power on the balcony. How beautiful it was, to feel her own Love against her skin. To know with certainty how strongly and fiercely she loved. For a moment, it had almost felt right to be Goddess.

And then everything had crumbled.

Serabel had *planned* this.

Not like that and not this way, but Serabel had *known* Amala would be next. If Amala had known before, perhaps... but finding out the way she had, so close to Madakahiri —

"Amala!"

She lifted her head, all hopes of finding Hawk vanishing as she noticed Medyr approach her, pacing fast across the empty corridor. He looked handsome in his priest attire, white robes and a decorative dagger strapped to his arm.

"Go back to the celebration," she told him. "You cannot miss it."

Medyr stopped in front of her, offering a hand she didn't take.

"Come back with me."

"I can't."

Amala met his golden eyes.

"Medyr, I can't be there. I can't stand it."

He paused for a moment, eyes trailing her face while he considered.

"Alright," he said in the end. "Come with me."

CHAPTER 61

H awk was too slow to reach the main room and missed his chance to sit next to Zale. He spent the whole ritual in the back, barely able to see. There were so many people. He had never experienced Madakahiri like that. After becoming Zale's Second — soon after moving to Aglatas — he had sat with the Prior in the front row ever since. Hawk liked Madakahiri, but he liked Verbamadeni more. Especially since meeting Amala.

He searched for Amala now but the multitude of people made her difficult to spot. Even finding Blade or Cairo would be great too; he didn't want to lose any of them in the crowd, especially not before they were drunk from Aarush's magic.

Since it was unlikely Blade could go more than two hours without smoking, he was probably outside.

He joined the long line of people eager to leave the temple hall, to reach the rest of the celebration outside. From the raised porch, there was a much better visual. Hawk spotted Blade, Cairo and Naressa across the plane down the columns, where the newly gifted stream bordered the temple.

He hoped they would stay there until he reached them. As he managed the crowd, he wasn't far when he halted at the call of his name.

"Hawk?"

He turned. A beautiful dark-skinned woman with feline eyes moved for him, a pleasant smile on her face.

"Wahine," he greeted.

"Have you seen Blade?"

"Yeah, I was trying to find him." He nodded in the direction of the pillars, offering his arm so she wouldn't lose him in the crowd.

"It was a beautiful ritual, wasn't it?" Wahine said happily. "Your High Priestess looked incredible under the sun. She looked *made* for the sun."

Hawk would have agreed if had he seen her officiate, though he trusted Wahine was right. Amala would have been breath-taking.

He had seen her on Air day: she had looked like the Goddess she was and he had fallen in love with her even more. He probably did every time he got to see her embrace her full role as High Priestess — she had a different type of confidence and her power whirled through the rows of people.

Wahine spotted Blade and ran into his arms.

"Hello, little drop."

"Where the hell were you?" Naressa asked Hawk, knotting her brows.

"Lost in the crowd," he grunted.

Cairo handed him a joint and he took it without hesitation. Yet he felt nervous. Restless. Uneasy.

"Hawk, chill," Naressa muttered, sensing his distress. "Is something wrong?"

He shook his head. He wasn't sure.

Naressa kept an eye on him as she finally smiled at Wahine.

"Hi, girl. How's stuff going at the orphanage?"

"It's calm," she shrugged. "I'm going back there soon. I'll have to keep an eye on the ones who came with me. There's no way I'll let them join the orgies."

Naressa laughed.

"So, you brought them to the boring part of the day?" Cairo said. "Way to get them into the whole spiritual thing."

Wahine chuckled. "The spiritual part *is* beautiful, the ceremony was so authentic. But me? I know absolutely nothing of their whole system. I didn't even know *he* was the High Priest."

"Medyr?" Blade echoed. "Yeah. Since when did you care about religious stuff?"

"Oh, I don't," she chuckled. "I would have addressed him properly, if I had known."

Hawk thought that was unusual. Wahine never cared much for titles, probably a consequence of the hierarchical bullying she endured as a child. A title didn't make a person and there were only some instances where Wahine would address people appropriately, often coaxing their Egos just the right amount to—

Strike a deal.

Realisation hit Hawk, his brain pacing faster than his heartbeat.

"When did you talk to him?"

Wahine shrugged.

"A couple months ago? He came to the Den."

His jaw dropped. Blade stopped smoking.

"He what?"

"He came to the Den." Wahine repeated, confused by the sudden change in their behaviour.

"What for?"

"What do you mean *what for*? I deal in poisons. He wanted some."

Hawk exchanged a brief glance with Naressa. Blade's jaw was set, serious eyes fixed on his sister.

"Why didn't you tell us?"

"Why would I tell you? I didn't even know who he was."

"Had you ever seen him before?" Cairo asked.

Wahine shook her head.

"No, but... wait, is this linked to your case?"

"Just answer the fucking question, Wahine." Blade snarled.

"God and Goddess, calm down! He was in a rush and paid a lot for me to deliver the poison right away."

"What poison?" Hawk asked.

"Anyeth."

☆

"I can't believe I spent half my life here and never knew about this tunnel." Amala said.

Medyr chuckled.

"I spent *all* my life here and had no idea it existed."

"Fair enough," she said with a giggle. "Do you and Hebs come down here often?"

"Sometimes."

Amala smirked. She liked the idea of her friend feeling safe with Medyr.

"Do you love her?"

His smile was quick in answer. "I do. I haven't told her yet so *don't you dare*." As he heard her faint laugh, his eyes lit up. "Do you feel better, now?"

Amala paused, leaning against the smooth wall.

"I know it sounds crazy. I should trust the divine energy more than anyone, but... I would have accepted anybody else but me. Why me?"

"I've told you already and I'll tell you again. I cannot think of anyone that deserves to be Goddess more than you do."

"But..."

"There's *no* but, Amala. Don't you see why you deserve it?"

She wanted to say no. She would've said no, had she not felt that love on her own skin not that long ago.

"It's not that." She admitted. "It's not just a matter of loving and deserving... I gave my life to the Goddess. I was ready — I *am* ready to serve her until my last breath. Surely no one with such a deep sense of worship *wishes* to be her instead. I never did. I wanted to serve her, not be her."

"Do you think some people deserve it more than others?"

"What do you mean?"

"Take Darnen and Aarush. Who deserved it more?"

Amala shook her head.

"I am no one to speak about this."

"You *are* the Goddess. No one *but* you can have a say on this."

"Even if I'm Goddess, I still don't have a say." She countered. "Darnen was incredible. But Aarush? He's good too. His soul needs to unwind, but it *is* settled on the good."

"You can't seriously believe that."

"If he's made vessel, there's a reason Medyr."

He was silent for a while.

"You have your answer, then." He said.

"What?"

"If you've been made vessel, Amala, there's a reason."

She was ready to ignore the tang of truth that pinched her soul. Instead, her eyes found his.

"Show me the Charal graffiti."

☼

"I *need* to speak with Aarush," Hawk repeated, "Now."

"He cannot see you now," the priest replied, for what was now the tenth time. "He's busy."

"I couldn't care less if he's fucking someone right now, open this door or get out of the way." He refrained from baring his teeth. One way or another, he needed to get to Aarush.

"What's going on?"

He turned, Blade followed. Hebex sauntered towards them, a red rose in her honeyed hair. She wore the glow that adorned each priestess during the God's festivities, each of her steps adequately measured.

"We need to talk with Aarush. Right now."

"I think Maeve is with him," she said, glancing at the priest who blocked the entrance. "Seth, what the fuck? You know who they are."

"Aarush won't be pleased if anyone gets in."

"Aarush will have a fucking orgasm if anyone walks in on him having sex," Hebex replied, quick to grab the door handle. Unquestioning of Hawk or Blade's request, she forced the doors open. There was a gasp, accompanied by a dark laugh; Hawk didn't need to see the scene before him to know what was going on.

"Apologies, my God." Hebex said for them, lips quirking in a smirk as she took in the view. A petite priestess was sitting on Aarush's lap, her curious eyes sparkling. "Captain Mercurian really needs to talk to you. He said it's urgent."

Aarush's golden eyes surveyed him, then Blade. The last time they had spoken was that day at the Raging Heart, but Hawk knew something had shifted in the God that day. The same expression was on his face now. Aarush knew Hawk wouldn't demand an audience merely to spite him. Whatever was going on must be serious.

"What's this about?" His voice betrayed the same hint of worry, despite attempting a look of annoyance.

Hebex nodded at the priestess with an apologetic glance.

"I think you guys should take a rain check and let the Captain do his work. Sorry, Maeve."

"That's alright," she said, stepping out of Aarush's lap. Her gaze lingered on Hawk. "Is everyone alright?"

"Hopefully," he said through gritted teeth. He waited for Maeve to leave the room, Hebex with her, then turned to Aarush.

"You said no one knew about the pact."

"No one knows," Aarush said impatiently. "The same way Serabel didn't tell Amala, I didn't tell a soul. No one else but us knew."

"What about Medyr?"

The God sighed.

"I already told you, he doesn't know either. He's not my biggest fan; I don't think he could have learned about it."

"Well, he did. He bought the anyeth."

Hawk had never seen Aarush look so surprised; the God was stunned into silence, his brain working overtime to process such information. Aarush almost died because of the anyeth: losing his mind for weeks, a warped cognition of time and space and life. He had not realised it brought Serabel to death, not even that she died on the same day until months later, and now... to learn Medyr was responsible?

Aarush blinked.

"How do you—"

"My twin is the Mistress of Venoms," Blade said with a shrug. Hawk had never seen him interact with the God before, but had a hunch Aarush would like him. His eyebrows indeed furrowed, as if he had heard the name before.

"And you think he bought the anyeth for me?"

Hawk sighed, close to losing patience.

"He bought it the same day you were poisoned, right after learning Serabel was taking an energy inhibitor. He must have known. He *must* have known that giving you the anyeth was going to trigger your pact and get Serabel killed."

"Serabel was taking an inhibitor? Wh—because she was sick?"

"Amala prepared her tea with Qelcena leaves." Hawk quickly explained. "There was no way for Serabel to send her energy back when you called."

Aarush took in the news with a slow blink. It *had* been his fault, he now realised. If he had known, perhaps, he wouldn't have called her, refusing to risk Serabel's life by activating the pact. A low murmur came from him a moment later.

"Medyr *hates* me. He thinks I don't know but I do. He's nothing like Amala was for Serabel. He does not admire me; he thinks I'm unfit for this role and doesn't even hide it."

"Which sounds like a good fucking reason to poison you." Hawk seethed.

"If he poisoned me to kill Serabel, then I'm next. He can't harm me, not personally — none of my priests can. But Amala could, especially now that she is..." *Goddess.*

Yet Aarush hesitated, as if unwilling to say the word. Instead, he raised his gaze on Hawk.

"*Does* Medyr know about—"

"He does." Hawk hoped Aarush wouldn't reveal Amala's divinity to Blade, not in such a moment — not without her allowing it.

But the God only said, "If Medyr had the guts to kill the Goddess, he won't hesitate in doing the same with me. He just needs to convince Amala to help him."

Blade exchanged a glance with Hawk, mirroring the worry on his face. "And where's Amala?"

The silence that stretched in the room felt painful. Hawk's breath caught, invasive thoughts flurrying with his midnight wind. He rushed out of the room with Blade on his heels, storming out of the doors in time to catch a glimpse of honeyed hair.

"Hebs!"

She turned to him, startled at his tone.

"Yes?"

"Where's Medyr?"

She bit the inside of her cheek, recalling. "Haven't seen him in a while. He said he was going to check on Amala."

"Do you know where they are?"

Hebex shook her head. "Why? Is everything okay?"

Hawk considered. How could he tell her that her own boyfriend possibly murdered her Goddess? What words would Amala choose in his place? But there was no time to think now — if Amala was with Medyr, if Aarush was right, he had to hurry and Hebex—

Hawk's grey eyes blinked studying the priestess, as the morbid realisation sunk in.

"You are his alibi."

"I'm what?"

Hebex wasn't at the temple the night Serabel died because she was with Medyr. Medyr didn't need to be *there* to trigger the blood pact, no. He needed to be somewhere else — *doing* something else, ensuring he was out of the way for as long as possible.

Hawk had always thought Hebex was far too extroverted for his liking, yet he could count on her. From that first moment at the Yonium, it was plain on her face: Amala was the person she cared about the most.

"Amala could be in danger, Hebs, I need to find her. Any idea where they might be?"

She shut her eyes, trying to concentrate. "I don't know where they went after the ritual, but Medyr likes the tunnel. And Amala hasn't seen it, yet."

The tunnel.

The goddamn tunnel *Hawk* had showed him.

Fuck. They could be anywhere along the path. Blade was already on the phone with Cairo as Hawk turned down another corridor, planning his next move. He needed to find Amala.

Aarush and Hebex? Their answers could wait.

Amala, Amala, Amala.

But as he tried to remember the path to the tunnel, he felt a sharp pull and found himself thrown off his steps. Hidden in the shadows of a darker alcove, he saw the gleam of a blade.

"What the f—"

There was a swish of long braided hair and a flash of white canines, then a faint spark. The Phoenix held the dagger in her hand, spinning it with disarming ease.

"Where is she?"

☼

Amala traced her fingers over the upward crescent moon etched into the wall, quite certain it was drawn with blood.

"I would have loved to meet them." she let herself admit.

"You might take over Serabel's mission, perhaps." Medyr suggested. He was observing other symbols, the flowy shape that meant *kuris*: blood.

"I know nothing about her plans, Medyr. She seemed more inclined to share them with anyone but me."

He didn't contradict her. It was true.

"You know what? You probably know more about her plans than I do." Amala turned her back to the wall and crossed to the graffiti on the other side.

"You're not wrong," Medyr mumbled.

Amala raised her gaze in the dim light of the tunnel.

"What do you mean?"

He stepped toward her. "I didn't say it in front of Hebs because I thought you wouldn't like that. But even before you told us the truth, I wondered about it."

He paused. Amala pursed her lips. "What?"

"If you were the next vessel."

"How could you know?"

She saw a flash of Medyr's teeth in the semi-darkness, then heard him chuckle.

"Serabel mentioned it a couple of times. At first, I thought you knew. Then I realised you had no idea and she was keeping it from you. But you know now, so it doesn't matter."

Amala wanted to counter that it *did* matter, actually. That she would have gladly liked to know before the moon shone on her on a frozen stream in Ulbaros. But she supposed there was no point, Medyr was right. She knew now. And there was nothing she could do about it.

Yet, to know that Serabel had told Medyr, *Medyr* and *not* her...

"I'd rather not talk about how Serabel didn't trust me enough with the truth — she trusted Aarush more than me!"

Although it pained Amala to admit it, she had thought she was the first choice for her Goddess. If Aarush's words were true, if Serabel was in love with her—

She couldn't think about that now. Those were exactly the thoughts that triggered her panic attack back at the temple. But that moment felt long ago; Amala had lost track of time as she descended through the tunnel. Had it been minutes? Hours?

It all felt the same.

"She cared about you," Medyr said. "And you were always there for her."

"Tell me about it," she sighed. "I knew her routine better than mine."

"Coconut oil and hibiscus tea."

She frowned at the mention of hibiscus tea. It had been *her* fault that Serabel was so low on energy the night she died — *Amala* had made her the tea. It didn't matter her Goddess had requested so, guilt consumed her. She didn't want to talk about it. How did Medyr know, anyway?

"It's alright to be mad at her, Amala," Medyr said from behind her, "Serabel kept so much from you. I understand if you feel angry. Even if she was your Goddess."

"I want to justify her... but sometimes I don't think I can."

"It's okay. It's reasonable."

"I would have liked to know more about the Charal," Amala admitted, observing the symbols of all the fierce women she would never have a chance to meet. Was Serabel helping them? Had she helped them at all? Her heart ached at the thought. Desperately, she wished to help them... but Serabel had only asked questions, *too* many question now unanswered forever.

"So many secrets and for what?" She murmured. "Me, this whole vessel story... the Charal."

"I bet she knew about this fucking tunnel too," Medyr muttered. "And that idiocy of a blood pact..."

"Yeah, that t—"

Amala's lips froze mid-sentence.

Aarush said Medyr didn't know about the blood pact.

But he did, apparently.

He knew about it.

He knew about the blood pact, and he knew about the hibiscus tea.

She gaped at him, realising way too much than she should've.

And, a second later, he realised it too.

CHAPTER 62

Amala froze, her body refusing to move from the spot next to the wall. Medyr stepped towards her and she flinched, regretting it a moment later. She wasn't sure what was going on but Hawk's voice rang clear in her mind.

Safety first. Find somewhere safe.

"I'm cold," she said, lips quivering. She hated the way her voice betrayed her fear.

Amala needed to find Hawk. She didn't know what she would do next, but she needed to tell Hawk that Medyr *knew* about the blood pact, that he knew too much.

"Can we go back?" she asked, daring to look at him.

Play dumb. Play fucking dumb, she told herself.

"So you can tell your boyfriend about it?"

Her heart was beating so fast she feared Medyr could hear it.

"What do you mean?" Amala asked, attempting to recompose.

"I've known you since we were kids, Amala. You're nice, not stupid."

"I'm... thanks?"

She needed to get out.

How far was the temple?

Which way should she go? Which temple was closer?

But she caught a glimpse of Medyr's face and saw what his eyes conveyed. The depth of his gaze almost scared her, and part of her knew he wouldn't willingly let her go.

"How do you know about their blood pact?" His voice rang cold.

Amala blinked in confusion.

What did he mean? Surely Medyr knew that—

No, she realised. He didn't. Medyr had no idea Aarush had confided in them about the blood pact. He couldn't know. He only knew what she had told him.

It had been a test, a hazard.

Medyr was willing to give up his own cover just to check what Amala knew and if she knew enough. And she had fallen for it. Because if she knew, it meant she could finally piece the puzzle together.

Glancing back at him, Amala tried to master the panic in her face.

"How do you know, Amala?"

Fuck, fuck, fuck.

She was speechless, unable to think of a lie.

What would Hawk do in her place?

Did he even know she wasn't at the temple? Had he noticed?

Medyr took another step as Amala's throat dried. She tried to speak and failed. She didn't interrupt contact with Medyr's gaze as she swallowed.

"Serabel—"

"Don't play with me. You just said Serabel didn't tell you about it." She couldn't breathe.

What could she say, without giving away everything that her and Hawk had uncovered? Without giving Medyr the option to cover up each truth before she was able to tell Hawk?

"Did Aarush tell you?" He insisted.

Amala quickly shook her head, far too unconvincingly.

"You can tell me, Amala." Medyr took another step. He faced her now, head on. He was much taller, forcing a lift of her chin to look him in the eyes. Though Amala was frozen in place, unable to summon her energy. Helioneis was likely far away probably, but it was worth a try. Her new energy. Her Goddess energy.

There was no way she could send it without Medyr realising, but it was the only option she had to try to reach Hawk. Closing her eyes, Amala summoned her energy from that deep, secret part inside of her.

Ready, it said, as though the divine part within her soul yearned to be used.

Amala basked in that feeling of power. She felt stronger. She was a Goddess.

Medyr couldn't hurt her. He couldn't fucking hurt her.

Amala let her energy go, directing it to the temple. To Hawk. It was a long shot, unsure if he would even receive it but she was out of options.

Medyr blinked, and she knew he felt it too.

"What did you do?" He asked, voice low.

"You're right." Amala said, "Aarush told me about the blood pact."

There was no strategy. She supposed she could distract him by giving him the answer he wanted, at least until Hawk found her. That or she would run at the first given chance.

"Did you send your energy to the temple?"

"I didn't." She swallowed again. "How do *you* know about the blood pact?"

"You know too fucking much." He muttered, ignoring her question.

"There's an investigation about it!" Amala snapped.

"How did you get to talk to Aarush? Did you—" his eyes darkened, pinning her in place. "Did you dance for him?"

Amala hated the blush that swept her cheeks.

"Yes."

Medyr's eyes narrowed, but then he laughed.

"I can't believe Captain Mercurian let his *mate* dance for Aarush."

"Hawk doesn't *let* me do anything," Amala retorted furiously. "I did it because *I* wanted answers."

"And what answers did you get?" He spat. "Were you happy to know that your Goddess died unable to resist it? That she didn't even know *why* she was dying?"

Amala's words died on her tongue.

She had refused to acknowledge Medyr's involvement — playing dumb, asking to leave — all of that to stop the unceasing feeling that he was responsible for everything.

"What did you do?" She breathed, chest heaving.

Could Medyr smell her fear?

"I've done nothing, Amala. *You* told me about the hibiscus tea."

She had. She recalled it now during his visit to the Yonium. Amala prepared the tea in front of him, careful to add the right quantity of Qelcena leaves. Medyr had known. How could she have forgotten?

The tea had inhibited Serabel, enough to make her unreachable when Aarush was...

"*You* poisoned Aarush?"

Medyr grinned, though it was a strange grin: not amused, no. Proud.

"I told you. You aren't stupid."

"You poisoned Aarush, knowing it would trigger the blood pact. Knowing it would kill Serabel?"

Medyr's face was unreadable, aside from a hint of pride Amala noted instantly. Was he proud of her for figuring it out? Was this a joke, was Amala missing some fundamental link in all of this?

"Why would you do it?" She whispered, lips wincing in disgust.

"For you, you ungrateful bitch."

The words hit her like a slap in the face. She bared her teeth at him.

"Take it *back*."

"Growing claws now, are we? After spending years pretending you had no idea what people said about you? I did it for *you*, but you're too busy feeling bad for them to open your eyes."

"What do you mean you did it for *me*? How could you think I would ever appreciate you killing my Goddess?"

Medyr snorted.

"I didn't kill anyone. And Serabel's death made *you* Goddess." His tone as he spoke Serabel's name made Amala wince, a silent anger shimmering in her icy gaze. He went on. "I knew it was going to happen. I knew you were next, she knew and was stupid enough to tell me her suspicions. Aarush knew too. Serabel just didn't have the fucking balls to do it."

Amala shook her head, refusing to acknowledge a single word. How could he have known? How could Serabel confide in *him* but not her? Her High Priestess. Medyr glimpsed the look on her face and gave a half smile, smug satisfaction clear on his features.

"Don't you see? They *never* cared about us. Aarush is an asshole; he never deserved to be God from the day I found out he was the new vessel. And Serabel — do you think she cared about you? Wouldn't she have told you her suspicions?"

Serabel was in love with you, Aarush had told her.

"But no," Medyr continued. "You act like a fucking ungrateful brat and blame me when I did you a favour, High Priestess."

A favour?

"What exactly did you think would happen? Did you think I would fucking thank you?"

"You weren't supposed to know about their blood pact. If anything, it's proof they didn't care about you enough to tell you the truth."

He couldn't be serious? To think Amala would ever disrespect her Goddess by thinking so low of her. She had learned Serabel's secrets on her own accord: it was clear now Serabel never trusted her, and though her heart ached at the realisation, even knowing she had been part of her Goddess' plans the whole time hadn't stopped Amala from forgiving her. She always did and always would.

Medyr knew nothing if he thought she felt anything from Serabel other than pure, undiluted love.

"What do you want from me, Medyr?"

"I want you to help me kill Aarush. I cannot kill him by myself, but you — as a Goddess — *you* can. You haven't sworn a pact to him. And once he's dead..." His silence stretched for a moment too long, Amala blinking in surprise as if she never expected to have such a realisation.

"You think you'll be next?"

"I *know* I'll be next."

"But how can you..."

"The High Priestess became Goddess. The High Priest shall be God too. If it worked once, it can work again."

He couldn't be serious. Amala would give up everything to return to when she was just High Priestess and Medyr would kill for the opposite? To *be* God?

"You liar." She hissed. "You said you did it for me but you're lying. You did this to test your fucking theory before making a move yourself."

"It wasn't my theory, it was *your* Goddess' theory."

"She was your Goddess too." Amala snapped. "And now I am."

"Finally, Amala." Medyr chuckled, the sound dark enough to make her shiver, "You just need to be brave, embody that power once and for all. Aren't you tired of the way Aarush treats you? He won't change just because you're Goddess, but I will."

"It doesn't work like that, Medyr. You cannot be God."

"Why can't I?"

"Because you *want* it. Have you learned nothing? That's not how a vessel works. It has never been about yourself. You should want your power for *others*. It's the only way you can make it work. You—" Amala paused, afraid her next words would risk her chance of getting out alive. Medyr peered down at her, almost in challenge.

"I?"

"You would *never* be picked as vessel."

He winced, her words finding their mark. His voice came out even lower a moment later. "I don't want the power for me. I want to be what I have worshipped my whole life. I want to be what Aarush doesn't deserve to be, but I do. I gave my life to the God."

"I gave my life to my Goddess too, but not like that."

"Then how?"

"Not with jealousy. With honesty."

Her words were followed by thick silence. But as Medyr took a step back, Amala released a breath: he would let her go. Finally, Medyr had come to his senses and was ready to let her go.

"Are you not even going to consider the possibility?"

Amala cocked her head, surprised he would ask her again. Stepping aside, she finally dared to move from the wall. Her voice resonated in the deserted tunnel.

"You can get lost. I'm not going to help you kill Aarush."

With a courage she didn't think she would find, Amala turned her back.

But his voice followed before she could take another step.

"You won't?" he repeated, "That's a shame. What would Hebex say?"

CHAPTER 63

There was no sound in the tunnel, except for the irregularity of Amala's breathing. Eyes adjusted to the semi-darkness, she searched Medyr's face for a lie.

"You—you *love* Hebs. You wouldn't hurt her."

"I do, you're right. And I won't hurt her. You will, if you rat me out."

"I mean, I'm sure she loves you, but she'll get over you once she finds out you killed our Goddess."

He chuckled again. Amala had started to hate when he did so.

"It's a shame she's the one who served Aarush the anyeth then, isn't it?"

Amala's blood ran cold. Not once had Medyr ever scared her but now, when she looked at him, her knees buckled. She needed to reach the wall to lean against it, to try and steady herself.

"What?"

"Do you seriously think Aarush would drink anything *I* give him? He's stupid, but not that stupid."

"So what? You told Hebs to do it?"

He grinned and Amala thanked the Goddess for the support of the wall, her body moments from crumbling beneath the rising fear within her.

"I asked her to prepare his wine while I checked on a ritual, told her the anyeth was some ecstasy drug Aarush liked."

"She's not stupid, she would have known it wasn't ecstasy."

"Well, that's on her. There's a whole footage of Hebex preparing the wine *and* serving it. You can thank Aarush's brilliant idea to set cameras around the temple for that."

Amala cursed. Her words came out louder than she thought.

"So what? Do you think this is gonna stop me from telling—" she paused before saying Hawk's name, "From revealing what happened?"

"If you want Hebex to stay out of jail, I guess you will."

"You wouldn't do this to her."

"Fucking try me, High Priestess."

Amala looked up — a habitual movement to check the sky. But there was no sky, only an endless ceiling consumed by darkness. Amala had no idea of the time now. Had she missed all the rituals? It couldn't be sunset yet, could it?

Had she missed *sunset*?

Was Hawk even searching for her?

Of course he is, she reassured herself.

Amala needed to wait until Hawk arrived without setting Medyr off. That would work. It had to work.

Buy some time.

But what would she do, then? Even if Hawk caught Medyr red-handed — what would happen to Hebex, then?

What was the alternative? Pretending it had never happened, all to protect her sister? Acting as though Medyr hadn't poisoned Aarush to kill Serabel, to test his theory in confirmation that *he* could be the next

God? Serabel had suffered an unjust fate, but so would Hebex if Amala exposed the truth.

Amala let it happen once — allowed her Goddess to die by revealing too much to Medyr. She wouldn't let it happen to her sister too. But what excuse could she conjure for Hawk? How could she lie to him after Hawk devoted months trying to discover the truth?

And how would he not notice that she was lying? He'd always seen all of her.

Later. Figure that out later.

Just get out.

"Your thoughts are loud," Medyr observed. He stood close — *too* damn close to her. "Care to share what's going on in your head?"

"I just don't understand how you would want to fail so many people that love you. Hebex loves you, Medyr. And you're a brother to me, for fuck's sake."

"If I were a brother to you, you would fucking help."

Amala ignored him, though he took a step closer as he continued.

"You have options. One, you help me kill Aarush. Or two, you rat me out and Hebex and I are sent to jail. I only *bought* the poison, which isn't illegal. Hebex was the one who gave it to him. Chances are we go to trial — they let me go, but keep her in."

"Do you seriously think you have more power over Harat than Hawk does?" Amala snorted.

"You don't want to testify against me, Amala."

"Or what?"

"Or I'll tell all your priestesses that you've been chosen to be Goddess and have kept it from them for weeks. They deserve to know, don't you think?"

Her heart sank. Amala had gathered enough in those past minutes to understand Medyr was ruthless, but she wasn't expecting that.

"You... you can't do that."

He couldn't. He *wouldn't*. She would lose all of her sisters — she would fail them and lose their trust and support. Amala wasn't ready to fail someone else, not after failing Serabel. But Medyr left her no choice.

Whatever option she chose, she would fail someone.

Her priestesses, Hawk, or Hebex.

And herself.

Herself and...

Time passed, but Amala lost track of the silence between them until Medyr raised an eyebrow, attempting to prompt an answer.

"What's the third option?"

He hesitated, but it was only a moment before he spoke again, his voice now low and gravelly.

"Give it up. Give your power to someone else."

Amala was confused to say the least. Give it up? Could she give it up?

Yes, was her instinctive thought.

Give it up. Anyone is worthier than us.

It couldn't be. She had felt that power merge within her: her soul, skin, heart, and bones fusing with that divine energy: the night under the Ulbaros' moon. If there was a way to give it up, she would know.

She would have tried.

"I don't think I can."

"You don't want to, you mean."

"If it was possible, Medyr, I would have done it the first day. Trust me."

She would have, at first, it was true; but now things were different.

My Goddess of Love, Hawk called her.

"Give the power to me." Medyr insisted.

"I can't, for fuck's sake! The Goddess must be someone who identifies as a woman."

"You don't actually believe that."

"I believe that keeping masculine and feminine separated is complete bullshit, *yes*, but it doesn't mean I can give my power to you."

It *was* bullshit — she had never believed it for a day.

Why was the Moon feminine and the Sun male? Why did the division of power revolve around being male or female? She despised the concept and didn't try to hide it.

"Everything you're saying goes against a millennia of divine power." She murmured.

"We can change that, Amala. We *can* change that. We—"

Medyr halted and Amala seized the opportunity to take a steadying breath. She was running out of ideas, afraid Medyr would harm her. Never would she have expected that to be possible before, but now she wasn't sure.

"Kill Aarush for me. Let me be God. And I'll make you Goddess of the Sun."

He would... what? Amala blinked. She couldn't help picturing herself in the temple: the sky shining through the tall windows, soothing her body — imagined standing on the balcony, back home, clearing the cloudy sky so she could see the sunrise.

Amala, Goddess of the Sun.

A part of her cried at the thought.

Would she finally be worthy — *feel* worthy — if she was Goddess of the Sun?

Would that unpleasant feeling of emptiness leave? A whisper said yes, only she knew it wasn't true. It didn't matter what power she had or what way she used it. It didn't matter if she could control the Sun and the clouds and the skies, witnessing all the sunrises and sunsets that she craved.

That wasn't the way to do it.

And Amala had never wished to be a Goddess in the first place.

The vision disappeared as dread pooled in her stomach.

"No, Medyr."

He took a final step, Amala now wedged between him and the wall.

"No?"

"Get the fuck away from me."

"No, you said?"

He didn't move, leaning in closer to her face. Amala's mind scrambled for purchase.

"No. I'm not going to do any of this. I'll shut up to protect Hebex, but I'm not—"

He snickered.

"Sweet, innocent Amala. Do you seriously think if *you* figured me out, the Captain won't? You can't stop that from happening."

"So what?" she breathed, fighting the urge to shove him away.

"I think it wouldn't hurt to have one less witness."

His words lingered in the air between them. He moved, and the dagger on his arm glimmered in the darkness. Amala's breath caught. Medyr *would* harm her and she cursed herself for thinking otherwise, for hoping he cared enough not to.

He was ready to *kill* Aarush — he was definitely going to harm her too.

Amala was still trying to master her Goddess power; she knew nothing of it, and there was no way to protect herself now.

But in that moment, as Medyr towered over her, she didn't feel like a Goddess at all. Not a Goddess, not a Goddess, *not* a Goddess — a woman, then.

Survival instincts kicking in, she did the only thing her brain could think of. Her knee struck quickly and precisely between his legs. He let slip a yelp of pain with some surprise too, as if he never believed her capable to do such a thing.

Amala ran.

The Yonium was off-limits. It was warded and she had no idea where the tunnel would lead to. She didn't even know how far she was, so went left. Toward Helioneis.

Medyr's pained voice cursed behind her, but she didn't stop.

Amala had no advantage over him, fearing she would soon grow tired: she was only buying time to figure out *how* to use her energy against him.

I summon you.

I summon you.

I summon you.

She felt it sparkle in her chest as her divine energy suddenly awakened.

Please, she begged, *Come to me.*

Amala ran for her life. Literally. The moment Medyr caught her, she was dead. Dead with no High Priestess to retain her energy, no one left to determine the next vessel, no one to care for her priestesses, no one to—

A branch, a harsh branch, brushed her ankle, and tried to wrap around it. Amala screamed in surprise and ran faster. *Shit.* Was Medyr going to chase her with his power?

Releasing a barrier of wind, Amala blocked the space behind her to prevent his magic from travelling through. She ran, eyes scanning the walls as if she could find a way out, an alley, a door — anything to help her desperate escape. But nothing: the only way to get out was to outrun Medyr.

His steps drew closer as she prayed her shield would slow him down, but it was no use. Energy and magic worked with emotion and she was too scared, too breathless, too terrified — her wind wouldn't protect her.

Another thread of ivy snaked on the floor, full of thorns and quick as a serpent. More emerged after, each pursuing her in chase. Amala tried to summon her wind but she couldn't — she groaned as the ivy wrapped around her ankle and pulled, yanking her to the ground. Knees bruising in the fall, she protected her face with her arms, elbows absorbing the impact on the cold floor. Amala made to stand up but the other branches seized her body, tightening until she was unable to move. Medyr's magic cornered her as he now strode in slower steps, enjoying the end of his chase.

Amala tried to stand but shit, the bruises hurt. Finally staring up at him, her true emotions shone. She didn't care how she appeared: a pleading Goddess. She would beg for her life, to see the Sun a final time.

"Please," she murmured, "Please, there's no need, I'll say nothing. I promise, I *promise*—" the words died in her throat as Medyr wrapped a hand around her neck, stealing her breath. Lifting her body until her toes scraped the floor, he shoved her against the wall.

"Your pretty doe eyes may work with Hawk, High Priestess, but he's not here now. Your *mate*," he blurted the words in disapproval. "Is not here. And I'm pretty sure he won't be here on time. Actually, I'm pretty certain I will be back long before someone finds your body."

She tried to breathe but she could barely inhale as his grip tightened on her throat. And she could only think of... she couldn't. She could think of anything as she tried — darkness circled her. Amala wanted to cry and fight, only she could do nothing.

Medyr let her go.

Amala gasped for air, as his body fell in front of her. Groaning in pain, he doubled over, recovered quickly, and spun around to face the attacker.

"Touch her again and you die."

No.

No.

No fucking way.

Amala whimpered in surprise, looking past Medyr to see for herself who approached them in the darkness.

The Phoenix.

☼

"Get away from her."

Medyr didn't.

Amala wanted to scream *move*, otherwise the Phoenix would kill him, but no words came. Unable to comprehend what was happening.

"Medyr, do what she says." Amala finally whispered.

"Shut the fuck up, Amala."

"Talk to her one more time, and I'm not gonna ask you again." The Phoenix said, dark eyes scanning Amala's body for injuries. *I'm okay,* Amala wanted to say, but she didn't think her voice would work. The Phoenix had come for her and now would kill Medyr. Perhaps she cared way too much for him, but Amala didn't want to watch him die.

"Medyr, *move,*" she pleaded, voice so feeble she thought he couldn't hear it. But he spat on the ground, dagger steady in his hand.

"I said shut up."

It's the fucking Phoenix, Amala wanted to scream, *she's going to kill you before you even blink.*

Medyr attacked first, but Amala knew it was a fight lost from the beginning. The Phoenix didn't allow him to get close before ducking to the side.

"Fucking stop," she hissed. "I will not kill you in front of her."

A spark of hope burst in Amala's chest. The Phoenix wasn't going to kill him, she—

Medyr moved again. Not to the Phoenix, this time, but towards the High Priestess. Amala glimpsed the blink of the dagger as he moved abruptly, faster than she ever thought he was able to. She felt a sting in her arm she cried out, but Medyr was down shortly after as his dagger clattered to the floor, far from them.

He didn't stand.

"What did you—" Amala started, wincing as she pressed a hand against her bicep — her wound. Blood rushed slick through her fingers.

"Are you hurt?"

"Did you—"

"Are you *hurt?*"

The Phoenix's voice echoed through the tunnel like thunder.

Amala shook her head, revealing her arm.

"He wasn't aiming, this is nothing. I can heal myself."

"He's not dead," she answered then. "Just out cold."

The Phoenix moved closer. Amala felt cold fingers on her skin and froze as her mate examined the cut, raising her other hand to light flames on her fingertips for better visual in the darkness. Why was her hand so cold? Shouldn't it be warm? She was made of fire...

Those fingers trailed to her neck.

"What about here?" She touched a spot and Amala winced.

"Is there a bruise?"

"A nasty one, but I've seen worse."

Amala held her breath as the Phoenix brushed her fingers against her skin, so lightly she may have imagined it. Only when she let go of her arm, Amala finally dared to meet her gaze.

"What are you doing here?" She murmured.

"Would you rather me have not come at all?"

Amala scoffed.

"No, I mean... how did you know where I was?"

The Phoenix surveyed her with those dark eyes.

"Your mate told me. He's on his way."

You're my mate.

She was close to saying it then.

What would happen, if she dared to?

Instead of speaking, Amala nodded and leaned against the wall, lowering to the floor. She hugged her knees as she sat. Hawk was coming. He would be there soon, and Amala would finally allow herself to cry in his arms.

CHAPTER 64

T he two women sat in silence for what felt an eternity.

Amala was certain the Phoenix wasn't breathing, or perhaps the own thumping of her heart drowned the sound. The mating bond twinged faintly in her chest. A thread made of fire that linked her soul to the woman beside her — supposedly, at least.

Amala couldn't feel anything at all coming from that thread. It burned though, so it was there.

The Phoenix had come to save her.

Hawk had told her where she was and she had come.

Did it mean something? Did the Phoenix recognize her as mate?

Her beautiful, hard face fixed on the opposite wall and Amala then realised she would likely never voice the word *mate* from her mouth. Was it even worth it? Why had the Phoenix saved her if she wanted nothing more?

Amala tilted her head, finding the Phoenix's dark eyes glued to her now instead.

Her heart beat faster.

"Thank you." She whispered.

Amala needed some comfort and the closest person was her mate, ignoring her from the moment they had met. The High Priestess barely extended her arm, before the Phoenix flinched and instantly moved away.

"Sorry," Amala whispered again.

The Phoenix said nothing. Glancing away, those eyes found Medyr's body still slumped against the opposite wall. She manipulated his robe to form bindings, tying his wrists and arms together. Amala was too shaken to point out the uselessness of those knots — anyone who knew about rope-play could spot that.

Amala repeated. "I'm sorry."

Though it didn't matter what she said, her mate never answered. Sitting together in the dark for an eternity of silence, she finally heard footsteps. Amala broke in a cry of relief once she heard Hawk call her name.

His voice.

The second it reached her ears, she knew she was safe. He was there; he had come for her. Hawk would hold Amala while she cried, wiping her tears and drying her cheeks with his wind.

"Hawk!" she called back.

Amala made to move but realised all the adrenaline, the energy which kept her alive was now completely gone. She was drained. The Phoenix shifted, rising to check on Medyr.

Footsteps grew closer, louder, echoing through the tunnel, and then they arrived. Hawk wasn't alone.

Hebex was with him. And Blade.

And... *Aarush*?

Had the God not been in Madakahiri just to go and find her?

Hebex reached her first. She knelt and hugged her without saying a word. And Amala, craving a hug, crumbled in her arms and sobbed.

"Hey, hey." Her sister whispered. "It's alright. You're safe. Hawk's here."

How could she start telling Hebex what had happened? Her voice trembled when she tried to talk, but Hebex held her tighter. It was Aarush who spoke next.

"What are *you* doing here?" He asked the Phoenix.

She simply glared.

"I found her."

Hawk didn't look surprised, but he didn't spare another glance before he was with Amala. Hebex moved away as he knelt before his mate, gently placing his hands on top of her knees, careful to avoid the bruises.

"I should have never let this happen, Amala mate."

"Medyr did it," was all she could say, trying to wipe her tears.

"I know. I figured it out at the temple but when I realised, you were gone already."

Her heart sank with relief. He *knew*.

Medyr was right. He knew. She didn't have to do anything, nor would she fail anyone. Hawk knew already.

"I've been so stupid, Hawk. I should have never let him lure me here."

"You weren't stupid, my Goddess of Love. You were hurt. And Medyr was your friend."

"Yeah, before he tried to kill me."

Hawk halted. His midnight wind snaked around her neck, soothing the bruise there.

"He tried?"

Amala nodded.

"If the Phoenix hadn't arrived when she did, he would have succeeded. Thank you for telling her where I was."

"Well, I didn't have much of a choice," he countered, and Amala saw a flash of a smile. "She cornered me and threatened to kill *me* if I didn't tell her."

Amala's lips parted in surprise, but she did her best not to look at the woman made of fire. Hawk had not just told her, *she* had asked him first.

She had asked him about her.

Hawk's wind surrounded Amala and she realised she would fall asleep soon, surrendering to exhaustion.

"Hebs is in trouble," she managed to say, words slurring. "Medyr—he made her..."

"I'll sort it out, my love. Hebex will be fine, I promise. You can sleep now."

No, she made to say, but she was already drifting.

"I've got you, Amala mate."

☼

She had not missed sunset.

Amala lay against a column, Hebex's head rested in her lap as the last sun of the day lit the room. Pink skies brushed with orange coated the window. Today, she didn't feel like watching the sunset alone. Absently stroking Hebex's blond hair, the pair sat in silence. But soon, they were joined.

Sinayla placed her head on Amala's shoulder. Seryn tugged at her ankle and hugged her waist.

Oh, how deeply she loved her sisters.

She loved them, loved them so much she had been afraid they wouldn't want all of it.

But they did, of course they did. And they loved her back.

"You didn't think I would pick Medyr over you, right?" Hebex asked.

Amala snorted.

"No, I didn't. I know you wouldn't."

"Great. Because you'll have to force my feelings out while I pretend not to be heartbroken."

Oh, Hebs, Amala thought, brushing her fingers against her cheek.

"We're here for you, my love." Seryn added.

They would heal together. Sinayla kissed Amala's shoulder tenderly.

"Besides Medyr being an asshole — are we going to ignore the fact you have found the next vessel?"

Amala released a breath; she wasn't ready for this conversation.

"I am sorry I didn't tell you. I felt guilty in every moment I kept it to myself, and yet—"

"Don't apologise, my Goddess. Your reasons don't need an explanation."

They did, Amala wanted to say, but she was shocked by the sound of the title from her sister's tongue.

My Goddess.

Amala expected her heart to crush under the words, but when she checked, her soul beamed. As if, for the first time, someone had finally addressed her the right way. The way she deserved.

"Aarush told you, didn't he?"

"I think Maeve overheard him talking to the Captain. We all noticed something was wrong when Hawk went searching for him. His wind searched for you everywhere. We wanted to help but we had no idea *what* was going on. People were searching for you and Medyr. It was so confusing... Maeve overheard Aarush talking about you and she was hysterical."

"Was she angry?" Amala breathed.

"What? No, of course not." Seryn intervened, toying with Amala's sunstone waist chain, "Just surprised. And happy. We all know no one deserves it more than you do. The divine energy knows too, apparently."

Hebex hummed her approval, breath tickling Amala's thighs.

"What happened after I left?" She asked.

Amala found herself asking the same question: Hebex left Helioneis to search for her and Medyr. But what about Madakahiri?

"I think the Prior knew something was off because some of his officers were on alert. Security was stricter than usual. But us — what's the redhead's name, Hawk's friend?" Sinayla asked.

"Naressa?"

"Her. She's *so* hot."

"I know," Amala hummed. "What did she do?"

"She was always around us, checking we were okay. Sometimes the other guy was here too. I think Hawk asked them to make sure we were safe."

Amala's heart skipped a beat: her mate was so thoughtful, even in the rush of the events, he cared for her sisters — her dearest thing in the whole world — and ensured they were protected. She sighed, knowing they deserved a full explanation.

"About the vessel..." she started, "I'm sorry, I really am. I wish I told you earlier, but I am glad I don't have to hide it anymore. From you, at least."

Seryn brushed her fingers against her cheek.

"You're the perfect vessel, Amala. I hope you know that."

"I'm not sure," she admitted. "But I trust that everything happens for a reason."

Her words lingered between the four of them, the unspoken promise to face it together, whatever the reason was. Hebex broke the silence, voice now curious.

"Was it really the Phoenix, the woman in the tunnel? What was she doing there?"

Oh. That, too.

Amala smirked, guilty. "I've kept a *bunch* of secrets, I guess..."

CHAPTER 65

A mala stared at the door. She didn't want to go in.

Seryn, by her side as she had always been, gently nudged her.

"What if I'm not ready?" Amala whispered, more to herself than to her sisters.

Sinayla tutted, slowly rocking Xantara in her arms.

"You know better than I do that being ready is *not* the point."

She sighed, knowing better than offering a counter. Sinayla was right and Amala had no excuses to procrastinate any longer. It had been over a week since the incident with Medyr. Amala needed to do this.

Pressing both hands against the door, she whispered. "I've never *not* knocked."

"Knock, if it makes you feel better," Seryn replied.

Amala knocked. Nothing happened, of course, as Serabel's rooms were empty.

She took a deep breath. Serabel wasn't in there. No one was in there and those rooms no longer belonged to Serabel.

Amala needed one more push. Hesitantly, she faced Hebex. The blond priestess curled her lips, half-amused, as if she expected that. Amala couldn't blame her though: she was very predictable lately.

"You don't have to accept Serabel's death now, Amala. No one is asking you that. No one is asking you to stop mourning just because we now know the truth. But you should accept... the other thing, my love." Hebex spoke softly, in a manner that Amala wasn't used to hearing. Often, it was the other way around.

"No one is asking you to move in or to sleep in there. No one will ever ask you that if you don't want it. But acknowledge that these are your rooms now. You are the Goddess of this temple, Amala."

I'm not, she wanted to say, but that was a lie.

She was.

After Madakahiri, she reunited her priestesses and told them the truth. Then, even though her whole body itched at the thought, she made them swear not to tell a soul until she was ready to accept her role. Until then, they would keep praying to the Goddess' energy with her as High Priestess.

Her priestesses had taken it exactly like she feared.

Ecstatically.

Amala didn't know what she had done to deserve such love — or maybe she knew, but wasn't ready to acknowledge it yet. Some of them she knew since birth; some had educated her and helped her become the person she was today.

She had shared kisses with some, shared more with others.

Some were her confidants.

But all of them were her sisters.

And she was their sister, before being their Goddess.

Finally, following the relentless approval from her sisters, she banished the part of her brain that acted as a constant reminder of how unworthy she was, and now — when the voice spoke — she tried not to listen.

It still was there, of course, and she doubted it would go away anytime soon. Perhaps it would just never leave.

But having her sisters by her side filled her heart with so much Love and goodness, she knew she could do this one step. If not for herself, for them.

So, Amala pushed open the door, and entered the Goddess' rooms.

☼

Hawk's phone buzzed.

Amala:
In Anemos now. Home in 2.

Howlite growled from the lack of attention, so Hawk scratched behind her ears.

Amala was coming back.

He knew he should have more faith, but he also didn't want to assume or expect she would stay with him, now she could return to the Yonium. Hawk loved having her around, but he always knew at some point she would go back. The temple had been her home since birth; she couldn't give up on it just like that. Especially now she was Goddess.

Hawk kept himself distracted by preparing Howlite's food until he heard Amala open the door.

"Hi," her sweet voice resonated in the living room.

Howlite momentarily paused, scratching against the wall. Amala wore her usual priestess attire and held a heavy-looking paper bag. Making her way to the kitchen, she offered Hawk a big smile.

"I brought you fresh lemons from our orchard."

"Really?"

She nodded, handing him the paper bag. "And there's a little note inside."

Hawk snorted, glancing at her as she washed her hands in the sink.

Placing the bag on the counter, he peered inside and found a piece of paper in between a multitude of lemons.

I love you. Like, a lot. It took me so long to say it aloud and now I've finally done it, my brain says it all the time. Lemons make me think of you, so I got you lemons. And I'm not going back to the Yonium. My priestesses need me, but I need you.

Amala ✿ ✿ ✿ ✿ ✿ ✿ ✿

He looked up, lips parted in surprise.

Amala was already smiling at him.

"You're staying?"

His voice came out softer than he wanted it to, unaware of how much he had hoped for this exact moment until now.

"I talked to my sisters. We need to heal from what happened together, which is why I will go there every day. But," she chewed the inside of her cheek, dubious. "I cannot live there. Not *now*. I can't sleep in there knowing I'm in the wrong room, the bed Serabel was in when she died." Amala paused, considering what to say next. "The Yonium is my home, but I'm not ready to be Goddess Amala just yet. I could never learn to love myself as a Goddess without you reminding me why I should."

Amala reached to hold his hand.

"I think I would feel worthy of being a Goddess, if I saw myself through your eyes."

Hawk couldn't believe his ears, giving her hand a gentle squeeze. He had no words, nothing to say except one beautiful promise.

"I'll convince you of that, Amala mate."

CHAPTER 66

E ven though he kept things as calm as possible while Amala tried to heal, Hawk had several matters to take care of in the week after Madakahiri. What had happened with Medyr spilled a few secrets: Amala and Hawk told Harat the truth as she held back the tears, reminiscing on the night in Ulbaros when she realised the next vessel had been found and how things unfolded afterwards. And now, Hawk's friends knew too.

He asked them not to tease Amala about it and, to his surprise, they followed his wishes. He doubted Amala would appreciate going from hot High Priestess to hot Goddess.

Today, the day after Amala decided to move in with him, he was at the Prior Palace — in his preferred office — trying to complete a bunch of paperwork. He could have asked any person below his rank to file the case instead but, the truth was, he didn't trust anyone enough to store information about Amala. Blade and Cairo were busy with paperwork too — undoubtedly the least exciting day of work since the beginning of the case.

Zale was in his office too. He stopped briefly — Eset had just called him and he needed to go back home — and was now eyeing the paperwork with a *I really don't envy your job* kind of face.

"I wanted to personally thank you for solving this case." He said.

"Don't, seriously," Hawk shrugged. Any other outcome would have probably hurt Amala *less*. He was glad it was over, but he wasn't happy.

"You did a great job, Hawk." Zale countered, "Stop fussing and enjoy the paperwork. You deserved it and you wouldn't be filing it unless the investigation was finished."

Hawk ignored the way Blade grinned at those words.

"There's still a lot to figure out," he said. "But for now, things are fine. Did you speak to Aarush?"

The Prior shrugged.

"He's doing just fine."

Hawk didn't have trouble believing that: the God and Medyr had never liked each other and, now Aarush could choose the next High Priest, he would probably pick someone more to his liking. He examined the report on his laptop once Zale left the office: Hawk never pressured Amala into revealing what had happened, but she was eager to get the whole interrogation out of the way, quick at answering each question, and determined to never speak of it again. The Phoenix filed a report too, answering all questions but one.

How had she gotten down in the tunnel before them?

The second he revealed Amala's whereabouts — where he *thought* she was — the Phoenix had disappeared. And then he found her in the tunnel with Amala, while Medyr was passed out on the floor. He still couldn't make sense out of it.

Maybe she had seen the blueprints too: she was well affiliated with the Embers, perhaps she had seen a different, extended version of the blueprints. Or maybe Hawk will never know.

☼

The Meads were always busy at noon.

Hawk allowed himself a quick break after completing the paperwork — a walk next to the Apàle to clear his head after the madness of the past week.

He was relieved to close the case, but couldn't help some kind of guilt to linger: was it even worth it, to feel satisfied, when Amala was suffering so much because of it?

To find out that Medyr was behind Serabel's murder had utterly destroyed, her and Hebex too: he couldn't imagine how the priestesses would feel, knowing that their Goddess had been murdered by someone so close in their circles — someone they looked up to.

Hawk should return to the Yonium soon. Amala was holding a commemoration for Serabel and had invited him. Some of the priests were invited, too. They all felt guilty, of course, for not realising how much of a shit Medyr was. And, even if they didn't know Amala was a Goddess, they looked at her now as High Priestess with no High Priest to guide them. Not yet.

Hawk wondered who Aarush would choose next. Regardless of his choice, he would no longer be Amala's counterpart. Not anymore. Aarush was her counterpart — her equal — and would be for the rest of her days.

Hawk would be by her side, helping her to understand her divinity — *why* she was chosen. If only she could see herself through his eyes, she would never second guess her divinity again.

Hawk was trying to remember where he parked his car when his phone buzzed.

Unknown:
I want to kill him. If you don't let me, I'll get him myself.

Tomorrow morning, at 5, Apàle Aquar Pier. You'll tell me what I need to know.

-Phoenix

CHAPTER 67

Over the past three months, Jaren had never given her a day off. Nor had she ever asked him for one. She had never asked him for anything.

And yet, after the events of the last few days, she had requested him to stay in Aglatas for a while. To check everything was okay.

The Phoenix rose from his bed, not bothering with a second glance in his direction.

"Leaving so soon?" He muttered after her.

"Go back to sleep, Jaren."

She didn't intend the harsh tone, but it probably came off as such. Jaren didn't seem to mind.

The massive mirror on the wall of Jaren's room reflected her image as she lowered to retrieve her clothes. She didn't like her body, not for a single day in her life. The Phoenix observed her naked figure with a frown of disgust, hoping Jaren wasn't watching her too. Though it wasn't like him to call her beautiful.

She didn't think anyone ever had.

Well, apart from her mother.

But her mother was a painful memory that hurt more than any wound; it wasn't worth the thought — she had a busy day. She was always busy, but at least her tasks kept the hateful voice in her head quiet. Some days, not having time to slow down and think was exactly what kept her going.

The Phoenix hated many things. For starters, she hated Jaren. She hated Pyramis. She hated the Embers, hated the Prior, Captain Mercurian and every other damn member of the Karale.

She hated the God, but hated the Goddess even more. She hated the cries of pain from her victims and, sometimes, she thought she hated killing them too.

She hated her body and the memories it brought her. Hated her life.

Hated the pain and any reminders of her weakness.

Most of all, she hated to hate.

But there were a bunch of things she did like. The way fire danced around her fingertips. The quiet that surrounded Aglatas at dawn, when no one was around and she could walk freely. She liked the moon, too.

And she liked her motorbike. She liked it a lot.

The roaring sound of wheels on asphalt was the only thing that calmed her head, as she drove away into the sunrise.

☼

She met the Captain by the river.

The cold, morning breeze barely seemed to bother him and *her* scent was all over him.

The Phoenix repressed the urge to bare her teeth: cinnamon, sugar, and sunlight. Her scent was so heady; the Captain seemed to guess the effect it had on her. Asshole. He had probably just finished fucking her, the Phoenix thought, allowing her a single moment to envision *her* body. The High Priestess had beautiful, short white hair that glowed in complete darkness. Those eyes were pure ice, though never looked spiteful: it was like ice that would melt, taking you with it.

She always wore a chain of crystals around her hips. Two chains. The Phoenix didn't know what the crystals were. She didn't know why she had allowed herself to think of her hips either.

"You'll find him on level 7. He's alone in his cell."

The Captain's voice was low, but she heard every word.

"Did he go to trial?"

Captain Mercurian shook his head. "He can try. Though there's no benefit of doubt if you kill a Goddess."

The Phoenix shrugged. Fair enough.

He passed over a small hard drive, where — according to the Captain — she would find everything she needed. His phone buzzed. Glancing at the screen with a smirk, his canines instantly protruded to his lower lip. He didn't bother hiding it. The Phoenix thought he would act differently in the company of someone else — he didn't seem a person who would usually show off his fangs.

Which probably meant the other person on the phone was *her*. The High Priestess.

It was definitely her.

Who else could make him react like that?

The Phoenix almost hoped it was her, for it would have been utterly ridiculous of him to react in such a way to anyone else, when he was blessed with *her* in his life.

"I'll make sure every footage of us right now will be altered," the Captain said.

"I don't care," she hissed. "I don't fucking care."

He said nothing. She turned away — or tried to, as her body seemed pinned in place. The Phoenix repressed a groan of frustration as that fire in her heart sparked and then pulled. She gritted her teeth, voice dangerously low as she asked, "How is she?"

Captain Mercurian repressed a grin. The Phoenix considered punching him in the face.

"You could ask her yourself, you know."

Never.

She had promised herself to never talk to the High Priestess.

"Forget it," she said, spinning on her heels and walking back to the motorbike.

It was a stupid fucking question and she shouldn't have asked. Damn her and her stupid brain—

"She's coping."

The Phoenix turned.

"Are you helping her?"

"Of course I am."

She sighed, ready to leave, to let the steady roar of her motorbike fill her head and drown her thoughts. Those hateful thoughts of icy eyes and threads of fire.

"Tell her you met me and I'll cut your tongue."

He did not seem impressed, though she supposed that was a good thing: the High Priestess needed someone like him by her side.

"Give me one good reason why I shouldn't and maybe I won't."

"She cannot know." The Phoenix breathed, hating the strain in her voice.

What reason could she give him? He *loved* her. More than anything.

He would tell her and the High Priestess would know.

But the Phoenix would do anything to prevent that.

"Don't tell her," she said again, eyes scanning the river. "Please."

☼

The High Priest was in the dungeon. The walls were thick, reinforced by layers of concrete and steel. And he was screaming.

Endlessly screaming.

The Phoenix let go of his carbonised finger.

"It burns, doesn't it?" She asked, flashing her canines at him.

"Fucking *stop*!" He cried in pain. "What do you need?"

She paused.

Considered.

"I need nothing from you."

"Then why am I here? Did they sentence me to *this*, instead of jail?"

"Oh, no," she smirked. "*I* sentenced you to this."

He screamed. The Phoenix didn't remember what his name was, but she didn't care.

In fact, she didn't want him to have a name — he didn't deserve one. All she wanted was for him to suffer, to hurt, to feel all the pain he caused to *her* — the woman made of light that deserved none of it.

Fingertips hissing with fire once more, her hand neared his face.

"You touched the High Priestess. You bruised her. You *hurt* her." He winced as the flames drew closer, but the Phoenix didn't move away. Didn't move forward either. "She was going to let you go. She told you to step away so that *I* wouldn't get to you. Even when you were about to kill her, she was trying to protect you. After you killed someone she cared about."

The Phoenix's eyes were dark like a night of New Moon, though her thoughts were clear.

Lucid.

Focused entirely on *her*.

The High Priestess with the icy eyes and the scent of sunrise.

Her memories replayed the memories of them in the tunnel: the High Priestess had apologised twice, reaching for her — trying. The Phoenix had moved away instead.

"Why the fuck do you care about her anyway?" The High Priest spat, his head jerking away from those fiery fingertips. "They got me in the end, didn't they? Amala and her damned *mate* made sure of that."

Her eyes glowed as he spoke the High Priestess' name. A thought surged in her mind, but she refused to let it form. Instead, she touched his face as fire seared into his skin.

"She is my mate, too." The Phoenix said. "And now I'm going to fucking kill you."

CHAPTER 68

T he night was quiet.

Amala had always thought no night could ever be as quiet as the Yonium, but Anemos was a fair contestant. The faint wind was the only sound, gusts of breeze sneaking under her hair. Hawk sat beside her.

Amala shifted her legs, skin touching the cold marble of the balcony as she freed some space for him.

He handed her a bowl full of pomegranate seeds and she threw him a grateful smile.

"I like the night, sometimes."

"Sometimes?"

"There's no sun at night. But sometimes I still like it."

There was something unspoken lingering between Amala and Hawk, dwindling in the days that followed Madakahiri. Somehow, they managed to ignore it, as though waiting to see who would take the first step. And tonight, Amala thought perhaps it was up to her.

"The night reminds me of home."

"The temple?"

She shook her head.

"No. A home I've never seen."

Some part of her shivered as she said it. Depending on her next words, there may be no coming back from it. Ever.

Hawk watched her, grey eyes gazing into her face and searing into her soul.

"Any other secrets?"

He knew. Amala had wondered for a while.

"I thought you knew," she just said.

"I don't. I know you're hiding something, Amala mate. But I'm not completely sure what it is."

Amala shrugged, a secretive smile curling her lips upward.

"I'm sorry for keeping secrets."

"I don't blame you for that."

"I didn't even know I had so many, until I realised you knew none of them."

"It doesn't matter now." Hawk replied, pure honesty in his words. "I never wanted to know your secrets until you were ready to tell me."

Hawk's words solidified the urge in her heart, the push she felt to tell him everything, to share every part of herself, even the parts she barely acknowledged aloud. Amala released a breath.

"While we followed this case, I've been listening more than I used to. I listened to what everyone said, even when I didn't like their words. To what the Protectors were saying, to what Aarush was saying. I don't think *she* told any of them, but—" Amala paused.

"What?"

"I think Serabel planned it that way for a reason. I think she planned for me to understand it all, as though she knew I would investigate too. After I find out about the vessel, I mean."

Hawk hummed, as if he had waited days for her to voice the words aloud.

"There *is* a thread," he observed, "That we haven't solved yet. And I have a feeling Serabel knew she was never going to be a part of her own plan, anyway."

"Yes," she breathed. "She wasn't because she couldn't."

He said nothing, only waited for Amala to take the lead. It would be a long story, this time. A story of years and years.

"Hawk."

This time, Amala's voice was different — serious in a way she had never been before.

"Hawk," Amala said again, "Each of my secrets is personal, yes. While I wouldn't like people to know, it wouldn't be the end of the world if it happened." She paused, eyes falling on the roofs around the balcony. When she continued, her voice was even lower. "But Hawk, if anyone else knows about this, I *will* die."

For carrying a secret
So deep in her soul

Those words were not about the divinity in her heart. And she had known, she had known *why* the prophecy was about her.

"I swear it, Amala mate. With my life, I will keep you safe."

Moon breather, the chant said.

"I know why Serabel thought I would be the next Goddess. It's not just the Love. It's not just the power. It's a debt coming to balance... how what is wrong is finally made right. The Love in my heart made me vessel, perhaps, but there's more. And I guess Serabel always knew. Now I know what she wanted me to do. Being a Goddess fulfils my half of the debt."

"Why would you take a debt upon yourself?"

"It's not personal. It's ancestral. *Kuris* is *kuris*."

Hawk stilled. Amala waited for him to figure it out.

But he said nothing.

"Dhara can find the Charal women, but she can't reunite them, Hawk."

"You lied to me."

"Yes." She breathed, "But not the way you think."

"Amala Abeile, you said."

She recalled the day after Serabel's death when he interrogated her at the Yonium.

"I told you to write High Priestess Amala."

"That wasn't true either."

Amala felt her body tense while Hawk gazed into her eyes, trying her best not to look away.

"I *am* High Priestess."

He *knew*. Hawk knew and, for some reason, had said nothing for the entire time. Was it because he loved her? Because he was waiting for her to tell him? She didn't know.

But when he grinned, a flash of his canines appearing in the darkness, she knew no one else deserved to know more than him.

Amala turned, exposing her back. She brought both hands to her neck, entwining her fingers into her hair. She swung her hair over one shoulder, exposing the top of her spine. She whispered to the Moon and the moon shone on her, flooding her skin with light.

And right there, on that spot below her neck... a faint birthmark appeared.

She felt her skin burn, but not with pain. Burning in a way she had always found pleasant because it reminded her of the truth. A truth she was safe enough to stop hiding. Even for a moment.

And then her skin stopped burning, and she heard Hawk's breath catch.

His eyes now fixed to that spot.

On her beautiful birthmark.

The crescent moon facing upwards.

Amala turned to him again and, this time, there was no hesitation in her whisper.

"My name is Amala Charal."

Acknowledgments

Dear Amala,

I know this is not I am supposed to write my acknowledgments, but truth is — this story wouldn't exist without you, so it only feels fair to start this final page like this.

You've been in my head for only a year, which is the shortest time for one my characters to convince me to write about them. Laila has been with me for 12 years, and I still haven't. Cassandra, you're next, I promise.

You know Amala, you're a cinnamon roll but you were so serious that night, on February 16th, when you whispered to me, *"Write my story."*

So I did, I wrote it, and I *published* it, which is even crazier because I had almost convinced myself I didn't really want to be an author... lies, of course. Writing stories is my lifelong dream. You gave me purpose, challenge, opening the doors of a new, beautiful world, allowing me to *write* again. Thank you for being such a beautiful goddess, Amala mate. Thank you for showing me and so many other people how true, deep, and real is our own divine energy. Tell Hawk I say hi.

Luca B, I know after all this time you still haven't learned what my writing face is (I'm not angry, just focused!), but seriously — thank you for never tying your hair in eight years. So I could write about a man who does it all the time.

Sara, you were the first person to read this story — thank you for listening to endless hours of world building, for your brilliant advice, and for your enthusiasm. You never made me doubt myself a single second, and I am so grateful. All the Oxford commas in this book are for you.

Yaska Sahara, you know you were the first person I told about Amala's story? We met for breakfast on my birthday and I wrote my first chapter just the night before, and somehow I couldn't keep it in. I knew this story was going to become a book and I wanted to keep it a secret, but then I couldn't. If you think the Phoenix sounds a bit like you, she does.

Mamma, stop calling it 'unicorn porn'. They're centaurs.

Eirini, thank you for sharing this past year with me. You're very special.

Thank you Eden, my beautiful editor, for your precious advice.

Elisha and Laura, thank you for your time, dedication, and support. And for being the first people to be shocked by the ending of this book (and Laura, thanks for drawing Aglatas' map. I love it!).

Abbie — thank you for sharing your beautiful energy with me.

Thank you to my amazing community, and thank to you, my special Reader, for reading my words. If you feel even just a tiny bit empowered by this story, then I achieved all my goals.

Now watch me keeping Phoenix's name a secret for an entire year. Good luck future me.

About the Author

Chiara Gala was born and raised in Rome, Italy, dreaming of stories and characters since she can remember.

Growing up writing stories in her notebooks, or keeping some of them secret in her thoughts, she graduated her Bachelors in Classics in Rome before moving to London, where she completed her Masters in Linguistics at UCL. Chiara has a deep sense of spirituality and self-love: her dream is for her readers to realise how strong and deep their own energy is, the same way she was inspired to write *The Goddess and the Hawk*.

When Chiara isn't writing, she's dancing, doing yoga, or talking to the characters in her head. They answer, of course.

They always do.

☼

Follow Chiara Gala on Instagram @authorchiaragala and TikTok @chiarawrites

And add *The Goddess and the Hawk* on Goodreads.

ISBN: 9798370997327

ASIN: B0BQZC4H4D

9 781739 299705